DANCING FOX
From the arms of an Indian Prince to the witch's gallows of New Plymouth, Chastity yearned for the only man who could set her heart free—and her soul on fire.

WHITE THUNDER
Through the wilderness of the English colonies, Edmund searched for the amber eyes and blazing beauty of the only woman who could still his restless spirit.

SOARING PASSION
And together they kept alive a feverish longing, kindled in one moment of perfect love and destined to rejoin them forever in a burning union beyond the bounds of earthly command!

SWEET ABANDON

WENDY LOZANO

AVON
PUBLISHERS OF BARD, CAMELOT AND DISCUS BOOKS

AVON BOOKS
A division of
The Hearst Corporation
959 Eighth Avenue
New York, New York 10019

for GiGi—
    who was always there

❧ One ❧

A SOFT REDDISH-GOLD CURL ESCAPED THE CONFINES OF her stiff white cap and danced teasingly in front of tawny eyes. Setting down her baskets, she impatiently snatched off the hated cap. Her heavy hair cascaded around her face and shoulders like a softly shimmering copper curtain. Next she sat down to take off her shoes and stockings. Wiggling her freed toes happily in the sun, she reached into one of the baskets half-filled with blackberries. She popped them into her mouth and relished their delicious freshness. A small, sticky trickle of purple juice started to run down her chin.

The elders would disapprove, she thought, catching the sweet droplets with her tongue. A giggle escaped her as she imagined Elder Parkinson, temporary head of the church in New Plymouth, meeting her there in the forest. He would stand tall as the fir tree in front of her, drawing the folds of his dark cloak close about him like black clouds that gather before a storm.

"Chastity Cummings," he would address her sternly, "tie back your hair decently and cover your feet. Let shame and not the sun burn your cheeks red and force your wicked eyes downward. Although you are not yet a grown woman, the almighty Lord perceives the seeds of sin in your heart. Repent your immodest and willful behavior before you end up as your cursed mother did. She opened herself to Satan, forsaking a good, God-fearing man and three innocent young children. Repent!"

Chastity shook herself out of the unpleasant daydream. Elder Parkinson scared and depressed her. He represented everything that made life dull and fearful: the

1

incessant prayers, the hushed voices, the drab Puritan clothing, the ceaseless self-examinations and accusations, and the reminder of ever-lurking evil.

The gloom of Plymouth had no place in the forest; she need not think of it. Chastity replaced the image of Elder Parkinson with that of Goodwife Cummings, her stepmother. It was plain, tired Goody Cummings who, sensing the restlessness welling up in Chastity, had quietly suggested she go into the woods to pick berries. Gratefully, Chastity had put away her sewing and slipped out of the dark house, for she loved the forest and rarely got an occasion to wander in it alone.

But today she was farther away from the settlement than usual. Her stepmother would be alarmed if she knew just how far. Picking up her baskets, shoes, and socks, Chastity pushed her way through the undergrowth. She was almost to her destination—Haunted Lake.

It lay before her, small and blue and still, surrounded on all sides by a thick tangle of bushes and trees. The Indians called it Puckweedjinees Lake, Lake of the Little Vanishers. Even white people claimed to have seen lights flicker and vanish over its surface, back in the days when New Plymouth was still a struggling settlement. So it came to be called Haunted Lake and was left alone by all, except Chastity. She loved the silent beauty of the place and the healing touch of the still waters. Sometimes, if she sat very still, she would watch as deer and otter came down to the water's edge to drink. Once she even had a curious squirrel climb in her lap.

Today, as on other days, she sat quietly and waited, watching shapeless clouds float lazily past. Soon an otter cautiously poked its head out of a burrow at the water's edge. Satisfied that there was no danger, it clambered up the mud bank. Three smaller heads popped out behind it.

The little otters scrambled back and forth on top of the bank. Suddenly Mother Otter gave one of them a hard push with her nose. With a surprised look on its face, it slid down the bank on its belly and splashed into the water. The mother barked, pushed the other two small ones in, and then slid down the mud herself after them. The youngsters playfully scampered back up and slid down all over again, one after another. Mother Otter went off looking for fish, leaving her offspring barking happily.

Chastity felt a giggle start in the back of her throat, and she willed it to stop, not wanting to frighten the performers away.

Two male cardinals flew out of the trees and over the lake. As they whirled and dove and circled each other, they were joined by a female. The two bright patches of scarlet and the one of reddish brown danced lightly in the air, and the sight was so lovely that Chastity sighed.

"Beautiful, is it not?" said a deep voice.

Chastity jumped up and spun around.

Behind her stood a man, a stranger. He was tall, taller than her father, who was one of the tallest men in the town, and looked to be in his early twenties. He was no Pilgrim; that was certain. She could tell by his soft buckskin clothing, moccasins, and the long black hair tied casually behind his neck with a leather thong. He was not an Indian either, she decided, for above his laughing mouth and aquiline nose, his eyes were a deep, rich blue. Over one shoulder he had slung a bow and a quiver full of arrows, and he carried a musket easily in his other hand.

"Upon my soul!" The stranger laughed, interrupting her thoughts. "Never have I been so carefully looked over by a young Puritan maid."

"Not so young as to excuse my manners," said Chastity with flushed cheeks. "Please forgive me, sir, but none come to Haunted Lake except myself. I believed that I was quite alone, and you startled me. I am Chastity Cummings, daughter of Thomas Cummings, the blacksmith. I have nothing to offer but some blackberries. You are welcome to them, if you have a taste."

"Forgive me, fair maiden," the stranger said with a gallant bow. "The sun was in my eyes, else I would have seen immediately that you are closer to woman than child. And I thank you for your berries, but I have recently eaten. Why is it that you come here alone? Are you not afraid of the Little Vanishers?"

"Pooh," she scoffed. "Firstly, I have never seen them, and secondly, what harm can be done by little lights? I am not afraid of anything." She sat down abruptly as if to prove it.

The dark stranger laughed and came closer. "You are a little lioness, or better yet, with your hair, a young fox!"

And indeed, she did look like a fox, with her long russet hair and slanted golden eyes. She was a maid bordering on womanhood and would soon be quite stunning, he decided. Pity she was a Puritan! What a waste of beauty!

"Will you sit, sir?" she interrupted his thoughts prettily. "Pray tell me, where is your home and what brings you to Haunted Lake today?"

"I have lived in many places," he replied, sitting Indian-style near her. "I was raised in England and have lived these past six years in the colonies. My home is wherever I find myself, sometimes in villages, sometimes in great cities. Right now it's here in the forest. I am on my way to Norwich, where I have dealings with the Wappinger Indians. This spot looked a fair place to camp for a few days. The game is plentiful and the water sweet. I hardly expected the company of a lovely young dryad."

"Dryad?" she questioned.

"A nymph of the wood," was the reply. "The myths say that the dryads were lovely maidens who lived inside the trees. The dryad was the tree's soul."

"That is a heathen belief!" she exclaimed. "It smacks of witchcraft! 'Tis a sin to tell such tales."

He shook his head sadly. The Puritans, who left Europe because of religious intolerance, were the most intolerant of all. "No, it is just a pretty story that dates back to the days of the ancient Greeks."

She doubted that, but this stranger was so interesting, so different from anyone she had ever known, that she stayed. Though she knew full well that she ought to leave, she was fascinated.

"What are you doing now?" she asked as he began rummaging in his pack.

"I shall show you." He took out three large stones, all smoothly chiseled, and laid them upon the ground. "Some Indians to the south of here taught me this. First we must find three young saplings—hardwood trees are the best."

"Like that one?" She pointed out a young oak near the edge of the lake.

"Yes, and those other two to your right," said he. "Now hand me one of those stones and watch carefully." He took the smooth rock from her hand, and digging around the foot of the sapling, embedded it deeply in the twisting roots. He did the same with the others. "There. In two or three years the roots will be firmly entwined around the stones. When I pass this way again, I shall have three strong tomahawks for gifts to the Wampanoags."

"I am sure they would do better with Bibles," the girl said primly. "One is being written in the Algonquian tongue."

He gazed at her for a moment, his warm mouth twisted into a smile. "A waste of time and labor. The Indians have no written language of any kind. Think for yourself, child! What on earth will Indians do with Bibles? Would you turn them all into what you Pilgrims call Praying Indians? Would you take away their land and their gods as well? You leave them nothing. They taught your people to fish and plant corn, and to hunt wild game. The Indians helped your people through the first hard winters and helped nurse your sick. Leave them their beliefs, as your people came to this new world to practice theirs."

Confused and annoyed, she replied stiffly, "I would remind you that I am not a child. And I am sure that the people of Plymouth only want to help the Wampanoags and all heathen tribes. Else they will burn in the endless fires of hell, as Elder Parkinson says."

To her consternation, he laughed. "You sound like a parrot! Who is this Elder Parkinson and what does he know of this land and its people? Since you insist that you are not a child, it is time that you begin to reflect and make your own decisions. You are the one who will have to live by them. Now, enough of serious things. Shall I help you gather more berries?"

Chastity looked down at her half-empty baskets. "I appreciate your kindness," she said, startled by his abrupt change of subject. "I must make haste to fill these and get home before my father does. He has forbidden me to come this far into the forest and will be sorely angry if I return late."

Together they headed into the undergrowth. He knew

the best places to look for blackberries, and soon both baskets were filled. Chastity wondered if he had lived in these woods before, or if his knowledge of Indian ways told him where the fattest berries hid. What a fascinating man! She watched as he agilely forded a stream, using a fallen log as a bridge. He moved like an animal, with a casual, natural grace that captivated her fancy. She tried to imitate his movements as she crossed the small stream, and was very aware of how clumsy she must seem to him.

"At least I did not fall," she consoled herself, peeking at him to see if he thought her ridiculous.

"Long skirts must be a bother," was all he said, and for some reason she blushed with pleasure.

He led her as far as the path to the settlement.

"You had best put on your shoes and socks," he cautioned with amusement. "I cannot think that your father would approve of your barefoot romp through the forest."

She plunked herself down and hastily pulled on the dark stockings. As she laced up her heavy shoes, she glanced coyly up at him, and innocent longing was plain in her amber eyes. He had to look away to hide a smile.

"Will you camp long at the lake?" she asked as he started to turn back into the woods.

"A few days, perhaps a week."

"God go with you," she called softly, jamming the white cap back over her tousled curls.

"Walk in beauty," was his soft reply.

Before the week was out, Chastity was able to sneak off again. This time she took with her a small loaf of bread and a piece of cheese. As she neared the lake, she wondered hopefully if her new friend would still be there. She walked as quietly as she could, wanting to surprise him.

He was lying next to the water's edge, his back to her. She hardly dared to breathe for fear of giving herself away.

"Good day, Chastity," he said without looking around.

"How did you know I was there?" she demanded. "I was ever so quiet."

He laughed and rolled over to face her. He noticed that her eyes sparkled with green when she was annoyed. The sun shone on her copper hair, and he thought that if it were not for her damn somber clothing, she would look as rich as a Titian painting. Even then, the ugly Puritan dress could not hide her softening contours and approaching womanhood. He felt a stirring in his body and had to remind himself that she was still just a girl, and for all her protesting, he must treat her as such.

"Your skirts rustled, you stepped on twigs, you pushed branches out of your way and let them snap back, you hurried and I heard your breathing, and you smell of soap. Shall I continue?"

Shaking her head, she sat down next to him. "What were you doing a moment ago?"

"Fishing," he said.

"With what?"

Instead of answering, he rolled over again and put his arm in the water. "Quiet," he ordered. It seemed to Chastity that an endless time passed. Suddenly, with a flip of his arm, he threw a fine, fat lake trout onto the bank.

She shrieked with surprise and delight. "How did you do that? Did you learn it from the Indians? Do you just grab them? Will you show me how? I want to learn."

"Calm down, Little Fox." He chuckled. "You will frighten off all the wildlife from here to Virginia. What I did is called 'tickling trout.' I did not learn this from the Indians, although I hate to disappoint you. The truth is that I learned it as a boy from an old poacher I caught on my grandfather's estate in England."

"Was he hanged?"

"Who, the poacher? Nay, I never reported him, and we grew to be friends. He was a good man—he only poached because he was hungry. Some laws are wrong and will always be broken. He taught me a great deal," he ended, half to himself. "Now, roll up your sleeve and put your arm in the water very slowly. Just relax and let your hand hang open. Good," he encouraged her. "Do not move, just let the water flow around your fingers. Fish are curious and not very intelligent. Soon one will swim up to investigate the strange thing in its territory. When it comes close to your palm, gently stroke its belly. Fish love that and will remain motionless. Then, grab it quickly and throw it up on the bank, far enough away so that it cannot flop back into the water."

Chastity held very still for what seemed to be hours. She felt a few nibbles on her fingers and once even managed to tickle a fish on what she supposed was its belly. But when she tried to grab it, the fish was gone. Meanwhile, her friend had caught another and had built up a small fire.

"Come, Chastity," he called. "It takes hours of patience and practice to learn to fish that way. Let us sit down and eat. Afterward I shall teach you to walk through the woods without sounding like a herd of frightened elk."

He rubbed a special root over the crispy skin of the fish, which gave the flesh a delicious taste. She took out the bread and cheese she had wrapped in her apron and broke off large chunks. She had not been hungry, but she ate every morsel, and even licked her fingers when she was through.

He smiled at her across the fire. "Was it good?"

"Oh, yes." She nodded happily. She helped him put out the fire and carefully bury the scraps and bones.

"The Indians believe that what comes from the earth must be returned to it. That way it can be replenished," he explained. "Besides, it keeps animals from raiding the camp."

He studied her briefly and then shook his head. "I cannot teach you to move quietly with those skirts. They rustle like trees in a windstorm."

"Wait!" she exclaimed as a solution occurred to her. Quickly she stripped off her shoes and knotted her stockings into a crude belt. Using it, she tied her heavy skirts up around her waist, leaving her shift dangling at her knees.

He had to laugh aloud, but it was a friendly sound.

"I imagine I do look silly," she agreed, giggling at the forbidden sight of her white legs, "but you have to own that it is more practical this way. Now, what do I do first?"

"Be quiet and listen." She cocked her head to one side and listened expectantly. "What did you hear?" he asked after several minutes.

"Nothing, just silence," she answered, puzzled.

"Nothing? Then you are deaf. Listen again."

This time she closed her eyes tightly to concentrate.

But when he repeated his question, she had to give him the same reply.

"Well, what did you hear then?" she demanded.

"I heard a frog jump into the water, the wind whispering in the leaves, a bird cry out a challenge, and the hum of a bee. There is honey nearby."

"I thought you meant something important," she accused him.

"Chastity, there is a world around us. In order to understand it, we must first be aware of it. It speaks to us, and we must learn its language."

He took her hand and she followed him along a faint deer path. She learned that moss tends to grow on the north side of the trees, where the hot, probing fingers of the sun rarely reach. If she walked close to the massive trunks where the earth was damp, the leaves and twigs did not crunch underfoot. He showed her how to start a fire without using a flint, and she beamed with pride as the first wisp of smoke curled upward from her tiny fire. She paid careful attention to everything he said and did, unconsciously mimicking the expressions on his handsome face.

"Do you think I shall ever do these things as well as you do?" she asked anxiously.

"With time, I am sure you will. You are young and learn quickly."

"I am not all that young!" She jumped up and stamped her small foot indignantly. "I am almost the age my mother was when she was wed."

"Little Fox, I do apologize." He laughed. "But you stand there with your skirts hitched up to your waist and your shift hanging down, and I cannot help but laugh. You expect me to treat you like a full-grown woman, but I confess I am at a loss. I have no idea how to act toward you! One moment you are a fetching young maid, and the next an enchanting woman. You bewilder me!"

She angrily untied her skirts and let them fall. "A gentleman would know what to do," she informed him, trying to muster her dignity. "A gentleman would never laugh at me."

He forced himself to be serious and patted the ground next to him. "Come and sit here and I shall treat you like the proper young lady that you are," he promised. Somewhat mollified, she sat down.

"I have greatly enjoyed the afternoon and your sweet company," he said disarmingly.

She eyed him suspiciously. "Do you still tease me?"

"Nay, Chastity." He swallowed a smile. "I am most sincere."

"Oh, then I thank you." Her amber eyes glowed beneath her fluttering lashes, and she leaned back on her elbows, her young breasts straining at the tight material of her bodice. He bit his lip as he saw her transformed into a woman again.

"Now it is you who teases me," he gently chided.

She flopped back on the leaves, all traces of flirtation gone. "Why did you say 'walk in beauty'?"

"It is the Indian way to say good-bye."

"What is the meaning?"

"The path of beauty is true understanding. Every living creature, each river, mountain, and tree, has a divine spark within. The Indians believe that we are all part of one family, born of Father Sky and Mother Earth. Everything has life, everything is sacred. If you understand this, you cannot help but walk in beauty."

She rolled over and grinned at him impishly. "Does that make you my brother?"

"That makes all men your brothers," he corrected her with a sparkle in his sapphire eyes.

She pondered for a few moments before commenting, "What strange beliefs. Why, they sound almost Christian!" She sat up, surprised by her own words.

He said nothing. He watched her mull over the new thoughts that were so foreign to her upbringing. She had a quick and curious intelligence, and he was drawn to her in spite of his good intentions. He caught himself and stood up, glancing at the sun. "We had best be off."

Reluctantly she rose and brushed the leaves from her dress. He led her along the deer path, pointing out tracks and droppings of different animals. She listened to him quietly, occasionally giving a toss of her rich curls to show that she understood. Where the path widened and joined the trail leading to the town, they walked in silence, side by side. Chastity's steps grew slower, as though she were unwilling to return, reluctant to reenter the drab world of reality. In sympathy with her feelings, the sky grew gray as they neared Plymouth. Sunbeams ceased their dancing on pale leaves and softly withdrew, as if strangely afraid to enter the town.

"I shall be leaving for Norwich before sunrise," he said softly as he reached to pluck a small leaf out of her hair.

She stared at him in dismay, not even trying to hide her disappointment. "I shall miss you more than you suspect," she said with a wistful sigh.

His fingers lost themselves in her heavy curls. His hand froze as golden eyes stared up at him. The forest was still, even the birds were silent, and she felt herself falling helplessly into the deep blue waters of his eyes. Very slowly he bent down and gently brushed her mouth with his hungry lips.

"Walk in beauty, Little Fox." Then he was gone.

Chastity's hand flew to her burning lips. A tear crept down her cheek. She knew she was in love, and she realized that she did not even know his name.

↭ *Two* ↭

"IDLE HANDS INVITE THE DEVIL," READ THE SAMPLER that ten-year-old Abigail labored over. She was working on a row of French knots and was having trouble seeing by the flickering firelight in the large kitchen.

"Leave be, daughter," said Anna Cummings. "Fine sewing should be done by God's own daylight. You and Patience fill the warming pan now and go off to bed."

Abigail obediently put away her sewing and stifled a yawn. She got the brass warming pan down from the brick wall that made up part of the chimney, and with long iron tongs reached into the fire and placed several red coals in the pan. As she carefully closed the lid, she called, "Are you coming, Patience?"

Patience looked up at her sister from where she sat on a stone bench set into the chimney. "I shall be up as soon as I finish carding this wool," she said with all the superiority of her eleven years. She deftly put her last handful of wool on one of the stiff brushes and combed the wool rapidly from one brush to the other. Finally, satisfied it was as clean as she could get it that night, she placed it in a large sack bulky with wool she had carded earlier that evening. As she started up the stairs to the loft where the three sisters slept, she turned.

"Chastity, are you coming?"

Chastity lifted her head. The passing years had seen her grow into a ravishing young woman. The glorious day she had spent in the forest was just a memory, tucked far back into the recesses of her mind. Although she sometimes allowed herself to daydream about the handsome stranger who kissed her, Chastity realized that

12

he had just been passing through and would probably not return. Like the other young women in Plymouth, she busied herself with her chores and duties at home, and awaited the day when she too would wed. Now she looked over at her young half-sister and shook her head. "I shall be up later."

"Do not neglect your prayers," came the gentle reminder from their mother.

Her stepmother looked almost pretty in the firelight, Chastity thought. It softened the tired lines around her eyes and the unhappy pull of her mouth. She was busily knitting caps for her husband and two stepsons and she sighed occasionally as she worked. As her fingers twisted and pulled the wool she was spinning into yarn, Chastity let her thoughts dwell on the young woman she called Mother Anna. She had been seventeen and an orphan when she first came to the house as a servant girl. She had slept in the loft with Chastity, who was then eight, and took care of her, her two older brothers, and the house. Sensing a good thing, Thomas, a calculating man, had married her. As far as Chastity could tell, the only real change in Mother Anna's life since her marriage was that she now slept downstairs in the master bedroom. It was a convenient marriage, but a cold one. Any dreams Anna might have had of romance were long dead. She was a good mother and stepmother, and Chastity knew that she had been lucky in her father's choice. He might have married someone who did not treat stepchildren half so kindly. From the moment she arrived, it was to Mother Anna that all the children had run with bruised knees and feelings. As the years passed, she seemed to sense when Chastity grew restless, and she would always think of an errand to get her out of the tense atmosphere of the house and into the fresh air outside. She even dared to intercede on Chastity's behalf when Thomas grew angry. And as Chastity grew older and more beautiful, this seemed to happen more often.

I should ask her about my mother again, thought Chastity. Mother Anna grew up in Plymouth, and I am sure she knew her. Perhaps she will believe me old enough to know the truth, and not dismiss my questions as she did when I was a child.

Benjamin and Joseph put away the wooden weaving bobbins that they had been whittling and announced that they were ready for bed. Thomas stood up and said that he would retire too. Anna quickly rose and hurried to fill the warming pan for their beds. Chastity looked at the three men of the family. Benjamin, the eldest, was tall and heavy like his father, and, like him, had brown hair and dull blue eyes. He was to marry in a few months; the banns had been posted on the meeting-house door. He worked with his father at the smithy, and Chastity thought he would probably make a reliable but boring husband.

Joseph was the religious one. There was even talk of sending him to Harvard, the only university in the New World, to study for the ministry. Chastity could remember when they hid in the woods together and played tricks on their slow older brother. All this childish fun had stopped when Joseph was ten and fell ill with a fever that lasted for weeks. When he recovered, he was completely different. He refused to play with other children and spent all his free time steeped in books and prayer. Joseph was handsome, in an intense and haunted way. But Chastity found she could not take him very seriously. Lately, for some reason that she did not understand, she was even uncomfortable when he was around.

"Come to bed, Anna," ordered her husband.

"Yes, Thomas, as soon as I tidy up," she replied. After the men left the room, she glanced apologetically at Chastity. "He does not mean to be gruff, it is just his way."

The girl tossed her hair. "It does not signify," she said noncommittally.

"He is a religious man and a good provider." Anna continued. "He is just a bit gruff sometimes."

"A bit gruff? Is that how you describe the way he was this morning? I came down the stairs from the loft too quickly and my skirts lifted too high. If he raised all that ruckus over seeing my ankle, I can imagine how *gruff* he would be if he saw my knee."

"Chastity!" Anna was shocked.

"Well, you know what I mean, Mother Anna. Everything I do seems to be sinful to him. Even my face upsets him."

Anna sat down slowly, her hands picking at an invisible thread in her skirt. "I think your looks remind him of your mother. It pains him deeply to remember her."

"Then tell me about her. Tell me so that I can understand why I am so hateful to him," Chastity begged. Feeling that her chance had come, she pressed, "And tell me the truth, Mother Anna, not that old story that she ran off with the Devil, for I do not believe a whit of that."

Anna gazed into the fire with a far-off look in her eyes. "She was beautiful, as beautiful as you are, but not quite so tall. Her eyes were blue. She was not born here, you know. Her parents brought her over here when she was a little younger than you are. They were highborn and unaccustomed to life in this wild country. They both died their second winter here, and the minister and his wife took your mother in. People say she could have had the pick of any man in the town. No one knew why she chose your father, although there are those who say that Benjamin was born too soon. But I must not gossip about what I do not know. At any rate, they settled down, and Benjamin, Joseph, and you were born, one right after another. She had always seemed dutiful; she went to church every Sabbath, kept a clean house, and taught all three of you to read the Bible.

"Then one day a ship from England came into Plymouth harbor. The captain was wonderfully handsome, I remember." Anna paused and smiled, coloring slightly. "All the girls in town thought him so. But he had eyes for none save your mother. Oh, I doubt that she actually encouraged him, but she did not really discourage him either. As reprimand for unwholesome thoughts, her name was called out at meeting. Your father was enraged. One morning, a few days before the ship was due to sail, she came into town, her face all bruised and swollen. I was there that morning buying fish at the dock, and I saw her with my own eyes. She marched straight on board that ship and never came down. The ship set sail that same afternoon."

Chastity's eyes flashed green. "He beat her?"

"I cannot swear to that, I only know what I saw."

"Was there never a word more? No letter or message?"

"The ship went down off the coast of Virginia, everyone on board went down with her. The minister said it was God's wrath punishing her wickedness. I am sure that it is sinfully wrong to leave a husband, no matter the reason, but I have always felt a little sorry for the poor woman." Anna rose.

"So forgive your father, Chastity. You look so much like her. I wonder sometimes if he does not blame himself in part for her death.

"I am off to bed before your father comes in to find out why I tarry. Bank the fire well when you go up."

Anna closed the kitchen door, leaving Chastity alone. The girl stared into the glowing coals, trying to picture her mother's face and her watery grave. Finally she got up, and with a long-handled shovel pushed all the coals to the back of the hearth and carefully covered them with ashes. It would never do to let the fire go out and have to borrow hot coals from a neighbor in the morning. She mounted the wood steps to the loft and climbed into bed beside her sleeping sisters.

Chastity did not sleep much that night, there was too much to think about.

The early-morning sunlight crept over the windowsill, spilled over the floorboards, and seeped into the brightly colored rag rug. It climbed up to the bed and warmed the sleeping girls. Reddish-gold lashes fluttered and Chastity awoke. Carefully, so as not to disturb her sisters, she slipped out of bed and tiptoed to the window. She touched the glass lovingly; Benjamin had put it in the summer before to replace the old oilskin. Glass was something of a luxury in Plymouth, and Chastity felt that she received a gift each morning when she woke up to see the sun outside her window. Even when the sky was gray, as Plymouth's sky was so often, she still felt blessed.

The window overlooked the small orchard behind the house. The snow was almost gone; a few patches lay here and there between gnarled roots. Soon the fruit trees would be in bloom and their gentle perfume would fill the air. She could never decide what time of year she loved the best; each had its own special beauty. Beyond the orchard lay the forest, still shadowed in the early dawn.

She remembered it was Saturday and hurriedly dressed, for there was a great deal to be done before the quilting bee. She stripped to the waist, and breaking the thin layer of ice that had formed in the china pitcher, poured the cold water into a matching basin and proceeded to wash. The water ran in rivulets down her neck and full breasts, bringing a flush to her creamy skin.

Her eye caught a flash of color beyond her window, and forgetting her nakedness, she moved closer to investigate. There, his scarlet waistcoat like a wound against the dark trees, stood her brother Joseph. How strange for him to be up and out so early! Chastity quickly stepped back lest he see her. Mother Anna had often chided her for washing in such an immodest way; she would have to remember to be more careful.

As she combed the sleepy snarls out of her long hair and wound it neatly into a bun at the nape of her neck, she thought about the terrible expression on her brother's face as he stared at the house. What private thoughts could be torturing him so? Whatever they were, he kept them well hidden. She would not intrude. She sent up a small prayer for him as she slipped into her gray wool dress. She quickly tied on her faded apron, which would be changed for a starched white one later, and climbed quietly downstairs to help her stepmother, who was already busy in the kitchen.

After the morning reading of the Scriptures and breakfast, the three men took their rifles and went to drill. New Plymouth had never had any trouble with the Wampanoags, the closest Indian tribe, because Massasoit, the chief, had signed treaties with both the town and the Massachusettes Bay Colony. Had it not been for the Wampanoags, the Pilgrims would have died that first terrible winter. The colony owed much to Massasoit's people. Lately, however, unrest could be felt, especially as the Pilgrims extended their settlements more and more upon Indian lands. William Bradford, governor of Plymouth, felt that Massasoit would keep the peace, but ever since the Pequot uprising in the north, he had declared Saturday drill mandatory.

Anna and the girls worked in the kitchen, preparing meals for that evening as well as for the next day. No work of any kind could be done on the Sabbath, which lasted from sundown on Saturday to sundown on Sunday. A turkey stew cooked in the huge iron pot that hung over the fire. To give it a richer taste, Anna added a woodcock that Benjamin had shot the day before plus a hungry pigeon that had wandered into his trap. At the last minute, she also threw in several ears of corn and some onions.

"Abigail, remove the wood from the fire and bank the coals so that the stew will simmer while we are gone," Anna instructed.

As Abigail obeyed, Anna, Chastity, and Patience cleaned up the kitchen. Then they changed into fresh aprons, donned their white caps and long woolen capes and gathering their precious English needles, they left the house. Chastity walked sedately up the dirt road at her stepmother's side as her sisters ran ahead. They came to the large main street of Plymouth and started up the hill, their feet crunching on the frozen ground. Few people were about, and the scene struck Chastity as lonely and very depressing. The dark shuttered buildings seemed to crouch on the hill like blind animals awaiting their prey. She found herself shuddering at the thought.

They passed by her father's smithy, the stables, and the meeting house, and arrived at the large square in the center of town. In the middle of the commons was a platform on which stood four cannon, each pointing a different direction. As they turned down the street to the right, the two young girls came running back.

"There is an Indian up there!" exclaimed Abigail, waving her hands wildly.

"Come see, Chastity," cried Patience.

Anna looked up the road. "Hush, child. He is a Praying Indian. Look, he has cut his hair. That shows that he has come to God and has been saved."

"Then he is not a savage anymore?" questioned Abigail in disappointment.

Uncomfortable with the question, Anna changed the subject. "Hurry now, girls. Sarah will be waiting."

They passed several plank houses, each with its own fenced-in vegetable garden. The fences were needed to keep out the animals, especially the domestic hogs that roamed the village. They stopped in front of the house where Benjamin's betrothed lived.

"Sarah! Sarah Miller!" they called.

The door was opened by a plain girl about Chastity's age.

"The Cummingses! Welcome. Come in and warm yourselves, we have already started." Sarah took their capes and hung them on pegs on the kitchen wall. She handed them four pewter mugs filled with steaming cider and returned to her seat.

The long kitchen table had been pushed to one side of the room. In its place was a large quilting frame. Solid oak benches were set around it, where Sarah, her mother, and several other girls and women from the village already sat. Chastity, Anna, and Patience slipped into the vacant seats. Abigail, whose stitching was not quite perfect, went to the end of the frame to baste down the hem of the quilt.

The topside of the quilt was of heavy cotton. Sarah had washed and bleached the material so many times that it was now a soft, snowy white. It was stretched out tightly over the frame; the drawn lines of the double-ring pattern that the women would sew showed faintly.

"It will be a lovely wedding quilt, Sarah," complimented Chastity.

The girl bent her head, her plain face flushed with pleasure at the praise. Her fingers flew over the tiny stitches.

"How is your son, Mary?" Anna addressed an older woman next to her.

"He is better now, God be praised," she replied. "He will be coming to meeting tomorrow."

"Chastity," a girl called from across the frame, "have you seen the new minister, Reverend John Cox? He is from Harvard and most comely of face. Best of all, he is unmarried!"

"He seems a godly man," commented Goody Miller.

"Aye, and more than that." The girl laughed.

"What does he look like?" asked Chastity.

"Lean and hungry, like Cassius," she answered in a false whisper. The girls giggled.

"Elizabeth! Hush!" the laughing girl's mother reprimanded. It is not fitting to laugh about a man of God! For shame!"

"Well, he is lean and probably hungry as well. Ministers cannot grow crops and are never paid well or even regularly. Anyway," she continued, "he is tall, has hair like flax, and pale blue eyes that give you the shivers."

"Where did you see him?" asked Anna.

"Talking to Governor Bradford and Elder Parkinson in the square yesterday."

"Please God, he will stay with us for a time, and not leave like the others. We have never been able to keep a minister long. Why, it must be over four years since we had a regular minister," commented Anna.

Goody Miller looked up. "That is because the town has never been prompt in paying them. A man cannot live on God's words alone, no matter how holy he be."

"This one is different," the woman called Mary cut in. "I hear he has asked for his house to be given to him outright! It was written into his contract with the town, along with his wages."

"No!" The women were shocked. A minister was usually allowed to live in the house provided by the town, but never to own it.

"Good for him!" exclaimed Chastity. "At least he will have something to call his own."

"And something to offer a wife," added Anna. She looked at Chastity's head, bent over her sewing. Her stepdaughter worried her. She was by far the prettiest and the most-sought-after girl in Plymouth. Her weaving was highly praised and fetched good prices. Yet here was plain Sarah, just the same age, marrying before her. Granted, Chastity was a bit headstrong and sometimes slightly immodest, but she was basically a good girl, and a strong husband would cure her few faults. However, so far she had shown no particular interest in the men that vied for her attention.

Ah, well, she thought to herself, all in God's good time.

The talk turned to plans for the wedding. Chastity had never been close to Sarah, but she believed that she and Benjamin would make a good couple. Both families approved heartily of the match, and the two young people had been courting in a quiet way for years. Once they were wed, their lives would likely continue much as before, he working at the smithy and she at home.

How dreadfully dull, thought Chastity. There must be more to life than being born, struggling, growing old, and dying. Unbidden, the image of the mysterious stranger at Haunted Lake rose before her. Even though almost three years had passed, Chastity could recall every detail of their wonderful day together in the forest. Life with a man like that could never be dull! Why, his very smile hinted at whole worlds of excitement! She closed her eyes and tried to recapture the burning sensation of his one devastating kiss. To be held by a man like that! To share his life, his love, his bed . . .

Blushing furiously, the lovely girl looked down and pretended to examine the fine stitches she had just made. In the early fall she had gone to the lake to collect bay-berries for candles. Out of something she described to herself as "plain curiosity," she had stopped to check the stones that she and the handsome young man had buried at the foot of the trees. The roots had grown tightly around them, holding them fast. Try as she would, Chastity could not budge them. She had thought with amusement at the time that it was like growing a toma-hawk from a seed.

As soon as the weather warms up a bit, I shall go and see if they are still there, she resolved in silence. But she was honest enough to admit to herself that her interest was not really buried at the foot of those tomahawk trees. Though Chastity had dreamt of the dark man with blue eyes and even caught herself searching the faces of strangers in town, hoping to see his face, she sensed that he was lost to the shadows of the forest and would prob-ably never return. And she was left with a town full of Puritan boys who seemed pale and boring when she compared them to his image.

"I hear that Governor Bradford has sent for Massasoit." Mary Ashley interrupted Chastity's thoughts. With a small shake of her head, Chastity hid the memory of her forest love back in the recesses of her heart and paid attention to the conversation.

"What for?" she asked.

"He has already sworn allegiance to Parliament and to Cromwell. Why does he come here?" questioned Eliza-beth. "I confess, I do not favor the idea of Indians in the town. They should stay where they belong."

"I agree," answered Goody Ashley. "They are all murdering heathens and should never be trusted."

Anna cleared her throat with disapproval and indicated the children with a nod of her head. "Do you know why they come, Mary?" she asked.

"Yes, and it is not about the treaty," answered Mary Ashley. "I have heard that the town wants to buy more Indian land. After all, we have more need of it than they do."

"When is Massasoit coming?" asked Abigail breathlessly. Indians always fascinated her.

"I imagine he will get here on Monday. Tomorrow is the Sabbath, and he is not allowed to travel." Mary Ashley spoke with authority. Her niece helped out at the governor's house and was the source of much of the news that came to the women in the colony.

"Oh, Mother, do let me go see him," begged Abigail, her dark eyes sparkling. "I have never seen a real chief. It will be so exciting."

"Please, Mother, I should like to go too," Patience joined her plea to her sister's.

"We shall see, children."

Chastity laughed. "I will take them, Mother Anna. I have seen Massasoit only once, and that was long ago. I remember only that he was quite an impressive figure."

The women chatted on for several hours. Shortly before sunset, they gathered their things together and set out for home. They had worked well together—the quilt was done.

That evening, as she set the table, Chastity looked at her father with new understanding. She had seen his temper often enough, and she could easily imagine him in a jealous rage. But she couldn't quite bring herself to see him as gentle and loving, which he must have been once.

She and Patience covered the long, narrow table with a linen cloth and put out a pile of matching napkins, while Abigail set out the large salt cellar next to a loaf of cornbread and filled wooden mugs with creamy milk. Each girl took a trencher, a large hollowed-out block of wood that served as a dish, and went to the fire, where Anna, pulling the chain holding the huge kettle and swinging it off the fire, filled them to the brim with the savory stew that had been simmering all day. The sisters carried the trenchers to the table and carefully set them down. In Plymouth, it was considered an ostentatious show of wealth for one person to eat alone from a trencher. The Cummingses, like most families, shared. One was placed before the parents, one in front of the two sons, and the third in front of the three girls.

Grasping a pewter spoon in his large fist, Thomas said grace. "Thank thee, Lord, for this good food which thou hast set before us. Thank thee for the strong roof over our heads and the good health that thou hast sent us. Thank thee for bringing us to this land and for making a way for us among the savages. Look down upon us and give us the strength to fight temptation and evil and to keep thy covenant. Amen."

Talk was discouraged at the table, and the family ate in silence. After dinner, the trenchers, mugs, and spoons were set aside to be rinsed out for the morrow. Chastity walked around the table, using a dried turkey wing to brush the crumbs into the voider she carried. The bits and scraps would be saved and later fed to the geese and hogs.

When everything was put away, the family gathered around the fireplace for Bible reading. Each family member took a turn reading verses aloud, for the Cummingses, like most Pilgrims, insisted on education for everyone, lest ignorance beget idleness. This was the waste of God's precious time and one of the worst of sins.

"Abhor one hour of idleness as you would one hour of drunkenness," was one of Thomas Cummings' favorite sayings.

Chastity enjoyed the Sabbath eve. She could stare dreamily into the fire and watch the burning embers change shape. When it came time for her to read, she did so in a moving voice that breathed life into the ancient words. After readings and family prayers, they retired for the night.

At nine o'clock on Sunday morning, everyone was summoned to meeting by the sound of the conch shell. Those who did not attend were heavily fined. The men wore tall stovepipe hats, and Chastity noted with amusement that all the women had taken special care with their appearance, for the new minister. She had splashed on only her usual amount of rosewater and had dressed as she always did for meeting, in a soft brown wool dress with a creamy white apron, and a cap with lace at the edges. The sun played in the strands of spun gold scattered in her copper hair and danced mischievously in her large eyes.

The Cummings family walked past the empty stocks and the whipping post on the meeting-house green, up to the church itself. It was a curious building. Although it was built on a wooden frame, the walls were made of mud and plaster and bound with grass. On the outside, it was covered with clapboards, but large patches of dark moss clung tenaciously in many places. The irregular glass windows were set at different levels and framed with heavy shutters, like heavily lidded eyes. On one wall were nailed seven wolf heads; the blood had dripped down and dried black on the wood. The town offered bounties on wolves, and the heads were left nailed to the meeting-house wall until they rotted away. On the door all kinds of notices were posted: announcements of town meetings, sales, intended marriages, and rewards for lost or stolen animals.

Inside were rows of unpainted benches on a sand floor. At the head of the aisle was the raised pulpit and the gallery steps, upon which all the boys sat with the tithing man to watch over them.

The men filed into one side, the women and girls sat on the other, the small girls on stools at their mothers' feet. Anna and Chastity had brought foot stoves, iron boxes with hot coals inside, to keep their feet warm, as there was no heat in the church. Poorer families brought their dogs, who were allowed to lie quietly on their owners' feet. The whipping master walked up and down the aisles to make sure that the cowering animals stayed in place.

Elder Parkinson led the singing. There were few printed hymnbooks, so he would read out each line, and the worshipers would sing it. The people of Plymouth enjoyed their singing and made up with enthusiasm what they lacked in musical ability. As there was neither piano nor organ in the meeting house, the singing often grated against the sensitive ear. Chastity's strong voice held the notes true, at times leading the other women's voices and at other times weaving above and below the melody in sweet harmony.

The Reverend John Cox introduced himself to the crowd. After a few opening statements he launched into his sermon, which was based on the Lost Tribe of Israel. Many Pilgrims believed that the Indians were originally white, their skins darkened by weather and dyes, descended from one of the lost tribes. As such, the challenge was to convert, civilize, and educate them as quickly as possible. Many others believed them to be the spawn of the Devil. The church had not yet handed down an official opinion.

Chastity eyed the minister with approval. It had been several years since the town had heard such a good sermon. His ice-blue eyes flashed as he spoke of the hideous trials and tortures that awaited the unconverted and the backsliders. He brushed his golden hair back from his brow, and his voice dropped when he told of the sorrow of never knowing the one true God. His voice had a hypnotizing effect. All the women and most of the men were wide-eyed, following his every word and each flourish of his long slender hands.

Sundays were long, the entire day given to worship. After three hours, the people left the meeting house and went to crude buildings nearby, where they unpacked and ate their lunches and relaxed their cramped muscles. The Cummingses had their own "break house" that Benjamin and Joseph had built. After an hour, everyone returned to the meeting house for four more hours of sermons, psalms, and public confessions. The small children grew restless, but whispering was severely punished, so they did their very best to remain still.

At the end of the day the townspeople filed out of the church, shaking hands with Reverend Cox, congratulating him on his sermon, and welcoming him to Plymouth town.

Chastity's father stretched out his large hand. "Thomas Cummings at your service, Reverend. We are glad to have you here and hope you will stay with us for many

years. That was fine preaching, very fine." He introduced his family.

Following the custom of welcoming unmarried ministers, Anna said graciously, "We expect you'll sup with
us as soon as you are settled in, sir."

"My wife sets a good table," said Thomas in a moment
of rare praise. "She has a way with herbs that will rival
any cooking you had in Boston."

John Cox smiled. "I would be pleasured, Goodwife
Cummings." His eyes took in the tall redheaded girl at
their side and his smile reached and lit his pale eyes.

Why, his eyes are the color of the shallows of
Haunted Lake when the sun dances on its surface! Blue
and silver at the same time! Chastity thought with surprise.

He took her small hand in his own and pressed it with
his slender fingers. "If all the ladies of New Plymouth
are as lovely and gracious as you two are, I am sure I
shall have no trouble in staying here to do God's work."
He held her hand a moment longer before letting go.

Chastity lowered her eyes and hid her hand back inside her cloak. She was used to fending off the clumsy
advances of the village boys, but this charming and
sophisticated minister was something new. To hide her
confusion, she excused herself and walked over to talk to
some friends.

"Did I not tell you he was handsome?" Elizabeth
greeted her with a question. "Many a girl will be setting
her cap for him, and many a supper invitation given, or
I miss my guess. He is coming to our house this Wednes-
day eve."

"Mother Anna has invited him as well. Everyone
seems quite taken with him."

"Even you, Chastity?"

The beautiful girl hesitated. "I do not know yet. He
certainly is fair, but . . . Have you noticed his eyes? They
are almost like blue ice. I have never seen anything like
them."

"Come along, girl," called her father, "it is time to go
home." Chastity excused herself and rejoined her family.

The next afternoon the three girls awaited the arrival
of Massasoit in the village square. Praying Indians had

brought the news that he was just outside the town, and the girls had hurried to the square, joining the other children on the large platform that held the four cannon.

"Here come the Indians!" cried a boy, looking down the hill from his perch atop one of the big guns.

Looking neither to right nor left, the Indians strode up the street, led by their sachem, the proud and terrible Massasoit. The chief was a remarkable sight. His long black hair was streaked with gray, and he wore a long cape of woven turkey feathers that swayed with his strong, steady strides. His boots were made of bearskin and embroidered with porcupine quills. Where his cape opened in front, the crowd could see his hammered copper breastplate. He carried a long spear in one hand, and in the other, a large shield upon which were painted his most daring exploits in battle.

A few steps behind the old chief walked Metacom, one of his sons. Around his head he wore a strip of bearskin that held his long hair back from his proud face and accentuated his high cheekbones. His hair was as black as a raven's wing, as were his bottomless eyes. From one ear hung a shell pendant carved into a hawk. He wore a soft leather tunic and pants and an elaborate wampum belt, over which a black bearskin, its mighty paws clasped in an embrace atop one of his shoulders, decorated his warrior's body. On his back he carried a leather quiver painted with strange symbols and filled with arrows tipped with eagle claws. He held a long bow casually in his hand and walked with the step of a man totally sure of himself at all times, a man born to rule.

Behind the two figures came nine warriors, each carrying a bow and arrows. No two were dressed alike. Some wore animal skins over their clothing; others wore only the fringed buckskin tunic and trousers. They all wore jewelry—carved shell and bone necklaces and beaded wampum bracelets and belts. It was truly a splendid sight.

The Indians walked up to the square where Governor Bradford was awaiting them. He greeted Massasoit formally and nodded to Metacom.

Lost in the pageant, Chastity gave a start when she felt a hand on her arm. Her brother Joseph stood next to her, a dark scowl on his face.

"Chastity, you are the only single woman here! It is

most unseemly for you to be here making a spectacle of yourself in front of these savages. Everyone is looking at you! Will you never learn? Take the children and go home immediately!"

She was about to argue, when she saw her father's angry face across the square. With a slight shrug of her slender shoulders she gathered the girls and turned to leave. Tilting her chin at a defiant angle, she walked slowly and gracefully through the small crowd of men and out of the square.

She was not aware that the deep black eyes of the Indian Metacom followed her every step.

❧ *Three* ❧

In late March the sun reached down and caressed the earth, which warmed and quickened, sending up delicate tendrils of life. Tiny buds swelled and burst into many-hued greens on the apple trees outside Chastity's window. Birds nested and bore their young, and as the days grew warmer, the deep grumping of frogs once again echoed in the swamps. In town, flowers bloomed in the small gardens that the Puritan women tended with loving pride. Heavy woolen clothing was laid aside and replaced by lighter cottons and linens.

Benjamin and Sarah were married and moved into a small house on the outskirts of the village. The townspeople gossiped about the wickedness of Thomas Morton, who set up a maypole in Merrymount and danced around it with heathen squaws. Even though he claimed it was for simple amusement and had naught to do with evil, the elders did not agree. They knew full well that the maypole was a symbol of the Devil, an invitation to night-flying hags. Since the crime of witchcraft was not proven against the man, he was not condemned but only excommunicated and driven from the town. The citizens prayed thanks that they had been spared the sinister taint of witchery.

John Cox had taken supper several times with the Cummings family since his arrival, and Anna noted with hope how his pale eyes lingered with pleasure on Chastity's fair face. The girl was not oblivious of his admiring glances; indeed, she seemed to have an inborn coquetry, although it could not actually be said that she encouraged his attentions.

Chastity grew lovelier with each passing day. As the sun warmed the earth, so it warmed her blood and like the earth, she bloomed and flourished. Sometimes it seemed as though she would go mad in the confines of the world that was permitted to her. She longed for something totally unknown, something her imagination could only guess at. She rebelled in small ways, taking a forbidden dance step or singing a few notes of some decidedly unreligious melody when no one was about, or defiantly weaving a single strand of soft yellow into the monotony of the dark brown threads upon her loom. She tried pathetically to fill her drab world with color, often bringing in flowers to lighten and brighten the drab rooms, only to watch the blossoms fade and die in the suffocating air of her home.

Unable to bear the confinement of the house any longer, she entered the kitchen one morning with a large woven basket. She put it down casually near the door and moved to do her tasks.

"What is that for?" asked her brother Joseph.

"I need some leaves for dyes. We should be ready to dye all the winter's wool soon."

"What about the leaves in the shed?" he asked suspiciously. "I saw you sorting them last night."

Chastity was startled, for she had gone the evening before and hidden the remaining hickory leaves, just to have an excuse to escape for a few hours.

"I did not realize you were spying on me, Joseph," she said coldly. "Had you taken the time to look properly, you would have seen that I am out of hickory for the brown dye, and field sorrel for the black. Weaving and dyeing are my specialties, remember?"

"See if you can find some young onions when you are out," requested Anna, rushing to soothe matters between brother and sister. Joseph seemed to find fault with Chastity so easily these days! "And you might keep your eyes open for some squash vines."

"Aye, and see if you can spot any honey," chimed in Patience, whose sweet tooth was well known.

Chastity gave a playful tug to one of her dark braids.

"If there is honey around, I shall find it for you," she promised.

Alone in the forest at last, she hugged herself with delight. First making sure that she was unseen, she pulled off her shoes and long black stockings, put her cap in the basket, and freed her long mane of copper hair. It tumbled around her shoulders and down her back. Laughing in gay abandon, she ran off through the trees. She knew exactly where the hickory and field sorrel grew, and sped there first. As she filled her basket with the pungent leaves, she remembered that she had seen some onion shoots at Haunted Lake the year before.

Following the old deer path, she kept alert for bees. Four or more would signal the presence of a hive in the nearby trees.

He had taught her that, the mysterious stranger. She wondered if he ever thought of her over the three and a half years since their meeting. She often dreamed that they would meet again, perhaps at meeting or at a barn-raising. He would see her across the crowd and slowly make his way through the people to come to her side. She would give him a slow, beautiful smile, and he would immediately confess that he had loved her all those years. They would find a way to go walking alone. He would take her in his arms, and once again his mouth would cover hers.

She felt giddy, a breathless, aching giddiness. The words of an old English folk song returned to her, and she sang aloud.

> Oh, Western Wind
> when wilt thou blow
> that the small rain down
> can rain?
> Oh that my love
> were in my arms
> and I in my bed
> again.

She crept through the undergrowth that surrounded the lake and came out near one of the tomahawk trees. The stone was still embedded in place.

"He must have forgotten." She laughed at the sound of her own voice in the stillness, and immediately felt a stab of loss. Had he forgotten her as well?

The lake was the same; only the seasons had changed. In the tall blue spruce above her head, a large blackbird scolded her, while a squirrel raced for safety among its many branches. Every shade of green was here, from the dark needles of the hemlock to the light yellow-green of the new pine and the silver-green of the aspen. The bushes were palettes of colors, with frail blossoms that would soon drop as their centers swelled into fruit.

With mounting excitement she dropped her basket and raced to a grassy knoll. She threw back her head and closed her tawny eyes, letting the sun lick her upturned face. Years of strict upbringing melted in the hot sun like wax. She felt wildly alive, and it was glorious. Slowly at first, and then gaining in speed and strength, her heel pounded out a rhythm on the virgin grass. Of their own volition, her arms rose slowly toward the sky, and her body began to sway. Following the ancient custom of her forgotten ancestors, Chastity began to dance.

Her hands wove intricate patterns in the still air, and she snapped her fingers to a secret rhythm. Unmindful of what she was doing, she reached back and undid her dress; it dropped to the ground like a slain bird. Still swaying, she shed her petticoats as though they were old skin and stood in her thin cotton shift. The sun accepted her homage and gently caressed her. The firm contours of her pale body strained at the homespun fabric, and grabbing a handful of material at the bodice, she ripped it down the front.

She stood naked—a young goddess. Her long hair fanned around her body like a glowing russet cloud. Head thrown back, eyes half-closed, she whirled about as if in a trance. She danced to music only she could hear. A low moan of pleasure escaped her lips as the golden sun sought out the secret places of her body. Tiny beads of perspiration gleamed on her smooth flesh, giving her skin the iridescence of pearl.

She danced down to the water's edge. Kneeling, she cupped her hands and drew the clear water to her mouth. The sweet liquid spilled down her chin and breasts. Her musical laughter sounded distant in her ears as she waded in, relishing the cool wetness lapping at her thighs. She went in deeper, and then paused to move her arms slowly and gracefully under the water. How good it felt! She glanced down and saw her breasts rising to meet the tiny wavelets that licked her pink nipples. She threw back her head for a moment and shuddered in excitement. Suddenly she sensed another's presence in her private paradise.

"You," she said calmly to the figure in her dream.

The tall figure in buckskin remained motionless.

"I knew you would come back."

Silence was her answer. Then she gave him her slow, beautiful smile.

"You have grown up, Chastity. My Little Fox has learned to dance. You are quite breathtaking." The man walked down to the water and held her with his deep blue eyes. "May I help you out?"

Totally unaware of anything but his look, she stretched out her hand, but she was still too far away. She came closer. Then something in his burning gaze touched her and she struggled to return to reality.

"Perhaps you had best hand me my dress and turn around," she said uncertainly.

"I shall hand you your dress, but I will not turn around for the world. I was here before you broke through the trees. I saw your dance and I kept still. Nay, Chastity," he concluded, "I will not turn round now."

"Do you expect me to stay here, then?" Was she mad? she wondered. Was this really happening, or was this part of her dream?

"If your temper matches your hair, I expect you to come storming out of the water and dress. Or not dress," he added softly as his glance lowered again to the rippling reflection of her body.

Like a lodestone to a magnet, Chastity began to wade in toward the shore. When she reached the bank, he silently held her crumpled dress out to her. She accepted it and pressed it against her skin. His eyes burned so that her throbbing body could almost feel their touch, and her breath came in tiny gasps.

"Now, either put that dress on or drop it," he commanded in a thick voice.

The dress fell to the ground.

"I have waited for you these three years," she said huskily.

He crushed her softness against him. His hungry mouth sought hers as his hands explored the mysteries of her hair. She was hardly aware of the rough feel of his clothes against her bare skin as she instinctively opened her mouth to welcome his tongue. A soft moan escaped her as her body responded to his touch. His head lowered, and she gasped with pleasure when her nipple felt the gentle, insistent flick of his tongue. Her legs bent under her, and they collapsed on the soft green moss.

In a quick movement he tore off his shirt, and she stared in fascination at his broad chest. She touched his dark nipples tentatively, and then more firmly as he hissed in pleasure. His mouth explored her neck and shoulders, depositing wet, dizzying kisses in her ear. His hand stroked the silken copper bush between her legs, and the fire in her loins rose to greet it. With his mouth fastened to hers, his fingers crept into the damp, dark crevice of delight.

"Yes, oh, yes," she murmured, unaware that she had spoken. She felt him hard against her thigh. It felt good. Mouth open, receiving, giving, she pressed her leg against this part of him and heard his answering moan. She felt the throbbing hardness between her opening legs, and her body arched up to receive him.

Pain! She bit her lips and tasted blood as her body tightened in fear and pain. But his thrusting continued and the pain lessened and then transformed itself into wild abandon. Her hips began to move, thrusting upward to meet his. One hand buried itself in his hair as the other squeezed the hard muscles of his buttocks. They moved faster and faster; her long legs wrapped themselves around his body. She was with him, of him. She longed to envelop him, to engulf him as he lunged deeper and deeper into her womb.

They climbed higher and faster, until she thought that she would die of pleasure. How could her body take more? A new fire awoke in her. She clenched her teeth and gave a mighty upward thrust. The wet slap of her flesh against his excited her to a new frenzy. The wave of passion seized her again and lifted her, and she felt herself being carried up and over a great peak. She gave a sob of joy as her partner responded with a long shuddering sigh, and they both lay still.

After long moments he leaned on his elbows to look down at her with tenderness. A light breeze licked at the salt sweat on her body, and she smiled up at him with the fullness of womanhood.

"You are the most beautiful creature I have ever known," he said in wonder, brushing a wisp of flaming hair from her face.

"And so are you." She smiled. "You are my mysterious stranger. Do you realize I do not even know your name?" She was laughing now, a dreamy, contented laugh that filled him with a rush of joy.

"Allow me to introduce myself, fair maid. I am Edmund Night, grandson of Lord Fairchild of Cornwall." He joined her laughter.

"Edmund! I could not have imagined a better name for you!"

He rolled to his side and laid one hand on her slender hip as he said, "Wait, sweet Dancing Fox, Edmund is but one of my names. In this world I am called Trapper Night, or just plain Night. On Indian lands, I am known as White Thunder."

"White Thunder." She tasted the strange name on her tongue. "That sounds fierce and almost awesome. But why do you have an Indian name?"

" 'Tis a long story, but I suppose you had better hear it." He shifted his weight to his elbow again and bent over her face, winding copper curls around his tan fingers.

"The story starts back in 1605, when the ship *Archangel* returned to England from a voyage to the New World. Aboard her were five Indians who had been taken captive. They were to be displayed at court as curiosities. Among the many who thronged the palace to glimpse the savages was a maid from the royal kitchens. It was a case of love at first sight. I do not know how she and the Indian ever managed to be alone, but manage they did, and a girl-child was born."

He paused and gently kissed her. "Is this too tedious for you?"

"Nay, I find it fascinating."

"Well," he continued, "for some reason, the maid was not dismissed, although the Indian was sent away. It was obvious that her child was his, with his dark skin and black eyes. She grew so lovely that when she was older she was given a post as maid to one of the queen's ladies-in-waiting. Through her mistress, the girl met and fell in love with the younger son of a lord. They loved each other deeply but knew that a sanctioned marriage was out of the question, even though he was a younger son. Lovely as she was, she was still a bastard born."

Chastity flinched; the dream began to flicker, but it held.

"Does the word offend you? Forgive me. I fear that truth is ofttimes offensive."

"Nay," came the soft protest, "pray continue."

"One dark night, since they knew that neither the lord nor the king would permit such a marriage, they eloped. It was the man's idea for he wanted her as his wife, not as his mistress. Several days' hard riding took them across the border into Scotland, where they were legally and very hastily wed. Upon their return to England the young couple went to the groom's father, hoping the lord would accept them. Instead, the raging nobleman had them thrown off his estates with only the clothing they wore. Finally, the disinherited couple ended up in London. He had neither money nor lands, nor credit. They were taken in by a kindly tavern owner. Until she discovered that she was pregnant, they both worked in the kitchen and stables. In 1628 a son was born. I was that child."

Chastity reached up and traced the firm line of his chin with adoring fingers, "What were you like as a child?"

"Happy, at first. The three of us lived in the loft above the tavern. I remember much laughter and music. Many nights my father would teach me to read by candlelight or tell me stories of his boyhood. My mother sat with us and would listen enraptured. I believe they loved each other deeply, and I always felt loved. I suppose that is all any child wants." He smiled at her, and she pressed closer, loving the child in the man.

"But when I was nine, tragedy struck. I was bedded down in the stables, keeping an eye on a mare that was due to foal. In the middle of the night, long after everyone was asleep, there was a fire, and the tavern went up in a flash. By the time the flames spread to the stables, there was nothing left of the other building but a burning skeleton. I was left in the street, without family, without friends."

"My poor love! How terrible! How did you ever survive?"

"I became a street brat, thieving, lying, and begging, like the rest." He sat up, and a frown crossed his handsome face. "I am not proud of some of the things that I did, but I did survive. One day, clumsy because of my hunger, I picked the pocket of an elderly man and was caught. Instead of turning me over to a constable, my captor took me to the corner alehouse and fed me. You can just imagine how terrified and confused I was." Edmund shook his head at the memory and added ruefully, "Of course, it did not affect my appetite much.

"After questioning me closely about my past, he introduced himself as my grandfather Lord Fairchild. It was like a child's fairy tale come true. He had kept an eye on my father during those years at the tavern and had even paid the owner to give him work and lodgings. His pride would not let him publicly forgive the hasty and unseemly marriage, but once his temper cooled, he concerned himself about the couple's welfare. After the fire, he had resolved to find me and bring me home. The old man had spent months looking for me—he must have searched every rat hole in London.

"He took me back to his country estate and raised me. I learned to ride and fence, to dance and make clever conversation, and all the things a gentleman must know. I wore satin breeches and almost forgot what it was like to go hungry. He even gave me his own ring to wear."

The ring he showed her was a sea serpent of reddish gold. Tiny rubies were its eyes, and its burnished scales glittered in the early-afternoon sun.

"In spite of the circumstances of my birth, I have always believed that I was the old man's favorite. He sent me to Cambridge to complete my studies, and then financed my expedition to this land."

"Why did you come here?" she asked. "Surely not just to trap."

Pensively he answered, "I think I really came here in search of my lost heritage. My excuse, of course, was fame and fortune. In a way, I have found both, but not in England's eyes."

"In whose, then, pray tell?"

"In the Indians', and in my own. That is what really matters," he added. "It is hard to explain, my love. I belong to both worlds now and travel back and forth between them. Both cultures have things of great value. I suppose you could say that the white man has knowledge, and the red man has wisdom. But that is a little too simple."

"Tell me about White Thunder," she reminded him softly.

"What impatience!" He chuckled as she playfully nibbled at his shoulder. "All right then, my name.

"You may not know this, but Indian names are sacred. A man may choose one because of a religious experience, or others may choose it for him because of something he has done. He may change it several times during his life, and none will ever ask why. I spent two winters with the Mohawks, and they gave me the name of White Thunder."

Chastity shuddered. "The Mohawks! Are they not the Indians to the west that are cannibals?"

"I have heard these wild tales, but in all the time I lived with them, I never saw anything to indicate that they were cannibals. They are brave and ferocious warriors, feared by all. They kill ruthlessly in battle instead of counting coup."

"Counting coup?" she questioned.

"A French word for 'blows.' When Indians fight among themselves, the object is not as much to kill as it is to disarm and shame the enemy. The bravest warriors rush into battle and try to touch or hit an enemy with their bare hands before they can be wounded. This is called counting coup. The Indian who has thus been touched usually retires from the battle in humiliation. It saves a lot of lives. The greatest mugwumps, or war captains, have their coups painted on their shields and quivers."

"I saw Metacom once. I could not understand the symbols on his quiver. Could they have been his coups?"

"Probably, he is a brave warrior and one day will be a great one. I counted coup on his father once, and then turned around and saved his life."

"Massasoit?" She clapped her hands with glee.

"The same." He grinned at her obvious delight. "Does that please you, my Dancing Fox?"

"Oh, yes. Why, he is the sagamore, the king of the Wampanoags. You must be very brave. Do you speak many Indian languages?"

"All the tribes for hundreds of miles are branches of the Algonquian nation. They all speak the same tongue; a few words are different or the accent is changed. I speak Algonquian and am understood at all the campfires in the northern colonies. Now you know my story. Are you ashamed to love a man with Indian blood?"

In answer, Chastity wrapped her arms around him, and holding him close, covered his face with fierce kisses. Her pulse began to quicken and her kisses became demanding as she felt her body begin to stir. A delicious weakness flooded through her, and she surrendered again to her passion. They made long, slow love in the afternoon sun.

The light crept across the sky as they lay together, his dark hair intertwined with hers. The shadows deepened and lengthened, and a lone bird's song hung in the air.

"The onions!" Chastity shot up.

"What?" Edmund leaped to his feet in alarm and reached for his knife all in one movement.

"Onions. I promised my stepmother that I would bring her some." She glanced up at the darkening sky. "I had no idea it was so late. I must get back."

"There are some shoots over there," he said, pointing to the edge of the wood. "Let me help you gather them." He slipped on his soft breeches, and she reached to pick up her clothes.

It was when she saw her ripped shift that the reality of what she had done struck her. Years of gray existence descended upon her with a rush, and she fell to her knees. With a cry of dismay she hugged her clothing against her to hide her nakedness.

"Chastity!" he cried with concern. "Are you hurt?"

"Nay, Edmund, do not look at me," she sobbed. "I am wicked. I have done an evil thing, a shameful, ugly thing. I am an abomination in God's holy sight!"

"What is this?" he asked, amazed. "You could never

be ugly! Not in God's sight, nor in any other's. You are like a wild creature of great beauty. You have done nothing evil or wicked." He bent down to take her in his arms, but she pulled back.

"First I danced like a harlot of Babylon . . ." She sobbed, and he saw large tears running down her cheeks.

"And did David not dance in the Bible?" he asked softly as he knelt beside her. "He danced for the same reason that you did, Chastity, because his heart was bursting with joy and love of life. He had no words to express his feelings to the heavens, so he spoke his happiness with his body."

"David danced with his clothes on!" She flashed him a miserable look. "The dancing was not my greatest sin."

"Is it a sin, then, to love?" He cupped her chin firmly in his hand, and she was too unhappy to resist.

"It is a sin to lie with a man unless wed to him. And I know it must be a terrible sin to enjoy it so. I am surely damned!"

He searched for the words to comfort her, fighting the impulse to take her in his arms. "Sweet Dancing Fox, what we feel for each other cannot be wrong," he whispered tenderly. But she turned from him and rose, stepping into her dress in a hurried, shameful movement.

"Chastity, do not turn from me. We must talk," he said.

"We have no time now," she replied, pulling the onions from the earth and wrapping them in a piece of her discarded shift.

"But talk we must, if not today then tomorrow." He walked over and helped her put the onions in her basket. "Now that you are grown, I have no intention of letting you slip away from me."

"And I could not if I tried, may God forgive me," she said. "But right now I have to hasten home or I shall not be allowed out again. My father and brother are dreadfully strict."

"Then I will meet you late tonight, when everyone is asleep."

"Oh, no!" She was horrified. "The law states that any woman out after nine at night is to be put in the stocks! I dare not risk it." She paled as she suddenly began to realize the terrible danger she would be in if anyone discovered her sinful secret.

"Barbaric custom!" he growled. Grabbing her shoulders roughly, he turned her around to face him squarely. "Chastity, I love you. I loved you three years ago, though it made me feel more guilty than I can say, and I love you still, now that you are grown."

She melted against him, tears of happiness and fear in her large eyes. "And I have loved you, Edmund, ever since you first kissed me. I have checked the tomahawks we planted, waiting for you to come back to me, though I must admit it was never quite like this in my dreams."

"I will never leave you again. That is, unless you want me to." He stroked her soft hair with something akin to wonder.

"I could never want that. Never, though I will burn in hell for all eternity for it. I shall be working in the orchard tomorrow. It is behind the house. Meet me there in the morning, and we will talk. No one will discover us there."

On the way back to Plymouth, Edmund watched her face closely with tender concern. She saw him looking and gave him a reassuring smile, but it hurt him to see the pain and fear in her eyes. Her newfound maturity and her guilt at the source of it gave her a new grace, making her even lovelier than before. He knew that she was the one he had been searching for, the woman who would share his life and his dreams.

"Why may I not just present myself at your door and ask to speak to you?" he questioned.

"Edmund"—she sighed wearily—"do you have any idea what would happen? I can see it now. A strange man with wild eyes, dressed like an Indian, calling at a Pilgrim door. Father would explode! Nay," she continued in a sober tone as she thought of her family, "we shall have to handle this most carefully. Here we are now."

They stopped at the edge of the woods behind her house. As tall as she was, Chastity still had to stretch up on her toes to reach his mouth. She clung to him fiercely, and then suddenly released her grasp and broke away.

"Till tomorrow, then?" she asked anxiously.

Edmund nodded. "Till tomorrow."

Bathed in the lilac twilight, she whirled around and ran up the path to her house.

He did not appear in the orchard the next morning. Chastity was struck anew with guilt and remorse. He thought her a harlot, she thought with fear. And no wonder; she had acted like one. She would never see him again. She would carry the knowledge of her lust through her lonely life and into her grave.

Chastity gave up waiting and went to the shed to put away the gardening tools. Here the air was heady with the perfume of rose, sweet clover, and wildflower petals stored with salt in a large basket for sachets. When she had gathered enough of the frail blossoms, she would add cinnamon, cloves, and rosemary and sew the mixture into small packets that would keep linens and clothing smelling fresh for months. Usually she loved the fragrance in the shed, but today she found it cloying and oppressive. A sigh escaped her as she stirred the pungent mixture. A shadow fell across the basket, and she looked up to see Edmund in the door.

"You came!" She threw herself into his open arms and pressed her cheek hard against his muscular chest. "I was afraid you would not."

"Nothing could keep me from my Dancing Fox," he teased her lovingly. "I saw a young man who looked something like you poking around the orchard. Knowing your desire for secrecy, I decided to meet you here, where no one would see us." He pushed her gently away and stationed himself where he could see outside and still remain unseen.

"It must have been Joseph. It is well you waited."

"I have given the matter much thought, my love. It would be easy through my acquaintants to get a letter of introduction to Governor Bradford. He could present me to your family as a man of good birth and standing. As an outsider, I presume that I would need some sort of evidence showing that I can support you."

"Support me?" Her breath caught in her throat.

"My sweet love, now that we are husband and wife in the eyes of the Lord, shall we not be the same in the eyes of the church? That is, if you will have me as husband."

"Have you!" She sprang up from the bench upon which

she had been sitting. "Dearest Edmund, I would be happy and proud to be your wife." Eyes aglow, she embraced him, and he kissed her soft lips reverently.

"And my plan? Do you judge it good?" he asked.

"Perfect. I do not see how Father can object to a friend of the governor's. You will have to take instruction, of course, and then join the church."

"Not so fast, Chastity. I have no intention of joining your church."

"Edmund!" she gasped in horror. "You are not a papist!"

"No," he replied, a worried frown breaking the symmetry of his dark face.

"Then why refuse instruction?" She anxiously searched his troubled expression.

"Much as I love you, I will not be a Puritan. I will not join a church where each member is encouraged to spy out the sins of others, lest God punish you all. You are not allowed to dance or sing or be joyous about anything except your religion. Why, look at your clothing! If God had intended the world to be gray and brown and black, He would have painted it in those colors."

"You forget that you are speaking of my faith," she said slowly, a chill creeping across her flesh.

He made a placating gesture with his hand. "Forgive me, I was too vehement. I know it is your faith, and I shall try to respect it. I will never interfere with your beliefs, Chastity, nor ask you to change them. If you truly love me, render me the same respect that I show you."

She withdrew to the corner of the shed and crossed her arms over his chest. "What are your beliefs?"

"I told you before, I am a product of two worlds. I am a Christian who believes that my God is also the God of the Indians. He is a God of laughter and love, of war and death, of beginnings and endings. I find Him more easily in the mountains and in the recesses of my own heart than I do in meeting house or in Scriptures."

"That is heresy! You will never be permitted to live in Plymouth! You will be whipped and then banished from the town. They would put you to death if you ever tried to return!" Her trembling voice came from the shadows.

"But I have no intention of living here. This land is huge. The Mohawks tell me of many tribes far to the west.

We have a whole continent to explore," he said with rising enthusiasm.

Chastity drew into the sunlight, but her lovely face was cold. "I was born here, and here I shall dwell, with my people and with my church. I love you, Edmund Night, but I will not marry a heathen."

"Sweet Jesus, woman! I am no heathen!" Edmund grabbed her and pulled her close. "Chastity, I love you. I am offering you a whole world. Please, please think on it. You cannot turn me away."

She looked up at his handsome face. Her own was flushed and wet with tears. "Go, Edmund. Leave me. I shall never love another man, nor will I ever marry. I will vow to sleep alone my whole life through. This is God's punishment for our sinful bliss. Oh that I had died last night in your arms and that this morning had never come!" Sobbing, she thrust him away.

"Chastity, I will not leave you like this. Look at me for a moment."

"Go!" She could not raise her eyes for fear that her great love would betray her. "Please, I can bear no more of this, my heart will break in pieces!"

He lifted his eyes in anguish to the heavens, his face contorted with pain. "All right, Chastity, it shall be as you wish. I shall leave you now, but I will not be far away. Here . . ." He took off his gold ring and pressed it into her palm. "Take time to think this through. If your thoughts change, or if you ever need me for anything, anything at all, give this ring to an Indian. The tribe does not matter. Just give this to an Indian and say my name, White Thunder. I swear I will come to you. Will you give me your word on it?"

She nodded but made no sound. She could not trust her voice to speak.

His eyes were a stormy blue as he kissed her tenderly on the forehead. "May you walk in beauty, Little Dancing Fox."

She watched his back disappear into the bright sunlight, and with it, all the beauty and gaiety in her heart. With sadness too great for tears, she collapsed and lay in a crumpled heap on the floor.

WENDY LAZEAR

[faded text from previous page showing through]

❧ *Four* ❧

"O SINNER, REPENT! REPENT ERE THE WRATH OF AN AN-
gry God fall upon your wicked head like flames from a
belching mountain. These flames that burn with a heat
so scorching they make the evil lust that burns in your
flesh seem like a summer sea breeze."

As the fearful phrases rang out in the meeting house,
Chastity gave a gasp and paled. How could the minister
know? Was he, perchance, hiding in the woods on the day
of her wanton dance? Or was the word "harlot" written in
flaming letters across her breast, for all to see and point
at? Despite the warmth of the day, she pulled her shawl
tight around her.

"The mighty Lord holds each man and woman over the
pit of hell, as one would hold a loathsome spider over the
fire. His wrath blazes. He cannot bear to have you in his
sight. You have infinitely offended him and are more
abominable than the most hateful of serpents.

"It is nothing but his holy hand that keeps you from the
fearful flames of hell. His hand alone offers one more
chance to repent.

"O sinner! Consider the awesome danger you are in.
His wrath is a great furnace, a wide and bottomless pit
of horror. You dangle over this terrible cavern by a slender thread. The flames of his anger singe the thread. Soon
they will send you plunging down to the very depths of
hell!

"Repent! Repent before his patience grows thin and
he casts you into eternal damnation."

Chastity kept her trembling lids lowered, but still she
could feel the penetrating blue eyes upon her, piercing

her heart like an icy dagger. Had her sin been so grievous? Would he never forgive her? Did he not smile upon lovers?

She and Edmund loved one another. That they could not be married, she felt no fault of hers. Yet, to be honest, he had not seduced her; she had come to him willingly, even joyously. The sin belonged to them both, but the fault must be hers. Wrapping her shame about her like a shroud, she silently swore to deny her sinful nature. She vowed to be dead to even the smallest pleasure of life.

She slowly realized that the sermon was not intended for her personally. The minister was speaking to all the congregation, and to judge from the stricken faces, she was not the only sinner there. Even Joseph had turned an ashy pale.

The long day finally drew to an end. Chastity tried to slip out the door unnoticed behind her family, but the Reverend John Cox espied her.

"Chastity, there you are. I have been wanting to talk to you. Good Sabbath to you also, Goodwife Cummings." He nodded at Anna, who stood by listening. "The Widow Hutchinson is ailing, and her poor daughter Elizabeth has all she can do to cope. I wonder if you two might find time to help?"

"Of course we will, Reverend," answered Anna immediately. "I shall speak to her right now." She moved over to where Elizabeth was standing with her younger sisters and brothers.

Left alone with the minister, Chastity made haste to murmur an excuse and start to leave.

"Wait! You are always in such a hurry to be off. Let me enjoy a moment of your sweet company. Why," he said as her large golden eyes reached his, "where is the bloom that usually graces your cheek? Why so pallid? I hope you are not ailing." He smiled slightly. "You spend too much time in the house. You should get out into the fresh air more often."

At these words, color flooded her cheeks and the minister's smile broadened as he misunderstood. "Perhaps I might be permitted to accompany you on a walk some afternoon?"

"I am most flattered, Reverend Cox—"

"John," he interrupted her.

"John, then." She struggled to regain her composure. "I am most flattered, John. But for the moment, I am terribly busy. I am about to dye the winter's wool, and there is my weaving, of course," she ended lamely.

His smile hardened. Was this girl actually refusing him? Used to the worshipful eyes of most of the female population of Plymouth, he decided it was only her delicate modesty that made her hesitate. Perhaps she was teasing him, he thought, hoping to better excite his interest. And so, with a bow and a slight smile, he said, "I shall not detain you, then."

Hurrying over to join her stepmother, Chastity was surprised to see a furious look on Elizabeth's pretty face.

What could I have done to anger her so? she wondered. But when she reached the small group, Elizabeth gave her a bright smile, and Chastity decided she was mistaken.

Later that night, Thomas Cummings spoke angrily to his oldest daughter. "I could hardly believe my ears! The minister courteously asks if he might walk with you, and you rudely insult him by saying you have no time! He will think you a servant in your own house, rather than the witless, ungrateful daughter you really are." His face grew red as he paced the kitchen floor. "Now, do not tell me that this educated and saintly man is not good enough for you. You are the envy of every girl in the town, though your nose be too high in the air to allow you to notice it."

"Perhaps she favors another," suggested her brother Benjamin, picking up the tools he had come to borrow.

"Who?" demanded Joseph. "What man could compare to John Cox?"

"There is no other," the lovely girl murmured.

"Why, then, do you refuse the minister's attentions?" her father demanded. "You should fall down on your knees and thank God that he has shown interest in you."

"I do not want to encourage his interest, Father." Chastity sat quietly, her hands still in her lap and her eyes staring into the dancing fire.

"You will encourage him if I order it!"

"Please." Anna tried to bring some calm to the stormy scene.

"Quiet, wife! I tell you right now, my fine young miss, if he asks me for your hand, I will give it. And if I do, you will make him a good, decent, God-fearing wife, or I shall know the reason why!"

"I will not marry him." She spoke softly but firmly.

"What? You will not? You *will* not?" He towered above her in rage. "Base ingratitude! Down on your knees, daughter of Jezebel!"

Trembling but decided, Chastity rose slowly to her feet. "Forgive me if I have angered you, Father, it was not my intention."

"Disobedient child! You will marry when I order it, and you will marry the man I choose for you!"

"If I were to marry, I would willingly take the husband you pick for me. But I have decided to spend my life in God's work, and I can do his will best by remaining unwed."

Disbelief spread across his face at her words. He stumbled to a chair and sat down heavily. "Never wed? I do not believe it. How will you live? What will you do?"

"I shall not become a burden on you, Father. My weaving sells well, and at good prices, and the title of spinster is an honorable one. I will spend my free time helping the needy and reading the Scriptures. I will devote my life to him, he who knows best what to do with it."

"My daughter unwed?" He shook his head as if dazed.

"Is my name not Chastity?" she concluded ironically, with a sad smile playing at the corners of her generous mouth.

"You would better do God's work by marrying one of his chosen saints," said Joseph. "If you stay single, you will only incite innocent men to impure thoughts. Marriage is what you women are born for." He dismissed his sister with an angry wave of his hand and followed his father out of the room.

"Father always has had a bad temper," said Benjamin gruffly. "And Joseph seems to have gotten worse since I married and moved out. They should not shout at you so. If you wish to stay single and serve God, you should be allowed to!" He reached down and patted his sister awkwardly. "Good night, little sister," he said. "Mother Anna." The woman nodded as he turned to leave, and then she rubbed her hand across her brow.

"Girls, up to bed now," she said wearily. "I would speak with your sister alone."

Patience and Abigail, although reluctant to leave, were too well-schooled to protest. With curious looks at their older sister, who was straightening the kitchen, they made their good-nights.

"When did you reach this decision?" Anna tried to catch Chastity's eye, but the girl would not look at her. Instead Chastity shrugged and picked up the heavy family Bible.

"A life of godly works could be comforting," she said thoughtfully as she traced the gold lettering with one finger.

"Comforting? A strange choice of words for a young, beautiful girl." Anna looked at her with curiosity. "You choose a lonely life, Chastity. Pray you, think on it. But be not rude to the minister. You know, I find him well-favored. In time, you may also."

She laid the Bible carefully on its stand. "Oh, he is handsome enough, and I know everyone thinks him a saint, but I could not love him."

"What has love to do with marriage? I made my choice gladly and am content with my lot. Do not be a silly, romantic child," Anna chided her. "Now, go up and sleep on my words. Pray for guidance."

"Mother Anna!" Chastity was exasperated. "He has not asked for my hand, nor even to hold it! All he did was to ask if he could walk with me sometime."

"Which is more than he has done to any other girl in Plymouth. He has his eye on you, and everyone but you knows it."

"I have not encouraged him!"

"No one is accusing you. Go to bed, Chastity. Perhaps the morning light will help to clear your head."

Her night was filled with dreams, but they were not of the flaxen-haired minister. Rather, she dreamed of dancing in the sunlight and of warm eyes like deep blue waters, where her tiny reflection bathed.

Elizabeth Hutchinson offered them a cup of precious tea when they arrived, but Anna, knowing how such a treasure was hoarded, refused.

"We have come to help, not to sit in idle gossip in the kitchen. I will go and check on your mother before I start to work."

Chastity watched the efficient movements of her step-mother with admiration and then turned to inquire after the widow's health.

"She has been abed for almost a week now. She is better, but slow in recovering. There is too much work to be done, and the children are too young to be much of a help, although they try." Elizabeth pushed a lock of blond hair out of her eyes, and with Chastity's help swung the heavy kettle full of hot water off the fire. The two of them together carried it outside to the back of the house, where the large washing tub was set up. They stood on opposite sides of the tub and began to soap the dirty clothes and then pound them with flat paddles, working the suds through the material. The day was sunny and warm, and soon both of their faces were shiny with sweat.

"Mother says it is time I marry; we sorely need more help around the place."

Chastity laughed. "I received just such a lecture myself last night."

Elizabeth shot her a worried look. "Have they picked a man for you yet?"

"I have no intention of wedding, not now, not ever."

"Chastity! How can you say that? Marriage is the only way of life for a woman."

"Not for me," the tall girl replied with a toss of her head. "Marriage is bondage, and I will not be bound to a man that I do not love."

"And what if you fall in love? Then will you change your mind?"

"That will never happen." Chastity set her lips in a firm line. "Anyway, the subject wearies me. Are you still walking out with Tom?"

"Nay," she scoffed, "he is just a boy."

"Why, Elizabeth Hutchinson! He is a full three years older than you are, and a fine miller. I thought sure he would be your choice."

"Nay, not he." She laughed merrily and started hanging out the clothes. When all the wet cloth was dripping in the early-summer sun, the girls moved to the small vegetable garden and began to weed. They made a pretty picture, the two lovely girls in their soft gray frocks and faded aprons. Chastity stooped to tie back a squash vine that threatened to break under its heavy load, her creamy skin flushed with the heat. She straightened up and undid the top two buttons at her neck. With her apron she wiped the drops of perspiration from her neck and face.

"The minister stopped by two days ago," said Elizabeth without looking up. "He said he came to ask after Mother."

"Yes, he told us that she was ill."

"He is such a brilliant man. Was that not a wonderful sermon on Sunday? God must have spoken to him."

Chastity squirmed uncomfortably. "It certainly was strong," was her only comment.

"Have you ever noticed the colors of his beard? The outside is the color of corn tassels in the sun, and the color gets deeper and deeper, reaching almost a golden brown inside. And the hair on his head is so blond it is almost white, like a metal that cannot decide if it is to be silver or gold."

"Why, Elizabeth! You are in love with John Cox!"

"Yes, I am," the girl replied dreamily, "and I think he favors me, Chastity, I really do. He smiles so warmly at me every time I see him, and he came to the house as well."

"But he came to see your mother," Chastity tried to warn her.

"Of course he did, he is such a good man. But he really wanted an excuse to see me." Elizabeth did not heed her friend's worried frown.

"Has he ever said anything to you about his feelings, shown you any sign?"

"Not yet. It would not be fitting, with Mother ill right now. But he will as soon as she is up and about, I know it. I have a confession to make. On All Hallows' Eve, a group of us got together to have our fortunes read. When I looked over my left shoulder into the looking glass, I saw a blond man with a beard! So you see, I know he is to be my husband."

"Elizabeth . . ." Chastity paused, uncertain of how to phrase what she wanted to say. "Be not too hasty. Fortune-telling is a game for children, and a wicked one at that. I know not who was in this little group of yours, and I have no wish to know. Fortune-telling is part of a witch's lore, and is evil. You should know better. Beware, Elizabeth, that you do not fall into the most dangerous of sins."

"Oh, Chastity," came the bright and hasty reply, "it was only a game for us too. I have naught to do with witches."

"Then if it was only a game," she said, reassured, "your vision could have been the trick of the moon. Perhaps the minister is only being kind and you mistake it for love."

"Are you jealous, Chastity?" Elizabeth turned a cold eye upon her. "You said you would never marry, never fall in love. Would you deny me my good fortune? It is no fault of mine that you choose to be nothing but a spinster all your life. I saw you talking to John after meeting. Could it be that you love him and he has refused you for me? I warn you not to cross me in this. There are ways to deal with you if you dare to."

"How could you think such things?" Deeply hurt and unable to show where her heart lay, Chastity replied tartly, "I wish you luck, Elizabeth Hutchinson, but I fear that you will find that his fancy is elsewhere." She turned and stalked into the house.

Anna was busy in the kitchen, pounding corn kernels into meal.

"Here, I will do that. You make the bread." Chastity took the bowl and mortar from her surprised stepmother and began pounding with a vengeance. After watching her for a worried moment, the good woman took the already sifted meal and added milk and eggs and began kneading and shaping the mass into small loaves.

Elizabeth entered the kitchen and filled the leather fire bucket that hung on the chimney wall with water. She cut a fat slice of bacon from the haunch hanging from the rafter and threw it into the kettle that was bubbling with the evening's meal. She began to prepare the fresh vegetables she had just gathered. For a long time the silence was broken only by the rhythmic pounding of the mortar. Finally Anna, uncomfortable in the tension between the two girls, and ignorant of its cause, sought to ease the situation.

"The rooms are badly in need of painting, Elizabeth. We have an extra basket of clam shells, and I shall tell the children to gather more. When ground into a powder, they make a fine paint. As you know, there is nothing like a fresh coat of paint to keep away the evil eye."

"Thank you, Goody Cummings. You are most kind."

Anna tried to draw the sullen girl out; she knew by the angry expression on Chastity's face not to bother her step-daughter just then. Anna shrugged and gave a final pat to the last loaf, placing it next to the others.

"There, you shall have bread enough for a few days." She checked the unusually large quantity of ground meal that Chastity had produced. "And meal enough for plenty more."

"Thank you for your help. I am sure Mother enjoyed your visit." Elizabeth turned blank eyes to Anna. A foot-step sounded on the gravel path outside the kitchen, and she went to open the door.

"Reverend Cox!" She flashed a triumphant look at the surprised Chastity and turned to show the minister her prettiest smile. "Pray come in. Mother will be so glad to see you."

She stepped back, and as the man crossed the thres-hold, his smile deepened.

"Elizabeth, what a pleasure. I feared I would find you out." He turned to Anna. "Goodwife Cummings, when-ever there is illness in the home, you can be counted upon to be there helping. Good afternoon, Chastity," he greeted her casually. "You have flour on your nose."

The girl blushed furiously as she rubbed her nose with her apron, and Elizabeth laughed out loud.

"I will bid good-bye to your mother," said Anna to the smirking blond girl.

John Cox crossed the kitchen and put the large basket he was carrying on the table. "Some of your other neigh-bors want to help but are busy with their own chores. They send the food in this basket and messages that they shall remember your mother in their prayers."

Elizabeth lifted the cloth. Inside lay donations of lob-ster, mussels, and breads, and even a pot of honey was nestled securely in the bundle. "How good our neighbors are!" she exclaimed.

"God commands us to love and help one another. 'Tis part of the covenant. Old Jane Scott sent an herb infusion. She says that three cups a day will help restore your moth-er's health."

Anna and Chastity gathered their things to leave.

"I shall accompany you ladies, if I may," said the minister, rising to his feet.

"Oh, you must see Mother, she will be so disappointed if you go," protested Elizabeth.

"Your mother is asleep, child. I do not think it wise to wake her just now." Anna turned to the minister with a pleased smile. "We would be happy for your company, sir."

The minister smiled, and they departed. Elizabeth stood by in helpless fury as the three took their leave. Their figures disappeared around the bend in the forest path back to town.

"It was most charitable of you both to help the Hutchinsons," John Cox said as they walked along. Head thrown back, he expounded on the virtues of charity until Anna interrupted him.

"I must rush home or supper will never be started. Take your time, Chastity," she called back, "it is a lovely day."

Chastity watched her stepmother hurry away with a mixture of annoyance at being left alone with John and amusement at the kindly woman's transparent guile.

Sun and shadow played hide-and-seek through the green leaves. Scents of flowers teased their senses, and the melody of the nearby brook sang in their ears. John had left the path and knelt down by the shining water. Cupping his hands, he let the liquid run over his fingers and fill the hollow he had formed. Chastity gracefully knelt by his side and followed suit, drinking deeply of the sweet water.

Her russet locks framed her face, and the sun was captured in her eyes. The breeze teased the lace at her exposed neck. Try as he might, John could not tear his gaze away from the soft white V of the skin exposed by her neckline. His eyes followed its plunge into the untold mysteries of her flesh. Without realizing what he was doing, he reached over and filled his hand with her luxurious hair.

Startled, she looked up and froze at the expression in his blue eyes. "John, you forget yourself!"

"Nay, Rose of Sharon, well I remember myself. 'Thou art all fair, my love. Thou hast ravished my heart.'"

"Let go of my hair!" she commanded.

"I cannot." His face was flushed and his breathing

heavy. "I am possessed." He began to twist her hair around his fist. With his other hand he reached over and grasped the open front of her bodice. With a pull, the buttons flew and the dress opened to her waist. " 'Thy breasts are like two young roes.' "

Frightened now, she tried to pull away, but her struggle only excited him more. He pulled back her head and she lashed out with her nails, clawing the air. He threw himself on top of her, pinning her to the grass. Her head whipped from side to side as she tried to avoid his heavy mouth. She sank her sharp teeth into his neck. With a curse he slapped her hard across the face.

"I will have you, Chastity! You cannot stop me."

"You are supposed to be a man of God!"

" 'The joints of thy thighs are like jewels.' " His voice rose as if in song. " 'Thy navel a round goblet, which wanteth not liquor . . . thy belly is a heap of wheat set about with lilies.' I shall come into thy garden." His breath came in pants and his pupils seemed to shrink and almost disappear.

"God help me," she moaned in terror.

"You bewitch me. I cannot help myself. The Devil is in you and makes my body burn!" With a cry he yanked her legs apart and forced himself upon her.

It was over. She lay like a crushed flower on the grass, her skirts crumpled around her like broken petals. Unable to move, she lay there as silent tears streamed down from her closed eyes. This too was part of God's punishment, she decided. For the rest of her life she would pay for her one day of sweet abandon.

John studied her as she struggled to sit up, surprised that he still found her beautiful. His desire momentarily spent, guilt began to fill the void that passion had left. He found himself angry with her for having inspired such an all-consuming desire. There was something almost evil about the girl, something that drove him wild with lust. How dare she incite these feelings? As he watched her fumbling to repair her disarry, he wondered if now that he had had her, he would be free of her spell. This temptress with flaming hair had burned within his mind's eye since the first time he had seen her. No amount of fasting or prayer had been able to drive her image out of his tortured dreams. She was still now, her tears had ceased, and her tawny eyes stared blankly at the sparkling water.

"Chastity?"

She turned to face him. No emotion showed on her finely chisled features.

"Be not afraid, I will not harm you."

"Is there something else to fear? What more can happen to me?"

He felt a stab of pity for the girl. He knelt beside her and took her cold hand. She did not try to draw it away; it lay passive between his, indifferent to his touch. Somehow the childlike innocence of her small pale hand moved him.

"We must pray, Chastity," he said firmly. "We must pray to the almighty Lord that he may look down upon us and forgive our great sin." He threw back his flaxen head, and still holding her hand in his, began to pray aloud.

"O great and mighty Lord, creator of heaven and earth. Thou who hath watched poor Adam tempted by a willful Eve and who witnessed their fall, thou who hath expelled them from Paradise and placed the great archangel Michael to bar the gate with flaming sword, forgive us our sin of lust.

"Thou who extinguished the fire of wickedness in men's hearts with thy fearful Deluge, thou who hath laid to waste the cities of Sodom and Gomorrah for their lewd and lascivious ways, destroy us not.

"Seest thou this young woman kneeling beside me and smite her not with thy awesome wrath. Thou knowest that women are weak and vain and easy tools of thy enemy Lucifer, who, in his evil cunning, would seek to use them to ensnare and destroy the souls of good men. Forgive her her wanton manner which invites the Devil to enter into her and carry out his terrible plan. Forgive her her golden eyes which befuddle a devout man's mind, and her sweet-smelling flesh that makes his senses reel.

"Shower her with thy blessed mercy, for truly she repents of her sins. Open up thy all-encompassing arms that she may come unto thee and delight in thy shining love.

"And forgive me, Omnipotent One, for falling prey to her seductive smile, and give me the courage and strength to fight the demon in her flesh. With thy grace I shall bring her struggling soul to salvation."

Chastity knelt there in the afternoon sun, nearly hypnotized by the power and beauty in his voice. How close, she felt, was she to eternal damnation! First she had, knowingly and willingly, given herself to a man who was half a savage, a man who did not even share her religious beliefs and who refused to enter into the covenent with God. Then, oh vilest of all sins, she had somehow tempted this great man who was the Lord's servant! She was an abomination in his holy sight!

Feverishly she began to pray for forgiveness.

He watched her copper lashes flutter against her pale skin as she prayed, and a strange smile hovered over his thin lips.

How innocent she looks now, he thought, how virginal. He felt desire, like an animal, reawaken and creep across his loins. With a mighty effort he fought it back. "Come, I shall see you safely home."

Together they found the buttons from her bodice and brushed off her rumpled dress. She clasped her bundle close to her breast to conceal the sight of her sinful flesh. She walked the path with her chin held high in determination to fight against her lustful nature. But her eyes were cast down, their glow muted and subdued.

Walking behind her, he felt his chest swell with the pride of ownership, but he took care not to show his thin smile. His eyes followed the flow of thick hair down her back and rested on the curve of her hips.

At last! he thought. Her fierce spirit is broken and she is mine, mine alone. No other man will ever touch her.

He stepped up next to her and took her arm to steady her so that she would not stumble and fall.

⊸§ *Five* §⊸

THE CHANGE IN CHASTITY WAS APPARENT TO HER ENTIRE family. Instead of the strong-minded, confident young woman that they were used to, a timid stranger went around wearing Chastity's face and doing her chores. In place of her melodic laughter, they heard long whispered prayers. Days of fasting had given her skin a translucent quality and her eyes a dreamy cast. In a way, she was lovelier than ever; her former vitality had given way to an ethereal air that hung gently about her. If she occasionally seemed forgetful, she was quickly forgiven, for her new manner was so modest that she could not help but be admired.

Indeed, so docile was she that Anna sometimes suspected her of shamming, but it was not so. She worked herself to the point of exhaustion, and only rested when Anna expressed fear that she would fall ill. She cared not a whit about sickness, but had no desire to be a burden on her stepmother. When Anna commented on the change in Chastity to her husband, he grunted that he was glad to see her get some sense. Nonetheless, Anna missed Chastity's exuberance and kept close watch on her.

For her part, Chastity moved in a strange world. Too much had happened to her in a few short days to leave her unscarred. Flung from the heights of ecstasy to the depths of terror, her battered spirit took refuge in her daily tasks. She could not think about what had happened too deeply or the horror would drive her mad. She would not allow herself to feel anything that might lead back to the terror. She remembered too clearly what had happened, but the reasons behind her experiences were unclear. Her bruises, physical and spiritual, she bore with stoicism, for she felt the pain was just. She had greatly sinned against God with both body and soul.

The days passed into months. She avoided people and preferred to stay close to the house, never venturing farther than the boundaries of the small orchard. When she was obliged to be with others, she remained aloof. She smiled and listened to the conversation but added little of her own.

Attendance at Sunday meeting was obligatory, so she could not totally avoid John Cox. She treated him with a distant respect that, while not obviously cold, was far from warm. It was as if the rape had stripped him of his identity. He was no longer John Cox, just simply the minister. When he did manage to catch her eye, he was left feeling that she saw a minister with no face, that her ear heard his words but not his voice. Love or hate he could have understood and would have spurned. Yet her elusiveness tantalized him; just when he thought he had conquered her, he found himself enslaved.

He knew that time cures all ills. Yet, as the maple trees decked themselves in fiery reds, and summer turned to fall, he could not shed the image of her silken hair and skin. As the days grew colder, he knew that his nights alone would grow longer. He wanted a woman to tend his hearth, to weave and sew as he read his sermons aloud on the long frozen evenings. He wanted someone to warm his empty bed and thaw the ice from his veins. He wanted a woman, a wife. He wanted Chastity. . . .

He had never defined his feelings to himself; they remained unuttered longings, vague but real. The man and the Puritan fought within him; first one rose to the top, and then the other. Sometimes he lay awake at night and imagined himself to be Anthony, while God and the Devil struggled for his soul. On the nights when God won, he would arise in a feverish sweat, fall to his knees, and pray until the first gray light crept into his room. When the Devil won the skirmish, he would toss and turn in his large bed, moaning softly, finally falling into an exhausted sleep.

Never before had he felt so unsure of what a woman was feeling, of what she would say. All summer long,

Chastity held the power to destroy him, to brand him a rapist, to send him to the stocks for whipping,—or worse —to drive him from New England and the church! That she had done none of these things was not due to love, nor even to fear, he knew. She seemed oblivious of the power she had over him. She simply did not care.

Nevertheless, he wanted her. He felt at times as though he were possessed. He ached to touch her smooth skin and fragrant hair, to caress her firm breasts and soft thigh. He believed that his feeling for her could be cleansed and sanctified only through marriage. Only when he truly owned her would his thirst be quenched, his passion consumed. He resolved to speak to her. After what had happened, he had to handle her carefully and gently, to woo and to win her.

Chastity never left the house alone, and John grew impatient. Finally he picked a time when he knew she was alone with her two younger sisters and went to the house.

She was stunned to find him at the door.

"My parents are not at home," she said demurely.

"It is you I have come to see, Chastity. Please let me come in and talk to you."

Doubt welled up in her golden eyes and spilled across her lovely face.

"Please. I only want to talk to you about something of great importance to us both."

Still she hesitated.

"Chastity, if you will not let me in, then come you outside. Call your sisters out where they can see us but not hear us. I shall not touch you, you have my word as a man of God."

She shrugged a graceful shoulder and called, "Patience! Abigail! Come out in front and weed the herb garden while I talk to the minister." The girls were glad to escape the tedium of practicing their catechism, and they rushed outside. A thin fog surrounded the area. Chastity leaned against the low gate set into the crude wooden fence that enclosed the house and yard. She gazed off into the gray distance and waited for him to break the silence.

"Chastity," he began, "I know that because of what

we did, what happened, you may see me in a harsh light." He tugged at his beard and waited for her reply. When none was forthcoming, he continued. "It is difficult to fight the evil inherent within ourselves. We tried but we failed that one time."

She appeared to be carefully examining the hem of her apron. The fog seemed to envelop her and a cold wind pulled at her skirts and made her shiver. He reached out to tilt up her chin, but remembered his promise and drew back his hand.

"Look at me," he said in a pleading voice.

She lifted her face and looked at him squarely, her eyes dispassionate and serene. He felt a terrible urge to shake her, slap her, force her to really *see* him. He clenched his jaw and with controlled effort stated, "You must know how I feel about you!"

Bewildered, she shook her head.

"I want you for my wife!" It came out in a rush, not at all the way he had carefully rehearsed. Inwardly he cursed his blunder.

Chastity was truly surprised. The thought that he might want to marry her had not occurred to her. Her hand flew to her throat, and unthinkingly she gasped, "No!"

"I did not mean to startle you like that," he confessed with confusion as he ran his slim fingers through his pale hair. "I had planned to lead up to it and let you get used to the idea."

"I never can!" She whirled away, but he caught her by the arm. "You said you would not touch me," she reproved him, drawing away.

Reluctantly he let go. "Then hear me out." Still fearing that she might run away, he let the words come pouring out.

"Chastity, what happened was wrong, I will not deny it. But the church forgives the act of fornication if there is a marriage. I am willing, nay, I want, to marry you. I offer you a good life, pleasing in God's sight. 'Tis nothing to scoff at, being married to a respected minister. You know I own my house. What few realize is that I also own the land around the parsonage. My contract with the town is long, and you will be well provided for. I am an educated man, a graduate of Harvard, and am welcome in almost all the homes in New England. I am seven years older than you are, which is what a husband should be. I hold you in high esteem and I"—pausing he looked down—"am most fond of you. You are the perfect choice to share my bed, to raise my children, and to help me in God's work." Finished, he looked at her hopefully.

She was slow to answer. "I am highly flattered and honored that you have chosen to ask me to marry you." She paused and searched his strange eyes. Would to God that they were the dark blue ones that she loved! But they were not. "I am unworthy. I know it would be a good life, but I cannot share it with you." He raised his hand in protest. "No," she said quickly "do not ask me why. It is sufficient for you to know that I cannot marry you."

"If you cannot give me the reason, it must have little value. There can be no one else. I would have heard the gossip." A thought occurred to him, and he turned to her with a raised eyebrow. "Surely it is not that you find me physically repellent?"

She shook her head. "You are a handsome man, John, you well know it. Please understand. It is nothing to do with you, but I will not marry."

He studied her determined face, puzzled. "I can see that I have been too hasty in speaking out," he slowly acknowledged. "But, frankly, you have left me little choice. I have had no opportunity to woo you in the manner of our local swains, with long walks and talks and a stolen kiss or two."

"It is not that, John." She sighed. "I simply cannot wed."

Until that moment he believed her refusal due to feminine vanity, that she resented the lack of a formal courtship. Now he did not know what to think. The look on her sweet face was almost wistful, and it gave him hope. He decided that it would be wise to retreat temporarily and give her time to reflect on his offer.

"You need time to think; I shall not press you for the moment. When you have decided, I will be at the parsonage."

He gave a slight bow. "I pray God to help you in your decision. Good day, Chastity." He waved to the children and headed off down the path, where he was swallowed up by the fog.

Chastity watched him go with mixed emotions. He had completely ignored her refusal. What an exasperating man! If only it had been Edmund standing there offering her a Christian life in Plymouth. How quickly she would have accepted!

Why is life so cruel? she wondered silently. The man she loved was lost to her because of his religious beliefs, and her suitor, though a man of God, she could never love.

I shall not marry him, nor any other, she reaffirmed to herself. Unless . . . But Chastity pushed the unwelcome thought away. It was only nerves, she told herself, that had interrupted her monthly flow; her belly was smooth and flat.

"It is only my nerves," she said aloud. As she went to the garden to help her sisters, she heard an unfamiliar voice call out.

"Please, wouldst thou give me some water?" A woman stood at the gate.

"Patience, draw some fresh water from the well," Chastity commanded. The stranger's face had taken on the gray tinge of the day. Alarmed, Chastity went to her. "Are you ill?"

"Only greatly fatigued," was the reply. She took the dipper and drank deeply. Despite the damp chill in the air, she poured a little water over her handkerchief and rubbed it across her face, leaving light streaks in the dust. "Ah," she sighed, "that is better. I thank thee most kindly."

Noticing Patience and Abigail staring openly at the exhausted woman, Chastity shooed them away. "Will you come in and sit a spell? It would do you good to rest." The woman did not look well; her dry skin stretched tightly across her bones, and her breath was labored.

"Thank thee again. I shall." She followed Chastity into the house and sank gratefully onto the bench in the warm kitchen. "It is good to be inside."

"Have you eaten?"

"Please, do not go to any trouble. 'Tis enough that thou hast given me water and a place by the fire to rest."

"Nonsense!" exclaimed Chastity as she filled a trencher from the iron pot that hung over the fire. "Eat this and then we can talk."

The woman gave her a warm smile. After a short prayer she began to eat greedily. Chastity did not want to appear rude by staring, so she busied herself with mending until the older woman was finished. "I feel much better now. My name is Hannah Foote."

"I am Chastity Cummings. Forgive me for being inquisitive, but in your prayers you made mention of a feast in the midst of your enemies."

Hannah had the grace to blush. "I did not intend to take advantage of thy hospitality unfairly. Perhaps I should have told thee before I entered thy house."

"Told me what?"

"That I am a Quaker."

That explained her strange speech and manner. The Quakers were a heretical sect that had been banished from the Massachusetts Bay Colony.

"Whatever are you doing here in New Plymouth?" Chastity asked with curiosity.

"I was whipped and forced out of Boston for spreading God's word. If I return there, I will be hanged. Most of us settled in Providence, in the Rhode Island Colony. But my husband and I had a mission. We had a new vision, one in which all God's children lived together in this new land, where each man was tolerant of his neighbors' beliefs, where each man lived bravely and no one spent his life spying out the sins of others. We started for Plymouth to spread God's word."

Her phrase gently tugged at a memory. Within Chastity there arose an image of a tanned face with sapphire eyes. She pulled herself back to the present with difficulty and realized that the woman was watching her curiously. "Where is your husband now?" she managed to ask.

"Dead, alas. We left Providence several months ago with few supplies and trusted to God to provide the rest. But my husband came too close to a she-bear with cubs. There was little left of him to bury."

"How dreadful for you!" Chastity cried.

"God works his will in strange ways." Hannah sighed. "He gives me the strength to continue alone, but I am not sure I could have walked much farther." She looked down at her swollen feet. "My boots gave out, as thou canst see."

"I am not at all sure that Plymouth will welcome you with any more warmth than the Bay Colony." Chastity seemed to be thinking aloud. "Of course, as yet there is no written law concerning Quakers, but the laws against heresy are many. This is a covenanted community."

"I shall stay in Plymouth, for my mission is here. But I had best leave thy house. Thou mayest be punished for helping me." Hannah rose painfully to her feet.

"Wait! Let me think!" ordered Chastity. "If you enter the town like this, you will likely be thrown into the stocks. You must have a plan."

"A plan?" Bewildered, the older woman sat down again. "I had not thought of it, but thou art right," she confessed.

"First off, where will you stay?"

"I do not know. I had thought that God would provide."

"Perhaps he has!" The first laugh in several months escaped her full lips. "There is a small cabin on the out-skirts of town. The owner died last winter, and no one has moved into it yet. I am sure that it is filthy and the gar-den in terrible shape, but it is a shelter. It would be ideal. The tools and garden things are likely still there."

"Blessed be the Lord," Hannah murmured in amaze-ment.

"You can go there now," Chastity continued eagerly. "I shall pack some things for you." She rushed out of the kitchen and returned in a moment carrying a basket. With a large knife she cut down a fat sausage that was hanging from the rafter and sliced a big ball of cheese into two parts. Hesitating only a second, she included a loaf of fresh bread and several apples from the family orchard. At the last moment she added a candle and a pair of her shoes that she had gotten from the other room.

That will have to do her, she thought. I shall have trouble enough explaining where these things went to, I dare not add more. She gave Hannah directions to the deserted cabin and walked her to the gate.

"I am most grateful to thee, but I admit that I do not understand why thou hast helped me so."

"I am not sure myself, except that you too are God's creature." Her pale face wrinkled in a frown of concentration, and she pushed her hair back out of her eyes. "There was someone once, you remind me of him. Oh, he was not a Quaker," she added quickly, "but something you said brought him back to me."

Hannah gave her a gentle smile. "Then God bless him, and God bless thee for thy charity. Fare thee well."

Chastity looked around to see if her sisters had observed any of this, but they were nowhere in sight.

"Good," she said aloud. "There will be less to explain."

Breakfast was over and the men had left for work. Chastity emptied the leftovers into a wooden pail for the hogs. Her pert nose wrinkled in distaste at the remains of the cold porridge smothered in maple syrup. Once she had considered this a real treat; this morning it only made her stomach churn.

She stifled a yawn and decided that she would have to get outside more often. The house left her feeling tired and depressed. Soon the heavy snows would come and there would be little pleasure in being out for long. As she plaited her tresses into a long braid she heard quarreling by the window and got up to look.

"I am old enough to go out alone! You went last year when you were just my age!" accused Abigail.

Patience stamped a small foot. "You silly goose, you do not even know where to begin to look!"

"I do too. You just look under chestnut trees! So there!"

Anna appeared. "Now, what is the fuss all about, children? Why such loud cries?"

"It is my turn to gather chestnuts, is it not, Mother?" Abigail wheedled, her eyes large and dark with the picture of roasted chestnuts on the hearth.

"She is too young," Patience countered. "She might get lost."

Anna settled the dispute easily. "You may both go. But be careful and be back by midday."

Abigail gave a delighted cry. "See?" she said to her sister.

"I said you may both go," reminded Anna.

Patience gave in gracefully and the two girls raced off hand in hand with braids flying.

"Mother Anna?" called Chastity through the window. "What needs doing outside today?"

"There is cod to be cleaned that Benjamin caught last night. His catch was large enough to share with us. They are in the barrel of water in the shed. Carry them outside into the sun."

Chastity nodded and took a knife, a wooden board, and the hog pail outside. She chose a sunny spot in the yard and went for the fish. Returning from the shed, she sat down facing the forest. She looked almost like a child as she flung her thick braid over her shoulder and out of her way. She put a large fish on the board, and grabbing it by the tail so it would not slide, she began to scale it. When she had finished, and the scales lay like tiny jewels in the grass, she cut off the head and tail with two whacks of her large knife. With an expert slice she split the fish open down the length of its belly. Reaching inside with a deft movement of her hand, she pulled out the entrails and threw them into the hog pail, along with the head and tail. The cleaned fish was laid on the grass, and she reached for another.

She worked quickly, letting her mind wander as her hands set up a rhythm. The pile of cleaned fish rose, as did the pile in the hog pail. The stench of fresh cod was overwhelming, and she felt her stomach heave. Looking down, she saw a large fish eye staring at her, and her hand full of bloody entrails. Hot bile rose in her throat, choking her. She closed her eyes and tried to get to her feet. She stood swaying for a moment, and a new wave of nausea hit her. She could feel it rise in her throat, flood her mouth, and come spewing out. She stood trembling, shaken by the violence of her reaction.

"Chastity!"

She turned around to see Anna staring at her. "I am fine, Mother Anna. I gather my stomach does not care for the perfume of fresh cod." She attempted a feeble laugh, but it rang hollow. Smells had never bothered her before. At least, not until lately.

She went to the well and washed her hands and face, ridding her mouth of its foul taste with sweet water. Suddenly she began to cry. It was no use pretending, she could lie to herself no longer. She was with child!

She looked up and saw her worried stepmother at her side. "Mother Anna," she said through her tears, "I am undone."

"Why, Chastity, what ever is wrong?" cried the older woman, gathering her against her breast. "What do you mean?"

Chastity turned a tearstained face to her. "I am with child, Mother Anna! I am going to have a baby!"

Anna recoiled from her as though she had been slapped. Her face drew pinched and white, and she stared at her stepdaughter with the face of a stranger. "Oh, Chastity! What have you done?" She moaned and shook her head from side to side. "I cannot believe what I hear! I have tried to be a good mother to you, to teach you right from wrong. I have loved you like my own. Where have I failed you?"

Chastity slumped to her knees and wrapped her arms around Anna's stout waist. "Please, Mother Anna," she begged wildly, "help me. I am lost."

"I never believed an unwed daughter of mine would be wearing her apron high. May the Lord forgive you."

"Mother Anna, what am I going to do?" A new wave of misery swept over her, and her sobs grew.

Anna stood listening to her cries. Finally she gently disengaged herself and said absently, "First, I think we need a good strong cup of tea."

Chastity obediently got up and followed her into the kitchen, but she could not stop her breath from coming in quick little sobs. She tried to compose herself as Anna prepared the tea and they both sat down at the kitchen table.

"Here, drink this," commanded Anna, thrusting a steaming pewter mug at Chastity, who blew on the tea and took tiny sips.

"I will not ask you how it happened," began Anna. She could not look at Chastity, but stared into her own mug. "I should have suspected. You have been so listless lately, and your appetite simply disappeared. I should have known by that, and by the shine in your hair and skin. But who would have thought . . . ?" She broke off as she saw the tortured expression on Chastity's frightened face. "How long have you known?"

"I have missed twice," said the girl, coloring at speaking such things aloud. "I kept telling myself that it was my nerves. I did not admit the truth to myself until just now when I was sick."

Anna threw her a wise look that was heavy with pity. "And does he know yet?"

"He?" Suddenly the truth of her precarious situation struck Chastity. He? Which one? She had no idea who had fathered this thing growing inside her.

"No, of course he could not know yet, if you just realized it yourself. Well, there is only one thing to be done. You must tell him and marry him as soon as possible, before you begin to show. Once you are safely wed, no one will point a finger. It will not be the first time it has happened in this town, nor the last," Anna concluded practically.

"Oh, Mother Anna, I cannot!" she wailed.

"Cannot? You have no choice, Chastity. You well know the punishment for fornication."

Indeed she did, though she had been trying not to think of it. A woman caught in fornication had two choices. If she were lucky, the man would marry her before she was denounced at meeting. If not, she was thrown into prison as soon as her crime was discovered. She was left in jail until her baby was born, then forced to stand in the stocks all day, babe in arms, while the villagers jeered her. She was then returned to prison until the child was six weeks old. At that time she was taken out and given a public whipping; forty lashes was the rule. Decent men and women shunned her forevermore, and often her child was taken away and given to others to raise, lest she corrupt its young soul. The thought of all this and the image of bleeding strips of flesh being flayed off her back almost made Chastity faint.

Reading her thoughts, Anna said, "You will not survive it, and if by some miracle you do, you would be shamed for the rest of your days. Do not even think on it."

Chastity was numb. Surely this was too much! Was she doomed to be punished forever? Was God so cruel?

"If you are afraid to speak to the man, I shall do it myself," Anna announced. "You have not sinned alone, remember. But he must be told quickly, there is no time to spare."

"Mother Anna, you do not understand. I cannot marry." Confused, the frightened girl clung to this one idea. "I cannot!"

"You should have thought on that earlier."

"Please, God, help me," she sobbed. She stared blindly into her tea, her hands twisting and pulling at her apron with a life of their own.

"You will not find the answer in your tea leaves. Now, calm yourself," Anna cautioned wearily. "You will hurt the babe."

"Hurt the babe! My God, the babe will be my death! I cannot breathe. I must get outside and think."

"Wait!"

"Nay, I must think what to do." She ran out of the house and raced down the path into the forest.

Anna remained where she was and gazed off into space. Chastity would calm down and come back when she was ready. Once the storm had passed, she would be sensible. How could she best help her in this tragic situation? What if the man were not willing, if he denied it, or if Chastity persisted in refusing to name him? She chewed on her lip and thought for a long time. She made a decision. She carefully rinsed the two cups and hid all traces of the precious tea. Then she took her shawl from its peg on the wall and carefully closed the kitchen door behind her as she started off to town.

Chastity ran on until her breath tore at her sides like sharp claws and forced her to collapse on a bed of drying leaves. She lay there panting, eyes slightly closed. All was silent. The only noise in the great forest around her was the sound of her labored breathing. She lay quite still, like a giant fallen leaf. Her hair had come unbraided and spread across her face and shoulders like a shimmering fan. Slowly regaining her senses, she rolled over and focused her eyes on the canopy of sunlight and scarlet leaves above her. A light breeze set the forest to whispering, and she watched a single brown leaf swirl gently down to rest near her.

She looked at her flat belly and grimaced. Soon it would be swollen and deformed, her sin known. She had seen a woman receive thirty lashes once. Although the poor sinner's back had finally healed, her mind and spirit had been forever broken, and she had died a few months later.

Despite her fears, Chastity knew she had to face her situation practically. There were only two possibilities for her—marriage or escape. It really did not matter who had fathered the child, poor little innocent. Suddenly she felt fiercely protective of the small life within her. It was *her* child! No one would take it from her! She would run away. . . . But where could she go? How could a pregnant woman, alone and with no money, possibly fend for herself?

Had she not been so totally miserable, she might have laughed at her foolishness. She sat up and watched a late robin alight on a branch to rest on his way south. She envied him his freedom. Unlike the small winged creature, she could not escape. She would have to stay in Plymouth. Now the question was purely one of survival.

John Cox was willing to marry her. Her stomach heaved at the thought, but she forced herself to think on. In his haste that day in the forest, he had not realized she was not a virgin, so he would assume the child was his. But was it his child? What if it had black hair? Her father had dark hair, she thought quickly; it could be explained away. She absently tore a leaf to shreds as she tried to imagine what life with John would be like.

From deep within her, the tears welled up and flowed. How could she live without love? With John, she and the child would be respected and cared for, their lives would not be luxurious, but certainly comfortable by Pilgrim standards. She could remain in the church and in the town where she grew up, near her family and friends. She would be mistress of her own home and envied by many. John must love her, or he would not have proposed, she assured herself. Perhaps in time she might even come to love him in return.

No, not love. She shuddered at the thought, and her mouth became dry. But with a comfortable, peaceful life for herself and the child, she might grow to like him. Anna was right, she was a silly, romantic child. Still, no matter how practically she looked at it, her very nature rebelled at the deception. She abhorred the idea of marrying John, suffering his touch, and living a lie. Must she lose her endangered soul in order to save her life?

She was doomed, cursed by God, as Eve had been before her. Eve and the treacherous serpent! An image began to grow in Chastity's head. She could almost see the serpent slowly unwinding from around the Tree of Life, sunlight shining on its golden scales. It coiled on the ground, swaying its glittering head, hypnotizing her with its fiery eyes. Of course! The sea serpent of Edmund's ring! She had buried it deep in the folds of linen she had stored in her hope chest, thinking never to look at it again.

She felt relief flood through her with the certainty that Edmund would help her. She would tell him the whole truth; there would be no lies. She found herself wondering for an instant if, knowing the truth, he would still want her. But surely he still loved her as she loved him. He would understand. Had he not said that he would be nearby, that she should send for him if she ever needed anything, anything at all? If he no longer loved her—and in the deepest part of her heart she could not even accept this idea—she knew that at least he would take her to safety. She would send for him, and everything would be all right.

In the meantime, she must think of a plan to stall for time. Mother Anna would be pressing her, and she must have time to wait for Edmund's arrival. But not too much time, she hoped.

The first thing to do was to retrieve the ring and send the message. With that in mind, Chastity turned toward home.

◦§ *Six* §◦

THE RING LAY IN HER BASKET, CAREFULLY CONCEALED in a napkin next to a jug of cider that she was taking to the smithy. This was the first excuse that she could think of for going into town. She walked slowly, trying to formulate a plan for sending her message. By the time she reached the main street, she still had no idea where to begin her search. She shivered and noticed that dark clouds had crept across the sun. Why was it that Plymouth always seemed gray? she wondered. A sense of foreboding gripped her. Then she saw the Indian.

He was lounging in the dirt outside the general store, and appeared to be asleep. Chastity's step faltered as she realized that she could hardly step up and speak to him directly; the gossip would be around town in an hour. But she was desperate, and Edmund had said with certainty that any Indian would do. Somehow, she must manage to get the ring to him. With determination she came close to the man and bent down as if to tighten the laces on her small boot.

"Follow me!" she hissed fiercely.

The old Indian opened his black eyes and stared at her impassively.

"Follow me!" she repeated urgently. She stood up, gave him a meaningful look, and walked into the alley behind the store. The shadow of the building looked inviting, and she pressed herself flat against the wall. What if he does not understand English? she thought with sudden panic. What do I do next? She had never felt quite so foolish before.

At that moment the Indian sauntered around the corner and looked at her curiously. What could this beautiful white woman want? Never before in his long life had one spoken to him in that way. He stood before her, waiting to find out why.

Chastity took in his tattered clothes and matted hair. Her only hope lay in his hands, though they were gnarled and filthy. More determined than ever, she drew herself up and asked, "Do you know the man they call White Thunder?"

The old man grunted, but whether in affirmation or denial, she could not tell.

"Do you speak English?"

"Me speak English, me Christian," he answered indignantly.

A Christian! Should she trust a Christian? The irony of her thought struck her, and she gave a quick, involuntary smile. The Indian took this as a sign of approval, and he nodded with satisfaction. Well, she would have to trust him. There was no other way left.

"What is your name, Old One?"

"Me Oliver," he said proudly, and for some reason the sound of the great Cromwell's name reassured her.

"Do you know White Thunder, Oliver?"

"Me know."

With a sigh of relief she reached into the basket and took out the ring. It lay glittering on her palm, and she extended her hand to him. "Take this to him."

He made no move to accept the ring; his ancient eyes shifted from it to her face.

"Please, take this ring. Give it to White Thunder and say, 'Help.' Please."

He took the ring and turned it over in his hand. He ran his finger across the serpent's scales, grunted, and then slipped it into a small leather pouch he wore around his neck. "Snake ring go to White Thunder, say help." He looked at her for confirmation.

"That is right. But quickly." She paused. How could she explain her urgency to the old man? "Fast, fast like the wind. Do you understand?" she asked anxiously.

The Indian nodded, and for the first time showed some expression on his wrinkled face. He could still remember the pangs of young lovers. White Thunder must love this woman-with-burning-hair. "Snake fly to White Thunder like wind," he reassured her.

"Thank God! Bless you, Oliver." Her face softened and lit with such a happy smile that the Indian almost smiled himself. Instead, he nodded and started out of the alley.

On an impulse, Chastity called after him, "Walk in beauty, Old One."

He paused for an instant, surprised at her using the Indian farewell. Deep within him, he finally smiled. The woman of White Thunder would have to be extraordinary.

Chastity stayed in the alley a few moments after he left. It would never do for anyone to see them coming out of there together. When she felt she had let enough time go by, she stepped out and continued her way up the street. The old Indian was nowhere in sight.

She stopped off at the smithy to deliver the cider to her father and brother. If they wondered at her visit, it did not show. They were too busy. The pounding of the hammer and the sharp hiss as the hot metal was plunged into cold water made conversation difficult, so she was soon able to slip away. She was surprised to find her stepmother gone when she got home, and wondered what had sent her away from the house.

Several hours earlier, Anna stood uncertainly outside a small house in the village. She resolutely grasped the heavy brass knocker and let it fall. The door was opened by a servant girl, who led her inside and asked her to be seated in the study.

Anna nervously looked around at the many books that lined two entire walls. The solid oak desk facing her made her feel insignificant, and she shrank inside her faded gray dress. She wasn't sure of how she would phrase what she had to say, and began to practice the wording softly to herself.

The door was flung open and John Cox strode into the room.

"Goodwife Cummings, how good it is to see you!" His face was flushed from the autumn air and his pale hair tousled, as he had just arrived home from a walk.

"Good day, Reverend Cox." She got to her feet quickly.

"Please, sit down. What can I do for you today?" he asked as he sat on the corner of the desk, dangling his long legs over the edge.

Anna had forgotten how she had planned to begin. She was an ignorant though warmhearted woman and felt uncomfortable surrounded with so much learning. "It is Chastity," she finally was able to blurt out.

His eyes narrowed, and his muscles tensed. To give himself time, he walked around and sat at his desk. This simple act served to create a physical barrier between them and to reinforce his superior position as a minister of God.

"What about Chastity?"

" 'Tis so shameful! She is with child!" Large tears began to run down her tired face.

"Are you certain?" The tone was cold.

"In truth. I well know the signs."

He leaned forward; his face had gone white, and two spots of red burned on his cheeks. "Has she named the man?"

"No. Not yet, at any rate."

A faint whistle of air escaped him as he slowly relaxed his muscles and leaned back in his large chair. "Why do you come to me, Goody Cummings?" he asked with some curiosity.

"Why, because you are the minister! To whom else should I turn, pray tell?" She wiped her tears with a weary hand. "What am I to do?"

His mind raced, but all he said was, "You know the law."

"Oh, no, Reverend, not that! Well I know it, and have just reminded Chastity of its harshness. But I have come to you for help. There must be some other solution. Please, please help us."

With a start, John realized that the study door was still open. He closed it and sat down again on the edge of the desk, where he could look down on the woman.

She was crying silently now and wringing her hands in despair. "She will be whipped to death—that is, if her father does not kill her first."

"There is one alternative," John suggested slowly.

"Yes"—she seized on it eagerly—"if done quickly enough." Her honest face clouded and she shook her head.

"That is the problem, Reverend Cox. She has not named the father, and she insists that she cannot wed."

"Cannot? Has she given you a reason?"

"None. I do not understand her." She stared at the floor.

"Nor do I," he murmured. "Let me think a moment." He crossed the room and stared out of the window as his thoughts flew. Why had she not named him? There was loyalty in the girl, then, he decided, a fine quality. What a wife she would make! Of course, now he understood everything. She had been frightened and confused; that was why she had refused him! A flush of victory stole across his pale face, and light glittered in his eyes. She was his now; the child sealed it. He would marry her quickly, but it must be arranged so that her family never considered him anything but innocent. He had his position to protect. He wheeled to face Anna.

"If she has used the word 'cannot,' then the man must either be dead or gone from the town forever," he said in a firm voice. "If he were already married, I would have heard of it by now."

"Dead or gone? Then she is truly lost. My poor little one!" Anna wailed.

"Perhaps not. She is talented and beautiful. Under other circumstances she would be considered a prize."

"Aye, and she knows her Bible, too. Her intelligence almost rivals that of a man. She would make any Pilgrim a wife to be proud of, except for"—she hesitated and looked up at him—"this one small thing."

He gave a short, sharp laugh. He must not play too easy. "A bastard cannot be referred to as a small thing, Goodwife Cummings." He sobered and added, "But in all else, I daresay you are right. I myself have many times looked upon her with favor."

"You?" she questioned in sly surprise.

"Of course, I had no idea that there was another man," he added hastily in feigned distress.

"Nor did anyone," she bitterly commented.

Satisfied with her reactions and sure his reputation was safe, he decided to go on to the next step. "Of course, she has fallen from grace and must answer to God for her sin."

Anna nodded dumbly.

"But in Chastity's case, I can see no reason to expose her to the village. She can atone privately and keep her shameful secret. It depends on the choice she must make."

"But the babe. How can that be kept a secret?" Anna watched him with questioning eyes.

"She must marry."

"But if the man is dead or gone, who will wed her? Who will save her and give the child a name?"

He took a deep breath. "I will," he announced quietly.

She was shocked. The most she had hoped for was good advice. He offered her salvation!

"Who better than a minister to see after her soul? Who better than a minister to see that the child is raised a decent Christian and its mother welcomed back into the fold?"

Anna threw herself at his feet and took his hand, covering it with tears and kisses. "You are an angel of mercy come in our hour of need. How can we ever repay you?"

"Get up, woman," he said gruffly, withdrawing his hand and trying to wipe it discreetly on his waistcoat. For a second he was touched by shame. "I am only a man. Do not say such things. I am sure that Chastity's hand will be payment enough. She will be grateful, and a grateful wife is a good wife. When all is said and done, God rewards us for our acts."

"How true." She marveled at his wisdom. "Will you speak to my husband? He knows nothing of the situation."

"Of course. But go you first and prepare him. Press upon him the need for haste." He dismissed her regally with a wave of his slender hand.

It was beginning to rain. He leaned his head against the window and watched a droplet run its crooked course down the pane. He smiled.

Little was said at supper. The children, sensing the tension in the air, ate quickly and asked permission to go upstairs. It was immediately granted. Chastity was left alone with her parents. Nervously she got up and began to clear the table.

"Sit down!" thundered Thomas Cummings.

Chastity sat meekly. She had hoped that Anna would not tell him of her condition, at least not right away. She glanced at her for support, but Anna busied herself folding the large napkins.

"I should have expected it from your mother's daughter!" Stung, she cast him a pleading glance, but he continued. "You look at me with her eyes turned yellow, and you flaunt your whoring body the same way she did."

"Father—"

"Silence! Slut!" he roared. Chastity bit her lip; she knew that to speak now would only goad him into violence. "I will not hear a word from your lying mouth. If it were not for your stepmother here, I would denounce you myself in Sunday's meeting!" Chastity risked a look at that silent woman. Was there hope for her, then?

"But our merciful Lord has offered you a chance to escape your due fate. I have spoken to the minister."

Not John, she thought in dismay. Please, God, not John!

"This saintly man has offered to keep dishonor from our name. He has agreed to marry you himself and raise the child as his own."

In spite of herself, Chastity could not help a snort of disgust. It was a mistake. In two strides her father was across the room. He drew back his huge hand and fetched her such a violent blow that she was thrown to the floor. Anna screamed.

He towered above her and could see the red marks of his fingers on her tender flesh. When he spoke, his voice was low, and all the more frightening for the cutting edge in it. "You will either have the banns posted on Sunday morning or I will administer the whipping myself! No daughter of mine shall bring public shame and scandal to this family!"

He spun around and grabbed the sobbing Anna by the arm. "Leave the whore be!" he commanded, and almost dragged his distraught wife out of the room.

Chastity lay on the floor too overwhelmed by the intensity of her feelings to budge. She had never felt true hatred before. How quick he had been to condemn her! It had never occurred to him that perhaps she had not been to blame. And what a sanctimonious hypocrite John Cox really was! She began to see clearly now. For the past two months her mind had been clouded with guilt and her reasoning blurred.

What had happened that day with John had *not* been her fault. She had not tempted him at all; the sin was totally his! Now that she understood, she wondered how she had been deluded into accepting the blame. She realized with a start that the man's voice had a mystical quality that could weave a spell around any unsuspecting woman.

The day with Edmund had been her own doing, she knew that. But instead of a feeling of repentance, she now hugged the memory of his hungry body to her in a fierce embrace.

All right then, the banns would have to be posted; it was the only way. She would have to pretend to go through with it. Edmund would probably not get here by Sunday, and she must not be locked in the prison when he arrived. Nor could she afford to cross her father and find if he really would carry through with his threat.

She calculated rapidly. The banns had to be read on three Sundays before they could be wed. Even if it were done on three successive Sundays, that would still take three weeks. If the wedding were the following week, that would still give Edmund plenty of time to receive the ring and return to save her. She would play the part of the obedient, repentant daughter until then, and then disappear with her lover right under their very eyes!

As she tidied the kitchen, she heard low voices arguing in her parents' bedroom. Cold furor shook her hands and made the coals rattle in the warming pan she held. Very well, then, she vowed, she would be as hard as her father was. She would survive. She began to plan what she would say to John.

The rain had slowed to a steady drizzle by breakfast the next morning. Anna bustled around the table, chatting brightly and trying to cover the silence. Thomas refused to look at or speak to his eldest daughter. She kept her eyes meekly on the gruel in the trencher she shared with her sisters.

Soon the men left for work. The women were settling down to their chores when Abigail rushed in, full of excitement.

"The minister is knocking at the front door! It must mean that someone is dead!"

Chastity's gag was answered with a sharp look from

her stepmother. "The front door is used on other occasions as well, silly child. Go and show the minister into the parlor," Anna ordered.

"The parlor!" Impressed, Abigail scampered out.

Chasity knew that all this ritual meant that John had come to formally propose. Unconsciously, her femininity asserted itself, and she reached up to smooth her hair. Anna nodded her head in approval and gave Chastity's cheeks a hard pinch. Color flooded into them.

"That is right; now, bite your lips." Satisfied with her appearance, the older woman asked anxiously, "Will you accept him, Chastity?"

"It seems I have no choice," she answered quietly.

Anna sighed with relief. "Everything is going to work out, you will see. I must prepare some tea."

I must fool him, too, Chastity reminded herself as she entered the parlor.

John was standing near the cold fireplace, resting his arm on the mantel. When he saw her, he immediately straightened and came to her side.

"I heard the news from your stepmother yesterday, Chastity. I want to help."

"So I have been informed," she said dryly. She caught herself and added, "My father spoke to me last night. It was unkind of you, John, to let me bear the guilt alone."

So she still had not told! Flushed with pleasure, he rushed to reassure her. "How could I help you if I too were accused of sin? This way I can reach down and raise you up. I could not do that if all the truth were known."

"You came here today for something?" She would not make it easy for him.

"To propose." With a flourish he knelt on one knee and took her hand in his. "Chastity Cummings, will you marry me and become my wife, have my children, and live with me until death?"

Chastity looked down at his pale hair and suppressed a smile. The position he was in now was slightly ridiculous, but it would never do to let him suspect her true feelings. "I will, John Cox."

If he expected her to fall into his arms, he was disappointed. She stood there regarding him with cool eyes. Feeling rather foolish, he got to his feet and was about to kiss her, when Anna came into the room. Grateful for the interruption, Chastity took the tea tray from her and set it on the table. As Anna poured, she asked John about the plans for the wedding.

"I am going to ask the minister from Duxbury to perform the ceremony. It is only a few hours' ride, and I am sure he will be willing."

"We must make you a wedding dress, Chastity," Anna said, turning to her stepdaughter.

"I will wear my grandmother's dress, as my mother did before me. It is packed in the old brown trunk in the loft with her other things."

"It may be in very poor condition. We will have to examine it. I know it will have to be lengthened," she stated doubtfully. She was not at all sure that it was a good idea for Chastity to wear the gown of a woman who had deserted her family and husband and run off with another man.

Chastity, who had no intention of spending the time until Edmund arrived sewing a dress she never planned to wear, said, "I am sure it will be fine. The lace on it is lovely."

"Perhaps there are some changes for my house that you would like to suggest, Chastity; it wants a woman's hand," John said. "Shall we go look at it? That way I can have everything arranged to your taste by the day of the wedding."

Chastity smiled sweetly at her betrothed. "You are most generous and thoughtful, John. I am a lucky girl. Mother Anna and I would enjoy that, thank you."

"Mother Anna?" He looked at her blankly and then regained his composure. "Of course, you are welcome too, Goodwife Cummings, if you are not too busy with your own house and family."

"I think it best if we are not seen alone again before the ceremony, John," Chastity said with feigned concern. "There will be talk enough because of the haste of the affair and the babe's early birth. Forgive me for speaking plainly," she added as she saw Anna wince, "but after all, we must not do anything that might cast a shadow on your good name." He searched her face quickly, but her tawny eyes were wide with innocence.

"That is wise of you, Chastity." Anna spoke with satisfaction. "It does my heart good to see you being so thoughtful and practical. I heartily agree."

Frustrated, the man sat back and scratched his beard, at a loss for words.

The banns were read for the first time that Sunday and then posted on the meeting-house door. The townspeople rushed up to congratulate them, and Chastity forced herself to stand there and smile. Her head throbbed and she hated the role she was playing. She had to remind herself that she was forced into this battle, for a battle it was. She drew strength from a crazy rhyme that had been repeating itself in her head all during the long day.

> If I am not to be wed
> I will be whipped dead.
> But I shall be gone
> If I keep my head.

Anna stood on one side of her and beamed proudly.

She seems to have forgotten the reason behind all this, Chastity thought bitterly, her face muscles stiff from smiling. But she could not remain angry at the kind woman, who was only trying to do her best for her stepdaughter.

Her father stood by her left. In contrast to his wife, his voice was gruff and his hearty handshake forced. He and Chastity had not exchanged a word since he stormed out of the kitchen that terrible night.

On the way home, Chastity lagged behind, wanting to be alone with her hopes and her fears.

He should be here in a few days, perhaps a week, she thought to herself joyously. She heard her name called softly and turned to see who addressed her.

Elizabeth stood behind her on the path, motionless, suspended in the twilight air.

"Elizabeth! I did not see you at meeting," Chastity greeted her with some trepidation. This was the girl who sincerely loved John.

"Oh, I was there. Indeed, friend, I was there." The lovely girl started to shake.

"Elizabeth, are you all right?" Chastity reached out to steady her.

"Touch me not, witch!"

"What!" Chastity was horrified.

"You bewitched him. You enticed him away from me," the blond hissed. "I am the one he loves. You have no right to marry him! I should be his bride!"

Chastity stood dumbfounded. Part of her wished to reassure Elizabeth that there would be no wedding, but when she saw the look of insane hatred on the other girl's face, she knew it would be useless.

"I am not wedded to him yet," she said as she stepped away.

"Oh, I may not be able to prevent that," said Elizabeth, following her. "But you will not live to enjoy his love for long, I promise you! I warned you that I had ways to deal with you!"

Chastity whirled around in amazement, but the path behind her was empty. Dusk seeped in, filling the spaces between the silent trees. In the town, a dog began to howl. Chastity hugged herself tightly, shivering uncontrollably in sudden fear.

The banns were read again the following Sunday. Chastity became more drawn and tense with each passing day. At night she would go from her bed and run to the window, only to find that the pebbles that she'd heard bounce against the pane were only her imagination. She paced the house and garden restlessly, eyes turned toward the forest.

She refused to try on the wedding dress, and Anna was forced to threaten to tell Thomas. She finally agreed to it, but it was her stepmother who stayed up at night to let down the hem and repair the torn lace. Each morning Chastity got up assuring herself that this day Edmund would come, and each night she lay awake listening and waiting for his step.

The banns were read for the third and final time. Chastity felt that she could not breathe. She spent the day praying earnestly for Edmund's arrival. As she came out of the meeting house for the noon break, she was amazed to see the old Indian Oliver sitting in the back. He was there in the last pew along with a few black slaves and other Praying Indians like himself. She almost went up and questioned him before she realized what she was doing!

He followed her outside and managed to sidle up to her when no one was standing near.

"Snake have wings," he said in an undertone as he bobbed his old head up and down.

So the message had gotten through! He must be on his way. She uttered a short, silent prayer of thanksgiving as she hurried to join her family.

The sun did not dawn the day of Chastity's wedding. Instead, from sullen clouds rain lashed across the village. She pressed her forehead against the windowpane and repeated to herself: He will come. He *will* come.

Anna came in and urged her to go downstairs and eat but she curtly refused. She would not leave this small, safe room where she had grown up. She stared into the rain, willing Edmund to appear at the forest's edge. Where was he? Her eyes burned and her heart ached as she pressed herself against the glass.

The door opened and a worried Anna entered. "It is time, Chastity. I shall help you dress."

"No! I will not do it!"

"Child, you have no choice. It is the wedding or the whip," she said softly. "It is too late now. Everyone is waiting at the church."

The church! Of course! Why had she not thought of that before? Edmund could hardly break into the house and carry her off in front of her father and brother. The old Indian had been at meeting and had heard the banns read. He must know that she was to be married today. He would have told Edmund! She must get to the church; Edmund was waiting for her there. He would announce to the whole town that she was *his* betrothed, and they would disappear into the forest forever.

"You are right, Anna. Help me get dressed. I do not wish to be late," she said as cheerfully as she could. Anna rushed to the bed where the lovely dress was spread out. She helped Chastity step into the imported satin and hook up the pearl buttons. Chastity's hair hung loose, and Anna brushed it till it glowed like the sun. She covered it with a lovely lace veil and stood back to admire the effect.

"Chastity, I have never seen a woman so beautiful," she said with simple sincerity.

Trying to imagine herself running through the woods in this costly white satin, Chastity smiled. "We had best be off."

The family rode in the wagon, although it was a short walk. Chastity sat up front between her parents, her dress and hair protected from the rain by her heavy black cape. There was a crowd outside the church, and Chastity eagerly searched the faces for the one she loved. When she did not see him, she decided that he must be inside or around the back, awaiting the perfect moment to present himself.

Her father led her firmly down the aisle, and the ceremony began.

Why does he not reveal himself? wondered Chastity with growing alarm.

"Look at them," whispered Patience. "Weddings are so romantic. Her head is like the color of the setting sun and his pale like the moon."

Anna hushed her daughter, but she wondered with foreboding what would happen in this forced union of fire and ice.

In a sonorous voice the minister from Duxbury intoned, "I now pronounce you man and wife."

The crowd murmured, and Anna suddenly gasped. Chastity had fainted dead away and dropped to the floor.

❧ Seven ❧

THE WIND PROWLED AROUND THE HOUSE LIKE AN ANImal seeking prey, howling as it slithered through cracks and crannies. Chastity put down the half-finished poppet she was making and stretched her tired back. It was still early, but the short hours of February sun had already disappeared. Her eyes stung from the smoke thrown off by the fat knot of pitch pine called candlewood that she used for light.

At the desk behind her, John worked on a new sermon. The shadow of the candle's flame danced across his lean face, giving him a dark and mysterious air. His quill flew across the page, crossing out a word here, adding a phrase there. He seemed to be totally absorbed in his work.

A wolf howled in the distance, and she shuddered. Due to the extreme cold of the winter and the lack of game, the wolves had drawn closer to the town, occasionally raiding the livestock of one of the outlying homes. Chastity was glad that the parsonage was close to the center of New Plymouth, and her thought flew to the musket that was kept above the kitchen door.

The fire sizzled and crackled in the hearth. She was not surprised to see the sap, forced by the flame out of one end of the log, freeze into ice when it hit the cold stone. She knelt awkwardly by the fireplace and filled the brass warming pan with coals.

"I am off to bed, John."

"Go along. I shall join you when I finish this," he said without looking up.

In the bedroom, Chastity thrust the warming pan between the sheets and passed it back and forth quickly, so as not to scorch the linen. A small fire was burning in the fireplace, but it seemed to throw off little heat. She changed into her woolen nightgown, pulling the soft material tight against her swollen belly. The babe would be born in about ten weeks, and although she tried to disguise her figure as much as possible, she was already getting curious glances. Of course, it would never do for anyone to say anything to her face. It was not for nothing that she was the minister's wife.

His wife! The words left a wretched taste in her mouth, like the mixture that is no longer cream but not yet cheese. The nausea that had plagued her earlier in her pregnancy returned. She grabbed a brush and vigorously stroked her hair.

Her thoughts centered on the more intimate side of their married life. The first night after the wedding had been a repetition of that day in the forest, except that this time she had not fought; she no longer had the right to. He had taken her as quickly and as roughly in bed as he had on the grass. Whenever he approached her it was the same, a hand rough on her breast, a panting in her ear, a violent thrusting of his slender hips, and then a grunt as he rolled off her and into sleep. She had thought that his desire would diminish as her belly grew, but the sight of her rounded belly and swollen breasts rarely failed to excite him.

She forced back the bile in her throat and realized that her head was throbbing again. If only it were Edmund coming through the door! For the briefest of moments she let herself picture him, arms open and sapphire eyes ablaze with passion.

No, she chided herself sternly. Such romantic fantasy is for children and fools. It only serves to make my life more barren than it already is.

Chastity knew that she had gambled and lost; Edmund had not come to save her, and she was wed to John Cox for life. But barren or not, it was her life and she would make the best of it. Her only prayer was that the arrival of the babe would help to soften the hurt and give meaning to the years ahead. Sometimes she pictured the child as a golden bundle of laughter, and other times as a warm, dark moppet with shy smiles. It would be better when the baby was born, she told herself—it had to be.

She looked at the nightstand, where the heavy family Bible lay. It was covered in soft brown leather and embossed with the same gold that made up its ornate clasp. It had been her father's wedding gift to them. There she sought solace in the first days of her empty marriage, but as time passed without change, she gave up looking for hope in its printed pages. She had honestly tried to be a good Christian wife. She had put on a brave face and worked to make the best of her situation, but her mask cracked and crumpled as the dreaded nights approached.

"I have finished the sermon." John entered the room, glowing with pleasure at himself. "What? You are not abed yet?"

"I was just finishing braiding my hair," she answered as she tried to hide her growing unease.

He sat on the bed and let his pale eyes follow her as she moved about the room. "You are quiet. Is the child bothering you?"

"Nay, I am just tired." She slipped quickly between the warm sheets.

"You seem sad. When I first met you, you used to smile all the time. Now you are like an old woman," he criticized.

"I do not mean to displease you, John," she said quietly.

"I must warn you against succumbing to melancholy, Chastity," he said in a severe tone. "It is but the skillful temptation of the Devil. It would be most unseemly for you, the minister's wife, to fall into this sin. Besides, cheerfulness is an obligation for a good wife." He leaned back and said half to himself, "The sin of melancholia. That would make a good subject for my next sermon."

Relieved that his thoughts seemed to be turned away from her, Chastity closed her eyes.

"Chastity, I am speaking to you." His voice broke in on her thoughts. When she did not answer, he reached down and put his hand on her covered thigh. In spite of herself, she flinched.

"Do you draw away from me, your husband?" he asked, amazed. "It is not possible!"

"It is my head again, John," she apologized. "It pounds so that I cannot think. I took a powder earlier, but it has not yet taken hold."

"You had a headache earlier in the week," he reminded her coldly. "I must confess, I thought your constitution stronger when I married you."

Chastity kept silent, hoping against hope that he would tire and lose interest in his game. As though sensing her thoughts, John slowly drew back the quilt and stroked her swollen breasts.

She sat up and stared at him, determined to speak.

"Well? What have you to say for yourself, wife?" he asked in the thick voice she dreaded.

She pulled the quilt up to cover herself, and blushed. "It is not easy to say what I am thinking, not for a woman." He crossed his arms and waited in impatient silence as she continued. "I think perhaps if you would be more patient with me, take more time . . ."

"Time?" he snapped. "What are you talking about?"

"Well, if you would kiss me first, or hold me, speak gently to me, and help me too—"

"Enough, woman! I am your husband," he said in an icy tone, "not some romantic fool who has to woo and win you. You are already won!"

"I only meant to say that my headaches might be less, that I might find more pleasure in your arms if we could discuss this problem," she said in appeasement.

"Problem? I have no problem." He stood up, and the coldness in his voice made her shrink under the coverlet. "And as for pleasure, I am shocked by your brazen immodesty! May I remind you, madam, of the facts? Physical desire is a curse, a disease that can only be cured by holy marriage, where the fires slowly dwindle and die away." He lectured her like a small child. "Pleasure indeed! You sound more like an infidel harlot than a God-fearing Puritan woman! It is not your duty or your place to search for pleasure, only to render me my rights as your husband."

She lay passively while he took his pleasure. She felt like the poppet that she sewed for the babe, made of faded scraps and tatters. Soon there was a grunt, the heavy weight rolled off her, and the man lay snoring at her side. Carefully, so as not to wake him, she moved over to the very edge of the bed so that no part of her body touched his. She gritted her teeth and felt her silent screams echo loudly in the dark room.

Chastity sat in the kitchen plucking the feathers from a fat goose given to the minister by a parishioner. The large body lay across her lap. She put the soft down in one bag and the larger feathers in another. They would be carefully washed and sewed into a coverlet for the new baby.

Emily, the servant girl, sat churning milk into butter. It was a long and hated task and she wore a sullen expression on her face. Chastity studied the girl's thick features and wondered again why she could not bring herself to like the girl. She was a hard worker and was clean, but there was something sly about her manner that Chastity could not pinpoint.

The girl got up to answer a knock on the door.

"Sarah and Benjamin! What a surprise!" Chastity lightly kissed her visitors and bade them sit.

"We have brought you a gift, Chastity," said Sarah with a twinkle in her eyes.

"Another surprise? Oh, I love them! What is it?"

Benjamin put the bundle he was carrying on the floor and pulled off with a flourish the cloth that was covering it. It was a small cradle set on rockers; its dark wood glowed richly in the light. Carefully carved wildflowers covered the headboard and formed a chain around its sides. As she looked at it, Chastity's eyes misted. It was truly a labor of love—carved by firelight in the long winter's nights, after full days at the forge.

"How lovely it is!" she said from the floor, where she was awkwardly kneeling to examine the flowers. "Why," she exclaimed with surprise, "you have carved all my favorite flowers!"

"I remembered that they were your favorites," Benjamin said shyly as he shuffled his large feet. "They are the ones you used to bring home from the forest."

She laughed as she remembered how frustrated she used to get as a child, when she arrived home to find the flowers, so fresh and lovely blooming in the woods, wilted and limp in her hands. She got up and hugged her brother to her, touched by his show of love.

"The child will sleep well there, Benjamin." She included Sarah in her embrace. "We thank you both."

Her brother blushed, for he was unused to demonstrations of affection. His wife smiled proudly at him as he rewound the long scarf around his neck and pulled on his woolen cap.

"I must get back to work. Sarah will keep you company for a spell." As he opened the door, he turned back toward his sister. "Some animal has been hunting around your house, Chastity. We found chicken feathers and some blood in the snow outside your door."

"Chicken feathers?" Chastity turned to Sarah in disbelief. "There are no chickens out in this weather."

"That is what they were, though," her sister-in-law asserted, "strange as it may be. There were no tracks—it must have happened last night before the snow began again."

"Were there any remains of the chicken?" Emily broke in. Her eyes darted from one face to the other, her expression strange.

"Not a sign, only a few feathers and some blood in the snow," replied Sarah. "We covered it up," she added to Chastity.

Chastity's mind flew back to a few months before, when the snow had not yet descended from the sky. She had gone out early in the morning, just after the sun had crept up, to draw water from the well. Lying coiled in the path, so close to the door that she had almost stepped on it, was a dead rattlesnake. Its back was broken in several places, and she had wondered vaguely at the time how it had managed to coil up in such a state, but she soon found other things to occupy her thoughts. She had almost forgotten the incident, but somehow, in the back of her mind, it became connected with the feathers and blood. She shuddered, as though some evil had cast a shadow over her house.

"Do not fret, for goodness' sake, it was probably just an owl," Sarah soothed.

"Probably." She agreed, but she was far from convinced.

The two women talked for several hours. When Sarah was ready to go, Chastity showed her the baby clothes she had been working on. Sarah admired the fine needlework with just a trace of envy. Although she and Benjamin had been married for over a year, there was still no sign of a child. She fingered the lace christening gown lovingly and smiled sadly.

Aware of her thoughts, Chastity was all the more appreciative of the delicately made cradle that now stood at the foot of the large bed. The long hours spent on the design and in bringing up the luxurious satin finish must have held a touch of bitterness that the gift was for another's child.

That evening Chastity was summoned by Mary Ashley's young son to nurse his ailing mother. She sat up the whole night beside the sick woman's bed. The fever finally broke and Chastity waited to see that Mary was out of danger before starting home in the gray dawn. A gust of freezing air cut through her cape and sent small flurries of snow scurrying ahead of her. As she neared her back door, she saw a strip of something red being tugged and twisted by the wind's icy breath. She examined it with curiosity and found it was a long red ribbon with three knots in it, each of which was pierced by a metal nail.

"How strange," she muttered as she wondered what it could be and who could have put it on her door. She pulled it down and put it in her pocket.

Emily had breakfast ready. As she lived on the outskirts of town, she often slept in the loft during bad weather. Chastity sat down next to the fire, pulled off her wet boots with difficulty, set them to dry, and eyed the steaming porridge. John entered the kitchen, inquiring about Goodwife Ashley. As Emily spooned food into the trenchers, Chastity remembered the ribbon. She drew it out of her pocket and laid it on the table.

A spoon clattered to the floor.

Chastity jumped and turned to see the girl backing off, her eyes wide with fear. "Why, Emily, whatever is the matter with you?"

But the girl did not answer. Instead she wheeled and ran out of the room.

"What in blazes has gotten into that silly wench's head?" John growled.

"I have no idea, but it seems to have something to do with this." Chastity pointed to the ribbon. "I found it hanging on the back door. Emily must know something about it. I shall question her when she calms down."

"Do that. I like it not when the household routine is upset." He barely glanced at the ribbon, and dismissed the whole affair as he wiped his spoon off on his napkin. "I will not be home till supper. First I must attend the town council meeting. I fear we will have trouble with the Quaker woman who came here several months ago. Several of the parishioners seem to be overly friendly to her, and I think that a sign of mischief."

"Has she broken any law, John?" Chastity asked with a frown. She had seen Hannah Foote on several occasions, but the older woman had maintained a discreet distance.

"Only that of good sense," he replied. "She should not have come to Plymouth.

"After the meeting, I have to stop by at the miller's. His tithing has dropped off, and it sets a bad example for the rest of the town. Then I shall stop by at Mary Ashley's to give her a word of comfort." He rose, wrapped his cloak about him, and left.

Chastity sighed wearily. She went into the bedroom and pulled a comforter and pillows off the bed. Returning to the kitchen, she laid them on the wide stone bench that was set into the fireplace wall. Emily was back at work, her face closed and her thoughts hidden.

"Emily, what is that?" asked Chastity, pointing to the ribbon that lay on the table.

The servant barely glanced at it. "It looks like a ribbon," she said guardedly.

"I know that." Chastity forced herself to be patient. "I want to know why it frightened you and how it came to be on my door."

"I am sure I do not know." The girl gave a sniff and turned back to her work.

"Emily, I want the truth. You need not worry, no one will hurt you. Just tell me why you were afraid."

The girl replied nervously, "I did not put it there. I have no idea who did."

The last part sounded sincere, thought Chastity. But it

was obvious that the girl had been frightened, and Chastity was determined to find out why.

"What does it mean, Emily?" she asked softly. "A red ribbon with three knots and three nails. What does that signify?" She turned it over in her hands.

Emily drew back and shook her head firmly. "I cannot say."

"Was it intended as some kind of message for you?" Chastity risked a guess, knowing in her heart that the answer would be negative.

"Nay, that could not be. I live at home," was the swift reply that said more than it appeared to say.

So it was intended for either her or John. "Have you seen something like this before?" She kept her voice low, hoping to lull the sullen girl's fears and thus win her confidence.

"Nay, never."

"But you do know what it is. You have heard about something like this, have you not, Emily?"

She paused and then reluctantly admitted that she had.

"What are the nails for?" Chastity coaxed.

"They are coffin nails."

Try as she might, Chastity could not get another word out of Emily. Instead, the distraught girl cried and pleaded to be allowed to go home for the day. Chastity finally gave her permission after obtaining Emily's promise to be back early the next day.

Coffin nails, she thought with dread as she curled up on the warm stone bench. "It would seem to smack of witchcraft! John and the elders will have to look into this." She fell into a fitful sleep, one filled with dreams.

She was far away in a strange place. The sun was pouring down through the tall trees, and a small brook sang softly nearby. She danced. And as she moved in carefree grace, the forest held its breath and wild animals bowed gravely at her passing. She heard a voice softly call her name, and she turned to see her beloved Edmund smiling at her.

"Chastity." A whisper . . . a breath of love . . . a hand on her forehead.

She woke with a start to find deep blue eyes close to her own. She smiled lazily.

"Edmund." It was a sigh. Suddenly she realized that she was awake, that he really was standing there in the flesh, in her husband's house.

"Edmund!"

"Hello, sweet Dancing Fox." His smile was an embrace and his deep voice was rich with love.

"What are you doing here?" She pulled the blanket close in fear. "My husband will kill us both."

"I heard you had wed." He looked toward the door. "I saw a man go out, I presume he was your husband. Is he due back soon?"

"No," she admitted.

His rich laughter filled the air and set her heart to racing. "Well, then, there is nothing to fear." He threw his leg over a chair and straddled it casually. The look he gave her was so bold, so secure, that Chastity wanted to scream. How could he be so calm when she felt the blood pounding so loud in her ears?

"Why are you here?" She forced herself to disguise her trembling voice.

"You sent for me. See?" He held up his fist, and the sea serpent winked its ruby eye at her.

"That was months ago, Edmund," she said dully, understanding at last. "It is too late now."

"Too late for what, Chastity?" His tone was quiet and serious.

"Too late to save me. I am doomed now. You did not come in time." Her golden eyes that had been dry for months began to fill with tears, and she tried to turn her head so that he would not see.

But with a bound he was by her side, cradling her head in his strong arms. "Do not cry, love. Hush now," he soothed her as he kissed her wet face. "Stop. Your tears will break my heart." He held her and stroked her copper hair until her breathing was regular again.

"I just got the ring nine days ago," he tried to make her understand. "I had given up hope and was in the far north helping to settle a territory dispute for the Abnaki Indians. I have no idea how many hands my ring passed through before it reached me. But when I got it, I jumped on a horse and came straight here. I rode one horse to death and half-killed another to reach you, only to find you married. But"—he tilted her chin up and looked deeply into her eyes, where emerald flecks were beginning to spin—"you do still love me, or am I wrong?"

She nodded wordlessly, and with a tiny moan her lips sought his.

After a few moments he gently pushed her away and said, "Now, tell me all that has passed."

"I do not even know where to begin," she said hopelessly.

"Start from where you sent me away," was the soft suggestion.

"A few days after you left, John, my husband, forced me."

"What do you mean, he forced you?"

"Just that." She swallowed and gathered the courage to continue. "We were alone on the path that cuts through the woods, and he forced himself upon me." Her voice dropped to a whisper.

"You mean he forced his attentions on you?"

"No!" She closed her eyes in exasperation and then made herself speak slowly and clearly. "He forced me sexually."

A blue vein throbbed in the man's temple, and his low voice was like steel. "I shall kill him."

"Nay, Edmund, you must not." She reached up and put her fingers against his lips.

"You love him, then?"

"No, but I do not hate him," she replied.

"What happened after that?" he asked grimly.

"I told no one, for I was afraid. I felt so guilty about what you and I had done that I thought I was being punished. And then I thought that it was all my fault. After all, he was a minister! Oh, I am explaining it all wrong; I am so confused." She looked at him sadly, and he squeezed her hand.

"I understand. Go on." And he did understand. He had seen strange things happen when people were raised to believe that everything natural was a sin.

"My stepmother found out I was with child, and I could not tell who the father was. So I sent for you—I knew that you would help, no matter how hurt you were."

"You are with child?" She nodded, and he traced the curve of her body as she let the blanket fall.

"But in the meantime my family went to John for advice, and he offered to marry me. When I refused, my father threatened to cry me out at meeting. I could not bear the thought of the whip, Edmund, I am just not that brave. So I pretended to agree, thinking to gain time till you arrived. But alas, you did not. John thinks the child is his, and perhaps it is. Only the Lord knows for sure."

"My poor love," he murmured as he kissed her shaking hands.

"I waited for you. Every day I prayed that you would come. Lord knows how I prayed! But you did not, and I was wed. And now you are here, and it is too late." She turned away in despair.

"Look at me, Chastity. It is not too late. Tell me what you want, and I shall see to it. I curse the events that forced me to leave this part of the country! Forgive me for not being here when you needed me. I cannot undo the past, my love, but I shall arrange the future."

"Edmund! Do you mean it? Are you sincere?"

"Test me," he challenged her. "Will you stay here with your pious prince of hypocrisy, or will you come with me?"

She hesitated. "And the child?"

"The child is yours. As I love you, I cannot help but love it. Perhaps I am its sire. It matters not. I shall be its father."

She threw her arms around his neck and held him close. "If only it were that easy." She sighed in his ear.

"It is. Listen, I have received news that my grandfather is very ill. He is an old man, and I owe him much. I want to be by his side when he dies. If we leave here tonight, we can make Tanbor in time to catch the boat to New Amsterdam. From there we shall sail to England. It will be tight, especially in your condition." He looked at her fondly. "I will buy a wagon so that you can ride comfortably."

"Edmund, you realize that I can never be your wife," she reminded him, fearing all the while that he might change his mind.

"You shall be my wife for all purposes. You have your

choice, lovely one. You may either marry me or not, as your conscience chooses. But I warn you, I intend to clothe you in silks and jewels and to introduce you to all as my wife, for that is what you are in my heart and that is what you always will be to me."

"I cannot marry you. I am already wed."

He said nothing, only looked at her.

"You must promise me one thing," she insisted. "You must not kill John. If he were to die, I would not shed a tear, but you must not be the one to end his life. Not because of me. 'Twould be more guilt than I could bear. Do you understand?"

He crossed to the table and began to toy with the saltcellar. "You seem to be very fond of the man. Are you sure that you want to leave him?"

She rose to her feet and stretched out her hands to him. "How can you doubt me? Can you not see the love I have for you written plainly on my face?"

"You loved me once before, yet you sent me away," he reminded her. "How am I to know that this time you are sure?"

"Look at me, Edmund." She sat on the bench beside him. "I love you, and you only. I will follow you anywhere on earth. Try me, give me another chance. Believe me, I have paid dearly for sending you away."

He searched her lovely face and thought rapidly. "I can give you a few hours. I wish it could be more, but we must leave by dawn at the latest or we will miss the tide. Pack just what you need for the journey, no more. I shall buy you the rest in New Amsterdam. I will be here with the first streak of morning light, before the town is astir."

"I shall be ready," she promised with joy.

"There is one thing more. We must have a signal in case you decide not to come with me. I have no desire to come charging in here and meet your husband."

"There is no need for a signal. I shall be there," she insisted happily.

"Nonetheless, we should have a signal." He searched the kitchen for an idea, and his eyes fell upon the red ribbon. "There"—he pointed to it—"tie that ribbon to your front door if you change your mind. I will see it and go to England alone."

"Never!" She kissed him passionately. "I am yours, I always have been."

So carried away were they that neither of them saw the shadow framed in the kitchen window. It passed silently.

"I must go buy the wagon and some supplies. Think well, and be sure of your decision." The sight of her upturned face filled him with such longing that he hesitated to leave. But he steeled himself; she had to know her own mind; there would be no turning back. More than anything he wanted this woman with flaming hair to be happy at his side.

He tenderly kissed her hands, her neck, her mouth, rich and full like a red pomegranate. "Until dawn, my sweet."

She clung to him for long seconds, unwilling to let him out of her sight for even a few hours. "Take me with you now," she begged with urgency.

"No." He was firm. "We have to be sure of ourselves and of each other. The decision you make will be for the rest of our lives."

She let go reluctantly. He was testing her love, and she really could not blame him. "I shall meet you before the first cock crows," she promised with a smile.

When he had gone, she flew into the bedroom to gather her things, her eyes dancing with happiness. She pulled a thick blanket out of a chest and began to pile her belongings on it.

"A nightgown, two dresses, a pair of boots, stockings," she counted out loud as she carefully folded the items. "My baby might well be born in the middle of the ocean!" She hastily grabbed a few of the tiny clothes she had made, as she had visions of herself in childbirh on the high seas. "I care not! As long as I am with Edmund." She sang as she packed, and her voice filled the dreary house with sweet music.

She studied the pile and eliminated a few things that could be easily bought in New Amsterdam. Rolling it all up into a bundle, she fastened it securely with a stout rope and hid it in the chest under the window seat in the parlor. The bedroom needed straightening and there was still some leftover goose for dinner. She decided to make dumplings and perhaps even something special for dessert. If she hurried, she might have time for a small nap, so that she would be rested and calm. John must suspect nothing until he woke to find the bed cold and her gone.

He was pensive at supper; the council meeting must not have gone well, she decided. He asked after Emily, and Chastity explained what had occurred. After the meal, they sat in the study; John read, and she somewhat guiltily darned a tear in his waistcoat.

Her yawns were genuine; there was no need for her to pretend fatigue. She had been up the whole night before with Mary Ashley and had only dozed for the briefest of moments during the day. She needed no excuse to retire early, but to her dismay, John followed her into the bedroom and watched her prepare for bed.

"You seem happy tonight," he almost seemed to accuse her. "Why are you smiling so much?"

"I was not aware that I was."

"That is exactly what I mean," he growled.

"Really, John." She turned a reproving glance on him. "First you are upset because I do not smile enough, and now you seem upset because I do."

"Your cheeks are flushed. And your eyes, they almost shine!" He watched her closely from where he lay sprawled on the bed.

"Why all the questions, John?" Her forehead wrinkled in a frown of puzzlement. "What exactly is the problem?"

"No problem, I was just curious." He stared at the rafters and then asked in a soft voice, "Where is the ribbon you showed me today?"

Chastity tried to ignore an uneasy feeling. "I think it is in the kitchen somewhere."

John left the room and returned in a few minutes, holding the strip of red satin in his hands. He sat down and began to take out the nails and slowly undo the knots.

"Emily told me they were coffin nails but would say nothing more," she said nervously as she plaited her long hair. "Think you it could have something do to with witchery?"

"Coffin nails. How appropriate."

"What?"

"Nothing." He smoothed out the strip between his

slender fingers. "Ribbons have many uses. For instance, they can be sewn into quilts, used to adorn dresses, woven into baby blankets." He came closer to her as he spoke, moving wih catlike grace. "They can be braided into love knots, and they can even be used to send messages."

Chastity faltered and looked at him with real fear.

"They can be worn around the neck, see?" He slipped it around her white throat and began to tighten it slowly.

"John! You are hurting me!"

His shrill laugh rasped along her nerves, but he let go of the ribbon and came around to face her. "That would never do, would it, my sweet Chastity? *Chastity!* What a mockery of a name!"

"I . . . I do not understand you," she stammered.

"I do not understand you," he imitated her in a high falsetto. "I will follow you anywhere, test me."

She looked at him in horror. He knew!

"Aye, Chastity, the two of you were so immersed in your lusting looks and whoring kisses that you did not even know I was there. Did you really think I would let you go?"

His voice had dropped to a whisper, and Chastity was terrified. She tried to back off, but he grabbed her by the wrist and held her fast.

"You can never get away from me, you are my wife. I own you, body and soul!" he hissed in her ear.

She broke away and ran to the other side of the bed, trying to keep furniture between them. "John, I know you are angry, and you have every right. Let me explain." She tried to keep her voice calm, to gain some control over what was happening.

"Angry?" He smiled, and the sight of that evil smile chilled her blood. "My wife a slut, my child a bastard, why should I be angry?" He slowly undid his belt and slapped it softly across his palm. "It seems I must teach you a lesson. I will make you an obedient, cheerful wife." The belt cut through the air and struck her shoulder with a sharp crack. She raced to the door but he was there before her. His eyes were like pinpoints and his breath came in fast little pants.

"Down on your knees, whore!" he roared. "The Lord

God omnipotent reigneth! Blessed is he that dasheth the whore of Babylon against the stones!"

"Come to your senses, John," she cried in terror. "You are a dead man if you harm me!"

"Am I? I shall show you who is dead." He fetched her such a mighty blow that she spun to the floor. "Slut!" he screamed as he took a fistful of her thick braid and pulled her to her feet. "Jezebel!" He slapped her repeatedly across the face, and she tasted blood. He flung her on the bed and began to undo his breeches. "I shall show you who is the master here!"

She crawled across the bed and steadied herself against the night table. With the back of her hand she wiped the blood away from her mouth as she sought desperately for something with which to defend herself.

He started around the foot of the bed, laughing wickedly. "Come, little Chastity, come to your beloved husband."

"Take not another step toward me, John! I warn you!"

His laughter grew, and he took another step. In desperation she seized the heavy Bible with both hands and flung it at him. The clasp caught on his cheek and tore open the flesh. He took a step backward to regain his balance, and his heel hooked on the rocker of the small cradle. With a splintering crash he fell on it. Blood dripped down his beard, and he moaned with pain, his leg twisted into a grotesque angle.

She raced around him and out the door; her only instinct was to escape. She did not even feel the cold as she raced down the moonlit path. She must find someplace to hide until dawn. Why had she not found out where Edmund was staying! She could never go to her father's house; he would straightaway return her to her husband. Panic seized her as she ran through the deserted town; her heavy body screamed with each step.

A shadow rose in front of her. Her heart missed a beat, and she almost lost her footing until she saw that it was Hannah, the Quaker.

"Chastity," she called. "It would seem the very demons of hell pursue thee."

"They do." The girl gasped for breath.

"Why, thou hast blood on thy face!"

"Hannah, save me," she begged. "Give me shelter for the night. I am in terrible danger and I would be gone by dawn."

"Of course, child. Come with me." She put her own cape about the girl's trembling shoulders and led her away.

When they arrived at the small cabin, Hannah stirred the coals and threw on some wood. Soon they had a blazing fire and were drinking warm herb tea.

"It was a lucky thing for thee that I was out, else thou wouldst be sleeping in the snow," said Hannah, seeing that Chastity was beginning to relax.

"I know," she murmured thankfully. She snuggled deeper into the wool blanket that Hannah had spread over her.

"Here, let me tend those cuts."

As the older woman dabbed her slit lip with witch hazel, Chastity asked with mild curiosity. "What were you doing out so late alone?"

"I was on my way home from a meeting."

"A meeting of Quakers?" Chastity stiffened.

"Aye, God has led me to a few good people who believe as I do." The woman smiled happily.

"Oh, Hannah, do be careful," the girl pleaded. "My husband spoke ill of you just today. 'Tis against the law for Quakers to meet now in Plymouth. You could be arrested and hanged!"

The older woman set her lips in a firm line. "We do what we have to do, and we do it alone. Life is worthless unless we follow our beliefs, whatever they may be."

Chastity mulled this in her mind, but she was so exhausted that she found herself dozing in the large chair by the fire. Hannah wisely asked her no questions and let her sleep.

A hand grabbed her bruised shoulder, and she winced.

"Shhh," warned Hannah, "make no sound." She was outlined in the moonlight that streamed through the window, and she held a finger to her lips. "I hear men's voices outside. They must be coming after thee."

Chastity sprang up in alarm. "He is mad! My husband is mad, and if he finds me he will kill me!"

"Quick, out the back door before they surround the

house." The two women crept to the kitchen door. "Here, take this." She thrust a knife into Chastity's hands. "Wrap the blanket around thee and hide in the forest till they have gone. After they search the house and find nothing, they will leave." The door opened with a loud squeak and Chastity held her breath.

There was a loud pounding on the front door, and Hannah gave her a shove. "Run!" she whispered fiercely.

Chastity ran for the edge of the woods, the blanket flapping behind her like dark wings. She hesitated at the first trees and looked behind her. There, in the white snow, outlined clearly by the full moon, were her tracks. In desperation she plunged deeper into the forest, forcing her way through the deep drifts. She ran until she could go no farther, her body twisting with pain and her lungs rasping in the winter night.

Leaning exhaustedly against the rough bark of a tree, she moistened her dry lips and fought the pain that tried to engulf her. She would stay there until just before dawn and then make her way to Edmund. If only he were there! With her! Realizing that she must keep awake, she stomped her numb feet and looked about her.

Slivers of moonlight pierced the dark trees and magnified the twisted limbs that seemed to loom threateningly above her. The silence was broken only by a pair of owls calling softly to each other. She shivered in fear, and, in spite of the intense cold, broke out in a fine sweat. The knife in her hands glowed dully in the eerie light, and its reflection seemed to bounce back at her, mirrored in yellow eyes.

Yellow eyes! With a throaty growl the wolf sprang, and Chastity felt a searing pain across her belly. An inhuman scream echoed through the trees as she sank the knife in the animal's furry throat and savagely twisted the blade. With a snarl the wolf fell dead at her feet.

Dazed, she stared at the bloody carcass, not knowing if the scream had been hers or the wolf's. From the shadows a gray body hurled itself at her back. With a soft thud she landed face down in the deep snow.

The first ashen finger of dawn crept into Plymouth and silently lit the dark town. A breeze played with a long red ribbon attached to the knocker on the parsonage door, making it flutter gaily in the ghostly light. A man watched its macabre dance with infinite sadness before turning heavily away. He climbed into a low wagon and rode off, the creaking of the stiff wheels echoing loudly in the cold morning air.

❧ *Eight* ❧

A SOFT MURMURING IN A STRANGE TONGUE SIFTED down to her as she struggled upward toward consciousness. She could just make out the shadows that seemed to dance in front of her, and smoke stung her half-opened eyes. She thought she saw a solemn baby staring down at her from where he hung high on the wall. Gentle hands raised her head and held a bitter liquid to her lips. She tasted it and spit it out. She thought she heard laughter as she slipped back into the deep blackness.

The fever came back, bringing with it painfully twisted visions. Faces from her past loomed before her. Her mother was there, laying a cool hand on her hot brow. John stared at her through icy eyes, blood still dripping from his beard. Her father was berating her for forgetting her catechism. Strange faces she had never seen before were there too, a young pockmarked Indian woman who chanted softly in a monotone, a wrinkled old woman surrounded in blue smoke, an old man with hawklike eyes. Edmund was there, too, but his sapphire eyes had turned the color of midnight. Twice she tried to get up but was held down. The pain was so great when she moved that she did not persist in her efforts. She had no idea when day faded into night, nor night into day.

Finally the fever broke and she lay soaked in her own sweat, her body weak and spent. Through her damp lashes Chastity saw that an Indian girl about her own age sponged her dry with soft doeskin. Seeing that she was conscious, the girl smiled and patted her reassuringly. She fell into her first real sleep in days.

When she woke up, she was alone. She tried to move,

but the thick bearskins that lay over her seemed to be weighing her down. She gave up the effort and examined her surroundings.

She was in a small circular building of some kind. There was a hole in the middle of the ceiling through which she could see the blue sky. The ceiling was made of branches that were lashed together and thatched with grass. By turning her head a little, she saw that the walls were made of young saplings set vertically right next to each other. The spaces between them were plastered with mud, and here and there hung long, gaily painted mats of reed and bark. On opposite sides of the building there were two low doorways, about three feet high, covered with animal skins that she did not recognize. More skins lay in heaps on two woven mats on the bare earth floor, like the one on which she was lying.

There was a small fire glowing in a ring of stones in the very center of the strange place; the smoke wafted slowly up and out the hole in the roof. Several blankets and hemp bags lay on the floor, but from her position Chastity could not see what they held.

She closed her eyes and began to explore the dull pain in her body, and discovered with a small shock that she was naked. Although her back hurt, she was able to move her head and arms, but when she tried to move her legs, pain knifed her in the belly. She let out a small cry and saw a hand push aside the skins on the door nearest her.

An Indian girl came in and squatted beside her. Black eyes stared at her with friendly curiosity as the strange girl felt her forehead. Satisfied that it was cool, she smiled and began to speak.

With shock Chastity realized that she could not grasp a single word the girl said. Seeing that she was not understood, the ebony-haired girl held up a finger and disappeared out the small door. She reentered immediately, followed by a woman a few years older than she. The woman straightened up, and Chastity could see that she wore a papoose board on her back. This she removed and hung up, baby and all, on the wall. She squatted down beside Chastity, who could see that her face was badly scarred from smallpox.

"You be plenty fine soon," she said as she held out something for Chastity to drink.

Grateful that she had found someone that she could talk to, Chastity took the horn cup and swallowed deeply. A cough almost choked her as she recognized the same bitter liquid that she had tasted before.

"Drink! Drink make you plenty better!" commanded the woman.

Chastity held her breath and obediently drank the foul-tasting stuff. She had so many questions that she did not know which to ask first, but decided on the easiest.

"Where am I?"

"Sowams," was the brief reply.

Sowams! That was the winter home of Massasoit, miles and miles away from Plymouth!

"How on earth did I get here?" she asked, bewildered.

"Metacom find you. Kill wolves. Wamsutta come, help bring you here to us."

So the owls she had heard in the woods had not been owls at all, but Indians. She had heard tell of such things.

The woman with the scarred face held up one of the skins that lay over the injured girl. "This wolf you kill. Metacom make you gift, for you plenty brave. This wolf mean, bad. Kill baby."

"Baby?" asked Chastity in dread. She did not really want to hear the answer.

"Baby born dead, torn from body." The woman sighed in sympathy. "Strong boy-child, hair like summer corn." She watched Chastity's face anxiously.

Tears rolled down her sunken cheeks, and she turned her face to the wall. A blond boy—he must have been John's son after all. And now he was dead. She would never hold him in her arms, kiss his little face, or hear his sweet laughter. Several minutes passed while she tried to absorb this. Finally she faced them again, and her voice was faint.

"How long have I been here?"

"Long time."

"How long?" she demanded impatiently. "A day, a week, what?"

"Long, long time," the woman insisted.

So Edmund must be on his way to England. He must

have waited outside the house for her and decided that she had changed her mind again. She would never see him again. Instead of coming to her aid, the memory of their last moments together cut into her, leaving her hurt and embittered. Her lips still felt his, hard upon hers, and she cried out with the pain of terrible, senseless loss. To have come so close! And now there was no hope; she had nothing left. Her past was dead, and so were all those who had lived there within. There was too much pain. She closed her eyes, and her grief was truly overwhelming.

Later in the day, a man came to see her. He seemed to be about sixty, but he moved with such fluid grace that it was hard for Chastity to judge. His black hair was salted with gray, but he held himself straight and tall. As he knelt by her side, his eyes were flat and cold.

He does not like me, she thought as he lifted up the skins to examine her wound.

Chastity protested in embarrassment at a strange man seeing her naked body, but the two women rushed to reassure her. Apparently he was the local doctor, she decided, because he examined her with a practiced hand.

Looking down, Chastity could see an ugly gash running across her belly. Tiny sticks of wood had been inserted under the skin, forcing the wound to stay open and drain. The man began to chant and shake a painted rattle that he held in his left hand, while with his right he reached into a small bag hanging at his side. He took out a hollow bone and some yellow dust, and putting the bone in his mouth like a whistle, blew the dust into the open wound.

Chastity watched with amazement. This was hardly the way that injured people were treated in New Plymouth, but since he was obviously the one who had been keeping her alive, she did not protest.

As if to answer her thoughts, the woman spoke. "Him powah. Him have manito, plenty big medicine. When Metacom bring you here, you dead. Him talk with powah, make plenty fine gifts. Powah make you better."

Chastity gave the stern man a timid smile, but he ignored her and resumed his chanting. After he had dusted off his hands and left, the two Indian women came and sat next to her.

"We talk, yes?" asked the older of the two.

Seeing Chastity's answering smile, she introduced herself and her friend, laying her hand first on her own breast and then on the other girl's. "Me Betty. Her Minone, mean Heather Flower."

"Minone." Chastity tried the exotic word. "How lovely! I am . . ." She paused, uncertain of what to say. She would never go back to Plymouth, so of what use was her Christian name here? "Dancing Fox," she concluded, which was as close as she dared to come to that precious, pain-filled memory.

Betty turned and said something in her own language to Minone, who clapped her hands with delight. Apparently they were pleased with her Indian name.

The baby began to cry with hunger, and Betty stood up to get him off the wall. She casually undid the top of her dress and began to nurse, and Chastity looked away in embarrassment. Not knowing what to do, she feigned sleep, and because of her weakened condition, pretense soon gave way to reality.

So she was not awake when Metacom entered the wigwam. His dark eyes studied her briefly as the two females answered his questions. He bent over and touched her copper hair with wonder. Then he issued a sharp command and left.

In the weeks that followed, while Chastity slowly regained her strength, she began to learn the language that had sounded so strange to her ear. Minone would gladly point out objects and name them, making a game of the words, while Betty would patiently prod her along and point out her errors. An ancient woman whom everyone addressed as "Grandmother" moved in with them, bringing her own mat, furs, and baskets. Although Chastity did not realize it, the old woman was there as a teacher and chaperon at Metacom's request.

Soon she knew enough words to be able to follow the gist of a conversation, and so learned more about her hosts. Betty had lived with a series of white trappers in Merrymount. That explained her knowledge of English and her English name. Chastity did not pry into Betty's reasons for leaving the town. She discovered that her own experiences were making her more tolerant and less sure of the definition of sin.

Minone's parents had died in the smallpox epidemic that had swept through the tribes of the Northeast some nineteen years before. Whole tribes had died from this white man's disease. Chastity remembered guiltily how the Pilgrims thanked God regularly for sending this disease and sweeping the land clean for them, the chosen people.

When she was strong enough to sit without tiring, Minone brought Chastity some clothing. She was pleased with the soft doeskin dress and touched by the girl's friendship. Seeing that she was able to express herself well in her new tongue, Betty moved back with her family, although she often dropped in during the day. Chastity enjoyed her visits. Betty's heart was as warm as her poor face was scarred.

The nights were spent around the fire in the small wigwam. Often neighbors would drop by to listen to Grandmother, for she was famous in the tribe as a storyteller, and had a gift of words that could draw tears or laughter from her listeners.

"Tell us about you and Red Deer," begged Minone one night. "How did he win you?"

The old woman showed her toothless grin and smacked her gums together as she remembered her first husband.

"In the old days, it was not easy for a young brave to get married. He had to sneak around like the tiny gray mouse to find his beloved alone. If she were well brought up, she would not speak to him, but she could smile at him just a little as if she wished to encourage him.

"When I was a young girl, I was very beautiful. My hides were the finest and the softest in the village. My thick braids were down to my knees and my skin was soft and smooth. My parents watched me carefully and made a rawhide bed for me to sleep upon at night. When they saw Red Deer wanted me, they tied me to my bed at night with thongs so he could not steal me away.

"He caught me one day as I went for water, and although I did not speak to him, I smiled, for he was tall and straight like the young pine and fair of face like the evening star. My smile so encouraged him that he went to my father and offered him five bearskins for me, three brown and two black.

"But my father waved him away, meaning for Red Deer to go away and quit talking foolishness like that.

"Now, that made Red Deer sick with love and longing. He went to his friend Moose Horn. Moose Horn said that he had some skins that Red Deer could borrow, and that when Red Deer got more, he could pay him back.

"So Red Deer went again to my father, and this time he offered him nine bearskins, four black and five brown. But my father waved him away again and would not say anything.

"Red Deer was so sick with love that he waited until he found me alone again. He asked me to run away with him and said he would fall over and die if I did not. But I said that I would not do any such thing; I wanted to be bought like a fine woman. In those days I thought a great deal of myself." The old woman grinned and bobbed her head up and down.

"Red Deer became so sick he could not eat a bite. He went around with his head hanging down and his shoulders bent. His family feared that he might drop down and die. But Moose Horn had another plan.

" 'Cousin,' he said, 'if you are man enough to do as I tell you, you may succeed yet. You must steal her and run away with her. After a time, you can return, and the old man cannot harm you, because she will be your woman. Probably she wants you to steal her anyway!'

"Red Deer agreed to the plan. They went away from the village, and Red Deer stripped naked. Then Moose Horn painted him solid white, and after that he painted black stripes all over the white. Red Deer looked terrible!

" 'Now,' said Moose Horn, 'if you get caught, everyone will think you are a bad spirit and will be too afraid to chase you.'

"When the night was getting old, they sneaked up to my father's wigwam. Moose Horn stayed outside to sound the alarm. Red Deer crept up by my bed and began to cut the thongs. But I was restless, and each time he cut a thong, it popped. Red Deer worked slowly and carefully, but when he got to the thongs on my thigh, he was seized with such a trembling that he scratched me with his knife.

"I woke up, and the first thing that I saw was a terrible

black-and-white-striped animal lying by my bed. I screamed and then my mother screamed and my father yelled. Red Deer jumped up, scared to death, and he almost knocked the wigwam down as he ran out.

"People came running from all over the village, with bows and axes and knives. Everyone was yelling.

"By now Red Deer was running so fast that he hardly touched the ground, and he looked so terrible that no one dared to kill him. We all thought he was a bad spirit. He made for the river and dove into a hollow log to hide.

"After many hours, when peace had again settled over the village, Moose Horn went down to the river and found his friend. They washed all the paint off Red Deer and sat down on the riverbank to talk about their troubles.

"Red Deer said that he would never go back to the village, he no longer cared what happened to him. The two of them decided to go off on the warpath, all alone.

"After several weeks they came across a Narragansett hunting party trespassing on Wampanoag ground. They killed the sentry and made off with as many fine furs as they could carry, plus three wampum belts.

"This time my father did not wave him away. He did not care about the skins and wampum. What he wanted was a son who was a real man, one who was brave, determined, and good.

"So Red Deer won me and told me this tale many seasons later, after our second son was born."

Chastity joined in the laughter as the old woman finished her story. She had sat in the shadows, but was still warm from the fire, as no one would be rude enough to pass between her and the flames. Listening to the stories each night, she gained insights into the Indian character and culture. Many things she still found puzzling, but most she came to accept.

The day she took her first steps, Minone sat down and cried.

"Why, Minone," she said, "you should be happy I am getting better. Why do you cry?"

"You will soon leave us, and like the snow goose, fly to find your own," the pretty girl said unhappily.

Dismayed, Chastity sat down abruptly. "May I not

stay here? I do not wish to return; there is nothing to return to. May I not stay here with you and Grandmother?"

Minone brightened. "You really wish to stay here with us? To live with the Wampanoags?"

"Is it permitted?" asked Chastity with growing hope.

"Grandmother! Grandmother!" Minone called, and the old woman thrust her gray head through the flaps at the door. "Dancing Fox wishes to remain with us, to wear the moccasins of the Indian."

Grandmother squatted down beside Chastity and grunted with pleasure. "It is good, the gods have answered our prayers."

Chastity reached out and held the wrinkled hand. "What must I do? Will Massasoit give his permission?"

The old woman clacked her gums together and nodded her head. "I will speak at the next council campfire. The powah will not like it, he has no love for the white skin. But if I adopt you, I think no one will speak out against it. Where is your man?" she asked suddenly.

"My man?"

"The one who made you great with child. Where is he?"

"My husband is in Plymouth, Grandmother."

"Does your heart sing for him?"

Chastity snorted in disgust. "Nay. I hate him. I hate and fear him, Old One. If I am sent back to him, I shall kill myself."

The old woman studied the younger one's face for a moment. "Your eyes speak truth, Dancing Fox. He must be a bad man, one who does not deserve a wife. You must divorce him."

"How?"

"When the council fires burn high and the chiefs have spoken, I will adopt you. Once that is done, you must stand up and announce that you have left your man and are now free."

"Is it that easy?"

"No one can make a woman live with a man unless she is a slave captured on the warpath," she explained patiently. "This is the law and the way of things. Metacom saved you, he did not capture you. You are free here; you are no man's slave."

"Then I shall divorce John gladly," she stated firmly. "And I must find Metacom and thank him for saving me."

The old woman drew back in horror, and Minone began to giggle. "No! No, Dancing Fox, you must not seek him out. And if he seeks you out and speaks to you when you are alone, you must not answer him."

Minone added, "If he comes up when we are together, you may say, 'See, Minone, here comes Metacom, the brave chief who saved me from the wolves.' But you must talk to me, not to him."

"You must make him a gift—I can show you how to make moccasins. I will give your gift to him from our family. He will know that you have made it, and in this way he will be thanked."

"Forgive me, Grandmother. I have so much to learn," said an embarrassed Chastity.

"The village will understand that you have not been raised in our ways," comforted the woman. "You have more freedom than a maiden, but less than a woman with a man. You are like a young deer who has lost its milk spots and not yet grown antlers for protection. You will learn in time; until then, let Minone guide you. Remember, a friend is called one-who-carries-your-troubles-on-her-back." She stood up and looked down at Chastity.

"Practice walking. You should step into the light of the council fire and stand there alone. Let no one say you were led."

Chastity practiced walking around the wigwam, and in a few days felt strong enough to go outside. She was surprised to find how cold it was. The wigwam kept out the cutting winds.

With Minone she walked around the village, pausing to rest on her arm when tired. Sowams was a fortified town circled by a stockade of upright logs, some of which were almost a hundred feet tall. Her friend explained that the trees were felled by lighting carefully controlled fires at the base of the trunks; large branches were removed the same way. Many dogs roamed the village, and Chastity shuddered at their wolflike looks. Minone soothed her fears by explaining that over the years many bitches had bred with wolves, but that the dogs were thoroughly domesticated. She was not reassured until she saw one licking the face of a young boy.

The village was busy and noisy. A group of boys played on a hill of snow, coasting down on strips of basswood bark. Chastity had never seen anything like it. They stood on one end of the narrow strip and held the other in their hands. Falls were answered with peals of laughter. A handsome warrior passed, carrying a load of firewood, and Minone blushed. He wore strange shoes, much longer than his foot and four times the width. They seemed to be made of some kind of net stretched between wooden rims, and kept him walking on the surface of the soft snow.

"That is Running Bear. He is a fine warrior."

Chastity looked at her friend with amusement. "If you may not talk to him, how will he notice you?"

"He is a friend of Metacom and his brother Wamsutta. I may talk to them, for they are my mother's nephews."

"Will they speak to Running Bear for you?"

"Oh, no. But they may lead him past the wigwam sometimes when I am sitting outside; there are many ways to arrange such things."

"If Grandmother adopts me, then may I speak to them also?"

"No, you will be of the Owl clan. We are of the Crow," she said proudly. "Of course, often maidens speak to men, but no one knows it. I have never done it unless he was kin, but if Running Bear were to surprise me one day, I might force myself." She giggled and looked sideways at Chastity. "You should not speak to a man who is not of your clan, but you may marry one."

Chastity stopped in surprise. Marry? She had not considered the possibility. "I do not think I shall marry again," she said slowly. "I loved greatly once, and now the man is far across the waters and will not return. It pains me to remember."

"We believe that a young woman should not sleep alone. There is time enough for that when she is old and her blood runs sluggish like the bear in winter. When a woman is of age to marry, she should marry. If her husband dies, she should wait awhile and then take another."

"It does seem practical," Chastity agreed as she suppressed a smile, "but I still doubt that I will do it."

"Your heart may heal with the passing moons. If you choose to have no man, I know one who will be sad."

"Who?"

But dark-eyed Minone only laughed and would not tell her.

The day of the council fire drew near, and minor sachems and mugwumps, or war captains, from adjoining towns came to Sowams. As they filed into the town with their followers, their clanspeople opened their homes to them. Unless actually at war, people sharing a clan were family, no matter the tribe.

Chastity grew more and more excited, and there was a festive air about the village. Minone helped her embroider her doeskin dress with shell beads and lent bracelets of carved bone.

That afternoon Minone was as happy as a child with a secret. She led Chastity outside where she could talk to her.

"Metacom has promised to have Running Deer sit right across the fire from me. Every time he looks into the fire, he will see my face!"

"Will there not be too many people?" questioned Chastity as she tried to untangle her long hair. "The town seems full enough to burst."

"No, since I am niece to Massasoit, I shall be in front. You will be too," she added gaily. "Grandmother holds a place of honor—she was Massasoit's father's sister."

Chastity had puzzled over clan lines and the many rules of behavior that followed them. "Then I shall be Massasoit's cousin?"

"Yes, but not an important one. It would have been different had Grandmother been his mother's sister. Now, let me do your hair. If we had husbands, they would do this for us every morning. But since we have none," she said playfully, "we must help each other."

Chastity laughed and sat patiently while Minone brushed her copper hair with a porcupine tail. She parted it expertly and made two long braids, wrapping the ends in strings of painted buckskin that were decorated with eagle feathers. She carefully painted the part in Chastity's hair white and then drew two large yellow circles on her cheeks.

"Yellow is for joy," she explained, "and white for peace." She added two white dots in the middle of each circle and three lines on her chin and then sat back to admire her work. Chastity wished for a mirror, but settled for the admiration she saw on the maiden's face. She had to smile when she thought of what they would say in Plymouth if they could see her. Well, they never would get the chance; after tonight she would be an Indian.

The flames of the council fire leaped high and their light flickered across the sea of painted faces. Chastity craned her neck to get a better view of the thin, black-robed Jesuit who was speaking. His accent was a bit thick, but his voice rang loud and clear as he asked the assembled chiefs for permission to stay in Sowams to preach the words of the true God.

His speech was long and eloquent; the Indians sat quietly and listened to each word. When he finally finished and sat down, Massasoit recognized the powah, Sassacus, who leaped to his feet in anger. Striding back and forth before the chiefs, his voice heavy with sarcasm, he declared his distaste for the white man's religion.

"Friends and Brother! It was the will of the Great Spirit that we meet here this night. He orders all things and has given us a fine night for our council. He has taken his garment from before the stars and blown on the fire that its flames might light our faces and show us truth. For all these favors, we thank the Great Spirit, and him alone.

"Brother! Continue to listen. You say that you have come to teach us to worship the Great Spirit agreeably to his mind, and if we do not take hold of your religion, we shall be unhappy for as long as the sun shall shine. You say that you are right and we are wrong. But how are we to know? You say that your religion is written in a book. We also have a religion, but we have no book. If this religion was intended for us, why did the Great Spirit not give us a book also, and the means to understand it?

"Brother! You say that there is only one way to worship and serve the Great Spirit. If there is but one way, why do you white people disagree about it so? Why not all agree, as you can all read what it tells you in your book?

"Brother! We have listened with attention to what you have said. You wish to live here with us and teach us the words of your god. You want an answer to your talk, and it is right that you should have one. You are a long way from home, and we do not wish to detain you. But the white man's heaven is repulsive to the Indian, and if the white man's hell suits him, why, he may keep it. I think there will be white people enough to fill it.

"Brother! You speak of your savior bleeding on a cross of trees. You say he died for us, that we must repent. I say if you white men killed your savior, it was very foolish. Make it up yourselves, we had nothing to do with it. If he had come among the Wampanoags, we would have treated him better.

"Brother! You have heard my answer to your talk, and this is all I have to say. I hope the Great Spirit will protect you on your journey home and return you safe to your friends."

As the angry powah sat down, the circle of Indians buzzed and many nodded in agreement. When no one else rose to speak, Massasoit himself stood.

He was an imposing figure in the dim light. His muscles gleamed with bear grease, and his face, painted red for power, showed no emotion as he turned to the Jesuit.

"Black Robe, we thank you for your speech. We shall watch with interest the religion of the white man. When the disagreements among you stop, we shall rejoice. We will wait until you are all in agreement. If then we find that your religion makes the white people more honest and less disposed to cheat the Indian, we will again hear your words." With a wave of his mighty arm Massasoit summoned two braves, who led the Jesuit away.

Chastity had been fascinated during the long speeches, but she began to grow weary as the hours wore on. She saw three young men staring at her from across the fire and thought that she recognized Metacom from that day in Plymouth so very long ago. The other two must be Wamsutta and Running Bear. She glanced over at Minone, who was smiling broadly at her. Self-consciously she touched the yellow paint on her cheeks and straightened her short skirt. This brought forth grins from Metacom's two friends, but he did not smile. He only looked at her with his mysterious black eyes.

With a start Chastity realized that the old woman had gotten up to address the council.

"Massasoit! Grand Sachem of the Wampanoags, brave chiefs, hear me! Among us is a young woman who wishes to live with us. She wishes to be my daughter, and my heart is glad. She was brought broken and bleeding to my lodge. She lay near death. We did not think she would live. But our mighty powah saved her with his great manito." She bowed briefly in the direction of Sassacus, who inclined his head indifferently.

"Where is this woman of whom you speak?" Massasoit demanded. "Let her come forth."

The old woman gestured to Chastity, who got stiffly to her feet. Now that the moment had come, she was afraid. What if she were to be sent away like the Jesuit? Where could she go? The crowd murmured as she approached Massasoit, for most of the people gathered had not seen her before.

"Is it your wish to stay in Sowams?" Massasoit remained seated and looked up at her.

"It is." Her voice was sweet and clear and she kept her eyes on the ground as she had been instructed.

"What are you called?"

"Dancing Fox, Great Sagamore."

"Why do you wish to stay here, Dancing Fox?"

She had not been prepared for that question and she searched for the answer. "Life in Plymouth is false, the people speak in two directions. They say one thing, but their hearts say another. I cannot live like that. I cannot go back. My life there is dead. Your people have been good to me, they have welcomed me with open hands and hearts. I wish to remain with them. They are good and true," she concluded simply. Had she said enough? Would Massasoit allow her to stay?

"Have you a man from your people who will come to claim you as his woman?"

"I did have, but I am no longer his woman. In my heart, I never was. I wish to divorce him." Chastity thought she saw the ghost of a twinkle in the great man's eyes, before she remembered and hurriedly dropped her own.

"Old Woman, is there a clansman who will protect her? Is there someone who will see that she has meat and does not starve, that she has skins and will not go bare in winter, that she has land and corn to plant in it?"

An old man stepped into the circle. "I, Witowash, elder of the Owl clan, accept this woman Dancing Fox as kin," he said in a reedy voice.

"Does anyone speak against this thing?" questioned Massasoit.

Chastity held her breath as the powah shifted his weight uncomfortably, but he remained silent.

"Then it is done!" came the judgment.

A short time later Chastity was surrounded by her new family.

ᦞ Nine ᦞ

IN THE WEEKS THAT FOLLOWED, CHASTITY WAS BE-
sieged by the women of the tribe. Even though she had
been in Sowams for almost two months, most of her
time had been spent inside, recuperating from her wound.
There were many women in the tribe who had never
seen a white female before. They stared at her golden
eyes and gingerly touched her flaming hair, as if afraid
that their fingers might be burned. Minone was always
at her side, to coach her in their customs and to explain
the intricacies of clan lines. The children especially liked
to gather around her as she worked, and they usually
found her stories of Puritan life quite hilarious.

"Is it true that the white men divide the day into
hours, like the moons of the year, and then divide the
hours again and yet again until the day is made up of
grains of sand?" she was asked one day as she made
suppawn, a thick cornmeal-and-milk porridge.

"Yes, the smallest grains are seconds, then minutes,
hours, days, weeks, months or moons, and then years."

"White people measure everything," a small boy assured his younger sister.

"Why?"

"Well, so that they know when something has to be
done," Chastity tried to explain to her young listeners.

But this sent the children into peals of laughter.

"The white man is silly," scorned the small girl. "Even
I know that the planting is done when the leaves of the
white oak are as large as a mouse's ear, and that we
move to our winter homes when Indian summer follows
squaw winter."

Chastity had no answer to that.

"Betty told us a story that I do not believe," said another child. "She said that when white men make a feast, they invite many and the food is varied and plentiful. But when the feast is over, the guest must pay for what he has eaten before he is allowed to leave the house! Is that true?"

She hesitated, wondering how to explain the concept of an inn to the children. She finally gave up and answered only. "It is the custom sometimes, and only in certain houses."

Tiny purple crocuses poked their heads through the white snow, and a bear was seen playing with her cubs by the river. Soon it was time to plant, and Minone took Chastity into the fields, for planting was women's work. Only tobacco was tended by men.

The girls cleared and broke ground with hoes that were made of large clamshells attached to wooden handles. Chastity already knew how to plant corn, as Squanto the Indian had taught the Pilgrims the secret when they first arrived in the New World. She carefully dug a shallow hole with the end of the hoe and dropped in five kernels of corn and a small fish. Minone worked on the other side of the row and alternated digging the holes with her. In this way the planting was soon done.

They went to the fields almost every day to weed and care for the young seedlings. When the corn was almost to their knees, they planted beans that had been carefully hoarded over the winter. They put them in the dark earth right next to the corn, so that the thick stalks would serve as natural beanpoles. They laughed and talked as they worked, and Minone told her stories from the times before the Pilgrims had landed on her people's shores.

One day, as she was bent over the rich black dirt, Chastity glanced up to see Metacom standing on a gentle hill by the field's edge, his arms wrapped in heavy leather and thrown up toward the sun. He wore only a red loincloth, and his bronze muscles rippled across his shoulders and thighs. Chastity watched in frank admiration as he threw back his dark head and let out a high, piercing whistle.

A black dot circled lazily in the blue sky. At the sound

of the whistle, it began to dive. Lower and lower it came, until she could see it was a fierce-looking hawk. With a gasp of fear she straightened up and signaled to Minone.

Her friend followed the direction of her eyes and smiled. "Watch," was all she said.

The hawk broke his dive a few feet away from Metacom's handsome face and landed lightly on his outstretched arm. The man stroked its feathered head and whispered a few words of endearment.

"Well, I have never seen anything like it!" exclaimed Chastity in amazement. "I heard tell that people in Europe hunt with falcons, but only the great kings and lords."

Minone eyed her strangely. "Metacom is a great lord and a prince. He may even be king one day, if his brother Wamsutta does not marry."

"What is he doing, hunting?"

"No, he is training the hawk to protect the fields. It will keep away the small birds and the rodents that steal our crops."

Impressed with the clever simplicity of the plan, she asked, "But what about the larger ones, the crow and such?"

"The crow is sacred—he may feed in peace." Chastity recognized the singsong quality in Minone's voice that meant a story was forthcoming. She was not disappointed.

"Long ago, when my people were many and hunger walked the land, before the honey bee came and signaled the arrival of the white man, we had no corn, no beans. One day a young brave was seeking his spirit. He painted his face white and sat on a mountaintop for many days. He did not eat, and drank only a little water. But no animal, no spirit, appeared to him, and his heart was heavy. Still he waited for his animal guide.

"After many days, when he was weak from fasting, the crow came to him from the southwest. In his right claw he carried a kernel of corn, in his left a bean. He gave them to the warrior with instructions on how to plant them. When he got home, there was much rejoicing and the people gave thanks.

"So you see, we cannot kill the crow, for he brought us the gift of life."

Chastity smiled warmly. These stories and legends

were an integral part of tribal life. Religion here was as natural as breathing the sweet air of the forest. There was a prayer and a song for everything, each time a seed was planted, an animal killed, or a tree felled. A tiny portion of the food was even offered to the fire before each meal, an offering of thanks. And the Pilgrims called these people the "spawn of the Devil"!

"The day grows hot and we are almost done. Let us go down to the river and cool ourselves."

Chastity agreed readily. One of the things she loved about her new life was the daily bathing. Every day when it was warm, and often even when it was very cold, the Indians trooped down to the river to bathe. Quite unashamedly, the women plunged in naked, together with the young children. Although the men did not bathe at the same time, it was hard for Chastity to adjust to this custom. The men occasionally passed the river while the women were in, but no fuss was made. She had at first bathed in her dress, too self-conscious to join in with the others. The Indian women teased her so that she had finally given in. It was strange. Once she had bathed naked like the others, no one noticed her.

Today she stripped off her dress with a single movement and slipped into the cool water. She undid her long braids and let her hair float gently around her like some new form of water plant. Children laughed as they splashed and dunked each other, and the soft hum of the women's voices played in the background. She lay back and let her mind wander.

She had started her gift of thanks for Metacom. Instead of moccasins, she had decided upon a medicine bag, which most of the men wore tied at their waists. She had learned that these were of great importance and contained articles sacred to the individual. The old woman had told her to gather the rushes that white people called Indian hemp and had showed her how to twist them into thread by rubbing them between her palm and thigh. She wove the creamy beige thread with care, and the result looked more like silk than hemp. Tonight, she decided, she would start the embroidery; she had learned to use porcupine quills for decoration by holding them in her mouth until they were soft and pliable.

Rolling over on her stomach, she took swift strokes that carried her a short way downstream. Swimming was another delight that she had learned from the Indians, although she did not yet feel proficient enough to swim alone.

It was July, the Moon-of-the-red-blooming-lilies, and many members of the tribe had gone to their summer homes by the ocean. As Chastity swam slowly back to join Minone, she thought of how her life had changed. She enjoyed a freedom that was new and luxurious to her. The work was hard, but similar in many ways to the work she had done in Plymouth. She took pride in her newly acquired skills, and if she occasionally had a secret wish for an English needle or for finespun linen sheets, it did not show. How could she help but be cheerful when she was surrounded by laughter and song?

The only custom thus far discovered to which she really objected was having to rub raccoon grease over her body. But, she admitted to herself as she wrung out her long hair, it certainly did help protect her from the hot sun and the many stinging insects that just seemed to wait to feast upon unprotected skin.

She climbed out of the river and lay on the bank, where the sun would quickly bake her dry. Minone impulsively grabbed her arm and held it next to her own.

"Look!" she commanded.

To Chastity's surprise, she saw that the skin on her arm was only a shade lighter than her friend's.

"We are both redskins!" she exclaimed with laughter.

"There is nothing red about my skin," she was corrected. "It is brown, a light brown, like a fawn." Minone joined in the laughter as words failed her. "Well, it is flesh colored." At Chastity's hoot, she added, "And you could never be an Indian with that hair! Look at yourself in the water."

A strange face peered at her from the gently rippling surface. Gone was her creamy complexion in which she had taken such pride. Her eyes gleamed a bright gold in her dark face, and her cheeks had thinned out some, giving her an untamed look. Over the months, the sun had bleached her thick hair. It was hard to tell now if it was red streaked with gold, or gold streaked with red.

"Why, my hair looks like the metal on my father's forge!"

"Hot metal hair! I shall call you Woman-with-hot-metal hair!" Minone exploded with laughter and collapsed on the soft grass.

Still staring at the stranger's reflection, Chastity began to chuckle, slowly at first and then louder and deeper, until she too collapsed with weakness.

They tried to fight down their giggles all the way back to the village. An old man looked up at them from where he sat carefully molding a clay pot with his knotted hands, and his wrinkled face broke into a smile as the two happy girls passed.

In the Moon-of-wild-rice, a maidens' ball game was announced.

"Tell me about it," Chastity requested one late afternoon as she sat weaving sweet grass into a split oaken bucket she had made. They had eaten, and the three of them sat outside the wigwam, bathed in the soft light of the fading sun.

Minone and Grandmother smiled at each other, and the girl said eagerly, "It is an exciting game. We will play, and all the young men in the village will watch. Of course, you may not play, but you will enjoy watching with the others."

"Why may I not join in?"

"Because it is a maiden's game." The old woman chuckled, and her large belly jiggled in mirth. "You sleep alone, but that does not make you a maiden."

Minone flashed her a grin and explained. "You see, we all gather outside the village. It is understood that each girl who rises to play is a maiden. If any man there wishes to challenge her virtue, he may. If he can prove that she has lain with him, she is shamed and driven away from the circle. But if the man accuses her falsely, he is taken away and thrown from a cliff."

"You mean killed?" Chastity was shocked.

The girl nodded her dark head as she carefully selected some long animal hairs from a pile at her side and braided them into the rope she was making. "Yes, you see, if she says she is a maiden when she is not, it is understandable. It is wrong to speak falsely, but in this case it is understandable. After all, this would lower her bride price. If the man accuses her without reason, he is not only false, but in this way he tries to hurt her and her family. So her relatives and friends punish him."

"Well, that would certainly punish him," Chastity commented dryly as she pushed away the finished bucket. "And where does all the fun come in?"

"In the game itself. Last year I almost won, but I was tripped inside the village."

"How is the game played?"

"There are two small balls attached with a thong. Each girl has a long stick with a hook on one end. The balls are thrown into the air, and we all try to catch them on our sticks. The one who catches them and then gets all the way home without losing the balls wins. You will laugh as you watch. We may not kick, or hit, or bite, but anything else is permitted."

"Remember the year that Laughing Lion fooled everyone?" reminded the old one with an amused snort.

Minone's dark eyes twinkled in amusement. "She was very clever. Her name was Yellow Bird then. The game had gone on all day with no one reaching home. As twilight fell, one girl made it to the village gate with the balls. Yellow Bird was hiding just inside. As the girl came through, Yellow Bird leaped out, screaming like a wounded mountain lion. The men had reported a lion nearby, so the girl dropped her stick in terror and ran away."

"And then Yellow Bird picked up the balls on her own stick and ran home. She won the prize and has been called Laughing Lion since that day," finished the old woman. "Massasoit is offering a fine pair of moccasins and vermilion as prizes this year. It should be a fine day," she said as she checked the red clouds in the west before stooping to enter the wigwam.

The girls gathered their things to follow her, but Minone grabbed Chastity's arm and held her back.

"Running Bear will notice me tomorrow if I have to hit him over the head with my stick!" she confided in a whisper.

The next day, everyone gathered in a clearing in the forest by the river. Many of the girls had painted their faces and removed all their jewelry and excess clothing, so that their movements would not be hampered. There was much joking and back-slapping as the young men placed bets on their favorites and tried to catch their attention. The strict rules of formality were somewhat relaxed, and the old women of the tribe teased men and maiden alike with open familiarity.

Chastity was a bit surprised at the frankness of some of the jokes and comments. In Plymouth, such things were considered lewd and left unsaid, at least in mixed company. But if the Indians took no offense at what was said, then neither would she.

The crowd formed a circle as each girl announced her intention to play. There was a hush as everyone looked around to see if the maiden would be challenged. When no man spoke out against the girl's virtue, the joking and laughter started again. Chastity was relieved when the last girl rose unchallenged and the game began. By the looks on the faces of some of the crowd, they were relieved as well.

The balls were thrown high into the air and caught on the stick of the tallest girl. They were immediately swept onto another stick as the squealing and laughter grew. From then on the action was fast. At one time Minone broke clear with the balls on her stick, but instead of heading toward Sowams, she turned and crashed into Running Bear, who was standing near. It looked like an accident, but Chastity smiled as the brave helped the girl to her feet, holding her just a bit closer than was strictly necessary.

"Dancing Fox, you will follow me." The powah, Sassacus, stood before her.

Chastity stood up, uncertain of what to do. When the old woman saw what was happening, she intervened.

"What do you wish of my granddaughter?" she demanded, thrusting her large bulk between them.

"Massasoit has sent for her, she is to come with me at once."

She shook her fist at him and loudly announced, "My granddaughter goes alone with no man, not even the powah!"

The ghost of a smile tugged at the corner of Sassacus' mouth. "Very well, old woman, come with her and protect her virtue." He turned and walked swiftly ahead of them.

In spite of her girth, the old woman was able to keep up with him, and she instructed Chastity as they hurried along. "Our sagamore is a great and wise man. This must be important or he would not send for a woman. If he asks you a question, you must answer. Today is an exception. You must look at him when you speak so that he may read the truth in your eyes and not think you false."

"Have I done something wrong?" Chastity was worried.

"We shall soon see."

The lodge of the famous chief was much larger and more luxurious than theirs. Chastity had a few seconds to notice the many painted mats that hung on the walls and the huge piles of deep furs as she entered. She trembled when she saw the great man sitting cross-legged on the floor, his two sons on either side of him, and Sassacus standing to one side. The powah's face was flushed with displeasure. From the tension in the air, Chastity assumed that she had interrupted an argument.

"There is the woman now," said Massasoit when she stood before him. "Let her answer your charges."

A cold flame leaped from the depths of the powah's black eyes as he pointed at her angrily. "This woman has taken an Indian name and wears Indian dress. She speaks our tongue, and the sun has turned her white skin to brown. But even the sun cannot make her one of our people!

"I say to you that this woman is white! Her skin is brown but her heart is white! We know the white man lies and cheats and tricks the Indian. Are we to believe that the white woman is any different from her man? When she opens her mouth, falsehoods will pour out, like snakes pour from the earth when the sun ends their winter sleep. Like the deadly venom of the viper, the poison in her words will eat away at us until we are no more."

"What say you to this, Dancing Fox? Are you white or Indian?" The powerful chief studied her gravely and remembering the old woman's warning, Chastity looked at him squarely.

"There is no answer to that, great Massasoit. The powah is right in part of what he says. I was born white and raised white, the sun cannot change that, nor can my dress and speech. But I love the life here and I love my Indian family." She hesitated and tried to hide the quiver in her voice. "I do not know if I am now more white or Indian, but I do know one thing. I know that my heart is true, no matter what color it is."

She flashed the powah an angry look, and as her anger rose, so did her courage. "I am not false, nor are my words. I can only speak the truth as I know it and see it, but if the powah says I lie, let him prove it!" she ended defiantly.

In the long pause that followed her speech, Chastity feared that she had gone too far. Gathered before her were the most powerful men in the tribe; they held the power of life and death over her. Glancing over at her grandmother, she saw the old woman's face showed shock and dismay.

"Have you more to say?" Massasoit studied his clay pipe and would not look at her.

She was sorely tempted to throw herself on his mercy, and saw clearly that the old woman was signaling her to do so. But at the last moment her stubborn pride reasserted itself and she faced the men bravely.

"Sometimes my temper makes me speak in haste, and then I am sorry for my words. But I am not sorry now. I have said only the truth. That is all I have to say."

Massasoit tapped his pipe carefully against a log before looking up at her. "You defend yourself well, child. You are brave and I respect that. Sit down, we shall speak."

"I will not listen to the words of a white woman!"

"Then you may leave," was Massasoit's calm reply. Wamsutta and Metacom looked at each other uneasily as the powah swept out of the wigwam, but their father spoke in a reassuring way.

"He is an old man and grows bitter with the seasons. Once the Indian was alone in this land and ours was the only way. Now the white man is here, and we must adjust our lives as the animals of the forest change theirs to fit the seasons. Sassacus does not see this.

"Dancing Fox," he turned to the girl in front of him, "I have called you here today that you might answer my questions. Will you help us?"

"If I am able."

"This, then, is the problem." Massasoit cleared a place in the dirt and began to draw a map. As Chastity came closer, she could see that lines were deeply etched in his tired face. This great statesman had been able to keep peace in his lifetime. Would Wamsutta, his proud heir, be so talented?

"Here is our land, here Sowams, here Plymouth," he said, making marks in the dirt. "We have received word that the whites want to buy more of our land. I wish to know three things. Why do they want the land? What will they do with it? And what will happen if I refuse?"

"I can only guess, Massasoit," she cautioned. "What exactly was said about the land?"

The sagamore signaled to Wamsutta. Among a people with no written language, memory was vital, and Wamsutta was known for this power. He closed his eyes and began to recite.

" 'Great and wise sachem Massasoit, sagamore and king of the Wampanoags. As governor of the Plymouth Colony, I send you my greetings and best wishes. The great white father across the waters remembers his son and sends him these gifts with his blessings.

" 'He is pleased with his son for keeping the peace as he promised and he reminds him to keep his feet on the road of peace.

" 'He orders his white children to meet with Massasoit to reaffirm this peace and to purchase more land, which will be paid for in wampum and awls. The great Massasoit is invited to Plymouth to negotiate the amount.

" 'Yours in God, the governor of Plymouth.' " Wamsutta finished and opened his eyes.

"How much land do they want?" asked Chastity.

Massasoit marked off a portion on the map. "Why do they want so much of our land?"

Chastity studied it; it was a goodly amount. "I can only imagine that there are more Pilgrims coming over the waters," she concluded at last.

"Will these people never stop coming?" demanded Wamsutta in anger. "They creep closer and closer to our towns. Their animals roam free on our lands and destroy our crops. Soon they will be in Sowams!"

"What say you to that, Dancing Fox? These people

breed like the mice in the fields, often and many. We have but few children in each family; we know that this is the best way. Every summer, more whites arrive from across the waters, while our numbers dwindle. When will they stop coming?" Metacom asked bluntly.

She looked up at him and, to her astonishment, began to blush at the obvious admiration in his black eyes. "I think that they will never stop. They believe this to be the chosen land for them. More and more settlers will come each year."

"The land is free to those who live on it, yet they wish to buy it. They say we keep the right to hunt and fish on the land we sell. Yet they plow and plant it so that there is no game left, and they dirty our rivers, so the fish leave. And then they tell us that we may not hunt or fish on their holy days. Will this too continue?" Massasoit frowned in puzzlement. The ideas were so foreign to him!

"I believe so. The Bible, their holy book, commands them to populate the earth and to cultivate the fruit of the soil. They will continue to plow and plant and fence their fields. As the towns grow, they will need more and more land."

"We must stop it now!" announced Wamsutta impatiently. "We must sell no more land! There will be none left for our children's children!"

Chastity squirmed uncomfortably and Metacom watched her carefully. "And what will happen then, Dancing Fox? What if we do refuse to sell our land?"

"I think they will take it from you," she admitted softly.

"Take it?" He pounced upon her words. "After all his words of peace, his promises? The white man would go to war to steal our land?"

"You must understand," she pleaded with the men. "They believe that what they do is right, that the Great Spirit wants them to have the land. They do not think of it as stealing. They believe that the land can only belong to a people who will work it. The Indians do not work the land, so many of the whites think that they should not have it."

"You work a slave, you cannot work the land." Wamsutta snorted in derision. "You accept what the land wants to give you, and you help it by putting a seed where you think it will grow. But you cannot work it. You say that they would go on the warpath because we do not mistreat our land as they do?"

"The white man is not a warrior. He would do well to paddle a canoe, but not to guide it," dismissed Metacom with disdain. "The Pequot were weak with disease and had no strong sagamore. That is how the white men destroyed them."

"But they have guns, my son," cautioned Massasoit. "Guns make weak men strong."

"They are still few. If the tribes band together, the whites would easily be defeated." Metacom spoke with clear conviction, his voice firm, his handsome face clear.

"No!" The sound of steel in the sagamore's voice caused Chastity to flinch. "I have given my word. I have promised peace, and peace it shall be. If we must sell land, then we shall do it. There will be peace as long as I have breath to speak. I charge you both, when I am gone and you lead this tribe, remember my words."

"There must be some way to deal with this, Father," said Metacom urgently. "We are like the fox who gnaws away at his own leg that is caught in a trap. He escapes the hunter, but he can no longer run and hunt for himself, and so he dies."

"Then we must learn the cunning of the fox. For I myself have seen an old one that ran on only three legs," Massasoit said wearily. "We will sell them lands we do not want, lands covered with stones that will break their plows and their backs as well. Lands far from the river, where beans will not sprout and the corn turns brown and dry."

"And they will clear the land of rocks and dig deep wells to find water. And when the fields are harvested and their children grown, they will want more land, and then still more." Wamsutta slapped his leg angrily, and his bitter words hung in the smoke-filled air.

Chastity bowed her head. He was right, and she knew it. The Pilgrims had started with only one hundred and one people some thirty years before, and half of them had died that first terrible winter. Now their population had increased to thousands.

"We cannot stop the thundering river when its waters

are swollen with melting snow." Massasoit sighed. "It is the same with the white man as it is with the river."

He stood up and towered over the seated girl. "Thank you, Dancing Fox, for your words. You were right, your heart speaks truth. It is not easy to be sagamore, chief of chiefs. When I was young like my sons, I saw only black or white, right or wrong. But now I see the grays of twilight, and I am no longer sure what is right. Perhaps this comes with age." He smiled sadly at her with quiet dignity and offered his hand to help her up. "Sons, see them home. I wish to be alone with my thoughts."

Chastity left the wigwam with the old woman and the two young men. As they walked through the silent village, the old one tugged at her skirt, and Chastity saw that her wrinkles had folded into a frown.

"You have made an enemy in the powah. Walk carefully and see that he does not tread on your shadow."

"He will not harm her, Grandmother," assured Metacom. "She is under my father's protection."

"He has strong medicine," she insisted with a shake of her gray head. "And the power of a powah reaches far."

"Sassacus hates the whites, Old One, but it is only because he has a great love for the Wampanoags. He believes the white settlers will one day destroy our life and drive us from our lands. But be at ease, Dancing Fox has done no wrong." Metacom brushed aside her objections and smiled at Chastity, who hurriedly dropped her eyes.

"Grandmother, I would speak with Dancing Fox." Wamsutta, who had been lost in thought, stopped impulsively.

"You will not, Wamsutta! The council is over and you are not your father!" She was aghast at the idea.

"Then speak you for me." Once Wamsutta got an idea, he did not let it go easily. "If I am to be clever like the white man and fight him with tricks instead of arrows, I need a special power, some kind of magic over them. The white man must not know my name, for that would give him power over me. I need a white man's name, one with power!"

Chastity stopped and looked at the impulsive young chief in surprise. The old woman poked her in the side and in a hiss reminded her of her forgotten manners.

"What kind of name do you think that Wamsutta would like, Grandmother?" she asked, feeling slightly ridiculous.

"Speak, my son. What kind of name would you like?"

"I want the name of a great warrior king, one who was a leader of men, who cut through problems and defeated his enemies. Thus I will trick the whites and they will fear me."

"It sounds like he speaks of Alexander the Great, Grandmother," said Chastity with a light laugh.

"Who was this man of whom you speak, child?"

"In the long-ago days, he was a great warrior who led mighty armies of braves. One day he came upon a cross-roads in the forest that was blocked by a large cart and axle. Now, the axle was bound to the cart with strong hemp, tied in so many knots that no one could untie it. It was said that he who untied the knots would be king of Macedonia, a great land of plenty. Wise men had spent years trying to undo those many knots, but none was clever enough to succeed.

"When Alexander came to the crossroads, he saw only a cart that blocked his way. He was very angry because his army could not pass. With an impatient blow of his long knife, he cut the hemp asunder and the cart rolled out of his way.

"He was made king of Macedonia and ruled over many lands for the remaining years of his life."

"Alexander," mused Wamsutta as he tried on the name for size. "It is good. It is fitting. I shall be King Alexander!" He let out a whoop of delight, and his dark eyes flashed.

Metacom grinned at his brother and then asked, "Did this Alexander have a brother, Grandmother?"

She turned to Chastity. "What was his brother's name?"

"I do not think he had a brother. I never read about one," said the girl, hating to disappoint Metacom.

"Had he no family, then, no clan?" demanded the old one. "Who trained him to be a warrior and gave him his first bow?"

"His father, Philip," Chastity remembered eagerly. "Philip was a great king too. There were several kings called Philip after him. They too were famous."

"Then you should be called Philip," said Wamsutta to Metacom, drawing himself up proudly. "Now we are protected."

"Since you are finished, we shall go," said the old woman in a querulous tone. "We have other things to do than to stand around talking to foolish young men." She sniffed and prodded Chastity in the back. "Come along, Dancing Fox. Let us see how the game proceeds." The two men laughed as she hustled off the lovely girl.

The game was over, and Minone was talking with some friends near the wigwam. She had not won, but her face was flushed and her voice animated. Chastity spied a group of braves nearby, Running Bear among them. They were whispering among themselves and smiling at the girls. The old woman saw them too and bore down upon the group of girls like a brooding quail.

"Go home, all of you! Minone, inside!" She waved her skirt at the men, who scattered in mock fear. "I have had enough of young braves sneaking around after my grand-daughters for one day. Get inside, both of you!"

Startled by her crossness, Chastity obeyed at once, but she was reassured by Minone's wink.

"Grandmother, we were only talking. It is not our fault if the men gathered near us. We did not speak to them."

"I am not so old that I have forgotten a maiden's tricks," she scolded her. "I hope you did not hurt yourself when you fell during the game. I saw that you needed help to rise."

Minone blushed at being caught, and started to make up an excuse.

"Never mind, child. There are more important things than vermilion. How do you think I caught Red Deer's eye?" She laughed as she saw the surprise on the girls' faces. "It is the way of maidens to make handsome braves notice them. But," she reminded them, "be careful not to go too far. You will lower your bride price and no one will want you."

She turned to Chastity and threw up her hands in despair. "And you, Dancing Fox, what am I to do with you?"

"Me, Grandmother? What have I done?"

"It is not so much what you have done as what you are. It is all right for men to pay attention to you when you

are old and ugly like me; then no harm will come to you."
She sucked the inside of her cheek with concern. "But
you attract men the way that honey draws the bear.
It is nothing you do, it is just because you are. You
have a manito, a power over men, and you do not even
know it. Why else would a great sagamore like Massasoit
listen when you speak and his son feast upon you with
his hungry eyes!"

"What?" She was bewildered.

"Yes, and even the powah is drawn to you in some
way, else his hate would not be so passionate. What were
the men like in your past, the one who called you his
squaw and the one you spoke of to Minone, the one who
went over the waters? Were they leaders among their
people?"

Chastity sat down in confusion. "The one who called
me his squaw was a leader of religion. But he was not a
good man," she added quickly.

"Good or bad, he was a powah," the old one stated
firmly. "I suspected as much. What of the other?"

"I do not know if the other was a leader, only that I
loved him terribly. But he did come from a family of
great leaders, back over the waters where he was born.
He was part Indian. Perhaps you know of him."

"His name?"

"White Thunder," she said with a rush of feeling.

"White Thunder! You mean He-who-wears-the-red-
eyed-snake?" When Chastity nodded, the two Indians
looked at each other in amazement.

"Even I have heard of White Thunder," Minone put it
timidly.

Chastity frowned and said, "He is gone and I do not
wish to remember him, for it brings me much pain. I
should not even have spoken his name."

"I was right when I said you had a power." The old
woman's eyes were half-closed and she seemed to be
gazing into eternity. "Your life has taken many strange
paths and there are more ahead of you. Take care, Little
Dancing Fox, you must learn to use your power well or
it will destroy you."

"I do not know what you are talking about!" Tears
stung her large eyes and she brushed them away angrily. "I have no power, I only want to live my life in

peace!" She ran out of the wigwam and Minone followed to comfort her.

"Do not cry, Dancing Fox, she is old and her mind wanders with the seasons." She put her arm around her friend's shoulders and stroked her face gently. "What she means is that you are very beautiful and men desire you. It is natural that they should."

"Forgive me, it has been a confusing day." Chastity sighed. "What happened between you and Running Bear?"

"Oh, it was wonderful!" The slim girl hugged Chastity in delight. "I bumped into him and fell. When he picked me up, he said, 'Are you hurt, Minone?' Minone! He called me by my name!" She whirled round and then added confidentially, "I shall tell you a secret. He is going to make an offer for me!"

"Did he tell you so? Minone! Did you speak to him?"

"Of course not, silly. But last night I had a dream where he offered many furs for me, and Grandmother smiled and put my hand in his."

"But that was only a dream, Minone. It may not happen in real life, you know."

Minone faced her with a sad, superior smile. "The spirits speak to us in dreams, Dancing Fox. You still have much to learn. Dreams always come true. If the dream is very bad, we pray and make sacrifices. Then the evil has not so great a power over us, the dream may be changed in some small way. But dreams always come true, always."

Taken aback, Chastity shrugged. "I hope you are right" was all she said to her friend.

"I am. Wait and see," answered the girl confidently.

A few days later Metacom presented them with a large beaver. He handed it to the old woman and said it was a gift from Massasoit.

"Massasoit indeed!" snorted the old one after the young chief had left. "Does he think that I have no eyes in my head, that age has shrunk my brains so that they rattle in my head like seeds in a dry gourd? Massasoit, ha!"

"What do you mean, Grandmother?" asked Chastity curiously.

"This is not from Massasoit, it is from Metacom. It was given to me, but the young rascal means for you to have it. Here, take it. I want none of it." She thrust the heavy bundle into Chastity's arms. "Metacom cannot fool me that easily. I have lived far too long for that."

In spite of her grumbling, the old woman helped eat the meat with relish, especially the tail, for beaver tail was a great delicacy.

❧ Ten ❧

IN PREPARING THE BEAVER, CHASTITY WAS ABLE TO USE many of her newly acquired skills. First the skin was carefully removed from the flesh, which was then stripped and hung to dry in the sun. The fat was scraped off the inside with a bone tool and stored along with the marrow from the bones. The following day she pegged the skin to the ground and scraped off all the hair, putting it in a basket to later weave into a belt. The inside of the skin was rubbed with a smelly mixture of boiled liver, brains, grease, and salt.

Minone helped her gather dry grasses to pile in the middle of the skin, and they poured hot water over it until the whole thing was thoroughly soaked. Next Chastity gathered in the four corners, tied it like a ball, and hung it from a tree to dry.

She was far from done. The skin had to be taken down, the grass shaken out of it, and all the moisture wrung out. She stretched it over a slanting wooden frame and scraped it again, taking care not to cut it. It was left there on the frame for a few days to dry and bleach in the sun. Some of the larger bones were saved to be carved into spoons and ornaments. The thicker sinews were used for thongs, while the others she treated for thread.

After a few days she took a rounded bone and rubbed the skin smooth. Minone helped her again with the final step. They took a string of sinew, stretched it tight between two trees, and threw the skin over it. Standing on either side, the girls drew it back and forth until it was as soft as velvet. Although Chastity had seen various stages of this done before, she had no idea that there was so much work involved.

As a matter of fact, she was almost discouraged when she saw the hunters return, their black heads adorned with the evergreen crowns that signaled a successful hunt.

Two large deer were laid on the ground outside their wigwam. Such a thing was unheard of, and the story soon spread around the village.

"Two deer, and not a man in the wigwam!" The old woman chuckled with pride. "We will not go hungry during the cold moons. The spirits have been good to us."

"Did the spirits drive the deer to our lodge and slay them outside the door?" teased Minone with laughing eyes.

"No, but they make young men sick with love. It certainly is a good thing to have two beautiful granddaughters."

The people who had spent the summer by the ocean moved back, and the entire tribe began to prepare for winter. While the men were gone hunting, the women busied themselves digging pits behind their homes. These had to be lined with grass mats and filled with nuts, corn, and beans for the hungry months ahead. Both acorns and corn were ground into a coarse meal and stored in painted baskets. The corncobs were either used to smoke the meats the men brought in or stored to use later in place of wood. Hides were quickly and expertly cured, and strips of meat hung drying in the sun. Many a long day was spent making clothing to keep out the biting winter wind.

Somehow Chastity found time to weave. The loom she used was upright and much simpler than the one she was used to in Plymouth, but she was still able to turn out excellent work. She delighted in experimenting with bright colors, especially the reds and oranges, and spent happy hours studying patterns from Indian pottery and face painting which she made come alive in her weaving. Her only frustration was in the lack of available wool, for sheep were rare. But she soon learned to combine a mixture of animal hairs and various soft, pliable plants.

She became famous in the village for her work; even Massasoit had one of her blankets. Other women tried to copy her style, but their efforts were poor imitations. They gathered around her as she worked, until the weather grew so cold that she had to move the loom inside.

In the Geese-going Moon, when the river began to freeze, the light birch bark canoes were pulled out of the water and laid up on logs until spring. The last pumpkins were stewed, and snowshoes were repaired.

Chastity tried walking on them when the snow covered the ground in white. Minone laughed as her friend tumbled head over shoes into a drift, and finally cautioned her not to lift her feet so high.

"You look like a mountain cat who has gotten his feet wet," she giggled. "Lift your feet only a little and slide the shoes along." Chastity did as she was told and was soon moving lightly on top of the snow.

One evening, as the three of them sat finishing their meal, a young man announced himself at the door. It was Running Bear, and the old woman signaled him to enter and sit. At the same time, she waved the two girls to the side of the small hut.

When Running Bear was seated in front of her, he cleared his throat and politely asked, "How is your health, Grandmother?"

"Only fair. My joints ache and creak in the cold, wet air, and my eyes are not as good as they once were. And you?"

"I am in good health."

"And your parents?"

"They are well also and send their greetings."

"How is your grandfather?" Noting the tightening of the impatient suitor's jaw, she grinned and continued. "He was a great warrior in his days and a handsome man. If it had not been for Red Deer, I would have married your grandfather and you would be my grandson! What do you think of that?" She cocked her head and peered at him like a fat old robin.

"The spirits smiled on Red Deer and not on my grandfather," he muttered through clenched teeth.

"Yes, they did," she agreed. "Now, how may I serve you?"

He leaned forward anxiously. "I have come to make an offer for your granddaughter, Wise One."

Minone pinched Chastity who squeezed her hand, and they both held their breath to hear what would be said next.

"Which granddaughter? I have two." It came out innocently enough, and Chastity hid her smile.

"Minone."

"Minone? I am surprised. I had thought that Dancing Fox would wed first. She is the older of the two and ready for a husband. The other one is still young."

The old woman was obviously enjoying his discomfort, but Running Bear insisted stubbornly, "My offer is for Minone."

"What do you offer?"

"I shall show you." He got up and went outside. The old woman threw the girls a wink and lit her pipe with a coal from the fire. Smoking was not common among women, but she was not a common woman.

Running Bear returned with a large bundle, untied it, and spread the contents before her proudly. "Seven bearskins, two black, five brown, five red-fox skins, two skins of the small winter white weasel, three of the raccoon, and a wampum bracelet and necklace of blue and white shells." The handsome brave stood back and smiled, confident of acceptance.

"Is that all?"

"All?" he stammered in surprise. "Is that not enough?"

She turned her wrinkled face up to him and snorted. "Young man, do not waste my time with foolishness. My granddaughter Minone is worth much more than this. She has the sweetest smile and the quickest laugh in the village. Her hides are soft and her baskets closely woven. Would you have me give her away for next to nothing?" She snorted again in disdain.

"Take away your trinkets. If you have a serious offer to make, come back. If not, try a girl with crossed eyes and black teeth, one who is lazy and dumb. Her family will accept these furs." She dismissed him with contempt, and the rejected suitor left sadly, too ashamed to even look at his beloved.

"Grandmother! They were beautiful furs!" cried Minone in anguish. "How could you turn him away like that?"

"Calm yourself, little Heather Flower, he will be back," soothed the old woman as she patted her hand.

"But why did you refuse?"

"Dry your eyes and I shall tell you." Minone obediently wiped her eyes and waited while the old one blew several smoke rings into the air.

"Rejection is good for a suitor, it makes his heart burn with love like a great fire in the forest. Running Bear has never been tested in war, he himself does not know how strong he is. Now he will have to prove it to himself as well as to me."

"But I love him, I want to be his squaw now," she wailed.

"Believe me, Minone," the old woman said to the unhappy girl, "I have lived many seasons and have had several husbands. I have no small share of wisdom in these matters. If he loves you, Running Bear will return a better man for what happened tonight."

"Just how old are you, Grandmother?" Chastity wondered.

"Younger than the forest but older than most of the trees." She smiled serenely.

"I mean actually, how old are you really? How many seasons?"

"How many seasons? How should I know? I never counted them. What a silly idea!"

"And you, Minone?" Chastity turned to her friend.

"Old enough to have a husband!" she sniffed.

As the winter passed, Minone learned to hide her impatience. Running Bear had gone to stay with friends among the Narragansetts soon after the rejection of his offer, and the reports coming back to Sowams were encouraging.

Thanks to their stores of provisions and the mildness of the weather, the Indians did not suffer during the months that snow covered the ground and the game hid. The land sale was concluded and the people of Plymouth seemed to be satisfied with the rocky soil that Massasoit had sold them.

But the great sachem was no longer as strong as he had once been; years of struggle and leadership had demanded a payment. Word passed quickly around the village that he had fallen severely ill and lay near death. People gathered in silent clusters around his lodge, and the powah spent days and nights at the sagamore's side. Finally he announced that there would be a medicine sing.

A large campfire was built outside the wigwam, and the whole tribe gathered. The oldest men sat in a large semicircle around the fire. The younger men formed a ring behind them, and the women and small children behind these. Someone began to pound on a drum, a slow, steady, monotonous beat, and several of the old men shook gourd rattles.

The powah came out of the building and, thrusting a torch into the fire, began a blessing. He carried the flame to the edge of the clearing, first to the north, then to the south, to the east, and to the west. He raised it to the stars and then held it close to the earth, calling upon the spirits of the six directions to help him. Massasoit was carried out and laid gently on furs near the burning logs.

Two lithe boys ran through the crowd, entered the ring, and raced to the fire. They each grabbed flaming torches in both hands and moving their feet in a shuffling dance, threw the burning lights into the air and performed the intricate art of fire juggling. As the arcs of flame curved over and around them like small comets, they quickened their steps and spun around, weaving patterns of fire in the dark night.

Chastity marveled at the beauty of the dance and was disappointed when it ended. But another boy, slightly older than his predecessors, took their place. He shook his rattle and eagle feathers fiercely as he danced barefoot in ever-tightening circles around the fire. She gasped as he leaped onto the logs and danced in the very fire itself! She expected to see his brief clothing go up in smoke and hear him cry out in pain, but no. Totally absorbed in his dance, the boy wore a trancelike look of serenity. After what appeared to be several minutes, he jumped out of the fire and walked to the second circle of young men and proudly took his place.

Sassacus began to sing. He sang of the stately pine and proud stag, both battle-scarred victors of the forest, of the great horned owl riding the night wind, and of majestic blue mountains that watched mighty rivers cut through the green land. He sang of the great man who lay on furs near the fire, of his years of leadership and fame.

Sometimes he sang in a strange tongue that his listeners could almost, but not quite, understand. His voice never ranged beyond a few notes, but combined with the rattles and drums, it cast an unearthly spell over the campfire. The rhythm of the drums echoed the blood pounding in her heart, the rattles the wind in her lungs, and Chastity felt her skin tingle and a kind of awe sweep over her as the singer's shadow grew larger and larger, until it seemed to cover the entire circle and leave only Masasoit in the light.

When the powah could sing no longer, an old man took his place. Soon after him, another, and then another, until the dark night crept away and it was dawn. They sang through the morning hours and into the afternoon. The tired sun sank slowly behind the horizon, and still the songs continued.

The midnight sky was pierced with distant stars when the powah rose to his feet. He held his hands over the fire, and a great green flame leaped up to lick at them. The weird light of the mysterious flame twisted his tired features into a ghostly mask.

"Massasoit will live! The evil is gone from him!"

A great sigh of relief escaped the crowd at his words. Slowly the Indians got up and made their way home, silent with hunger and fatigue. Not a word was spoken, no child cried. Their beloved leader was safe.

Chastity's legs were so numb and cramped that she could barely hobble back to the wigwam. She collapsed upon the furs, too exhausted to speak, and fell into a deep sleep.

The next day, Sowams was back to normal. Massasoit was improving rapidly and would soon be up and about. Laughter again floated lazily in the early spring air like the elusive fragrance of wildflowers.

It was time to plant, and Chastity and Minone set out for the fields, hoes slung over their shoulders. Chastity was asking her about some of the other miraculous cures that the powah had produced, when Metacom startled her by stepping out from behind a tree.

"Running Bear sends you his greetings, cousin," he said to Minone.

"You have seen him?"

"I saw him before my father became ill. Your sweetheart is trading with the whites for blue wampum, that your grandmother might smile upon his offer."

She darkened with pleasure but struggled to feign indifference. "You may tell Running Bear not to be away from Sowams for too long. There are many strong braves here who are good hunters and need wives. I cannot wait forever."

He laughed, and his white teeth gleamed against his bronze skin. "I shall tell him so."

Minone joined in the laughter and threw a wink at Chastity, who was trying hard not to look at Metacom.

"Cousin, I would speak with Dancing Fox. Will you leave us?"

"Cousin, I cannot, and you well know it," scolded Minone.

"Then, fair Dancing Fox, I speak directly to you. Will you hear my words?"

In spite of herself, Chastity was very drawn to this handsome young chief who stood before her. But she was not sure if she wanted to be left alone with him. She signaled her uncertainty to Minone, who opted for romance and promptly abandoned her.

"I shall stand over there by those rocks," she announced.

When she had moved off and could no longer hear, Metacom began to speak. "Dancing Fox, I would tell you of my feelings, but my words are weak like the wings of a fledgling bird. They would fail me and I would fall. This is a song of my people, the words are my words, they come from my heart. Rise up with the eagle wings and look down into the deepest corners of my heart."

Chastity sat on a fallen log and listened.

Awake! Awake to me, flower of the forest, sky-treading bird of the mountains. Awake, wonderful honey-eyed one.

When you look at me I am satisfied, as the flowers that drink dew. The breath of your mouth is the fragrance of flowers in the morning; your breath is their fragrance at evening in the Moon-of-fading-leaf. Do the red streams of my veins not run toward you as the forest streams to the sun in the Moon-of-bright-nights? When you are beside me, my heart sings; a branch it is dancing before the wind spirit in the Moon-of-strawberries.

When you frown upon me, beloved, my heart grows dark—a shining river the shadows of clouds darken. Then, with your smile, comes the sun and makes to look like gold the furrows the cold wind draws in the water's face.

Myself! Behold me! Blood of my beating heart. Earth smiles, the waters smile, even the sky-of-clouds smiles. But I, I lose the way of smiling when you are not near.

Awake! Awake to me, my beloved.

She could not speak; she simply sat there staring at the ground. When she was finally able to break the spell and look up, he had disappeared.

"Grandmother," Chastity said later that evening, "I would talk with you." The old woman nodded her head and Chastity continued. "I believe that Metacom intends to make an offer for me."

"Are you surprised?"

"Well, yes, in a way," she admitted.

"Then you are foolish, Dancing Fox," she said between puffs on her pipe.

"Explain, Old One, I do not understand." She put down the flax she was twisting and moved closer.

"He saved you from the wolves and he brought you here. Not to Plymouth, which was where your people were, and very close, but here, to Sowams."

"Yes, I had not thought of that." She had to admit that this was strange.

"He gave the powah many gifts to cure you, and he asked me to adopt you."

"He did?" She hesitated. "But I was the one who wanted to stay here."

"He hoped that you would. And so did I." She chuckled.

"But I do not know if I wish to marry him, even if he has planned it all along."

"Do you find him attractive?"

Chastity's golden eyes lowered as she reluctantly admitted that she did.

"Then listen to me, Dancing Fox, I will tell you what I have learned. After Red Deer died, I thought that I would die too. Birds no longer sang for me, flowers lost their perfume, food was dry, and water was not sweet. The snows came and went and came again. Still my heart was heavy.

"Then Red Deer's mother came to me and she scolded me. 'Red Deer would not want you like this,' she said. 'How can he go hunting in that Other Place when you hold him to you with your sorrow? There is a time to be sad, but that time is over.' She was right, there was truth in her words. I took another husband.

"Oh, it was not like the first time. My blood did not burn, my heart did not sing for him. But he was a good husband to me and we were happy.

"I have outlived four husbands, all good men. I have loved each one. Perhaps you cannot understand this, but it is so. This kind of love grows with time, only after you are his woman. With a good man, it grows like rows of golden corn in the sun. Metacom is a good man."

"I know he is, and I respect him," Chastity agreed. "But must I marry?"

Grandmother drew on her pipe and studied the girl. "No one will force you, Dancing Fox. But there are things to consider. I am old, I will not see many more seasons. If you have no man, who will protect you when I am gone? Who will speak out for you? Who will hunt for you, bring you meat to eat and skins to tan?"

"We have meat now." She was not convinced.

"And who do you think brings it? I do not draw the bow."

"Metacom?"

"Metacom and his friends who seek to please him."

"I had thought it came from the members of the Owl clan," she confessed.

"You did not think." A large blue smoke ring drifted up toward the hole in the ceiling, and they watched it in silence. "There is more, Dancing Fox. You have lain in a man's arms. You have buried your head in his chest, and your body has melted into his. You have smelled the sweet man-smell and tasted the honey of his skin. Do you really wish to spend your days and your nights alone?

"Tell me that you have not known these things. Tell me that you do not miss them, that your heart does not cry out during the secret hours of the night, and I will be silent." The old woman peered at her and saw the stricken look on her lovely face. "Metacom has spoken to you?"

"Today," Chastity whispered.

"And what did you do?"

"Nothing. I sat there like a frightened rabbit while he made love to me with his words. I could not even look at him."

The gray head bobbed in satisfaction. "That was wise, child. He will wait a few days and approach you again for your answer. You have time to think."

"Grandmother, what shall I do? I am so confused!"

"I cannot help you. Each of us must choose our own path and, in the end, we all must walk alone."

"If I decide to accept, must I tell him of my past, of my husband in New Plymouth and of my love for White Thunder?"

"No, the past is past. He knows there was a man; you were no maiden when he brought you here. He needs to know no more than this. Remember, the bird who opens her beak to sing cannot carry grass to make a nest."

"I feel rushed, Grandmother. I am not ready to decide. How long will Metacom wait before he speaks again?"

"A few days perhaps," said the old woman. "He has been waiting for you these many moons, and his blood must now burn hot and pound loud in his veins. He has been patient up to now. There are many women who would gladly leave their lodges to follow him."

"I know I am lucky," said Chastity miserably, "but I have to be sure of my own feelings. And I am not yet sure. If he asks me tomorrow, I will have to refuse, though I spend tear-filled nights in the seasons to come."

Minone came in, and the conversation ended. Chastity could not confide her doubts to the younger girl, whose head was so full of romance that she would not have understood at all.

Although Chastity woke early the next morning, Grandmother and Minone had risen long before her, so she found herself alone in the wigwam and hurried to start the day's chores. She was just finishing a light breakfast when the old woman returned.

She smiled at Chastity as she put a large bundle on the floor. "There is much to do. Today we go to visit my youngest sister, Awashuncks."

"I did not realize you had family nearby, Grandmother," said Chastity curiously. "You have never spoken of a sister."

"Once I had many sisters, now I have only Awashuncks. I have outlived the rest, but it will take more than just the passing seasons to close her eyes in final sleep. She is stronger than most, and the path she chose is a strange one. It is not a path I would choose, or could choose. I could not walk in her moccasins."

"Now I am truly curious, Old One," said Chastity with a laugh. "What manner of path did this strong sister choose?"

"To be sachem, Dancing Fox. My sister Awashuncks is the squaw sachem of the Sakonnets."

"Sachem!" Chastity's large eyes were dark with amazement. "A woman sachem, a female sagamore? How can this be? Do the chiefs listen to her at the council fires? Do the mugwumps support her words?"

"All this you shall learn for yourself, Dancing Fox." The old woman chuckled. "Sowams is not the world, child, no more than Plymouth was. Different peoples have different ways. Who is to say what is best? Not I. I am far too old and have seen too much. Now," she concluded, "help me prepare for the journey."

"Will it be long?" The girl could not keep the hope from her voice.

"Three days by canoe paddling with the river, almost four against it. Of course, we will visit several days with my sister."

Chastity suddenly realized the reason behind the journey, and relief flooded through her. "You are giving me a most precious gift, Grandmother," she said gratefully.

"Gift?" The old woman chose not to understand her. "And what gift it is I give you, Child?"

"Time, Grandmother. Time to discover my true feelings about sharing my life with a man. Time to consider Metacom's offer and avoid refusing in haste."

"The idea was mine," admitted the old one seriously, "but the gift is from Metacom. We will travel in his long canoe, with his blessings, and two of his braves go with us to act as our guides and protectors. The man loves you very deeply, Dancing Fox."

Chastity said nothing, but her cheeks flushed a golden rose with pleasure.

❧ *Eleven* ❧

CHASTITY SAT IN THE BOTTOM OF THE LONG BIRCH-
bark canoe and let her fingertips trace swirls in the water.
The boat was packed with bundles of supplies, yet there
was plenty of room for the two of them plus two young
braves. Chastity watched as the warrior in the bow gracefully twisted his light paddle and sliced the water in a
sweeping forward stroke. So agile was he that his paddle
never left the water. The only sound to be heard was
that of the river splitting over and around an occasional
rock that pierced its shining surface.

How kind of Metacom to pick braves from the Owl
clan as guides, she thought to herself. That way she
could look at them and even talk to them directly without
fear of breaking taboo and bringing shame upon herself
and her adopted family. Of course, she realized with
sudden insight, being clan-kin, these braves could not
possibly be any competition for the handsome chief. No
wonder Metacom was a leader in his own right! She
chuckled out loud at his wisdom. "You have happy
thoughts, child." The old woman turned and smiled.
"Would that I had your youth and disposition! My old
bones creak with the boredom of sitting in this canoe,
and I have not had a single smoke since we left Sowams.
Soon I shall sit in my sister's lodge. She packs a good
pipe, though her cooking is not to be eaten."

"Grandmother," began Chastity in puzzlement, "did
you not once tell me that you were an only child? I do
not understand. How comes it that an only child can
have many sisters?"

"I *was* an only child," said the old one defensively. "My

stories are always true. I was an only child until I married Red Deer. When I left my parents' lodge, they adopted a young orphan boy. Soon after that, my mother had two baby girls. She never recovered her strength from their birth, and she died some moons later. My father needed a squaw to take care of the children, so he married my mother's youngest sister, Runs-like-wind. Although it is our custom to have but a few children, Runs-like-wind gave him six. Awashuncks was the youngest of those six.

"Now you know how an only child can have sisters," she said tartly. "And beyond that bend is the village of this only child's youngest sister."

"I surrender, Wise One." Chastity hooted in laughter. "I will never question your words again."

The old woman nodded in smug satisfaction, just as the light canoe swept beyond the trees and the village of the Sakonnets came into view.

At first glance the village looked like Sowams. It was hidden entirely behind a stockade that was itself surrounded by carefully tended crop fields. There were many Indians at the landing to greet them, for the word of her visitors' approach had been swiftly carried to Awashuncks. The squaw sachem herself was not there to welcome the visitors, but she had sent her powah to represent her.

"Welcome to our village," he said, extending a hand to Grandmother as she waddled out of the canoe that suddenly seemed too small for her. "I am called Many Feathers. Awashuncks sends you greetings and asks that you follow me."

Knowing Sassacus' dislike of her, Chastity tried to read the expression on the powah's face, but all she could detect was lively curiosity. She and the old woman followed their new guide to the lodge that was to be theirs during their stay.

"Our wise sachem asks that you make yourselves comfortable while there is still light," said Many Feathers. "Your braves will sleep elsewhere; they have kin in the village. You will be sent for when it is time to eat." He pointed to a pile of rugs and another of gourds filled with fresh water. "If you are in need of anything, you need only ask. I have placed my grandson here to serve you."

The two women thanked him and entered the guest lodge, while the proud young grandson of the powah stood guard outside.

As they were refreshing themselves from the long journey, Chastity heard the throaty rasping that was the Indians' polite way of requesting permission to enter. She gave it immediately, and their young servant entered, carrying a large basket.

"This is for you, Old One, although the Beautiful One may have some too," he said respectfully, lowering his mop of black hair. "Our sagamore sends it that it may please you and remind you of happy days gone by. She said that it was a favorite of your father's."

The old woman lifted the lid on the basket and then grinned wide in delight. "May the spirits smile upon my sister and fill her seasons with joy! Come, Dancing Fox. This is a taste you will never forget."

"What is it, Grandmother?" asked Chastity, trying to see around the woman's broad back.

"Golden corn exploded over the fire and covered with the sticky sweet syrup of the great maple tree. It is the taste of my childhood, the taste of a time of peace and plenty. It is the food of Hawenneyu, the god of the spirits." She could speak no more, as her mouth was filled with the delicious treat.

The two sisters greeted each other affectionately. Awashuncks was tall and slim. The squaw sachem wore a woman's soft dress but, apart from a thin braid that swung free on one side of her head, her graying hair was worn long and loose, like that of a man. When she turned and smiled at Chastity, the girl could see that Awashuncks must have been quite beautiful in her youth, for she was still a handsome woman.

Her lodge was similar in size and decoration to that of Massasoit, and as the three of them sat down to eat, Chastity glanced quickly around her. Her eyes swept over the piles of thick furs, rested briefly on the large framed rawhide that seemed to serve as a bed, and touched lightly upon the two men that were sitting against the opposite wall. Abruptly she felt herself stiffen, and she stared at the men in disbelief.

One of them was white!

He must have felt her eyes on him, for he broke off his conversation and smiled at her, giving her a polite nod of the head. Chastity inclined her head in return, relieved to see that the man was a stranger. Nonetheless, it was a shock to see a white man dressed in Indian clothing and looking as though he belonged there as much as she did.

With a small start Chastity realized that the sachem was waiting for her to speak and knew that she had missed the question and would have to ask for it to be repeated.

"Forgive me, wise Awashuncks," she said somewhat guiltily, "I was so surprised at seeing a white man here that I was not listening."

"It matters not, Dancing Fox," said the sachem graciously. "The man whose presence surprised you is one of my husbands. Perhaps you would talk to him. It gives him pleasure to speak in his own tongue, and I have never had the patience to learn it. Indeed, it sounds harsh and clumsy to my ears," she admitted with a smile. She beckoned to her white husband, who quickly came and sat by her side.

"I thought my eyes belied me," he said to Chastity in English. "I have seen many a strange sight since living with the Sakonnets, but none so strange as a redheaded Indian!" His warm grin added to Chastity's confusion.

"Is he of the Owl clan, Grandmother? May I speak to him?"

Awashuncks gave her sister a strange look. "You have trained her well. Did she come to you a child?" Although her words were polite, Chastity suddenly felt as though the sachem had lost all interest in her, as though she had just failed some kind of a test.

Grandmother must have sensed the same thing, for her answer was quick and pointed. "She came to me woman enough to interest the famous Metacom. We travel in his canoe."

"She is lovely," conceded Awashuncks. "It is no wonder she excites his interest."

"Not only his interest. He wishes to make her his squaw." The Old One sat back and drew on her pipe in satisfaction. "She has manito, do you not feel it?"

Awashuncks looked at Chastity again, and the girl

felt that she was being weighed. Finally the sachem seemed to find something she approved of, for she grunted softly and nodded. "My husband is not of the Owl clan, child, but you break no law by speaking with him. You are both white. In a sense, you are kin." She turned back to her sister, dismissing the two of them.

"Now that that is settled, my name is Tom," said the man in friendliness. "Tom Morton."

For a moment Chastity was taken aback. Where had she heard that name before? "Be you of the Bay Colony?" she asked cautiously.

"Nay. Several years ago I lived in Merrymount, misnamed though the town may be. The Pilgrims' sour faces and bitter ways drove me off. They hate a hearty laugh and swear that any kind of fun is Devil-sent." He grinned and threw her a wink. "I was only celebrating the planting. If they cared not for my tame dance around the pole, they should see me dance around the Sakonnets' fire!"

"Tom Morton! Of course!" Chastity's laugh joined his. "You were expelled for dancing around the maypole! I mind the gossip well!" She remembered in shame that a few short years before she had condemned the man as heartily as any, and all sight unseen. How time was changing her!

The talk carried on until the fire grew small and Grandmother began to yawn lazily. "There is time for one more pipe and one more log, while you tell Dancing Fox how you became sachem," she suggested.

"I would not fill her pretty head with serious talk." Awashuncks smiled. "What need has she of tales of leadership and power?"

"Massasoit did not feel that way when he sent for her to ask her advice," grumbled her sister. "He saw beyond the pretty face. You grow old, Awashuncks. Your eyes grow dim. Perhaps when you have seen the seasons I have, you will begin to understand. Come, Dancing Fox," she said crossly, "let us return to our lodge and sleep."

Confused, Chastity got to her feet to help the old woman rise.

"You disappoint me, Little Sister. You were beautiful once, yet no one thought you a fool." She smacked her gums in disapproval and started to leave the lodge.

"Wait." The squaw sachem rose and addressed Chastity. "Massasoit sought your counsel?"

"Yes," admitted the puzzled girl.

"You travel in his son's canoe?" When Chastity nodded, Awashuncks seemed to come to a decision. "Tomorrow I shall send for you. I will speak to you alone. You shall learn the truth, as my sister wishes. Perhaps you will never need the wisdom I will give you, but then perhaps it will serve you well in the seasons to come." Her single braid swung gently as she turned to speak to Tom Morton, and Chastity knew they were dismissed.

"What is this story, Grandmother?" asked Chastity when they were safely back in their lodge. "Why is it so mysterious, and why did she decide to tell it to me?"

"Even I have never heard her story through," confessed the Old One. "Perhaps you remind her of herself. I do not know." The old woman shook her head. She is the only woman to ever rule as sachem. You are greatly honored."

"Sit down, Dancing Fox," said Awashuncks when they were alone. "I shall begin at the beginning. It is hard to put into words. I have done what I have had to do, and I have walked the path the spirits chose for me. Do not judge me while I speak, for the time may come when you find that our moccasins leave the same track in the snow. Listen, that you may learn from my words.

"I was married to Winnaco when I was but a young maid. He was old in seasons, but he was chief of the Sakonnets and my parents were pleased with the match. I believe that Winnaco first wanted me so that I might give him sons. His own sons had died on the warpath and his other wives were old and their juices no longer flowed. He did all he could to please me. He took me everywhere with him and even let me sit and listen when the chiefs took council. You see, he loved me and he could not bear to be parted from me. I would have liked to give him children, especially the sons he longed for. But it was not to be. The few times that I began to swell with child, I grew weak and sick. Soon the child was lost. I suggested that he take another wife, but he refused. He said he was too old to start again.

"Instead, he began to talk and to explain things to me.

I always had a quick mind, and he began to train it. Sometimes I believe he thought of me as the son we could not have. Other times, I was his wife." Awashuncks colored slightly with pleasure at the old memories.

"He taught me many things, but two stand clear in my mind that I wish to tell you. He taught me that I must always keep my word, for that is all of me that most will ever know. And he taught me that everyone has a price, be it wampum, power, fame, or love.

"Toward the end, he grew sick and passed long days lying on his furs. Many of the decisions he made during those days were my decisions. He had taught me well. I had had a taste of power, and his sickness gave me time to think and plan. I decided not to return to my mother's lodge upon his death. Winnaco had been a good husband, but I would not lose myself in the forest as some widowed squaws do. Having been treated as an equal, I would not marry another man who would treat me as less.

"The night Winnaco went with the spirits, I made my first move. There were only three strong men who could stop me. The powah and the two greatest mugwumps had the power to destroy my plans. The rest of the Sakonnets would follow the path chosen by these three. Left alone, these men might challenge one another, and the sagamore would be selected through the ritual duel. I would not allow this to be. I would be sagamore. I would be the first squaw sachem!

"I knew that Many Feathers wanted power, for that is the nature of all powahs. But I did not know if he would be satisfied with just religious power and nothing more. I spoke to him and told him my thoughts. I said that ruling should be left to women and dreaming to men, which is as I believe. When women get old, they fear nothing. Nothing and no one. They only speak truth, for they cannot be bothered to speak otherwise.

"At first, Many Feathers laughed at me. Then he saw that I was serious. I promised him the power of the spirits for him, his son, and his son's sons. And then Many Feathers grew serious himself. I left him thinking about the possibilities of that kind of power, and I went to the first mugwump.

"This man's name was Kewa, and he had long looked

upon me with hunger. During my husband's life, he had shown respect, but I knew that his flesh burned for me. So I gave him what he wanted. And in return, he promised to support me at the council fire.

"The other mugwump, Little Eagle, had daughters but no sons. If he had had grown sons, I do not think he would have joined with me. A man without ambitions will find them for a son. But I promised to make his grandsons mine, to school them in power and leadership and to make the best of them sachem after me.

"Although the words were never spoken, I knew the men thought they would rule me. If I gained power and they ruled me, they ruled the Sakonnets. I said nothing of this to them. I waited until the council fire.

"When the fire grew low and voices high in disagreement, I stepped into the sacred circle. I said that Winnaco had trained me to rule the Sakonnets. I promised them peace. I swore that no more sons should die on the warpath. It was a sign of how confused they were that they did not laugh me out of the circle. But each minute they let me stay, my case grew stronger. They did not realize what strength their indecision gave me.

"Many Feathers stood behind me and said that he had had a dream. In his dream, I was squaw sachem and the Sakonnets prospered.

"Little Eagle then stood, and he too swore allegiance to me. The young braves loved Little Eagle, and many of them came over to my side because of him. All was going as planned.

"Then Kewa stood up and laughed. 'A woman rule over men?' His laughter was cold. 'Why, she will destroy our enemies. She will cut them down with her sharp tongue! This is a fool's plan. How can Awashuncks keep peace when no woman can even keep her word?' He laughed again, and he spit on the earth in insult. It was a mistake.

"It was either win now or be driven from the tribe in shame. I had no choice. The laughter started to spread. I vowed I would not lose so easily!

" 'Kewa fears women,' I mocked him. 'Would you have a coward rule? Come, Kewa, see how my blade bites deeper than my sharp tongue!' And I drew my knife.

"In the silence that followed, I began to regret my impulse. If Kewa refused to fight me, I had lost. If he even showed his weapon, he was lost, for he would have acknowledged me as an equal.

" 'Come, Kewa,' I cried softly, 'do your man-balls hide in your body with fear? The women whisper that your knife is dull. Is that why you do not show it? Are you that afraid? Is that why your skin is so pale and white?'

"With a furious growl he sprang at me. Even delivered by a woman, these were insults that he could not brush aside and still save face. I was so light that I danced to one side of the man, leaving a trail of scarlet along his arm. He looked at it in disbelief, and then at me in pure hatred. He pulled out his knife and circled me warily. He was a big man. I knew that he could beat me easily and quickly. I had never learned the art of fighting. But my husband had taught me how to think.

"With a cry, I half-fell to the ground, supporting myself on one hand. Kewa saw his chance and threw himself at me. It should have been over then, but like the quail that limps to save her chicks, I had planned this move. The sand that I threw at him filled his eyes and blinded him, giving me the moment I needed. With both hands I plunged my knife into his side and ripped his body open from one side to the other.

"The screams were terrible. Both of us were covered with blood. Then I stood up, and my people knew that I had won. To challenge a mugwump and win was an act of courage that was respected. No one else questioned my right to rule.

"Seasons later, Many Feathers asked me why I had killed Kewa. He said it would have been enough to wound and shame him. At the time, I thought it was because I was not trained to fight. I did not know how to wound, only how to kill.

"But there was more to it than that. I had given Kewa my body, and he had betrayed me. He was my enemy. He broke his word. I knew then that I had wanted Kewa dead. It would have shamed him too much to be bested by a woman, and he would have sought revenge. I did not want live enemies. Both my heart and my head wanted him dead. I would not have forgiven him.

"I think Winnaco would be proud of me now. But he would scold me for Kewa. I did not rightly judge his price. I almost paid for that with my life.

"I have kept my word to the Sakonnets. We walk the path of peace and plenty. No man rules me, nor my people through me. It has been a lonely path, though not without rewards. But the loneliness sometimes grows large within me. Many Feathers and Little Eagle are good men, they have kept their word. But they do not bring me ease when the loneliness grows big. And so I take a new husband, but he must not be a very strong man. I will not be ruled, even by love.

"I grow old. My power will pass on to other hands. But I will be remembered. I speak to you of this because someone should know. Truth is like the moonlight, it gets lost when given in pieces.

"My sister is right, Dancing Fox. You could walk the path of power. You have manito. But the path is rough and difficult. The rewards are great, but there is a price you must pay. There is always a price."

Awashuncks fell silent, and Chastity realized it was time to leave.

As she walked back to the guest lodge, she considered that Awashuncks had paid too high a price. The story made her out to be cold and calculating. How could she have given herself to Kewa in so casual a way? And having once given herself, how could she have turned on him in such blood-filled violence?

Chastity shook her head in disbelief. She would never be like that. Nothing was worth such a price. She would give herself only in love. She remembered why she was in Awashuncks' village then and caught her full lip between white teeth.

What would she decide about Metacom? Of course, if she gave herself to him, it would not be like Awashuncks and Kewa. But would what she felt for the young prince turn into love, the kind of love that her body and soul ached for? She wanted so much, and until now she had been forced to settle for so little. Well, high ideals were all very well and good for children and maidens, but sometimes one had to be practical in order to survive in this world. Perhaps she had been too harsh in judging

Awashuncks. Who could know the depths of the sachem's sufferings?

Chastity was so lost in her thoughts that she walked directly into two men. She stumbled and was caught in powerful arms. She looked up and found herself mirrored in a pair of laughing brown eyes.

⊷ *Twelve* ⊶

"Mon dieu! what have we here? beauty among the beasts?"

Chastity mumbled an apology before she realized that the voice spoke in English. The accent was soft, with a musical lilt, and left her with the desire to hear the voice again.

"Tom," the voice continued, "is she a member of your tribe?" If so, I will join *tout de suite.*"

"Take care, André," came Tom Morton's easy reply. "Dancing Fox speaks English far better than you do."

The men smiled at Chastity, and the foreigner spoke again. "You will forgive a poor Frenchman, no? I had no intention to offend. But to find such a *bijou,* a jewel as you say, here in the wilderness! You are not angry with me, please?"

Chastity had to laugh at the woebegone expression on his face. "Nay"—she shook her head merrily—"a compliment like that cannot anger me. Indeed, I have never been called a—what was it? A *bijou?*"

"But that is what you are!" the man exclaimed. "You are a precious jewel, not glowing soft like the ruby, nor bright and common like the diamond. You are dangerous and exciting like the fire opal!"

Chastity felt embarrassed and pleased at the same time. But she did not know quite how to handle this romantic stranger. He was handsome enough, she decided, with his laughing eyes and his curly brown hair that refused to lie tamely against his head. He looked so eager to please, and at the same time so experienced! So she

166

smiled at him because she enjoyed his flattery, but she turned to Tom to speak.

"I have just left Awashuncks. What an unusual woman!"

"Aye, that she is," he agreed. "But she has been good to me and I have no complaint. If I drink a bit too much or enjoy watching the maidens at work, she does not nag. Sometimes I wonder which of us is the heathen."

"Tom, *mon ami*," said his companion impatiently as he poked him in the side, "will you not introduce me? Must I stand here like a tree while you speak with this beauty?"

"Dancing Fox"—Tom smiled—"this is my friend André. He is a trapper and a Frenchman, so there are two reasons not to trust him very much."

"But you just said he was your friend," protested Chastity.

"And that he is. But there is not a woman alive that I would trust with him," was the reply. Chastity looked from one man to the other, trying to decide if Tom were serious.

"He exaggerates, Bijou," claimed the Frenchman with a shrug. "He is jealous because the women of his country seem to like me. It is not my fault." He smiled disarmingly. "I do not force myself upon them, you know?"

"You do not fight them off, either." Tom laughed as he clapped his friend on the back.

André looked at him in amazement. "Would you have me refuse and hurt the woman's feelings? What animals you Englishmen are! Forgive us, mademoiselle." He turned back to Chastity. "This subject must bore you, no? Perhaps you would be kind enough to show a stranger around your village?"

"There he goes, Dancing Fox. Pay him no mind. André has visited on and off regularly since I married Awashuncks. He knows his way around the village as well as I do." Tom grinned with amusement, and André shook his head ruefully.

"And he calls himself my friend! Bijou, take pity on me."

"From what I hear, sir, pity is not what you are interested in," replied Chastity teasingly. "If what you want

is a pair of adoring eyes and soft, panting sighs, why, I
suggest you get yourself a puppy!" With a light laugh she
darted away.

"She is a fire opal, *mon ami*," André whispered. "I
must have her."

"You have competition, then. She is being courted by
a Wampanoag prince and is under my wife's protection."
Tom Morton shook his head discouragingly. "If you try
anything, you will not live to regret it."

"Ah, but I am a patient man. All things come to the
man who waits, no?" André shrugged and laughed. "So
I wait."

"There will be a squaw dance in a few days, my
friend. You will see her there."

"And she will see me. Perhaps that is more important,
no?" said the Frenchman strangely.

Their young guide gave Chastity a tour around the
village, and she confirmed her original impression. It was
much like Sowams. So much so that Chastity caught
herself turning to make comments to Minone, and she
wondered if she were homesick. Home. Sowams *was*
home to her now. It was more than a place to live, her
lodge, her family . . .

She broke off her thoughts, as she was not quite ready
to investigate these feelings that she was experiencing.

That evening, at the campfire after the meal, she saw
the Frenchman again. Sensing that Grandmother was an
alert and careful chaperon, the man did not even try to
approach Chastity. But the looks he sent the girl were
heavy with meaning, and their boldness caused her to
lower her eyes. She could not decide if she were more
embarrassed or flattered by his obvious desire. Grandmother, although she could not help but notice what was
going on, said nothing that night. Chastity's behavior was
almost maidenly. Almost, but not quite.

Chastity was in no great hurry to return to Sowams,
and when she heard there was to be a squaw dance, she
begged that they stay a few extra days. The Wampanoags did not have squaw dances. The custom had
come to the Sakonnets from the tribes to the distant west,
and Awashuncks had adopted it readily. Since it was the

only chance that Chastity would have to participate, the old woman finally agreed to delay their return.

"Do you fully understand the rules?" she asked of the girl.

"Only that the women ask the men to dance and that they dance together in the circle," she responded.

"But that is only a small part," cautioned Grandmother with a wag of her fat finger. "First you must catch your man. All the unmarried braves run and hide in the shadows. They will pretend that they have no desire to dance with you. You must seek out your choice and put your hand on his arm. Once you have done this, the man must follow you back to the fire and dance with you. When he is tired of dancing, he will ask you what his ransom is to be."

"His ransom?" asked Chastity in surprise.

"Of course." The old woman chuckled. "His freedom must have a price. You must set the price, but you must do it wisely. From the older braves you must ask for a wampum bead, perhaps even two. From the younger, a feather or something small that catches your eye. If you ask too much and they cannot pay, they will be humiliated. If you ask too little, they will be insulted. You must judge carefully."

"But what if I judge wrong?" demanded the worried girl.

"Then the man will continue to dance with you. It is a game, Dancing Fox, only a game that men and women play."

Chastity shook her copper head and laughed merrily. "I had almost forgotten," she admitted.

"It is time you begin to remember." Grandmother seemed pleased.

Chastity dreamed of a man that night. At first she did not recognize him. His face was not too clear, and kept sliding in and out of focus. She chased the man through the shadows and finally managed to lay her hand on his arm. When she had led him back to the fire to dance, she saw that it was Metacom. The rush of excitement she felt in her dream was powerful enough to waken her. She lay there trying to sort out her puzzled reactions. Was Metacom really her choice?

André was sitting with Awashuncks and Tom when Chastity arrived at the campfire. The Frenchman must have been telling a humorous story, for when he finished speaking, all three of them began to laugh heartily. Almost unconsciously Chastity waited for him to turn and smile in her direction, and to her surprise, she felt slightly annoyed when he failed to notice her.

She sat down with a group of women of mixed ages. The older women were helping the younger ones plan their strategies for the dance. There was much joking and laughter, and Chastity quickly regained her humor among the gaiety of the company.

"Let the dance begin!" commanded Awashuncks, and as if by magic the unmarried men melted into the shadows. Several braves started to pound on drums of all sizes, while the other married men sat around smoking and talking. Chastity decided to sit and observe for a little while.

A maiden arrived at the fire with her captive, and they began to dance. From the happy look on the brave's face, he had not tried to hide overly well. Soon the couple was joined by others. In shuffling steps they formed two circles, with the women on the inside. The partners danced side by side in a counterclockwise direction.

"Tonight we wish to hold back the sun," Chastity was told.

She saw Tom go over and hand drinks to the drummers and then take a healthy swig from the jug himself. Knowing that the Indians did not make any strong liquor themselves, she asked what was in the jug.

"Something that our sachem's husband has discovered. He makes it from the berries of the red sumac," a woman told her. "He mixes it with sugar from the maple tree and lets it stand. The taste makes the eyes water and burn, yet it gives the drummers strength to play all night. Sometimes it makes them happy, and sometimes they grow wild like the grizzly bear. But then they fall asleep and the wildness leaves them."

From that, Chastity knew that Tom Morton was mak-

ing some kind of alcohol, and she wondered if he were
unhappy with his life among the Sakonnets. Did he miss
his old life and his friends? She glanced in André's direction, but he was gone.

Just then she saw a laughing girl lead him to the fire.
He was smiling at her. She was a pretty thing, Chastity
grudgingly admitted to herself. Annoyed, she leaped to
her feet and went in search of a dancing partner.

She saw a male figure at the outskirts of the circle.
Seeing her approach, the figure darted off and she sped
after it. The shadows closed in, and she was forced to a
walk. She was about to give up when she heard a soft
laugh and made out the figure of a man leaning against
the back of a lodge.

"Are you waiting for me?" she asked in amazement.

"It would not do to run too fast," said the shadow.
"How then could I be caught?"

Laughing, Chastity went over and touched the stranger
on the arm. He followed her meekly back to the fire.
Once there, she saw that her prisoner was very young,
just past the threshold of manhood. He was proud of
being caught by such a beauty, and as if to prove it, he
began to dance with vigor.

"If you are bored, we could disappear into the forest,"
he offered after some time. "Rules are relaxed tonight,
and it is permitted. Many couples do."

"Not this time, thank you." She laughed, delighted by
his total lack of guile. "I wish to dance tonight."

Finally she set his ransom at one feather, and after
protesting dramatically, the pleased young man paid
happily and disappeared into the shadows again. She sat
down to rest and saw that Grandmother had joined in the
fun.

The old woman had caught a man as skinny as she was
fat. He was begging for release, but she steadfastly refused, claiming that if she had the strength for the dance,
he should as well. Other older women pointed and
laughed, making ribald remarks and challenging each
other to do as well.

"I am not so old as I had thought!" cried the grandmother to Chastity with a broad grin. "Find a partner,
child and join me!"

Out of the corner of her eye Chastity saw a figure slip into the shadows behind a large pine. When she reached the tree, the figure had disappeared. The crack of a stick to her left caught her attention, and she plunged on in that direction. She was soon rewarded by the sight of a blanketed back ahead of her. Determined not to be eluded, she lengthened her stride, but the figure began to race. She lost sight of him and stopped in uncertainty, when the moon broke through the trees and outlined a strange figure.

There he was, sitting on the ground, blanket over his head and holding branches in his hands. He was disguised as a bush! At this comical sight Chastity began to chuckle, and she threw herself at the figure in bubbling laughter.

"I have you now," she cried. "You will have to follow me back!"

"Bijou! But, is it you?" It was the voice of the Frenchman, all innocent in surprise.

"André?"

"Mon Dieu! I thought it was a she-devil come after me! Had I known it was my fire opal, I would not have run!" He threw back the blanket and grinned up at her. Although she knew he was teasing her, Chastity could not stop laughing.

"You look so silly as a bush!" She collapsed weakly next to him on the ground.

"And you so lovely as a huntress," he whispered after a moment.

Suddenly Chastity felt uncomfortable at his closeness. The forest seemed very still and the campfire far away. She felt totally alone with this man. He made no move to touch her, but she could feel the tension between them almost as if it were a physical being.

"Come, let us return to the dance," she suggested nervously. "I have caught you fair and square."

"If that is your only desire." The man shrugged slightly in disappointment and then turned and smiled at her disarmingly. "I am your prisoner. I must follow you anywhere, no?"

Chastity felt many eyes upon them when they returned

to the circle. Had they been gone too long? But Grand-mother nodded at her reassuringly.

After they had danced many times around the circle, Chastity felt it was time to set the ransom.

"Two wampum beads," she demanded.

"If I had such wealth, I would give it willingly, you know? But I am a poor man," exclaimed André.

Chastity looked at him quickly. Had she humiliated him by asking too much? To her amazement, she saw that he was laughing. He was teasing her! With this, she became determined.

"Two beads or you shall dance till dawn," she stated firmly, giving her head a pert toss. "Your freedom will not come cheaply, Frenchman. You made me run too much for that."

"Then dance I must," he cried in feigned misery. "What a terrible fate, no?" The couples around them laughed heartily.

"I will lend you the beads, Frenchman," called an old squaw in cackling laughter. "You can pay me back when you get the chance."

"No, kind lady, I must refuse," he answered gaily. "I cannot borrow from a woman. Frenchmen have pride, you know?" His eyes twinkled, and others joined in the laughter.

"Perhaps you should lower the price, Dancing Fox," shouted the women.

"Never!" cried the girl, entering into the game. "Freedom is much too precious a thing!" She shook her head with spirit and they continued to dance.

Many couples had disappeared into the forest, and still Chastity danced with the Frenchman. She was getting tired of the shuffling steps, but not of the game. There was something exciting here that intrigued her. Suddenly she realized that Awashuncks stood before them.

"Dancing Fox will accept your word for the beads," said the sachem in polite formality.

Knowing that he had prolonged the dance more than was correct, André bowed. "Then you have my word on it, Dancing Fox. And I thank you for my freedom." He turned and left the circle.

"Perhaps you would rejoin your grandmother," suggested the handsome woman gently. Although nothing

was said in words, Chastity felt that she had been reprimanded.

"I think it is time to return to Sowams," said Grandmother late that night. "We have been here longer than I
planned."

"Did I do something wrong?" Chastity felt that something was wrong and decided to bring it out in the open.

"I do not think so. Did something happen with the
Frenchman? Something of which I was not aware?"

"No, nothing happened. But I found that it was flattering to have a man respond to me so," she admitted
with a shy smile. "It made me feel warm and alive again.
I hope I did not seem too bold. I was just enjoying myself."

"No, child, not really. I understood what you felt, and
so did my sister." The old woman grunted. "But if you
are to awaken to your womanhood again, I would rather
that it not be around that Frenchman."

"Is that what is happening to me?" asked Chastity
curiously. "Is that why I feel this way?"

"I think I recognize the signs." Grandmother smiled.
"It means that your heart has passed through its winter's
sleep, Dancing Fox. It is spring again. Are you ready to
return?"

Suddenly Chastity realized that she was. Her home
was in Sowams. Her future was there. The past was over
and done, and she could not mourn forever. She knew
that she would never love another as she had loved
Edmund, but she knew that she was tired of being alone.
The winter was over. The old woman watched as the
lovely young one nodded happily.

Chastity saw Metacom a few days after their return.
He was on the narrow path running back to Sowams from
the river. She was carrying two large pails balanced on
a pole over her shoulders, and the water sloshed over the
rims when she came to a sudden halt. Without saying a
word, Metacom took the buckets and walked in front of
her toward the village.

She was surprised at the sudden rush of warmth that
filled her. Seeing him completed her homecoming. She

was truly pleased to see him and knew that he was an important and exciting part of her life.

The brief loincloth he wore flapped gently against his powerful thighs and his body shone like bronze in the sun. Chastity could not help but watch the muscles play across his back and shoulders, and she wondered what it would be like to be swept up in his strong arms.

When he reached the wigwam, he set the water down outside the low door and turned to face her. Still silent, he grasped her chin firmly in his large hand and looked long into her amber eyes. He ran his thumb gently over her full lips, and a vein throbbed in his temple. Tiny diamond pinpoints burned in his bottomless eyes, and she caught her breath at his desire. Without looking away, he let his hand fall.

She smiled. She was so happy that she smiled, and he understood.

That evening he came to the wigwam with two large bundles. He would not sit with the old woman, but remained standing, proud and sure, as befitted a prince.

"Grandmother, I have come to make you an offer for Dancing Fox. I would make her mine."

"What is your offer, Metacom?"

Without answering, he cut the thongs that held the bundles and stood back. "See for yourself, Old One."

"Ten and five bearskins, all black! Three deer, two moose, five fox, seven of the white weasel!" There was awe in the old woman's voice as she counted. There had never been a bride price like this!

"And this," Metacom said as he casually kicked the smaller bundle toward her.

Inside the small skin lay wampum bracelets, necklaces, and belts, all adorned with the shell of the precious blue clam. Even Minone could not repress an exclamation of surprise when she saw all that wealth.

"There is enough for all of you," said Metacom in a haughty voice. "Let no one say that this family loses when Dancing Fox joins mine."

"Metacom, you take the pleasure out of an old woman's days," Grandmother grumbled crossly. "How can I refuse these gifts? How can I send you away? The offer Running Bear made, I could refuse, but this"—she pointed to the gifts—"would buy many wives."

She turned to the girls. "Rise, Dancing Fox, here is your husband."

Chastity stood up and walked slowly to Metacom. The old woman took her hand and laid it in that of the young chief.

"My granddaughter is yours, Metacom. Treat her well. May the spirits guide you both, that you may walk in beauty all the days of your lives."

Chastity could feel the heat in his hand as it tightened around hers and his hungry eyes feasted on her upturned face. When he spoke, his voice was thick and husky.

"Prepare her. In three days I shall come for her."

Chastity began to shake after he left. She shook so violently that Minone wrapped one of the black bearskins around her with a worried frown.

"What says your heart, Dancing Fox?" asked Grandmother, noticing the girl's trembling.

"My heart feels fear, Old One. I cannot see the reason, but I am afraid. Suddenly I feel threatened. My life will change."

"Of course it will change!" cried Minone impatiently. "You will have a husband!"

"Is it Metacom you fear?" Grandmother asked with a worried glance at the pale girl.

"No, not Metacom." She started to smile but began to shake again. "I cannot explain, for I do not understand it myself."

"When you are in your husband's arms, you will forget your fears," soothed the old woman. "You have been alone too long; this is just a reaction to your awakening. It means that your heart is ready to sing again."

When the fire burned low and Chastity lay asleep on her bed of furs, she had another dream. She was in a valley where the grass was green and thick. Feeling thirsty, she knelt beside a sweetly singing brook and dipped her hands in the clear water.

"Drink that and you will die," a soft voice whispered in her ear. She looked up to see a huge black snake coiled under a bush.

In her dream, she reached for an apple that hung from a bough above the stream.

"Eat that and you will die," hissed the snake.

She began to run away, but everywhere she looked she saw the snake, its red tongue flickering and its flat head swaying from side to side.

"If you leave this place you will die of hunger and thirst," it warned.

She woke up and felt something warm and sticky on her cheek, and she tasted the salty taste of blood.

"Blast!" she said in English as she got up to look for a rag.

"What is it?" Minone leaped up in alarm.

"Go back to sleep, Minone. It is nothing serious, a nose-bleed. I used to get them as a child. Forgive me for disturbing your rest."

Instead of lying down, Minone looked at her in horror and went over to where Grandmother lay snoring on her furs.

"Awake! Awake, Old One!" The girl shook the sleeping woman soundly. "It is Dancing Fox. There is blood coming from her nose!" The two women looked at each other in fear, and then at Chastity, who began to laugh.

"But it is nothing, Grandmother, only a nosebleed. It has almost stopped." She took a handful of water from a gourd and splashed it over her face. "See? It is over now."

"An omen, it is an omen," muttered Minone with a shudder.

"Hush, Minone," ordered the old woman, gaining control of herself. "She is right, it is nothing. You will tell no one. It is not worth mentioning," she said sharply as Chastity sank down again onto her bed.

The next day when Betty stopped to congratulate her, she remembered the mysterious alarm that had been shown during the night.

"Betty, what does it mean when a person's nose bleeds? Is it something important?"

"It warns of death, Dancing Fox. Whose nose has bled?" she asked with morbid curiosity.

"No one's. It was a story that Grandmother told last night. I did not understand it, and I forgot to ask her the significance."

"It is an evil omen. If it ever happens to you, you must go to the powah at once. He will make sacrifices. But Metacom will teach you all this. How lucky you are!"

Chastity thanked Betty and moved away. Lucky? At

the moment, she was no longer sure. Metacom was a good man and would make her happy; that she knew. Why, then, the fear? Why the sudden longing for help? Only one thing was really clear to her. She certainly could not go to the powah. He was the last person on earth who would help her.

⊷ *Thirteen* ⊷

"RUNNING BEAR IS BACK!" MINONE ANNOUNCED BREATH-lessly as she rushed up to Chastity. "And he is more hand-some than ever!"

Chastity smiled at the enthusiasm in the girl's voice, and questioned, "Where is he? Did he speak to you?"

"No, he is across the river with Metacom and some of their friends. Oh, Dancing Fox, soon we shall both have husbands! He must have come back because he is ready to make a new offer."

As the girls walked slowly through the village, Chastity glanced at her friend with a small frown. "Are you sure that is why he has come back?" she asked.

"Of course, why else? That is our way. Besides, you forget my dream. This time, Grandmother will accept him." She looked at the redhead with mischief. "Are you not curious about what they are doing?"

"Who?"

"Metacom, Running Bear, and the others! Are my words like the breeze that blows past you and leaves no mark?"

Chastity stopped and shook her head as if to clear her thoughts. "Forgive me, Minone, I was thinking about something that Betty said. Tell me, what are they doing across the river?"

"They are putting up your wigwam!"

"Across the river?" Chastity showed her surprise.

"Of course. You would not want to spend your Moon-of-honey in the village," she scoffed. "From the look of the trees they have felled, Metacom has been at work for several days. He knew his offer would be accepted. That

179

must be why he said the wedding would be in only three days. He knew the lodge would be done."

"Minone," Chastity said slowly as they neared their home, "perhaps you should tell me exactly what will happen. These marriage customs are new to me."

"You have had a husband before, you know what will happen. You should be telling me."

Chastity grinned and pulled the laughing girl's thick braid. "I am speaking about the ceremony, Clever One, not after. I can handle that without your help."

Minone sank to the ground beside Grandmother, who was leaning against the wigwam sewing. She merely nodded at them and grunted, as her mouth was full of porcupine quills. Chastity sat down as well and examined the moccasins the old woman was making.

"How soft they are," she exclaimed, "and yet how strong." The woman pointed at the shoes and then at Chastity.

"For me? But my moccasins are still good."

"You must wear all new clothing for the wedding," explained Minone. "You will shine like the morning star. Today we must start on your dress."

"Tell me exactly what will happen."

"When your wigwam is done, Metacom will send a message. Then Grandmother and I will carry all your things to your new home. Early the morning of your wedding, you will bathe in the river. You should enter the water at the moment the sun rises. Four maidens will accompany you to wash your hair and rub you with raccoon grease."

"Could I not leave off the grease for just one day?" Chastity begged.

"And be burned and bitten so that Metacom will not be able to touch you?" Minone was shocked, and the old woman firmly shook her head from side to side.

Chastity shrugged. Much as she was tempted to follow her own inclination in this matter, she did not want to do anything that would upset her family or Metacom.

"We will help grease your skin," Minone continued, "and then bring you back here, where you will dress. I will braid your hair and paint your face for the last time. After that, it will be the duty and the pleasure of your husband." She paused for effect for a moment. "When you hear the drums, it will mean that Metacom is on his way to you. The whole village will line up and make a path from his wigwam to ours. Massasoit will call us out; first I will go out, then Grandmother, and then you. Massasoit will take your hand and give it to his son.

"Since Metacom is the son of our sachem and a chief himself, he will lead you to the place of the council fire. There will be feasting and singing and dancing all day, as well as contests of skill and much storytelling."

The old woman rocked happily, her eyes lit with warm memories. She took the last quill out of her mouth and flattened it with her broad thumbnail.

"At the first faint glow of the evening star, the two of you will walk quietly away together," she said softly. "But first, you must make your dress. One that will be worthy of the jewelry that Metacom gave you. Fetch one of the new deerskins, and we will help."

The three of them worked busily, first cutting the skirt carefully with a sharp knife and then the small vest. The old woman took her time sewing so that she would not snap the flint needle, while the two girls cut the long fringe that would hang gracefully against her body. They worked until the light began to fade and then reluctantly went inside.

They were up with the sun. The old woman sent Minone with one of the weasel skins to trade with a family who had spent the previous summer by the ocean. The girl came back proudly bearing a sack of small shells, which they proceeded to sew in intricate patterns on the dress. When they were finally finished, it was folded gently and laid aside, and then they checked Chastity's few belongings.

The blankets she had woven were carefully piled next to her loom, although she insisted that Minone and the old woman each take one. Next came her baskets, mats, and buckets. Grandmother gave her a clay pot, a horn spoon, and a few gourd cups, telling her that Metacom would make her more. That was part of a man's work. She had a few furs, the skin from the wolf that had attacked her, the beaver, and a few more she had acquired over the year and a half she had lived in Sowams. On top of all these lay the knife that Hannah had thrust into her hands a lifetime ago. The old woman gave her own hairbrush to Chastity, who marveled at the graceful design carved into the handle.

"It was a gift from one of my husbands. The third, I think. No matter, it was made with love, and with love I give it to you. When Metacom brushes your hair-of-fire, you will remember me, and you will tell your children of the fat old woman who took you in."

When Wamsutta came with the news that the wigwam was ready, Chastity tried to conceal her restlessness. Sensing what was happening, the old woman asked her to start supper while they carried her possessions to the wigwam, and Chastity agreed readily, for she wanted something to keep herself busy.

Dusk in the forest was the gentlest time of day, a time when violet shadows blended rock into fern. Chastity made her way to the river to refill the water pail. A whippoorwill gave a soft plaintive cry, and she smiled, remembering the days when she had found its call unsettling. She loved the damp smell of dusk and the music of the twilight sounds. A small breeze rustled the leaves, and the tree in front of her suddenly seemed to move. Chastity froze.

"Forgive me, Dancing Fox, I did not mean to startle you."

It was Metacom, and Chastity smiled uncertainly. Was she permitted to speak to him now? After all, it was the eve of their wedding. The dark chief seemed to understand her silent confusion, and he moved closer to her.

"Let me help you," he said simply as he took the bucket from her hand. Chastity followed him down the path to the river, wondering how many taboos she would break by speaking. Finally she could stand the silence no longer.

"I thought you would be across the river," she ventured, and was rewarded by seeing a flame leap into his black eyes.

"No." He knelt to fill the bucket, and Chastity found herself kneeling as well. "Wamsutta is there now. My brother takes my place with your family. He entertains them."

Chastity searched his face with curiosity, and surprised a fleeting smile. Why, he has tricked Grandmother! she thought to herself. What happens now? She started to rise, but the man reached out and touched her hair gently.

"Your hair-of-fire burns dark tonight," he said, and Chastity heard the catch in his throat.

It was almost as if she were powerless to move. With a quick tug Metacom undid the bindings on her braids and let her hair hang free. He slipped his hand through her curls and gently stroked the nape of her slender neck. She felt her skin begin to tingle and a weakness threaten to flood her body.

"It warms me," he murmured, and his other hand stole into her locks to join its mate. His proud face was softened in the fading light, and his hair was the color of midnight. Chastity bit her lower lip as she stared into his hungry eyes. It had been so long!

He cupped her face in his dark hands and drew it slowly and purposefully to his. She caught her breath as his dry mouth brushed against hers, testing, teasing, awakening her long-slumbering senses. Something in her began to swell, to rise and twist with pleasure. She gave a soft, panting moan.

Metacom's hands dropped slowly to her breasts, tracing ever-decreasing circles around her taut nipples. His tongue played in her ear, leaving her dizzy and breathless. She found her arms sliding around his naked shoulders and her body pressed against his.

His fingertips danced down and around her sides, coming to a butterfly's brief rest on the bare flesh of her thighs. The thing inside her seemed to take control, and her fingers dug demands into his muscles and left small white scratches across his mahogany back. He pulled her closer, burying his head in the long hair that cascaded down her shoulders and over her breasts.

Suddenly, with an abruptness that made her gasp, Metacom pushed her away. He rocked back on his heels and stared at her through the dusk that filled the forest.

"Metacom?" she whispered in confusion.

He shook his head as though to clear it, and she was silenced. He devoured her body with burning eyes, that body that cried out to be touched, to be kissed. But he made no move to touch her, to kiss her. He simply caressed her with his eyes. Finally he reached out again, but only to trace the curve of her cheek gently with the back of his hand.

"Tomorrow!" he promised them both fiercely. "When you are mine. Then I shall make our bodies one."

Chastity understood then. But understanding did not help to still her pounding heart. She stood up quickly, trying to disguise her newly awakened desire. Metacom was forced to do the same.

"The Old One will be back at her fire," he said softly. "We must go."

They walked the path quietly. There was no sound save the silent clamoring of Chastity's senses. At the lodge that had been her home, he put down the bucket and briefly touched her hand.

"Blood of my heart," he whispered, and stepped back into the shadows.

Grandmother and Minone were inside, and Chastity was glad. She had no desire to be left alone with her thoughts just then. Nothing was said about the beans that were late in cooking, or about the flush of her cheeks.

Minone was full of talk about Chastity's new home. "What a wonderful place to start a life with someone you love! You can hear the river sing and the trees whisper love songs. How lucky you are, Dancing Fox!"

Chastity attempted a smile, even though her thoughts were tumbled and confused. How readily she had responded to Metacom's touch! It was as though she had been asleep for years. No, she corrected herself, only since that treasured day at Haunted Lake. How many lifetimes ago was that? she wondered. Would she ever recover from losing Edmund? Even thinking his name brought a stab of pain to her heart. Why had she responded so to Metacom's touch? Was this love too? She stared blindly into the fire.

"Do you know the story of the Fox Woman?" asked the old woman, seeking to distract her. When the girls both replied that they did not, she lit her pipe and settled back.

"Once, long ago, there was a young hunter who lived alone. He had proved himself in battle and so was entitled to tobacco and a wife, but none of the girls in his village made his heart sing. So he built his wigwam in the forest and lived alone.

"Now, he began to find that when he returned home

after an absence, his lodge had been visited. It had been swept and everything had been put in order. His clothes were hung up to air, and a nice hot meal was always waiting for him.

"One day he decided to see who was doing these things, so instead of going off to hunt, he hid himself under some bushes and waited. He waited all the morning until the sun stood overhead and there were no shadows on the ground.

"Then he saw a fox enter the house. Thinking it was going to steal his food, he crept silently in after it, an arrow notched in his bow. But upon entering, he saw a most beautiful woman dressed in skin clothing of a wondrous make. A fox skin hung over a line to air. The woman looked like an Indian, except for her long hair, which was reddish-gold.

"The young man asked her if it was she who had done the things for him, cleaned his lodge and prepared his food. She replied that she was his wife and it was her duty to do them. She hoped that she had done them to his satisfaction and that he was pleased.

"He was very pleased indeed, and surprised as well. His new wife was much lovelier than any maiden he had ever seen. They lived together as man and wife for a short time.

"But after a few days he began to notice a musty smell about the house and inquired of her what it was.

"'I emit that odor,' she said, 'and if you are going to find fault with me for it, I will leave.' And with that she tore off her clothing, slipped into her fox skin, and dashed off. She has never been disposed to visit a man since that time."

The girls chuckled with her and then banked the coals before preparing for bed.

"I shall wake you very early," said Minone, lying down on her furs.

"I probably will still be awake," came Chastity's answer from the darkness.

Sure enough, a few hours later, the old woman woke to see Chastity going out. Following, she found the girl sitting on the ground outside the wigwam.

"I could not sleep," Chastity confessed when she saw her.

"Is your heart so heavy, child?"

"How can I say what I feel?" She stared into the dark night. "I know that this is the best thing to do, considering my circumstances. My heart is indeed drawn to Metacom, but, to be honest, I fear my body is more attracted than my heart. Does this make me wicked?"

"No . . ." Chastity heard the old woman sigh in the darkness. "Only human. Metacom is a good man, love will come."

"The strange thing is that I believe you. I believe that the kind of love you speak of will come, that perhaps it has already started."

"Then?"

"Will it be enough?" she whispered. "You see, I cannot forget the other."

"And you would be a fool to forget. He was part of your past, and that past helped make you what you are now. Cherish your past, but do not live in it," warned the sleepy voice. "Is there more?"

"A sort of lurking hint of danger. That is the part that I cannot understand. It is as though something or someone were waiting for me."

"Metacom will protect you. You will be the wife of a chief tomorrow, the daughter-in-law of our grand sachem. There will be no danger, no one will be able to harm you. Come inside now," she said as she got up clumsily. "I will give you something to help your slumber."

Chastity gratefully took the cup that she was handed and drained it. She soon sank into a dreamless sleep.

As the sun's pink fingers reached out and gently touched the rippling surface of the river, Chastity plunged in and began the ritual preparations for the marriage. The water was chilly, but she enjoyed it and was in no hurry to get out. When at last she had had enough, she swam lazily back to the shallows and joined her friends.

All four of them took off their dresses and waded in to help with her hair. With such an abundance of help, it took much longer than usual, but finally her copper tresses were declared clean. The girls rubbed her feet and hands with the fine yellow sand from the riverbed until her skin was soft and pink. Next, regretfully, came the grease.

She slipped into her old dress, and the four girls encircled her so that she would meet no male on her way back to the lodge. She would have preferred to stay and dry her hair in the sun, but was whisked inside to rub it with a small skin.

If Chastity was unusually quiet, the other girls made up for it with their whispered teasings and soft giggles. She looked around for breakfast, but was informed that no food would be eaten until after the ceremony.

"I shall faint with hunger before then," she joked.

"See that you do not," warned Grandmother sternly. "It would be a most unfortunate omen."

The three maidens returned to their homes, and Minone helped her into her dress. The soft skirt was overlapped at one side and showed a healthy amount of her tanned thigh when she sat. The small vest fitted tightly over her full breasts, and the long fringe hung down to the end of the skirt. Next came the wampum jewelry and the embroidered moccasins. Judging by the briefness of her outfit, she had thought it would be light, but it weighed more than she had expected.

Minone carefully brushed Chastity's long hair, separating the red snarls gently with her fingers and stroking it until each strand glowed. She plaited them into neat braids and deftly tied the ends with thongs that were decorated with the same shells that were on the wedding dress.

Next came the face painting. Taking only yellow paint, Minone painted the part line in Chastity's hair. Dipping her fingers into the liquid again, she drew a thick line across her cheeks and the bridge of her nose, and then a circle on her chin with four small radiating lines.

The old woman grunted her approval. "Now you must pray," she instructed Chastity. "Pray to the spirits of the sun and stars, of the wind and rain. Pray to the owl and to the crow. Pray for patience and understanding, for laughter, and for love. Speak to the spirits, Dancing Fox. It is almost time."

Pray? But to whom? Chastity had learned the Indian prayers and songs to the spirits, but now the jealous God of her childhood sprang into her thoughts, and she was confused. Did he accept her divorce? Would she be living in sin in his eyes? Was the Great Spirit of the Indians really the God of the Pilgrims, as she had been taught as a child? The Indians did not accept the God of David and Abraham, did he still accept the Indians as his children? She tried to reason it out. When she was a child, God had looked very much like Elder Parkinson, only bigger. As she grew, his features dimmed, but his angry, vengeful aura remained. She had lived most of her life according to what she believed to be his wishes. And what had it gotten her?

Very little, she reflected honestly: a father who could not bear the sight of her, a forced marriage to a man she despised, and a child torn from her womb by wolves. She had left the God of her childhood back in New Plymouth.

Out here there were many spirits. The Indians believed that they were everywhere, in everything. Hawenneyu was the Great Spirit, but his word was no more absolute than was that of the Indian sachem. Was he real? She twisted the long fringe of her vest around her fingers as she searched for answers to her questions. Did God and Hawenneyu create, or were they created by men? She trembled as she dared to wonder if the answers to these questions really mattered. Perhaps the truth lay somewhere between the two worlds, lost in the hazy blue smoke of fiery sermons and sacred pipes. Maybe this truth was something that mankind had half-forgotten, which drifted back in tantalizing fragments, or perhaps it was something that mankind had not yet dreamed.

To this nameless something Chastity sent her prayers. So engrossed had she been in her thoughts that she did not notice the deep call of the drum.

"They come." Minone sprang to her feet, her black eyes dancing with excitement. She helped Chastity up and straightened her clothes.

"You shine like the evening star in the Moon-of-wild-rice." The old woman's voice cracked, as her eyes brimmed with proud tears.

Chastity nervously wiped her moist palms against her skirt and bit her lips. The drums grew louder and were joined by the rattle of gourds. Again her heart echoed the beat of the drums, and the very walls of the wigwam seemed to pulsate with rhythm. And then . . .

Silence. Men's voices were suddenly raised in anger, and the women looked at each other in bewilderment.

Finally Grandmother could wait no more, and she

thrust her head out the door to see what was happening. When she drew it back, her broad face was ashen and she trembled.

"It is the powah. He has returned from the forest and painted his face in mourning. He is demanding a council!"

"And Massasoit?" whispered Minone in dread.

"He is undecided." She threw Chastity an anxious look with the command to remain where she was, as she went outside.

"What is he doing? Why does he interrupt my wedding?"

Minone motioned to her to be silent, and the two of them crept to the door to listen. Abruptly the skin flap was flung aside and a warrior entered.

"You will come to the council," he said to Chastity.

Chastity looked at Minone for support, but the girl shrugged. "I do not understand either, Dancing Fox. This has never happened before."

The man followed Chastity outside, and she soon found herself surrounded by four braves, much as she had been on the way back from the river. Only this time there was no teasing, no smiles.

Massasoit was sitting next to Wamsutta, a hard expression on his proud face. Metacom strode angrily back and forth. When he saw Chastity, he gave her a small smile of encouragement, and she felt the knot of fear in her throat loosen.

Then she saw Sassacus. He had painted half his face blue, the other half black, and his eyes glittered in the bright sun like polished obsidian. He stood alone in the center of the circle and motioned for Chastity to sit on his left. She did so, and was somewhat comforted to see that her grandmother had forced her way through the guards and was seated slightly behind her. Minone seemed to have disappeared into the crowd.

"Begin, Sassacus. And be sure your words have weight enough to excuse your actions on my son's wedding day," snapped Massasoit.

"Mighty Sachem, young Chiefs, brothers! My heart is heavy beyond tears. I falter when I think of the terrible words I must speak, and I fear my voice will break. But I am your powah. I must protect you if I can." He threw his arms out as if to embrace his listeners.

"My people! I have had a dream. A terrible dream! When I woke, my body was weak and wet with fear, like that of a young child. I went into the forest and prayed. You must hear my dream. You must know the truth.

"I dreamed that Metacom took this woman to wive and there was much feasting. After some months, it was known that a child would be born. But as the seed grew within the woman's belly, so the light dimmed in our great sagamore's eye. Massasoit was dead before winter!"

A muttering could be heard in the crowd, and Massasoit shifted his weight uncomfortably.

"If my dream had ended there, I would not have spoken on this day. Death is a part of life, the way of all things. But there is more grief.

"Wamsutta became sachem. Before long, the white man demanded more Indian land. When our new sagamore refused, he was invited to their town for council and thrown into their jail! There he caught the white man's fever, and he was allowed to come home only to die!"

Chastity saw the fear creep into Wamsutta's eyes, and Metacom's worried frown. She felt her skin begin to crawl on the back of her neck, and she strained to hear the next words.

"My people! Metacom was our new leader, and across the land he was known as King Philip. With this woman at his side"—he pointed accusingly at Chastity—"he gave many concessions to peace. Too many, for the white men broke their promises, and their treaties were written on the wet sand that is swiftly smoothed by the waters of greed. And still we smoked the bitter calumet of peace.

"Without warning or provocation, these evil men stormed Sowams. No messages were sent, no arrows wrapped in snakeskin, no wampum belts dyed red. In the middle of the night, death exploded among us. I saw mothers struck down with babes at their breasts, children falling like ice in a winter storm, warriors murdered before they could string their bows. The flames from our burning lodges turned the night into day, and the earth was soaked with the blood of her children.

"My people! Tremble with me. I saw all this and more.

"I saw Metacom escape with some of our strongest braves. I saw him go to our brothers and ask for help. And I saw the Wampanoags, the Nipmucks, and the powerful

Narragansetts unite to avenge the bloody slaughter of our people. I cannot speak of the battles I saw, the broken bodies, the bleeding scalps. I am your powah, and I am afraid.

"I saw Metacom shot in the back. He died without singing his death song. I saw his body cut into pieces and his flesh into strips. There was no one to mourn him, no one to speed his soul on its lonely path. Our men were hunted down and shot like deer, our women murdered in their beds, our children sold into slavery.

"My people!" His voice, which had been loud and strong, broke, and he finished almost in a whisper. "The Nipmucks, the Narragansetts, the Wampanoags, the tribes that had lived in these forests since the beginning of time, were no more."

He slowly sank to the ground, overcome with grief. The wailing of women brought Chastity back to reality. Not a person there remained unaffected. Some cried openly, others tore their clothes and rubbed dirt on their faces, while still others stared blankly ahead of them in shock. Even the mighty sagamore was severely shaken, and when he found his voice, it was thick with pain.

"Your vision is truly terrible, Powah. The horror you describe is unbearable. Is there no way we can prevent this, no sacrifice we can make?"

Sassacus remained silent, his head buried in his chest.

With a trembling voice Metacom asked, "Was there no more, wise Sassacus? Was there no hint of hope for us?"

"There was more, young chief, and it was very strange." He lifted his head and looked straight at Metacom. "There is one chance."

He stood up, and his eyes swept across the crowd, pausing for an instant on Chastity. She stiffened as she read the bitter hatred and contempt in his glance. The trap was ready to be sprung.

"After my dream, I could not sleep. I went into the woods and built a sweat lodge. There I fasted and I prayed. When I could take no more, when the air burned my skin and scorched my lungs, my animal guide came to me. I told him of my dream and asked him the questions you now ask me. Finally he nodded his wise head and answered.

"I will help your people, but you must prove to me that they are worthy of my help. I will not aid the Praying Indians, nor those who live in the white man's towns. But I will help my brothers the Wampanoags, if they are true of heart. Massasoit and his sons are my brothers. I wish them no harm. If their line is to continue and they are to lead their people, they must have wives who are decent and pure. They must have women who will give birth to brave warriors and great chiefs, strong women who will advise their husbands with wisdom, women fit to be wives of your sachem. Give me the woman who is to be Metacom's wife, I will test her.'"

Metacom sprang up from where he had been sitting and cried, "She is fit! She needs no test!"

"If she is fit, there is no need to fear." Sassacus stood up and addressed the crowd. "My people! The spirit spoke to me and said he would test this woman. He said that if her heart is pure, he will help to save the Wampanoags. What say you to this?"

The crowd roared its approval. Chastity felt like screaming. Could they not see that he was lying?

"Great Massasoit"—Sassacus addressed his leader confidently—"what say you? Your people want me to test this woman. Do I have your permission?"

The old sagamore struggled for a moment, but Sassacus had forced him into a corner and he had no choice. What was the life of one when balanced against many?

"Prepare the test," he agreed.

The four guards encircled Chastity. She saw Grandmother in hurried conference with Minone, who rushed away. The powah strode off toward his wigwam, and Metacom, breaking all taboos, came over to reassure her.

"Feel no fear, beloved, you will pass the test."

"But he is lying! He hates me, and he is lying! Metacom, if you love me as you say, save me," she pleaded.

"Your mind is clouded with fear. Sassacus does not lie. You will see how easily you pass; we know your heart is pure. Be brave, my love, there is nothing to fear," he chided her gently.

"I would bless my granddaughter," said the old woman loudly as Minone returned. She pushed her way through the guards and reached the frightened girl's side.

Chastity held out her hands helplessly, and as the old

woman took them, she felt something hard pressed into her palm. Her hand closed quickly over it as she was pulled to the woman's ample bosom.

"Beware, his spirit is the snake," she whispered in Chastity's ear. "That is senega I gave you, snakeroot. Rub your hands well with it and then hide it with care. . . .

"Bless you, Dancing Fox," she said in a loud voice. "You are strong and true. Soon all will know it." She left her and returned to her place in the crowd.

Chastity sat down and furiously rubbed her hands with the gnarled root. She tried to do it under the fringe of her vest so that no one would see, and she did not dare to even look at her hands. There was a stir as the crowd parted and she saw Sassacus returning, carrying a large sack at arm's length. Quickly she dug a small hole in the soft dirt beneath her and thrust the root into it, carefully pushing the earth over to cover it.

"Dancing Fox, rise," he commanded as he laid the sack gently on the ground. As she stood up, he slowly reached inside, and to Chastity's horror, took out a large evil-looking viper. He held it firmly in one hand and with the other stroked it slowly with an eagle feather.

"Come, little brother," he cooed softly as it coiled around his arm like green-and-yellow bracelets.

Chastity watched in fascinated terror. The snake did not strike and she decided that the powah must have rubbed his body with senega. That must mean that it worked. It was the only hope she had left, and she knew it was slim.

"Tell me, wise Powah . . ." she said, and he looked at her in surprise. "The spirit said he would help the Wampanoags if I am brave and my heart is true. Did he say if he would let me live? Am I to be Metacom's wife or your personal sacrifice?"

Despite the fear in her voice, it rang clear in the still blue air, and the Indians stared at her in wonder. A faint frown appeared on the powah's face as he realized that he had underestimated her, and Metacom stepped forward hesitantly.

"Stand back, young chief. This is between the spirits and Dancing Fox," the older man ordered. He turned to Chastity, and the slight curve of a smile twisted his thin mouth. "Let water be brought, that the smell of food on her hands not excite the serpent!"

"No!" Convinced that he had guessed her secret, Chastity rushed on. "There is no need. I have not eaten or touched food today. Proceed with your test, Powah, and then we shall continue with the wedding."

"You are brave," he said admiringly. "Nevertheless, the scent of sweat may linger on your skin. Bring water!" he roared, and a boy leaped to obey.

Chastity stood frozen, pinned to the spot by the sight of the man's flat eyes and the undulating tail of the snake. Her mouth was dry with fright, and as the boy poured water over her shaking hands, she felt the sweat trickle down her body. She looked to Metacom for help, but he stood confused and powerless behind her tormentor. She was lost.

"Take the snake, Dancing Fox, and hold it to your breast as you would a child. Show us that you are fit to be the daughter-in-law of our honored sachem and the mother of future kings!"

As if hypnotized, Chastity slowly stretched out her arms. Closer and closer they came to the flat, swaying head and the lidless eyes that watched her.

A shot rang out.

She screamed as the upper half of the snake went flying through the air and she was splattered with blood and bits of flesh. The men leaped up, and the powah whirled around furiously. Excited cries broke out, and all was confusion. Chastity turned and looked to where the people were pointing.

There, seated on a jet-black horse, his leg thrown casually over the horn of the saddle, and calmly blowing the smoke from the barrel of his gun, was Edmund.

"I never did like snakes," he said.

❦ *Fourteen* ❧

"WHITE THUNDER!" THE ASTONISHED WORDS CAME FROM Massasoit. The powah shook with rage and spit out the order for Edmund to be seized. Chastity's heart stood still as she saw a group of braves cautiously surround him, but Edmund appeared not to notice.

He acted as though the two of them were all alone. She stared at him, wide-eyed and intense, and the look that he returned was like a physical embrace. She felt herself blush with pleasure and embarrassment. For an instant she forgot the danger that she, and now he, were in. He could not get enough of looking at her, devouring, enveloping her with his deep blue stare. She stood there motionless, totally absorbed in his gaze.

Suddenly the spell was shattered. She watched as the men surrounded his horse, their hands poised on their knives. He studied the scene slowly and deliberately with a sardonic smile.

"Seize him!" ordered the powah again, furious that he had not been obeyed at once.

"Stop!" Massasoit held up his arms. The braves drew back. The powerful sagamore and the rider eyed each other for a moment, each wishing to avoid a battle, but each determined to win. It was Edmund who spoke first.

"Great Sachem, you owe me a life."

Massasoit nodded in assent, wondering the reason behind all this. "You are right, my brother. But is this why you come riding into my camp shooting your gun? It is a bad time you have chosen. Evil things are at hand."

"I was here, I heard the powah's dream." He glanced at Metacom, who in turn was studying him closely. The

look that Edmund had exchanged with Chastity had not
gone unobserved.

"I have settled disputes among the Indians before,"
the horseman continued. "Let us talk, as brothers
should."

"My people!" Sassacus cried wildly. "This man defies
the spirits! He should not be allowed to live!"

"I defy no spirits," he answered calmly. "I shot a poisonous viper, not a spirit. And now I would talk with your
sachem."

"We will speak." The powah was about to argue when
Massasoit cut him short. "I may be dead by winter, Sassacus, but until then I am your sachem, sagamore of the
Wampanoags. I shall speak with my brother White Thunder. Let the pipe and the calumet be brought!"

Edmund dismounted and squatted in front of the aging
leader and his two sons. This time it was the powah who
strode angrily back and forth. Chastity felt her knees begin to buckle under her and sat down quickly in order to
avoid falling. A wrinkled hand stole into hers, and she
realized that Grandmother had crept up beside her. The
two of them sat in silence, trying to catch every word of
the conversation that was going on in front of them.

At first it consisted of the polite formula reserved for
such circumstances. Edmund presented Massasoit with
a small mirror that he had brought with him, and the Indian eyed it with curiosity. Then the pipe was carefully
packed with calumet and lit. Massasoit took a long drag
on it and blew the smoke in the six directions. He passed
the clay pipe to his sons, who smoked on it and passed it
to Edmund. After inhaling deeply, he returned it to Massasoit. The wily sachem then handed it to Sassacus, who
was thus trapped by ceremony into sitting down peace-
fully and joining the council of men.

Pleased at his success, Massasoit addressed Edmund.
"I have agreed to this meeting out of respect for you,
White Thunder. Your name is known in many corners of
this land. You have settled many disputes, among both
Indian and white. Your deeds are told around campfires
at night, and the wind carries your fame to far-off ears.
You are known as a great man, but great too is the prob-
lem before us. I wish no harm to this woman, but what am
I to do? If you heard the powah's dream, you heard what

is to befall us. If the spirits demand a test, I cannot forbid
it."

"What was the test, powah, to embrace the snake or to
live after its poisonous kiss?" Edmund asked the angry
man.

Seeing the trap, the Indian priest hedged cautiously.
"The spirit did not say. It only said to give the woman to
him."

"So she might have passed the test and still died?"

"I do not know," he grumbled. "Sometimes spirits
speak in riddles. But this I know: if the woman is to be the
wife of Metacom, she must first pass the test!"

"What are your thoughts on this, Metacom?" Edmund
turned to face the young chief. Black eyes caught his in a
defiant challenge, and for the first time in his life Edmund
felt the cold caress of jealousy wash over him like a giant
wave, leaving him suddenly weak. Chastity, his Chastity, was in love with this man! This emotion was totally
new to him, and he fought to control it as he studied his
rival.

Had the small hands he loved played in that dark hair?
Had golden lights glittered through her half-closed lashes,
as the man before him pressed his body against hers, and
had she moaned her sweet moan of pleasure?

The cold jealousy was consumed by burning anger,
and Edmund suddenly realized that his muscles were
rigid, his body ready to spring. With a mighty effort he
willed himself to relax. There was too much at stake for
him to allow himself these feelings. Somehow he must
make some sense of all this.

For his part, Metacom studied his father's friend with
great suspicion. Who was White Thunder to gaze upon
Dancing Fox? His look had been familiar and tender,
a look that had reached out and touched her soft skin in a
way that Metacom alone should. Was this the man she
had divorced?

"If the powah says that Dancing Fox must be tested, it
must be so," challenged Metacom loudly. "She is brave
—you all saw her reach for the snake. She will pass the
test for purity and courage and then she will be my wife!"

"Even Hawenneyu needs the help of the sky gods to
see," said Edmund, shaking his head in disbelief. He
realized that Metacom loved Chastity, but he could also

see that the young chief would stand by and watch her die without understanding the politics of what was happening.

"She would pass the test for courage, and then the snake would strike and you would have a dead bride, Metacom," he said dryly. "Your test would seem to be slightly faulty."

"I cannot believe that what you say is true," said Metacom. "The spirits are just, they do not lie and cheat. But"—he turned to look at the powah, and there was a new and dangerous light in his black stare—"sometimes men do. If Dancing Fox passes the test and dies, then so dies Sassacus—slowly and painfully. Let this be understood!"

The air was quiet with deadly challenge, and even Massasoit sat in shocked disbelief.

"There is another way," Edmund suggested carefully. "I do not believe that the spirits would test this woman if she were an Indian. Is this not so, Powah?"

Sassacus avoided Metacom's eye as he admitted that this was true. "Then the spirits would know that her heart was our heart, her strengths our strengths."

"The solution is simple then, wise Massasoit. This is not the woman that Hawenneyu has chosen to be Metacom's wife!" Edmund sat back and watched the men's reactions. Metacom was furious and defiant, while the powah nodded in righteous agreement. To Edmund's surprise, he saw that Massasoit was secretly relieved, although he took pains to hide this from his son. Edmund wondered about this for a moment until he realized that the sachem, too, believed in the fearful dream, and even though Massasoit did not wish to see Chastity harmed, he would not permit an open clash between his son and his powerful priest.

"You owe me a life, great King. Now I claim it. Give me this woman and I will take her away from here. Your debt will be paid in full."

"No!" Metacom leaned forward, his muscles taut with furor. "She is not a slave to be given away or lost in gambling! She cannot be used in payment for a debt! She will not go with you, she is mine!"

"Is she?" inquired Edmund in deadly dispute. "I thought she belonged to no one as yet."

"She will not be forced!" insisted the angry chief threateningly.

"You misunderstand me, Metacom. I would not wish to see her forced to do anything, not even to take a test she did not wish to take." Edmund's voice was low and dangerous, and Massasoit hurried to interrupt before the two men sprang at each other.

"Let the woman decide!" At his signal, Chastity was led to where they were sitting. The men rose to face her, Edmund and Metacom eyeing each other warily.

"Dancing Fox," Massasoit addressed her, "you have the choice. Do you wish to take the spirit's test and, if you live, become my son's wife? Or do you wish to leave this place with my friend and brother, the man called White Thunder?" Taking pity on the girl who had been through so much on what was supposed to have been the happiest of days, he gently added, "Whichever you choose, my child, you have my blessing."

Chastity looked from one man to the other in dismay. Metacom had given her so much! Through his efforts she had found the happiness and security that had been denied her. As she gazed into his bottomless eyes, she knew that the young chief loved her deeply, and she was forced to admit that she felt something for him in return.

Life with Edmund would be risky. Even if he still felt as he had in Plymouth, there would be obstacles. In the white man's world, she was still another man's wife. Would he be able to truly accept her after her stay in Sowams? Would it really be possible to start anew?

But as Chastity searched his rugged face, she knew that her decision had been made long ago. Even if there had been no powah, no serpent, no test, her path would have been clear. Her hand belonged in Edmund's, her heart beat within his breast.

"White Thunder," she said quietly. And then again louder, "White Thunder."

She sensed Edmund relax, but was dismayed when Metacom turned on his heel and strode off.

"I must explain to him," she murmured as she ran after the young chief.

Sweet Jesus! thought Edmund to himself. He would allow her to be put to death, and she loves him still! I shall never understand that woman!

With the whole crowd looking on in amazement, Chastity grabbed Metacom's arm. He shook her off, but she put herself between him and the door of his lodge as he attempted to enter. Finally he stopped, but he kept his eyes on the ground and would not look at her.

"Metacom," she begged, "you must understand. You knew I had a life before you brought me here. White Thunder is a part of that life, part of my past."

"You renounced him at the council fire. Why could you not divorce him from your heart?" asked the man in quiet pain.

"Nay, Metacom, not he," she protested, now understanding his confusion. "I divorced my husband, not White Thunder." Metacom still would not look at her, and Chastity felt tears fill her eyes at the realization of how she was hurting him.

"I believed this man gone from my life forever. But now, you see, he is back, and I cannot help myself."

"And what of last night?" His voice was low, and she had to lean forward to hear him. "Did it mean nothing to you?"

"Last night was last night, Metacom," she said helplessly. "But my world has changed since then. What I felt was real last night, but it was not what I feel for White Thunder. Perhaps I was wrong to agree to be your wife, but I truly believed that it would work out and we would be happy. I never dreamed that I would see him again"— she gestured at Edmund, who watched from a distance with a frown. "I believed that part of my life was over forever. It really is best that he has come back now, and not after you and I were wed. For you see, Metacom, I am powerless in the face of what I feel for him, what I always will feel for him. I am like the river that, whether it will or no, must rush to the sea and be one with it. I beg you to try to understand."

"And if he had never come back?" Metacom whispered through tight lips.

"If he had not come today, I would have been dead by evening. The powah's test was designed so that I could not live. I pray that someday you will understand this."

"And if there had been no test?"

"Then I would have become your wife, and you my sea," she answered simply.

He looked at her then, and his dark eyes were filled with such immense pain that she put her hand gently on his shoulder."

"Do not touch me," he whispered in anguish. "I cannot bear it." He shuddered slightly and then took a deep breath. He straightened his shoulders and lifted his proud head high; she was reminded of the first day that she saw him walking slowly and regally into Plymouth.

"Come!" he commanded.

Chastity followed him back to the circle of men, full of respect and admiration. King Philip—the name suited him. He would be a great leader, the greatest of all the Wampanoags.

"I give you this woman," Metacom said to Edmund with a slight emphasis on the first word. "Treat her well, my brother, as you value your life. May the spirits guide you on your path and smile upon you, that you may both walk in beauty."

A brave brought up Edmund's black stallion. He swung lightly into the saddle and reached down his strong arms to lift Chastity up behind him. The horse reared at the unaccustomed weight, and Chastity grabbed Edmund around the waist to keep from falling off, while the Indians gathered around them laughed.

Searching the crowd, Chastity spied the old woman.

"Grandmother!" she cried.

The woman wiped her bright eyes with the back of her gnarled hand. "Follow your star, my granddaughter," she called. "Let it guide you and light your path."

Chastity nodded happily and wrapped her arms tightly around Edmund. With a slight bow to Massasoit, he lightly touched the stallion's flanks, and they galloped out of Sowams.

For a long time they did not speak; the stallion moved smoothly, and Chastity luxuriated in the feeling of the powerful muscles under her and the ease with which he ran. She buried her face in Edmund's broad back, rubbing her cheek gently against the soft spun linen of his shirt, feeling safe at last. When he considered the distance between them and the Indian camp sufficient, Edmund slowed the horse down to a fast walk.

The narrow path that they followed wove in and out of

the soft green light of the forest. Sun and shadow played tag, and Chastity laughed aloud in pure delight. The sun was slightly behind them, telling her that they were headed east. They were not going to Tanbor then, which lay to the south. She wondered vaguely about their destination.

Coming across a small stream, an offshoot of the Sakonnet River which ran past Sowams, Edmund halted the horse and jumped off. When he turned to help her down, she thought she saw his nose wrinkle slightly in distaste.

Slipping back into English, he said with a trace of defensive derision, "I found you more attractive when you smelled of rosewater. Perhaps you would care to bathe?"

She had forgotten the raccoon grease, so carefully rubbed into her skin that morning! She realized that she must be a sight; months of living with the Indians had accustomed her to the smelly grease, strange face painting, and seminudity. She blushed as she thought how she must appear to him, and suddenly she realized he understood the meaning of the bridal symbols painted in bright yellow on her skin.

Sensing her embarrassment, he smiled. "You look more like a pagan priestess than the young Puritan maiden who once invited me to sit down next to her at Haunted Lake." Then his face clouded and he looked away. "I shall fix us something to eat. There should be some soap you can use in my saddlebag."

Chastity watched him move away, and frowned. Why had he not taken her into his arms? Why was he withdrawing from her? As she scrubbed away the grease and paint, she wondered if he had perhaps found another. No, after all, Edmund had arrived and discovered her on the point of becoming the young chief's wife. No wonder he was so distant!

So many questions crowded into her mind that she did not know where to begin. How had he found her? What had happened in the months that they had been separated? Where were they going? As she returned to where the horse cropped the long grass, she debated how best to get through the defenses he had obviously set up against his feelings for her.

"Here," he said as she sat down a few feet away from

him, "have some jerky—it is venison. Tonight we shall eat a hot meal, and tomorrow, with any luck, you should be back in Plymouth."

"Plymouth!" She was aghast. "You cannot be serious!"

"But I am. Look, Chastity," he tried to explain patiently as he fought with his own conflicting emotions, "I interfered with your wedding to Metacom only because the test meant your certain death. Otherwise I should have left Sowams without your even knowing I was there. But I could not let you die. Now you cannot go back there, so I shall return you safely to your own people." He stood up and brushed his hands on his pants. "What more can you ask of me?"

"I had thought . . . But no, it was a foolish dream."

He saw the trembling of her full lips and felt the fire in his veins. "You had thought what?"

Her love for him made her bolder than she had believed possible. Throwing her pride to the wind, she said quietly. "I love you, Edmund. When you appeared out of the air and challenged Sassacus, I thought that it meant that you loved me still."

"Love you?" he cried in anguish. "Love you, Chastity? You are the essence of everything I love in life! You are laughter and song, passion and tears. You are the mate of my heart, of my soul. You are my very breath!" She took a step toward him, but he stepped back to avoid her.

"You say you love me, but each time I find you, you send me away. Married to one man, I find you today about to become the wife of another! And yet you say you love me? I do not want this kind of love. I cannot bear it!"

"Wait, Edmund, I did not send you away the last time."

"I saw the ribbon."

"You *what?* The one we had arranged on as a signal? But I did not hang it on the door."

"Nevertheless, I saw it there," he insisted.

"John must have put it there. That diabolical man!" She looked at Edmund pleadingly. "Let me tell you the whole story and you may judge for yourself."

He listened as she explained all that had happened since that day he had appeared in her house in Plymouth and offered her her freedom. As she spoke, his tanned face became even darker with anger. She told him about John's savage behavior, how Hannah had offered her shelter, and how Metacom had saved her from the wolves and arranged for her adoption. She told him about the baby and the wise old woman who had been her grandmother, gentle Minone, and about the lasting enmity of Sassacus.

"I have only one question," he said when she had finished. "It concerns Metacom. Did you love him?"

She searched within herself for the answer. Whatever the truth was, she would deliver it to him unflinchingly, even if it meant losing him. He was too much of a man, and she loved and respected him far too well to tie him to her with deceit.

"I was beginning to," she admitted quietly. "I felt a kind of love. Metacom was very much in love with me, and I acknowledge that I found him extremely attractive. But I will not ask you to forgive me for this." She tossed her head with a touch of defiance, and the jealousy he suffered was tinged with admiration. "I believed you to be in England, never to return. Remember, I am a woman, with a woman's needs and desires. My life had to go on."

Seeing that he hung back, she asked gently, "Can you tell me in truth that you knew no woman in the time we were apart?"

"No." He hesitated and then shook his head with a rueful grin. "No, I cannot tell you that."

"Edmund, you must understand. I had lost everything —you, the babe I carried, even my sense of self. Metacom gave me my life back; he gave me a family who loved me, a way of living, and most important, he gave me hope when I had none. Had you not returned and the powah not arranged his evil test, I think that Metacom and I would have been happy together. I cannot and will not deny that there was something true and valid there.

"But he was not you, and it never would have been the same. When I saw you sitting calmly on your black horse, staring at me with your wonderful warm eyes, I knew I had to be with you, whatever the price. I know that a woman cannot ever truly belong to a man, but I know that I belong *with* you. I cannot give myself to you, but I can give *of* myself, I can share myself with you, if you will let me. Does this mean anything to you?" She put out her hand tentatively.

And found herself crushed against his hard chest while he devoured her mouth with fierce kisses. His hungry fingers found the fastenings on her vest, and she moaned with pleasure as they melted into the golden-green glow of the silent forest.

She leaned on her elbow next to him, delicately tracing the features of his handsome face with her fingertips while she marveled at his beauty. Her gaze wandered from the strong jaw up to the high brow, lingering lovingly on the thick black lashes through which she caught a fleeting glimmer of blue laughter. In places, his skin was almost transparent. She could see the tiny veins in his eyelids, which seemed to catch and reflect the warm color of his eyes, as though he had carefully applied the thinnest coat of paint upon them.

How brave and how true he was, and how her heart had leaped to her throat and choked her with fear after he shot that hideous snake! In that act of valor he had gambled his life for hers. Chastity had never felt so treasured or so loved.

She traced the large veins that twisted down his forearm, half-wishing she were a sculptor, that she might capture the raw beauty of his strength, and of his gentleness. How very strong a man must be to allow his gentleness to show. How blessed she was, and how very much she loved him.

For his part, Edmund thought he had never seen such delicious loveliness. He was a man of the world and a connoisseur of women, but never had he known one quite like the beauty at his side. She possessed the body of a courtesan and the logic of a scholar. In fact, her clear intelligence and sharp wit made her a choice companion, and he was rather surprised to discover that her boldness and honesty served to further seduce his heart, if that were possible. Puritan, dryad, Indian, ageless child, seductress—she was all this and much, much more to him. The thought that this delightful creature preferred him above all others was like a rich, heady wine, and he reached up and pulled her to him, so that she lay with her head on his chest.

"How fast your heart beats, dearest White Thunder. It seems as though it would burst."

"It well may," he teased, wrapping her curls around his fingers like bright copper rings. "First with fear at how close I came to losing you forever, and then with happiness that I have found you again."

"How did you find me?" she asked, perplexed.

He chuckled softly, and she loved the warm sound. "I was staying with the Narrangansetts when a visiting brave announced his departure for home. It seems that his friend was to marry a woman with burning hair known as Dancing Fox. Having known only one redhead with that name, one I gave you myself, I simply had to investigate."

"How lucky we are that you did! But I thought you had gone to England."

"I did." He sighed and stretched his powerful body. "I was at my grandfather's side when he passed away."

She touched his face tenderly, seeing the sorrow written there.

"It was a peaceful death, Chastity, I was glad for that. The old man had a full life. I think he was tired and ready to go. He had little left to live for when he died. The world as he knew it was destroyed. King Charles was executed, and Cromwell king in all but name. England is a dangerous place for the nobility right now, and my grandfather was too old and stubborn to change his ways. He would have ended up in the Tower. He told me that he had held on only to see me, and I thank the Lord I was able to get there in time."

He sat up and began to pull on his clothes. Following his lead, Chastity did the same, though reluctantly.

"Will we go back there, Edmund?"

"I think not. It is not wise at the moment—the country is split asunder. The Roundheads, damn their eyes, persecute all opposition. There is still talk of setting young Charles upon his father's throne, in hopes that Bonnie Prince Charlie will bring peace to the country. Both Ireland and Scotland declared for him, to their regret. They forgot to reckon with Cromwell. The reins of government will not easily be torn from his iron fist, and it may all end in more bloodshed. No one can say. Nay, unless things change drastically, we will not go to England."

"Where, then?"

"Well, you have your choice, fair mistress." He made a low bow and swept an imaginary hat from his dark head. "The Virginia colony grows stronger every day, and life there is considerably more comfortable than here. I own some lands that I have never seen. We will never be poor. My grandfather left his estates and title to my cousin but settled a goodly amount on me. Virginia is a beautiful place, rolling green hills, mild winters, and rich earth, a place where every seed that falls into the ground takes root. We could live there happily.

"But as I told you once, this country is huge, larger than anyone imagines. There are fresh-water oceans to the west and more land beyond them. You might choose to explore awhile before settling down. I have been to the edge of these inland seas and seen the tops of blue mountains. Alone, I could spend the rest of my days there. But it would hardly be a life of comfort for you, continually on the move, no home, no friends.

"Say the word and we will ride off to Virginia. One part of me would willingly take up farming."

She weighed it carefully in her mind as he searched her tawny eyes, trying to follow her thoughts.

"There is a freedom here in the forest I have never known in town," she said thoughtfully, "a freedom just to be oneself."

" 'Tis a heady feeling, I know what you mean," he agreed.

"The laws of nature are strict, but they are the laws of survival. Look, Edmund, behind you!"

She pointed through the trees. A young deer, discernible in the shadowy light by its pale milk spots, was nibbling happily on tender leaves. With a startled leap it disappeared, leaving only the waving forest ferns to mark its passage.

"I love it here!" Chastity exclaimed. "Everything is so alive! Oh, Edmund, show me these inland seas and blue mountains that call to you. Take me to your virgin forests. Let us explore while we are young and strong, before we are blessed with children or grow too old to love the taste of adventure. Someday we shall go to your land in Virginia, but not yet."

His rugged face lit up at her words. She flung her arms around his neck and pressed against him.

"But, Master Edmund Night, you have forgotten one very important thing."

"And what is that, pray tell?" he murmured, rubbing his lips across her brow.

"I was promised a Moon-of-honey."

He laughed and held her far enough away to drink from her golden eyes. "Our whole life shall be a Moon-of-honey, my little greedy one."

"I am greedy. And I want a whole month with you here, before we set out into the wilderness. I want time to explore the mysteries of you before we explore the mysteries of this land. Please, Edmund." She looked at him lovingly. "Just for a little while. It does not have to be a whole month—a week or so will do."

"Is that time enough to solve the mysteries of my soul?" He laughed. "All right, we shall stay here long enough to gather some provisions; I have only enough for one. And you could use some other clothes. That outfit you are wearing is delicious, but hardly practical. Have you learned to tan skins?"

"Almost as well as any woman in Sowams! Oh, Edmund, thank you!" She twirled away and pointed. "We can put our wigwam there."

"Slow down, Chastity," he said with a smile. "It would be better a little farther away from the trail. I shall build it downstream a bit."

"And I shall help," she said firmly.

"Follow me then, Dancing Fox. We shall build a palace of love for our forest bower!" He shouldered the saddle-bags, and Chastity took hold of the bridle and led the stallion downstream after him.

They picked a spot that was well hidden from the trail and close to the water. Instead of a wigwam, Edmund built a lean-to between two saplings. Unlike the Indians, he used a small ax that he carried strapped to his saddle, so their shelter was built before nightfall. While he was working, Chastity made a snare and set it in a bush a short way off. She cut armloads of leafy ferns and fashioned a soft bed for them. Then she set to work scraping a place bare for their fire, lining it carefully with stones that she picked out of the stream, so that the fire would not spread.

Suddenly there was a great commotion in the bush, and they ran to see the cause. Caught fast in her snare was an angry bronze-tailed turkey, who lunged frantically as he tried to escape. Fortunately she had fastened the rope securely to a tree, or they would have gone without supper.

They feasted that night and, when they were done, they suspended the rest of the food from a tall tree, far out of reach of any hungry animal. She sat curled in Edmund's powerful arms as they watched the flames of the campfire lick across the glowing pine logs. Her body fit so perfectly, so naturally against his. She turned her head slightly and buried her lips in the flickering shadows on his throat. He gathered her even closer to him, and she gave a hungry shudder of anticipation.

"Take care, Dancing Fox," he warned her with a low growl, "lest I become an uncontrollable animal burning with insatiable desire!"

In answer, her tongue darted out and traced a pulsating vein down his neck and into the deep hollow at his throat. She felt his lips on her hair and his hand stealing up to encircle her round breast. A small gasp escaped her as he gently teased her ear with his tongue and teeth, and she pressed against his chest hungrily. Her wandering fingers found his nipples, hard under his shirt, at the same time that his mouth found hers. His kiss was long and demanding, and she felt a flood of sensations sweep over her. As she slid deeper into his arms, she deliberately raised one knee in delicious provocation.

Suddenly his hands were rough and hard, but instead of hurting her, they drove her to new passion. She thrust her tongue in his mouth and tasted of it greedily. With more daring than she dreamed she possessed, her hands dropped to his lap and gently explored his groin. His answering moan was muffled as he buried his head between her breasts. She pulled at the fastenings of his pants, her skin feverish from the hungry kisses he left around her nipples.

Without a sound his pants opened and her hands flew in to caress that part of him that brought her so much pleasure. He responded to the light touch of her fingers as she stroked the soft velvet skin, fondled the rounded

crown, and followed the throbbing veins down to the base
into the dark hair that curled around it. She watched in
wonder as it seemed to grow to fit her loving hands.

She had not even realized that she was naked, so en-
tranced was she with what she touched. But she knew it
now, as Edmund bent over and pressed his face into her
small belly, leaving a trail of wet kisses along her scar.
His tongue came closer and closer to her throbbing center.
Strong fingers gently penetrated her secrets, and she cried
out in delight as she felt his tongue on her thigh. His
breath was loud as he gently massaged and manipulated
her, and she felt herself opening to him like a rose.

Suddenly his mouth was upon her, and her body tingled
with the intensity of the pleasure and pain pulsating
through her. But at the same time that she tensed, her
hands held his head in place and he dove deeper into her,
drinking of her secret essence.

She lay there moving rhythmically. She let herself flow
with their passion, riding the waves as he guided her ever
upward. Her breath came in tiny sobs as each new crest
of delight was reached, and she was carried higher, until
her whole body throbbed with liquid fire.

Her name, like the whisper of the sea, escaped his lips
as he rose and enveloped her burning body with his. She
opened and absorbed him as he sank into her flesh. She
wrapped her legs around him tightly as he moved within
her, convulsing them both in small, passionate shudders.
He devoured her hungrily, mouth, throat, breasts. His
hands twisted her thick hair into love knots as the light
from the fire danced across their intertwined bodies. She
licked the sweat on his body. Her nails dug into the flesh
on his back.

Higher and closer and harder and faster they moved.
Time and stars and forest and fire all exploded in a gigan-
tic burst of color. Panting, they held each other.

And then they were two again. The fire had died to
embers, and they lay together and watched the warm
glowing shapes in contented silence. Everything had just
been said.

Sweet-smelling days ripened into delicious love-filled
nights in their private paradise. They spent joyous hours
talking, sharing their childhoods, funny forgotten memories, treasured secrets, hidden pains.

Chastity remembered forgotten moments of her past and found it richer than she had realized. It was like the time she had discovered her mother's trunk tucked away under the eaves of the loft. Throwing back the heavy lid, she had plunged her arms into the faded clothes, smelling the scent of rosewater that still lingered on the soft materials. Drifting back on the perfume came images of a lovely smile and sparkling eyes. She shared this and other secrets with Edmund. It felt right and whole. How terribly lonely she had been before him, and she had never really realized it!

Two idyllic weeks passed. Although he appeared to be content to stay in their hidden bower forever, Chastity began to sense a slight restlessness in him that manifested itself in small ways. Another woman might not have noticed, but Chastity was living in a state of heightened awareness where all her perceptions were magnified. She realized that she too was looking forward to their adventures with eagerness. Once this thought had crystallized in her mind, she spoke.

"These weeks have been the most beautiful and the most peaceful of my life, Edmund. But now I am ready to climb your mountains and drink from your fresh-water seas. I am ready to leave."

His boyish grin delighted her, and she congratulated herself on having read him correctly. How lucky she was that they were so much alike in what they wanted!

"I did not want to rush you, but I am ready too," he confessed. "Let us ride into Portsmouth today to buy our supplies. I should be able to get a decent horse for you there. We can spend the night in the town and set off tomorrow morning." He halted as her face darkened and she frowned.

"Do you think that is wise?" she asked hesitantly.

"What do you mean, my love?"

"My going to Portsmouth. I have a strong feeling that I should avoid towns in this colony. Who knows what has been said about me? You know how news travels and is twisted. At the very least, I am considered a runaway wife. Why, I might even have killed John," she whispered as the thought struck her for the first time. "The last I saw him, he was lying in a pool of his own blood and screaming!"

"I hope you did," he growled.

"Oh, no, Edmund! To wish him dead as I did is bad enough, but to have killed him would be terrible!"

"Forgive me, Chastity, you are right. I suppose that I did not really mean what I said. I fail to be reasonable where that man is concerned."

"Edmund, I cannot go into town. I may be wanted for murder."

" 'Twould take more than a Bible to kill him, I wager. But forgive me, my love, I shall say no more." Edmund gazed up and checked the sun's position. "It is early, I could make it into town and back before night. Would you rather stay here than come along?"

"I think it would be best. You check out the notices on the meeting-house door and listen to the gossip. That way, we will know if anyone is looking for me."

"You are not afraid to stay in the forest alone?" he questioned.

"Of course not." She helped him button up his shirt and looked up at him teasingly. "Will you miss me?"

"Terribly!" He lifted her up and swung her around in the air with a laugh.

As she checked the girth to make sure that the saddle would not slip, Chastity reminded him to buy salt. "Our supply is very low," she said.

"Salt, a horse, and a ribbon for your hair, my lady." He let his eyes rest on her beloved face for a moment and then reached into his saddlebag and drew out a pistol.

"I am sure that you will have no need for this, but take it. I will feel better knowing that you have it."

"To protect me from ferocious chipmunks?" She laughed.

"To keep you safe until I return." He cupped her face in his hands and kissed her lips gently but thoroughly. "I shall be back for supper," he said as he swung himself into the saddle.

After he had gone, Chastity set about preparing for their journey. There were still a few ears of corn left, although they had long ago lost their freshness. She put the cobs in the hot ashes and left them to cook, as she had learned to do in Sowams. The Indians treated corn this way to take on long trips; in an emergency, one handful of this food would give a person enough energy for a whole day.

When the corn was thoroughly parched, she sifted it from the ashes, using a small loosely woven mat that she had made one afternoon as Edmund lay fishing. The corn was laid on a large stone swept clean of moss and dirt while she searched for a rock that would fit comfortably into her hand. Finally finding one to her liking, Chastity sat down and began to pound the corn into a heavy powder.

The sun filtered down through the tall trees as Chastity worked and thought how surprised Edmund would be when he saw how she had spent her hours alone. She would show him that she was suited to the adventurous life they had planned.

The muffled pounding of stone upon stone set up a steady rhythm. Her thoughts drifted into daydreams. Fragments of a song that she had heard before leaving Plymouth came into her consciousness, and she began to sing.

> His hair was black, his eye was blue
> His arm was strong, his word was true
> I wish in my heart I was with you
> Johnny has gone for a soldier.
>
> Shule, shule, shule agra
> Only death can ease my woe
> Since the love of my life from me did go
> Go thee, thu McVourneen Slaun.
>
> I sold my rod, I sold my reel
> I even sold my spinning wheel
> To buy my love a sword of steel
> Johnny is gone for a soldier.
>
> King Charles was routed in the fray
> The wild geese went with him away
> My love went too that dreary day
> Johnny is gone for a soldier.
>
> I shall dye my petticoat, dye it red
> And round this world I will beg my bread

Till I find my love, alive or dead
Johnny is gone for a soldier.

Shule, shule, shule agra
Only death can ease my woe
Since the love of my life from me did go
Go thee, thu McVourneen Slaun.

In the silence that followed her song, Chastity thought she heard a noise. She turned in that direction. There! The soft nickering of a horse! Edmund could not have returned so soon. She remembered the pistol, tossed carelessly on top of the ferns in the lean-to. Too late she raced for safety.

A horse cut her off as she ran toward the lean-to. Whirling around, she saw another rider break through the trees behind her. It was impossible to run; she would be overtaken immediately. Her only chance was to try to brazen it out, and all the time work her way over to the gun.

"God be with you, gentlemen," she said, forcing her voice to be calm. "We do not often get strangers."

"We?" The man in front of her spit a stream of brown tobacco into the bushes and peered at her. "Seems to me like you are alone."

"Not really." She made herself smile at him. "My husband is fishing a little ways upstream. I am surprised you did not see him." She inched her way toward the shelter, but the man on the horse did not move.

"You see anyone, Jake?" he called to his companion.

"Nope." The man behind her dismounted and began to walk toward Chastity. "You reckon she is the one?"

"I reckon. She fits the description."

"What description?" Chastity felt a weight in her hand and realized that she still carried the rock she had used to pound the corn. It made a poor weapon against two men. If only she could distract them long enough to get the pistol!

"Chastity Cox, wife of John Cox, Plymouth's preacher." Seeing her eyes widen in fear, he added, "That's her, all right. Look at that red hair and them yellow eyes."

The man called Jake whistled in admiration. He was

close to her now and reached out a dirty hand to touch her bare skin.

"Watch it, Jake, none of that. She is dangerous. Remember what the notice said she done to the last man what touched her! Now, missy," he said to the terrified girl, "we'll just have to take you back with us to Plymouth. We're going to get that reward."

Plymouth!

She hurled the rock at the speaker's head. He was caught unawares and, as she lunged toward the shelter, she saw the man tumble from his horse from the corner of her eye. She was brought up short and felt her arms pinned to her sides in a steel vise as the other man grabbed her from behind. With a vicious backward kick she broke free. Howling with pain, the man spun her around and slapped her across the face. Smiling sadistically, he drew back his arm and landed a hard punch in her stomach.

Chastity doubled over in pain, fighting for breath.

"Knock the bitch out," she heard the other man order. "It will save us time and trouble."

A heavy pistol butt cracked against her skull and she was propelled into blackness.

⊷ *Fifteen* ⊷

CHASTITY SLOWLY BECAME AWARE OF THE JOLTING gait of the horse. With every step the animal took, pain gripped her anew. The ground passed before her eyes, and she realized that she had been unceremoniously tied and thrown across the horse's back, like a large sack of flour. Her wrists were bound together behind her back; she could feel the thongs cut into her soft flesh when she tried to move. The blood that pounded in her throbbing head made her gag, and she was afraid that she would be violently ill. A convulsion shook her weak frame, and she slipped back into blissful unconsciousness.

She came to again when the men stopped to make camp for the night, and found herself lying on soft pine needles under a tall tree. Chastity kept very still and watched her two captors through half-closed lashes as they talked.

"You think that girl is as dangerous as they said in the reward notice?" asked the man called Jake.

"Maybe not," replied his companion. "Them Puritans always stretch the truth some. But we better not take any chances. Money is money."

"Hope she comes around soon. I could use some female company." Jake laughed and slapped his thigh. "A man gets mighty lonesome in these woods."

Deep within her, Chastity shuddered.

"You leave her alone, Jake," grunted the man as he threw another log on the fire. "You already hit her too hard. The poster said *alive*. If she dies, she is no good to us."

"Killing ain't what I had in mind." Jake giggled obscenely and leered in her direction.

"I said for you to leave her alone, and I mean it, Jake. Alive and safe in Plymouth, that girl is money in our pockets. I want that reward," he warned threateningly as he wiped tobacco juice from his square chin and glared at his companion.

Jake shuffled his feet in disgust and then grumbled, "You never let me have my fun. All right," he added hastily as the larger man scowled darkly, "whatever you say. She is too skinny for my taste anyway. I like my women with some meat on them."

"Good. Now, go see if she has come to yet."

As Jake ambled toward her, Chastity decided there was no longer any point in dissimulating. As long as the big man at the fire was in charge, she was safe from Jake's animal desires. But she had to figure out a way to escape. She had no intention of returning to Plymouth. By now Edmund would have returned to their camp and found her gone. Having lived among the Indians, he would rightly read the signs in the forest and know that she had been taken prisoner by whites. An Indian would not have had a horse to leave tracks, nor would he have failed to see the gun she had so carelessly left in the shelter. Besides, these bounty hunters had spoken of a reward notice. Edmund would have read it too, and would know that she was on her unwilling way back to that hated town. He would come after her, and then these men would have the devil to pay!

On the big man's orders, Jake untied her hands and brought her to the fire, where she eagerly drank water from a skin bag. When she had had her fill, she turned to the man with an idea.

"If it is money you are interested in," she began, "my husband will pay twice what is offered for me. I swear it. Return me to him safely and you will not regret it." Chastity tried to maintain the story she had started when the men first appeared at her camp, and she thought she saw a flicker of interest in the man's eye.

"And which husband is that?" he asked.

Too late she realized that they had never believed her. The blow on her head must have rattled her brains. These men knew her for a runaway wife. Worse yet, they probably knew her for a murdering runaway wife. Why else would there be a reward?

Jake snorted as he leaned over the fire. "You take us for fools. If you had a boyfriend back there in the forest, he was only some Indian, and Indians have no money. Besides, a man does not have to pay for a woman like you. If he wants her, he just takes her."

"You see," said the big man, getting to his feet, "we do know who you are, Chastity Cox. I reckon the Puritans will give you your due. They say you are a terrible sinner, and seeing you, I can believe it." He looked her up and down, and for the first time she felt naked and exposed in her Indian garb.

"You might as well save your breath," he said. "There is nothing you can say that would keep me from returning you to Plymouth. Nothing personal, you know. If you behave yourself, you will get there safe and sound. If not" —he shrugged his large shoulders—"my friend Jake here might forget himself and decide to teach you a lesson.

"Tie her up again, Jake," he ordered. "One of us best stand watch tonight in case her boyfriend shows up. You get some sleep and I will wake you if I get tired."

This time they tied Chastity's ankles as well as her wrists, and try as she might, she could not even work any slack into her bindings. Her only comfort was that now her hands were tied in front of her. It was easier to lie down that way, but no matter how she strained, there was nothing she could do to free herself. She resigned herself to passing the night a prisoner. Surely they would untie at least her ankles in the morning! Perhaps then an opportunity for escape would present itself. With this in mind, Chastity dropped off into an exhausted sleep.

She woke up in fearful silence. Something was wrong. When her eyes became accustomed to the dark, she made out the shape of a man looming over her and heard the harsh panting of desire.

"Make a sound and you are dead," came a male voice, and she knew it was Jake who threatened her. She glanced quickly at the low fire, but the big man was nowhere to be seen.

"He is out scouting." Jake read her thoughts. "He figured I was fast asleep and that you were safe. He was wrong on both counts. Now, he will not be back for a spell, and I intend for us to have some fun." He knelt down by the terrified girl, and she almost retched at the stink of his body.

"If you scream, this knife in my hand might slip and cut your pretty face up a bit." Moonlight gleamed dully on the knife blade he held above her throat. She flinched violently as she felt his rough hand pull at the thongs that held together her small vest.

Something had changed in Chastity. The fear that threatened to overwhelm her took specific shape, and suddenly she knew that she was stronger than it was. With this realization, her fear turned to outrage.

Not again, she thought to herself in cold fury. I will not allow this to happen again! This animal will have to kill me! I will not be raped again! She steeled herself to wait. In a moment or two the man would be vulnerable.

Thinking that she cowered in fear, the man grunted with desire. "You know you want me. You like it rough like this?" With twisted passion Jake tore away the doeskin that covered her breasts. The sight of her flesh in the caressing moonlight drove him to a frenzy, and he slashed at the bindings that held her legs together and sealed her from him.

This was the moment she had been waiting for.

Doubling up her knees, Chastity kicked the man full in the face, and at the same time she let out a scream that echoed through the dark trees. The force of the blow knocked Jake over on his back, and the defiant girl leaped to her feet. Where was the rifle? She raced toward the fire, but the gun was not there. Jake's partner must have taken it with him.

A furious roar caused Chastity to spin around. Jake was coming toward her, and murder was written across his ugly face. She quickly put the fire between them, and they circled it warily. Although her wrists were still tied together, she grabbed a glowing brand from the fire and thrust it at the man in deadly seriousness.

"Keep away from me!" she warned.

Jake grinned evilly, and just then Chastity saw his partner run into the small clearing.

"What the devil is going on here?"

"She tried to get away," said Jake quickly. "I aim to teach her a lesson like you said."

"Not true!" cried Chastity. "I was asleep and this animal attacked me." She was careful to keep the fire between her and the two men.

"Women always cause trouble," said the man in disgust. "If you want her that bad, Jake, you had better take her and be done with it." Seeing Jake's hungry expression, he added, "Just make sure she is alive when you finish. I want that money."

"Help me catch her, then," wheedled Jake. "She fights like a squaw." The man nodded, and the two of them came at Chastity from different directions. She knew she had lost.

"Forgive me, *messieurs*, but your game bores me," came a voice from the shadows.

She knew that accent! Chastity wheeled about as the French trapper that she had met at the Sakonnet camp stepped into the clearing.

"André! It is you!"

"Bijou?" The man was amazed. "I heard a woman's scream; I never dreamed that it was you. Ah, *messieurs*" —he turned to the bounty hunters—"now I am truly angry. You play cat and mouse with my fire opal. I cannot allow this."

"Oh, André! Thank God!" Chastity ran to his side, and he smiled at her.

"Mind the rifle, Bijou," he cautioned. "Take the knife from my belt and cut your ropes."

"There is a reward out on her, trapper. Help us get her to Plymouth, and you can have a share," offered the big man.

"Fools!" The Frenchman sneered. "Can you not see that the woman herself is reward enough? *Mon Dieu*, I think all Englishmen are blind! No, do not move," he warned the bounty hunter, who had started to raise the barrel of his rifle. "I will shoot you very quickly if I have to, you know? Empty your guns and throw the bullets over there."

With muttered curses the two men unloaded their guns and threw their bullets on the ground. Chastity ran to collect them and then returned to safety at André's side.

"Now, you will please take off your boots," he ordered the stunned men. When they had done as he commanded, the Frenchman threw the footwear into the fire and watched it burn with satisfaction. "That will slow you down, no? Take their horses, Bijou. We might as well travel in comfort."

Chastity laughed gaily. Now that she was out of danger, her good humor had returned. She came back with the horses and held the reins while André mounted.

Suddenly Jake lunged! But before he could reach the girl, André fired. The man screamed and clutched at his shoulder; spurting blood ran out from between his fingers.

"You are a dead man, Frenchie," growled the big man from between clenched jaws. "I will track you down and kill you myself. That is a promise."

"Perhaps, *monsieur*." André shrugged as Chastity mounted her horse. "We all must die one day, no?"

"Now, Bijou," he said a few minutes later as they rode through a stream, "we must get you to safety. I have a cabin not too far away. It is small, but I think you will be grateful for its shelter, no? We will go there, and then you can tell me your story."

"But I must return to our camp," protested Chastity. "Edmund must be beside himself with worry."

"Edmund?" She did not notice the look of disappointment on the Frenchman's face. "But of course, there must be a man. Ah, well, first we will hide you safely away from danger, and then we will send for your friend. You cannot return to your camp now. That is exactly what those men we just left would expect. Have no fear, *ma petite*, no one can trace us to my cabin. I am too clever a woodsman. You are hungry?" He smiled at her as he changed the subject. "There is some good rabbit stew."

Chastity suddenly realized that she was famished. "All right, André, perhaps you are right. It would be safer to go to your cabin first. Then we will send word to Edmund."

By the time they arrived at the small building, Chastity's hunger had turned to a dull ache and the girl collapsed on the bed in exhaustion, unable to taste the promised stew. The last thing she saw was the Frenchman's boyish smile as he tucked a blanket around her shoulders.

"Sleep well, Bijou," he whispered, and she drifted off. In the morning she told him briefly of the events leading up to her capture. It seemed to grow more complicated in the telling, and she flushed at what André might be thinking. Seeing the soft rose flush on her cheeks, the man sighed to himself and reached out to lay his hand lightly on her arm.

"So you see, André, I owe you double thanks," she said. "First because you saved me from that animal's filthy pawing, and second because you saved me from unspeakable horrors in Plymouth. I know not what awaits me there. I fear I must have killed John, although I swear to you that that was not my intention. I only wanted to get away." She shook her head at the painful memory, and André squeezed her hand lightly in compassion.

"We must get word to Edmund," she continued urgently. "He will take me away from this part of the country." Seeing the strange expression in the man's eyes, she hurried to add, "Oh, please do not worry. Everything will work out. I do not mean to be a burden on you." She smiled softly, and suddenly the room seemed full of sunlight. André turned from her so that she could not read his face.

"You could never be a burden." He fiddled with a trap that needed repair.

"Will you send for Edmund today?" she asked hopefully.

"If that is your wish," he answered in a tight voice. She looked up quickly, but his face was still turned away.

"André?" she asked. "Is something wrong?"

"No, Bijou." He turned to her and was smiling again. "I will send word today and at the same time buy some supplies. If your friend has gone on to Plymouth, it may take him a few days to receive your message. We will eat well and enjoy ourselves while we wait, no?"

She nodded happily and then busied herself with the breakfast dishes.

After André had gone, she explored outside the small cabin. He had left his rifle, which she carried with her, although the place was so secluded she felt slightly foolish. But Chastity had learned her lesson well, and so she kept the loaded gun with her at all times.

She gathered some wildflowers, jack-in-the-pulpits, Queen Anne's lace, and tiny bluebells, thinking to brighten the table, and then she stumbled across a wild-strawberry patch. The berries were so ripe and luscious that she was sorely tempted to eat them then and there. Instead, she fashioned a small basket of moss and took her treasures back to the cabin.

The structure was small, obviously made for just one person. Inside were a bed, table, bench, and in front of the small fireplace, the chair where André had spent the previous night. Better than a wigwam, Chastity decided, but just barely. She surveyed the room with a home-maker's eye. At least wigwams were clean! The table and hearth were sticky with grease from dinners past, and the sod floor was in dire need of sweeping. The mattress badly wanted a beating and airing. As a matter of fact, the whole cabin would benefit from an airing, she decided as she put her flowers in water and set to work.

When André returned late in the day, he was very moved by the picture of domestic tranquillity that greeted him. Chastity sat in the chair in front of a well-scrubbed hearth, where a steaming pot gave off the delicious odors of wild spices. Her copper head was bent over a rip she was mending in his spare shirt.

"What is this?" he asked loudly to cover up his emotions. "Everything is so clean! I think I am in a dream or in the wrong cabin!"

Chastity laughed as she rose to unpack the supplies he had brought. "I had nothing to do while you were gone, so I decided to be of some use. I hope you brought more grain. I used the last for bread." She gestured to the table, where two golden-crusted loaves sat cooling.

"I must leave you alone more often," he teased. "Soon you will turn this place into a real home."

"It needs a woman's touch." She glowed at his obvious pleasure. "You should take a wife, André, then you would have a real home and not be lonely."

He looked at her intently for a moment and then reached into his saddlebag. "I have a surprise as well. It pleases you?" He turned and handed her a length of pale homespun. "There is a needle and some thread there. I thought you would like a change of clothing."

"How wonderful!" she exclaimed. "I must admit I am tired of this Indian dress. How very kind and thoughtful you are!" She hugged the cloth to her chest and smiled up at him, delighted by his gift.

André looked down quickly, afraid his eyes would betray his rising emotions. "I like you in fringe, Bijou," he tried to say lightly, "but I think perhaps I will like you in homespun too."

"I am sure that Edmund will repay you for your generous hospitality. I know the supplies were costly, and I do not wish you to suffer from your good deed."

He sat down heavily on the bed, and when he was able to look at her, his face had lost its boyish charm. "No matter. I sold one of the horses. There was money to spare." His voice was wooden, but Chastity plunged on, too excited to be aware of the change in him.

"Was there news of Edmund in town?"

"No." His answer was short.

"He has likely headed straight for Plymouth then," she continued brightly. "He must have read the reward poster by now. Did you send the message there? Is it done?"

"Everything has been taken care of." André lay back on the mattress, his curly head resting on his hands. As Chastity got up to see to their supper, he fixed his eyes on her slim back. Whatever he was thinking was hidden from her.

In spite of her impatience to be reunited with Edmund, Chastity found the days passed quickly. André was a charming and generous host, and in the evenings they sat before the fire and he amused her with tales of his boyhood in France. She was beginning to feel a warmth toward him that she would have felt toward a dear friend or a younger brother. If he fell strangely silent sometimes, she dismissed it as moodiness. It was understandable, she thought, because the poor man was so used to being alone. What a shame in one so young! He really should seek a wife.

She had finished her gown of homespun, and wore it with great pleasure. The pale color set off her sun-kissed skin, and the soft folds of material, though more concealing than her doeskin, were every bit as flattering. She wore her thick hair gathered and tied at the nape of her slender neck. Sometimes Chastity caught André sneaking a sidelong glance at her, and for a second she would feel uncomfortable. But he never made a move to touch her, nor did he stir from the chair where he slept at night, so her discomfort was quickly dispelled.

Nevertheless, she was impatient to be away, and she mentioned this to André one morning.

"Do you know how long I have been here now, André?"

"No," he answered guardedly. "I have not counted the days."

"Well, I have, and it has been exactly ten days since you rescued me."

"Has it been that long?" He feigned amazement. "I can hardly believe it. It has gone quickly and pleasantly, no?"

"I cannot help but be worried, André. Edmund should have come for me before this."

André continued rubbing grease into the harness of a trap. "Perhaps he has changed his mind," he suggested. "Perhaps he has gone on without you, Bijou."

"Never." The girl smiled confidently. "We have been through that before. You forget that Edmund loves me. It would be like leaving part of himself behind." She sipped the precious tea that André had bought for her when he got the supplies.

"Love is unpredictable. It makes one do strange things," he muttered.

"If Edmund had gotten the message, he would have been here days ago," she said firmly. André's hand paused in midair and then reached out for more grease. "Will you send another message to him? I truly fear the first went astray. Please, André."

"And if I do and he still does not come? It should show you something, no?" André asked softly.

"I cannot imagine that," she said slowly. "If Edmund received the message you sent . . ." She turned and looked abruptly at André, who was staring intently at the harness in his hand. "André? You did *send* the message, did you not?"

"I told you that everything was taken care of," he said in a low voice, but she noticed that he did not look up at her.

"Yes, you did. But does that mean you sent the message?" Chastity walked toward him slowly and stood staring down at his crown of brown curls. "André, I must insist that you answer me!"

He raised his face then, and Chastity was sick with dismay.

"No, Bijou, I did not send your message." He smiled winningly at her, as though he had not betrayed her trust.

"Why?" she demanded. "What kind of a man are you?"

"Ah, but that is simple. I am a man in love. Be reasonable," he begged. "I could not just turn you over to another man, you know? I want you to be mine alone."

"But I love him," Chastity cried angrily, "and I do not love you!"

André shrugged his shoulders and then with slow deliberateness rose and walked over to where his rifle hung above the frame of the door. He smiled at her slyly as he removed the firing pin and pocketed it. "You do not give me a chance. You have not been unhappy these past ten days. I hoped we would have more time together before you found me out. I think you were growing fond of me, no? Could you not try to love me, just *un peu*, a little bit?"

"Listen, André," she tried to explain patiently, as though to a child, "you have been good to me and I am fond of you. But what I feel for Edmund is totally different. I love him deeply. I want to spend my life with him. Do you understand what I am saying?"

"You will learn to love me, Bijou," he assured her with confidence. "I have patience. I will give you time."

"No!" She was exasperated. "I will not learn to love you! And I will not stay here with you!" She whirled around and crossed the room.

"But you have no choice." He smiled at her innocence. "You would never find your way through the forest to a town. And if you did"—he shook his head—"they would hang you for murder. You yourself told me so. Even the Indians will not take you back now. You have no place to go. You have only André."

The Frenchman was probably right, she thought, to her dismay. Where could she go? Nonetheless, Chastity had no intention of staying with him one second longer than necessary, and she knew she would have to have some kind of a plan.

"We could be very happy, Bijou." André laid his hands gently on her shoulders and looked into her golden-green eyes hopefully.

"You are no better than those brutes who captured me!" She hurled the insult at him. "Why do you not force me and get it over with?"

The man flinched as though her blow had been a physical one. "How can you say that?" he cried. "I love you. Do you know what that means? I am no animal to take you against your will. You must come to me smiling, of your own accord." He put his hands behind him and added softly, "I will wait for that day with much impatience, *ma chérie.*"

"Then you will wait your foolish life away!" she said sharply.

"Perhaps." He smiled in secret amusement.

Nothing that Chastity said or did changed the Frenchman's plan. Her fury provoked his humor, her tears his loving solicitude. He ignored her silence and continued talking to her as though nothing were wrong. She even tried to frighten him by refusing to eat, but after almost forty-three hours she gave in and devoured the delicious meal he was tempting her with.

Finally Chastity realized that he would not be swayed. She would have to escape somehow and try to find Edmund on her own. André no longer left the rifle with her, and he took the remaining horse on the few occasions that he went hunting. She resolved to escape in spite of the obstacles, and set the date for the next time he went out for the day. She did not have long to wait.

As soon as he was out of sight and Chastity was sure he would not return for several hours, she threw some food into a light bundle, filled a skin with fresh water, and tied it around her shoulder with the fringe from her vest. She had long since rejected André's gift of homespun. It had cost her a small pang of regret to abandon it at the time, but she had decided that she would not give him the pleasure of seeing her in his gift. She carefully slipped a knife into the band of her skirt. She knew that she would need it for food and shelter in the forest; she remembered her last escape and prayed that she would not need the weapon for anything else.

At first she followed the path, but then she spied a faint animal trail and plunged into the undergrowth. She tried to remember all she had learned of forest lore, but the most important thing to her was to put distance between herself and her love-smitten captor. She set her course by the sun and traveled east, knowing that eventually she would have to reach the sea. Indians of various tribes spent the summer there, and she hoped she could ask for shelter and help in finding the man known as White Thunder.

The day grew hot and Chastity careless. Stopping to bathe her face in a small stream, she knelt without pausing to inspect the area. Steel teeth bit into her ankle as the trap she had sprung closed with a snap.

She would not let herself scream. Searing pain blinded her as she tried to pry open the metal jaws. They would not budge. She pulled at the trap, but it was securely chained to a tree. She could not even hack away at the harness, for the trap was designed for the razor-sharp teeth of the beaver. A whimper of pain escaped her as she fought helplessly to free herself.

André found her at dusk. He was gentle and considerate, not even reproaching her for her attempted escape. All he did was to point out that he was a hunter and a trapper, and with that she knew he was telling her that he would always be able to follow her trail. It was a kind of threat, however gently he phrased it; she was still his prisoner. André tenderly lifted the injured girl in his arms and started the long walk back to the cabin.

Chastity was lucky. No bones were broken, and after a few days, the swelling in her ankle began to subside and she was able to stand alone again. But André spent more and more time with her, until she felt that she could not breathe.

"I know that you will try again, Bijou," he said one evening as he carefully unwrapped the binding from her foot. "But I will always find you, you know? It would be better for both of us if you would try to love me. Is it so very hard to do?"

Chastity shook her head in frustration. The man was even more stubborn than she was! Imagine him thinking that she could ever love him! Even had he not behaved like such a scoundrel, her heart belonged to another. If only she were a man! She quickly dismissed this thought with wry humor. If she were a man, she would not be in this predicament to start with!

The image of Awashuncks came to her, and for the first time she felt a kinship with the strange woman. Of course, the squaw sachem's goal had been that of power, and hers was her freedom. Awashuncks had not hesitated in giving herself to the traitor Kewa. She had considered it part of the price of power. What was the price of freedom? If it came to that, Chastity was not entirely sure if she could follow the sachem's lead.

Perhaps it need not go that far. If only she could lull André's suspicions while her ankle healed, she might have a chance to make good her escape. She looked down at his rich curls and sighed deeply. He certainly was not an honorable man, yet neither was he wholly evil. He had saved her from the bounty hunters and Plymouth's jail and had not tried to force himself upon her. But in failing to notify Edmund and keeping her a prisoner, André had betrayed her friendship and trust.

What was it that Awashuncks had said? *I have done what I had to do, and I have walked the path the spirits chose for me.* Well, so would she, Chastity decided. She hoped she need not go too far to deceive André. But when the time came, she too would do what she had to do. She would gain her freedom. But she knew that she must proceed with intelligence and caution. As foolish as André might seem about love, the man was no fool. With this in mind, she gave him a lazy smile.

"It would be hard to love you, André, but not altogether impossible." She paused for effect and saw that he was searching her face with dawning hope. She warned herself not to seem overly interested.

"You are handsome in a boyish way, and sometimes you are even kind. But love cannot be forced, and I fear I could never love my jailer, however kind and handsome he be."

He raised her small foot to his mouth and laid a moist kiss on the curved instep. "I would do anything for you, Bijou. Anything but set you free. This I cannot do. You understand, no?"

Chastity quickly pulled her foot away, giving a little yelp of pain. It would never do to let him know how quickly her ankle was healing.

"Forgive me, *ma chére*," André cried miserably. "I had no idea there was still so much pain and tenderness. I am a clumsy fool." Chastity pouted prettily and allowed him to fuss over her.

"Will you help me to the bed, André?" she asked later when the last embers burned red. "I fear my ankle is somewhat worse." As he helped support her weight, Chastity leaned against him more than was strictly necessary and was rewarded by hearing him catch his breath with suppressed desire. She smiled softly, and he watched the shadows play across her face with growing hope.

"Dream of me, *ma chére*," he whispered to her. "Dream of the love I have for you, the love I wish to give you. Do not hate me."

"No, André," she murmured in feigned sleepiness. "I cannot hate you. It is too tiresome to treat you as my enemy, especially when that is not what I truly feel." She raised her lashes and gave him a sweet amber look. "I am so confused." She sighed and turned her face to the wall, leaving the Frenchman alone with himself. She had to smile when she heard the door open and close. André had gone to cool himself off in the dark summer night.

The following days, Chastity walked the thin line between seductress and innocent, pretending to be drawn to the man against her will. She wisely made no open moves to arouse his suspicion; she was neither too eager nor too cold. Sometimes her glance would follow him with just a trace of obvious wistfulness as he moved about the small cabin, and she would make a point of quickly looking away as soon as he noticed her. She took care to sing aloud as he puttered around outside the open window. Let him believe her growing content with her lot. No more the heavy heartfelt sighs at the mention of Edmund's sweet name. Let the Frenchman grow confident, she told herself, for then he would grow careless.

At times Chastity almost felt herself pitying the enamored trapper as he eagerly rushed to please and win her. Other times she did not much like herself for the role she was playing. But she hardened herself against such weak feelings. She would be free!

"We finished all the meat yesterday," André said worriedly one afternoon as they sat outside enjoying the sun. "I should go out checking the traps."

Sensing his uncertainty, Chastity turned to him with a small frown. "Must you go? I hate to be left alone with this injured ankle. It still has not healed properly."

André leaned back against the tree and stared into its leafy canopy. "You have the cane I made for you," he reminded her, "and you need not go outside the cabin. In fact, I think it better that you do not."

"Little fear of that!" she exclaimed. "It would be just my luck to run into savages, and with this crippled foot, they would take me captive for sure. What would happen to me then?" She gave a grimace of fear, and he promptly forgot the months she had spent living happily as one of the tribe. "Stay with me, André. Forget your traps, at least until my foot is healed." She hoped she had not overdone her helplessness, and she watched for his reaction.

She need not have worried. *"Ma pauvre,"* he soothed in condescension, "you women are so fearful. Stay in the cabin and you will be safe, I promise you. I must check the traps. If we do not get meat now when it is plentiful, what will we eat this winter? We must think ahead. Never fear. I, André, will take care of you. And when your ankle is better, you will come with me and keep me company, no?" He reached over and took her hand in his, and Chastity knew that now was not the moment to pull it free.

He helped her to rise, and taking her arm, led the limping girl into the cabin. He sat her down on the edge of the bed and devoured her eagerly with his eyes.

"Do not leave me alone for too long, André," she said quickly, fearing that the moment had come when her bluff would be called. Was it a bluff? "Let me start supper now —you will want an early-morning start."

Again he shook his head. "I have waited so long, Bijou," he murmured. "So very long. No man could wait longer."

"I am not certain I am ready yet. I am not sure." She tried to stall for time. What price freedom?

"Ah, but I am long ready, *ma chére* opal of fire." He
raised her hand to his lips and turned it over, slowly teasing her fingers open with his teeth. "My heart is yours, and
I cannot wait. Truly I cannot." He pressed burning kisses
into her soft palm, and his tongue left a moist trail up her
tingling wrist. His face was flushed and soft with love
and promise.

The door flew open. Before either of them had a
chance to react, the crack of a rifle filled the room. Chastity gasped in horror as André's body was propelled past
her and hurled to the floor. His face was no longer young.
It was no longer soft. What used to be the back of his
head was now a terrible gaping hole. As his life spilled red
across the sod floor, an animal scream tore from her
throat. All in one movement she swept up André's knife
and lunged toward the door, but her weak ankle gave
way and she missed the big man who stood there.

"Knock her out, Jake," she heard him say, "and make
sure she stays out until we reach Plymouth."

ঙ§ *Sixteen* ঽ৶

At first she thought she was in hell, one that was damp and dark and silent. She cautiously touched her throbbing head and discovered several large bumps; apparently she had been hit more than once. Wincing with pain, she gingerly explored a cut on her forehead that was caked with dried blood, and decided that, although painful, it was not serious. Her eyes gradually became accustomed to the dim light that filtered through chinks in the wall, and she began to make out her surroundings. She was in a small room with no windows. The outline of a door caught her attention, and she attempted to rise. It was then she realized that her leg was shackled and chained to a large iron ring set into the wall. Ignoring the shooting pain that made the slightest effort a trial, she pulled at the chain with both hands, but it held fast. Giving up momentarily, she sat back on the moldy straw to think.

A small shape darted along the wall and went behind the slop bucket to her right, and an involuntary shudder went through her as she heard the squeal of a rat. She drew her legs up under her and thought back to the last thing she could remember.

Poor André! The vision of the Frenchman's shattered skull returned to her, and her muffled sob sounded in the dark. Although she had not loved him in the least, he had loved her. Somehow that fact made her feel possessive and protective about him. He had not been an evil man, more like a willful child, she decided with a touch of tenderness. She remembered his face the day he gave her the gift of homespun, but she could not hold that pleasant image before her. The memory of his blood at her feet too soon returned to fill her mind. To be sure, André had not deserved his ugly death.

But it was her own death that must preoccupy her thoughts now. Surely this black and stinking place was the Plymouth jail. She shivered, and it was not just from the cold. What would become of her now? It had been some time since the bounty hunters had first captured her. Had Edmund given up? Did he think her dead?

She bit savagely into the soft flesh of her hand. She would not allow herself to think along those lines. She would have faith in him, in his love for her. She could not afford to despair now, not with what lay before her. But in all reality, she admitted, unless Edmund could save her, she was miserably lost. She faced that fact bravely.

How would he be able to find her now, and how could he rescue her from her cell? Could one lone man storm a town guarded by cannon and a militia? Of course not. Edmund would use his Indian cunning; he would wait and watch and plan. And then he would somehow free her. He had to! She held on to this hope fiercely. Meanwhile, she must compose herself and be ready to face her accusers. She would need all her wits about her.

Time dragged by slowly. What seemed hours later, the door was opened slightly and food was thrown in. Chastity called out but received no reply; she only saw a hand reach out to close the door. As the heavy bolt fell into place, she eyed the food distastefully. It was fairly fresh, but she could not bring herself to eat it. Fearing that it would attract the rat, she threw it to the other side of the cell.

Chastity, dressed in her brief doeskin, was cold. No blanket had been provided, so she pushed her disgust aside and burrowed deep down into the musty straw. The last sound she heard before falling asleep was the sound of rats fighting over her discarded food.

The sound of the heavy door swinging open on its rusty hinges brought her wide-awake. The bright light blinded her for several moments, and she could see only a large shape moving toward her. She found herself caught up in a huge bearlike hug and she recognized the voice of her brother Benjamin.

"Chastity, what has happened to you?"

"Oh, Benjamin, thank the Lord it is you!"

"Are you all right?" he questioned as he saw the dried blood that matted her hair against her face.

She dismissed the question with an impatient gesture and asked anxiously, "Why am I here? Of what crime am I accused?"

"Best sit down, little sister. I fear the news is bad."

Chastity obediently sat down and looked up at him expectantly. Embarrassed by the amount of flesh that her Indian dress lay bare, Benjamin looked away, and his words sounded more harsh than he intended.

"You are to be questioned by the magistrates today. They will decide if the evidence warrants a trial."

"John is dead, then," she said woodenly.

"Dead? Nay, he is as alive as you are, though you left him crippled in one leg."

"Then why am I in jail? Surely I was not brought back here just because I left my husband?"

"You really have no idea?" he asked awkwardly.

"Of course not, Benjamin. I have been gone nearly two years. How could I know?"

He settled on the straw next to her and began in his slow way. "They say terrible things about you, Chastity, things I cannot believe."

"What things? Come to the point."

"That you tried to do in your husband with spells, and failing that, flew away to the wilds with your demon lover!"

"Rubbish!" she snorted. "Who would believe such tales?"

"Lightly, sister. There is them that remember a cow going dry or a babe falling sick after you passed by."

"Well, if that is the evidence against me, I am in little danger, Benjamin." She smiled and squeezed his arm reassuringly.

But he shook his large head and kept his worried frown. "You fail to understand, Chastity. Your own husband has cried out on you! 'Tis the minister himself who says he saw his witch-wife in the Devil's embrace!"

Understanding began to penetrate her aching head, and with it came cold fury at the man who had denounced her. Unable to face losing her to a rival, John must have spun an intricate web of lies that left her caught fast. Who would doubt the word of the minister?

"What is to be done?" she whispered as the reality of her situation struck her.

"You shall get a fair hearing. I know you are no witch, and there are other sensible people in this town who refuse to listen to such gossip. Of course . . ." He looked away, his heavy face flushed with embarrassment.

"Speak, Benjamin, hold nothing back," she pleaded.

"It is Father. He says that witchcraft is in your blood and admonishes God-fearing citizens to beware the redheaded witch. He refuses to see you and has forbidden Mother Anna and the girls to do so."

She shrugged; she had long since grown indifferent to this particular pain. "He has always hated me, for I remind him of our mother. Yet, I would have thought he would have the decency to wait for the trial before crying out on me. What does Mother Anna say?"

"She says nothing. She tries to shelter the girls as best she can and to remind them that God is your judge. It is hard for her. She loves you truly and feels torn in two by duty."

"I well believe it. Father is not a gentle husband."

They were interrupted by the constables who came to take her to the hearing at the meeting house.

She walked proudly and defiantly through the assembled crowd. She heard the whispers as she was led up the main aisle, and realized that her old friends and neighbors must be astonished by her appearance and costume. She could distinguish the face of Elizabeth and was shocked to see it lined with hate. Chastity wondered if it had not been Elizabeth, demented by jealousy over John, who had hung the ribbon and coffin nails on her door.

"The witch flaunts herself before our men today," she heard Elizabeth whisper, "but soon she will dangle from the gallows tree!"

She glared behind her but was roughly restrained by one of the constables who feared her evil eye and shoved her onto one of the benches in the front of the room. Three of the most respected elders sat as magistrates, and another served as clerk of court. Chastity risked a look at the crowded benches and spotted many familiar faces. Her father was there; his face could have been carved of stone for all the expression it showed. As this was not a religious meeting, Mother Anna sat at his side, her eyes lowered. Abigail and Patience sat next to her. Chastity ventured a quick smile at them, but they hurriedly looked away. Her brother Joseph sat next to a young man whose eyes burned with the same feverish intensity as his did. She noticed he was taking notes of the proceedings and wondered who he was. Benjamin, his wife Sarah beside him, gave her a nod of encouragement and then turned to watch the man who was entering the meeting house.

The passing months had not dealt kindly with John Cox. He looked haggard and hardened and walked in halting steps, dragging one leg behind him. Chastity caught her breath when he turned to look at her, and could not resist a guilty twinge of satisfaction when she saw the ragged scar that ran down his cheek and was lost in his beard. Their eyes locked for a long moment, and he was the first to look away. He took his seat as Elder Parkinson rose to open the hearing with a prayer.

The first testimony was vague. Emily, the servant girl who had worked for her, told of the chicken feathers and blood and of the red ribbon. The crowd stirred at the mention of coffin nails. Then she said her mistress had the power to see out of the back of her head. The women in Plymouth who had servants or slaves knew that they often felt this way.

Next came several witnesses who spoke of cows going dry, plows breaking, sheep running wild, and children falling sick. Although some of these things had happened as long as ten years before, all of the people remembered that Chastity had been nearby when they had occurred.

Then the magistrates called Joseph Cummings to the stand. In surprise Chastity watched her brother get up. This surprise turned to revulsion as she listened to his testimony.

"She has the Devil's own power over good men's imaginations and dreams," he stated in accusation.

"Explain yourself," ordered the elders.

"She makes herself attractive to men, and even though it not be their will, they are drawn to her. Many is the night she would come to me as I lay fast asleep. With a look from her strange eyes, she would seal my lips so that I could not pray, and then she would slip into bed with me. She had a terrible strength that would overpower me! She would put her hands on me and I could not stop it! Much as I fought, the evil abomination would still take place!"

"Foul incest! This is a most grave accusation. What say you, Chastity Cox?" The room was deathly still as Chastity rose to defend herself.

"I am truly shocked by my brother's words! If he had these evil dreams—for dreams they were, and not reality —it was none of my doing! And if men find me attractive, it is because God has seen fit to make me so, not the Devil! I cannot control the dreams of young men, nor indeed of anyone. Perhaps it *was* the Devil, I know not. He that appeared in the shape of the saintly Samuel may appear in anyone's shape, I suppose. It had naught to do with me!"

"And the Devil himself may quote Scriptures. How strange that you should seek a passage that reminds us of the Witch of Endor. Perhaps you should pause to think before you speak," warned the magistrates.

"I marvel that your Honors listen to these rumors; I scorn them. These people belie me!" Anger shook her voice, and she fought to remain calm. The crowd stared at her as though she were a monster from another realm—and with her matted hair, strange and dirty clothes, and wild eyes, she might well have been mistaken for one. She clenched her fists, digging her nails into the soft palms of her hands, hoping that the pain she inflicted upon herself would help her to keep her temper in check.

"Your Honors, cows go dry and babes fall ill—that is the way of things and always will be. If a plow breaks, the farmer would better spend his time looking for a stone than for a witch. Of the things that Emily has told, most are true. I did find the ribbon and the other things at my house. But I found them there, I did not place them there. If they be of witchcraft, I know not their purpose or origin."

"When did you last partake of the Lord's Supper?"

Knowing that it would be in her disfavor, but having no choice, Chastity told the truth. "Just before I left Plymouth."

"Almost two years ago?"

She admitted it and saw the scowling looks of disapproval.

"Where have you been that you could not attend meetings?"

"In Sowams." Again the crowd began to buzz, and Chastity knew that another mark had been scored against her.

"You have been living with the heathens, the Wampanoags?"

"May it please your Honors, I had been attacked by wolves. The Indians found me and saved me."

But the magistrates' sympathies were not so easily swayed. "And so they took you to Sowams instead of bringing you home? Did you make any attempt to escape that unholy place?"

"Nay," she admitted, and then hurried to add, "I was very ill for a long time. Anyway, I had no place to run to."

"You seem to forget that you had a lawful husband. Why did you not seek to return to him?"

"I feared him. I had run away that night because I feared for my life." Chastity looked over at John, who was sitting with his hands clasped in prayer. A shaft of sunlight was streaming through the window and played about his golden head like a halo. Knowing his flair for the dramatic, she wondered if he had chosen that spot by the window for that purpose.

"You feared this saintly man, our good minister?" asked Elder Parkinson incredulously.

"We had a fearful fight, a serious one. Hannah Foote can bear me witness," Chastity said eagerly as she remembered the kindly Quaker. "She saw my sorry condition and helped me to escape."

The magistrates looked at each other in concern. One of the men shook his head and said, "Hannah Foote was hanged for heresy soon after you left Plymouth. It does you little credit to call her to witness. We all know that the most serious forms of witchcraft begin in heresy."

Chastity groaned inwardly at the thought of her gentle friend hanging from the gallows tree, but she knew that she could not afford to let her weakness show.

"If you were these many months in Sowams, explain

how you came to be found in the cabin, indeed, in the very arms of a Frenchman, known womanizer, horse thief, and papist." The elder's voice shook with accusation, and Chastity felt looks of fear and loathing directed at her.

"Please, your Honors, it was not of my doing. Let me explain."

"Do so," she was commanded. "No decent woman would have found herself in that position."

"I was in a small camp with the Indians," she improvised, "when I was surprised alone by the two men who brought me here. They took me captive and started toward Plymouth. That night, the one called Jake woke me." She paused and saw the men staring hungrily at her. Even some of the women were bent forward in greedy anticipation.

No, she thought to herself, I will not satisfy their ugly curiosity with details.

"The next thing I knew, the Frenchman was there with his rifle drawn," she said aloud.

"But it was reported that you called him by name," interrupted the magistrates, reading from a crumpled sheet.

"I probably did. I had met him once while visiting the Sakonnets," she admitted.

"The Sakonnets too," she heard murmured. Another mark was entered against her.

"He told me he would help me escape, but he tricked me and took me to his cabin, where he held me prisoner."

"A willing prisoner, then, to be in his arms." The elder in charge shook his head slowly. "We are not foolish. We are men of the world, Mistress Cox."

"But you do not understand! Forgive me, your Honors," she said, seeing the angry glances, "but I was not in his arms because I wished to be."

"He forced you, then?"

"No," she admitted with honesty, "it never came to that. I wish you would understand! Had I been a man, I would have fought with my fists and won my freedom. But I am a woman, and so I had to use a woman's weapons. I had already tried to escape and failed. When the men broke in, I was fighting. I was using the weapons the good Lord gave me."

"Do not blaspheme with his holy name!" an elder roared. "In spite of what you say, you were found consorting with a man of the Devil! Do you deny that he was a horse thief?"

"Nay," she admitted meekly.

"Had he not sold the horse in his greed for gold, you might never have been found," the magistrates answered one question for her. André had been so sure that his tiny cabin was safe! "Do you deny that he was a papist?"

"I do not know," she said in confusion. "We never spoke of religion. I cannot say if he was a papist or no. He did not try to convert me."

"All these days alone together and nary a mention of God? This by your own mouth?" The elders were shocked. "How can you then expect us to disbelieve the testimony brought against you? You are a sinner by your own admission!"

"Please, your honors, I may be a sinner in your eyes, but I am not a witch! Perhaps I have been misguided, but you can plainly see that there is no real testimony against me."

"We shall be the judges of that!" Chastity knew that she had made a serious error. "Reverend John Cox, take the stand."

John stood up, and almost every eye in the meeting house was fastened upon him. Chastity saw Joseph whisper something to his friend, who was writing furiously. The minister came forward solemnly, his crippled leg scraping a crooked path in the sand floor. He sat down awkwardly, bathed in the crowd's pity. He turned to the magistrates in anticipation.

"Just tell us what you wrote in your deposition," he was told. "You need not face the accused if the sight of her disturbs you overmuch."

"Your Honors, I married the prisoner in good faith, believing her a decent Christian soul. At first I suspected nothing, though many nights I awoke to find her absent, her side of the bed cold. When she would return, her cheeks would be flushed, and a strange acidlike smell emanated from her. She always explained it by saying that she could not sleep and had drunk an infusion. I thought no more about it, though sometimes I thought I heard the back door open and close. I cherished her as the Book commands, and was a good husband to her.

"The day she left, I found signs of witchcraft about the place, the ribbon that my servant girl spoke of, evil-smelling spices hidden in the kitchen, and a poppet half-finished. I grant that these things must have been intended for spells, yet I cannot believe that my wife meant to kill me, as some would have it. In spite of her evil pact, part of her loved me still and wished me no great harm. Though she be a witch, I shall not break charity with her and call her a murderess!

"But I get ahead of myself. I found these things and intended to question her about them. I came home that day from visiting a sick parishioner, and to my shock, found my wife in the arms of a stranger! At first I thought him an Indian and her a prisoner. I was about to sound the alarm when he turned, and I saw that his eyes were a deep, unholy blue." John paused for a moment to let the crowd absorb this piece of information.

"I heard the woman who was my wife laugh, and to my greatest horror, saw the kitchen filled with evil imps! They ran about her like children, singing abominable blasphemies, scampering along the beams of the ceiling. One flew through the air and landed on the shoulder of the creature I then recognized as the Prince of Hell himself!"

"Lies!" Chastity jumped to her feet and cried. "Your Honors, this man belies me!"

"Hold your tongue, woman, or you shall be gagged!" The order thundered through the meeting house, and Chastity was grabbed rudely by the shoulders and thrust back down on the bench. "You will have the chance to speak later. Pray continue, Reverend Cox."

"Your Honors, forgive me if I falter." John ran his slender hand through his hair and stared into space. "I remember trying to take my wife by the hand and free her from the spell, but she laughed at my pleadings and pushed me away. I ran into the bedroom for the Bible, knowing that only God's holy words and his merciful light could save her, but they followed me there. She begged me to join their wicked company and offered me great power and wealth. When I refused, the Master of

Evil thrust himself upon me and we wrestled for my very soul."

The crowd gasped and leaned forward, devouring every word. Some of this had been gossiped about in town, but to hear it from the man himself was different. A child whimpered in fear, and a sudden wind rattled the lead casements and wailed Devil songs under the eaves.

"I know not how long we fought." John's voice was lower now, and not another human noise could be heard in the room. "The imps clawed at my clothes and screamed the foulest of words in my ears. With a mighty kick of his cloven hoof, my adversary shattered my leg and I fell. Then I heard this woman, his wicked hand-maiden and my lawful wife, say, 'Leave him, master. We will return another day.'

"Before my amazed eyes I saw them turn into large black crows and fly out the window! The room was filled with smoke and the stink of brimstone. I clasped the Bible to my breast and thanked the almighty God for my salvation." John stopped, and a powerful shudder ran through his lean frame.

"She does not cry!" rang out a woman's voice. "Witches cannot ever cry!"

"What say you now, Chastity Cox?" a magistrate called out.

"I do not cry because my anger has burned away my tears. Your Honors, good people of New Plymouth, these are all lies." She turned an impassioned gaze upon the crowd. "This man has spoken not one word of truth. Or rather, he has twisted the semblance of truth to suit his own purpose. I deny all that he has said!"

"May I speak?" The young man next to Joseph rose from his seat.

"Identify yourself," Elder Parkinson said, frowning at the interloper.

"I am Increase Mather from Boston, fellow student at Harvard with the brother of the accused witch."

The magistrates consulted among themselves, and one said, "Young Mather, your reputation for godliness and scholarship is known here in Plymouth. If you have any light to shed upon this sorry matter, pray do so."

"There are several basic tests for witches, your Honors, and so far, the prisoner has not failed all of these. Has she been seen in the company of witches or of the Abominable One? Has she a familiar spirit? Has she tried to recruit converts to the Devil's service? Does she bear a witchmark? And, the infallible test, can she say the Lord's Prayer? It is not enough that one person accuses her of one of these things, no matter how saintly he be."

"The prisoner will recite the Lord's Prayer, and if she be guilty, we will all be witness! God will discover her!" The order rang clear in the courtroom, and Chastity choked back a hysterical impulse to laugh. These people were all mad!

"Our Father, which art in heaven, hallowed be—"

"Hollowed! She said 'hollowed'!" It was Elizabeth Hutchinson who cried. She sprang up and pointed an accusing finger at Chastity. "The witch is unveiled!"

The magistrates called for order, but by now the place was in an uproar. People argued in heated voices over which word had been used, while children began to cry and Chastity tried to make herself be heard. A dog started to bark outside, and soon others joined in. In all the clamor, the pounding of the gavel fell upon unhearing ears. The magistrates were at a loss to bring the hearing to order.

Only two people remained silent. Increase Mather scribbled notes furiously, and John Cox hungrily followed Chastity's every expression and gesture with an icy blue stare.

Unable to proceed, the elders ordered Chastity returned to her cell, where she sat in helpless fury. She received no food that day nor the next, for the court had called for a general day of fasting and penitence. She searched in vain for the food that she had thrown away, but the rats had long since carried it off. Time passed as she carefully went through every detail of the hearing, reminding herself thankfully that it had just been an interrogation and not the trial itself.

Several weeks passed, and Chastity struggled to keep her sanity. She tried to remember the many parts of the Bible she had memorized as a child, hymns and old songs, the math tables, anything she could think of to keep her mind busy and herself from falling into the

blackest despair. Once a day the door to her cell was
thrown open and the curious allowed to stare in at her,
as though she were an animal on display. At first she
had tried talking to these people, but they would not listen. Some put their hands over their ears; others simply
jeered at her. She soon realized that only those who believed her a witch came to the prison, and she learned
to say nothing to them when she saw that her every word
was mocked and twisted in the retelling.

The worst of all indignities was when a group of
women arrived, sent by the magistrates to examine her
for witchmarks. They stripped her body naked and sub-
jected even her most intimate parts to the prick of a pin,
looking for a spot that had no feeling, that token dead-
ness that sealed her to the Devil. Furious at such an outrage, and a painful one at that, Chastity had fought
them. They had her arms and legs bound in irons, so
she was easily overcome by the group of determined and
righteous women.

A few days after this torture, Benjamin finally came
to see her.

"Chastity," he began hesitantly, "before I speak of
the trial, I want you to do one thing for me. Say the
Lord's Prayer."

Chastity was so grateful to see him that she simply
nodded with understanding at his doubts, and recited it
through, word perfect.

"God be praised!" His face crinkled into a smile.
"Sarah made me ask. I knew you were no witch. But
neither of us was sure which word we heard you say during the hearing."

"Tell me what they are saying in town. What is the
gossip?"

"There are mixed feelings, sister, though there be
many that think you a witch since the hearing." He
reached over and patted her shoulder. "But take heart,
they have sent to Boston for your judges; they will be
impartial and fair. All is not lost yet."

"Talk to Joseph," she urged. "Persuade him that I had
naught to do with his evil dreams. Apart from John, who
will never change, Joseph's is the most damning testimony."

Benjamin shrugged his big shoulders helplessly. "I

have tried, but he will not discuss it. He was always strange, you know, ever since his illness, and this past year at Harvard has made him worse. I no longer know him as my brother."

"Pray try again. Who else speaks loud against me?"

"Your husband says little, but what he says condemns you. He asks that people pray, so that you might see the light and repent and confess. 'Tis Elizabeth Hutchinson that puzzles me. I thought she was your girlhood friend."

"Nay." Chastity shook her tangled head. "She has loved John since first he came to Plymouth. She once warned me she would do me grave harm if I married him. Would that I had listened to her! What is she saying?"

"It is not so much what she says as what she hints at. Well, I always thought her a sly piece of baggage. Have you any proof that she threatened you?"

"Nay, none. She told me in private." Chastity rested her chin on her knees and hugged her legs. "Benjamin, what will they do to me? Is there any hope at all?"

"There is still something that I do not understand," he said evasively. "Your husband is our minister, a man of God, and I will hear no word against him. He is a God-fearing Christian, yet he cries out on you and calls you witch. If you be no creature of the Devil's, why does he say that you are? And why did you tell the court that you feared him enough to run away?"

Chastity studied her brother briefly, as she debated telling him the whole truth. If he refused to believe John's part in it, she would be condemning herself uselessly. Although loving and kind, Benjamin was stern and righteous when it came to moral questions, and he would never forgive her. It would only pain and confuse him and do her cause harm.

"Benjamin," she began, thinking quickly, "remember that the Devil is called the Prince of Darkness, the Lord of Hell. Would not a prince choose a worthy opponent? Would Satan not choose to ensnare a good and honorable man? The wicked man is already his!"

Light began to glow in his dull eyes.

"If the Devil wanted to conquer Plymouth," she continued, "he would begin by trying to delude the minister, the man who guides all our souls!"

"And you feared him for this?" There was still some doubt.

"Nay, that was simply an argument between husband and wife." She hated having to lie to him. "You know how easily excited we women can be."

"Sweet Jesus, save us! What a terrible calamity has fallen upon your chosen people! What an evil delusion the Devil has thrown over poor John's eyes! He wrestled for his soul and thought it saved, but he has been tricked into believing you a witch. Our souls are in mortal danger! If we condemn you who are innocent, we are all damned!" He fell to his knees and began to pray.

A little surprised and more than a little ashamed, Chastity watched him. She had not intended to take it quite that far, but it was to her advantage that her brother had done so. In a sense, she decided guiltily, what he had said was even almost true. When he finished his praying, he smiled at her, and Chastity could see the relief in his eyes.

"You are no Ann Hibbons, you will not hang."

Puzzled, she asked, "Who is Ann Hibbons?"

"She is a witch in Boston, sentenced to hang next month. Joseph's friend Mather was at her trial and is beginning to make a name for himself in witch-hunting. That is why the magistrates listened to his list of points so carefully. Ann Hibbons failed every point on that list, and her guilt was plain to all. Besides," he added with confidence, "she had no family to defend her name. I shall speak to the elders and explain how the Evil One is deceiving your husband. He will not listen to me, the poor deluded man—he is already put out by having to pay two shillings a week for your board and irons. We will concentrate first on saving your life and then on saving his endangered soul.

"Sarah will bring you some decent clothes. You cannot appear before the judges in that," he said, gesturing toward her filthy dress. In all the weeks she had been imprisoned, she had not been given a change of clothing. "And I will pay the jailer to give you hot water and some soap."

He got up and gazed fondly down on his sister. "Do

not worry, I will get you out of this stink hole, and soon you will be home again."

Chastity smiled up at him, but her heart was heavy. For all his love and good intentions, Benjamin thought in a slow and plodding manner. John would cut him to pieces with his biting tongue, make him seem a stammering idiot, and appear to be a saint while doing so.

There was an unusual face in the crowd of people who came to stare at her the following day. Chastity recognized the wizened old Indian who had sent the ring on its long path to Edmund. He apparently did not recognize her, and though she tried to signal to him, he made no response. He glanced incuriously about the cell and then seemed lost in a dream. When the jailer said that it was time to leave, the people began to push out of the dismal cell.

The ancient Indian studied the moldy straw and announced in a clear voice, "Need rain. Much rain. Thunder come, bring rain."

A woman tittered, and the jailer shoved the Indian roughly outside. It was taken for granted that the old man was senile, wanting to water moldy straw, and no one noticed the flush of hope that sent Chastity's cheeks to blooming.

Edmund was on his way! Much rain—that must mean help; he was coming with help to save her! God bless the old warrior!

For the first time, laughter sounded in the small cell. The jailer, thinking the lovely witch gone mad, shook his head as he shot home the heavy bolt on the door.

Chastity clung to this message of hope with desperation. She needed it when the women came again to re-examine her for witchmarks.

✑ Seventeen ✐

SHE SAT ON THE PRISONER'S BENCH TRYING TO LOOK AS innocent and as modest as possible. Her hair had been carefully washed and brushed and then folded into a neat copper bun at the nape of her slender neck. She had scrubbed her soft skin until it was raw, trying to rid herself of the stink of her cell. Although no longer accustomed to the many layers of drab cloth that went into the long dress she wore, she kept her hands clasped demurely in front of her and looked the proper, decent Pilgrim woman.

The meeting house was so full that many people had to sit outside, fighting among themselves for positions by the open windows to better hear what was going on. There was almost a holiday air about the place, as whole families from outlying villages arrived to take in the day's events.

The senior judge from Boston had a forbidding aspect to him; very stern but honest, Chastity decided as she stole a glimpse of him through her lowered lashes. The other two judges had presided over the hearing, Elder Parkinson having excused himself for reasons of illness. A jury had been selected from the chartered members of the colony, men who were known and respected.

After the opening prayer Chastity requested that the court appoint a counsel for her, modestly explaining that she was totally unlearned in law.

"This is a court of law, not a political debate," she was sternly informed. "If you are innocent, God himself will defend you."

Stung by the unjustness of the reprimand, she bit her lip and remained silent while the judges reviewed the testimony given at the hearing. To her dismay, she began to realize that these men were accepting the records of her interrogation as facts already proven! The only new business was to be the hearing of testimony collected since the original examination, and the deliberations of the jury!

The oldest matron from the group that had searched her was called up to testify. She nodded her head with grim satisfaction and announced their findings.

"Indeed, your Honors, we did spot the Devil's mark on this woman. It took the form of a witch's teat, located behind her left ear. When pierced with our sharpest needle, the prisoner felt nothing, and the next time we examined her, it had withered away to dry skin!"

Next the judge read aloud a deposition written by Benjamin, swearing to Chastity's good character and advancing the suggestion that perhaps the Devil, seeking to tempt the good souls of Plymouth, had first succeeded in deluding the minister. The jury was visibly impressed by the document, and Chastity felt the stirrings of hope.

This was quashed when Elizabeth Hutchinson took the stand.

"As long as three years ago, the prisoner tried to lure me with fortune-telling," she claimed. "She kept telling me that there was no harm in trying projects, as though that were not the first step toward heresy. But I refused her, and finally she left off her pestering.

"I know naught of the spells she wove while living with her saintly husband, for I shunned her company. But I do know this. She visited me not five nights ago!"

In the back of the room a woman began to laugh hysterically. An imprisoned witch was able to slip out of her chains and go visiting by night! No one was safe! An angry rumble broke out in the room, and the judge rapped for silence.

Elizabeth continued in wide-eyed innocence. "I was banking the coals and preparing to retire when I saw her standing in the corner of my kitchen. At first I could not believe my eyes, but then she laughed and I knew she was really there.

" 'Come, Elizabeth,' she said to me, 'have no fear.
We are friends, remember?'

"I avowed as how no witch could be any friend of
mine. I told her that she would be hanged, that Plymouth
wanted no part of witchery and hags.

" 'Come now,' she chided me, 'do you really think my
master will let the dolts hang me? Nay, he will confuse
them and I will be set free."

"To my great disgust, I saw that she suckled a toad!
'Do you find my son attractive?' she asked with a mock-
ing laugh. 'I am privileged in that my demon offspring is
also my familiar.'

"I wondered how that could be, and she asked scorn-
fully, 'Have you never heard of copulation with incubi?
Aye, I can see from the fearful expression on your face
that you have. Well, you may remember that when I left
Plymouth I was with child. This is my son!' She thrust
the loathsome creature toward me, and I saw it smile
evilly.

" 'Get thee behind me, Satan!' I screamed, but she
and her hideous familiar did not move.

" 'Not until I have got what I came for,' she said. 'We
have much to offer you, my master and I. Wealth, power,
fame, love, take your pick, they are all yours for the
asking.' "

The crowd hung on her every word. Never in the his-
tory of New Plymouth had such a tale been told. There
was a palpable tension in the room, and it would have
surprised no one had the Devil suddenly appeared,
wrapped in all his malevolent glory. So great was the
fear, that several spectators sniffed the air suspiciously
for traces of sulfur, others clutched their Bibles to their
breasts, while the jury looked about uneasily.

Elizabeth raised her blond head, and her voice carried
to those who sat breathlessly outside. " 'Just write your
name there in the Black Man's book,' she said, and she
held out a large book and an iron pen. I knew that if I
signed, my soul was lost forever, I refused, and she grew
furious.

" 'Fool!' she spit at me. 'You cannot refuse me! You
dare not!' The toad in her arms began to swell and grow.
Before my horrified eyes, he grew as large as a sheep!

" 'Elder Parkinson annoyed me,' said the witch, 'and

so I struck him down! When he dies, let his death be a warning to you. I will return in nine days, and I will not be refused!'

"There was a clap of thunder, and she and her wicked familiar vanished into yellow smoke!" Elizabeth sat back, pleased with the commotion she had caused. She caught John looking at her, his pale face twisted in surprised confusion, and she had the grace to blush.

"She has failed the tests," announced Joseph Cummings loudly, and Increase Mather nodded solemnly. With a start of horror, Chastity realized that one by one Elizabeth had carefully covered every point on the scholar's list.

A woman screamed. Little Abigail, unable to bear the tension any longer, had slipped to the floor and lay there twitching.

"She has bewitched the child!" shouted Elizabeth, who jumped to her feet and pointed an accusing finger at Chastity.

As the impressionable young girl was carried from the meeting house, Thomas Cummings stood up, rage burning his eyes. "That witch is no daughter of mine!" he roared. "She is the spawn of her witch mother and the Devil!"

"Now the Devil is indeed in Plymouth," cried Chastity, giving Elizabeth a hard and meaningful look.

Thus she did condemn herself.

The jury was out only a brief time, and the verdict came as a surprise to no one.

"Guilty as charged!" The words sang in the hushed air, and the townsfolk were finally able to sigh with relief.

Chastity, her face tinged with the gray of her dress, stood on her feet facing the judges. Although she had half-expected it, the verdict still came as a blow to her. There was a rushing sound in her ears, and she hid her shaking hands in her skirts.

"Chastity Cox, you have been found guilty of witchcraft," pronounced the stern judge from Boston. "Yet, before we pass sentence upon you, it behooves us to remember that all men are sinners. And if all men, even more so women. Salvation lies, therefore, not in innocence, but in redemption and repentence. It is written in the Bible, 'Though your sins be as scarlet, they shall be white as snow; though they be red like crimson, they shall be as wool.' "

In the judge's tone there was no pity for the lovely creature before him, only misguided justice. "Will you now confess to your crimes and truly repent? Think carefully—it means your life."

"Your Honors, I cannot confess to that which I did not do." Tears of helplessness threatened, and she shook her head and thrust out her chin. "Would you have me belie myself?"

"Enough!" The judge had lost patience with her. Who was this stubborn girl to refuse God's blessed mercy? "Three days hence, you will be taken to Gallows Hill and hanged from the neck until you are dead!"

Back in her dark cell, Chastity calculated her chances. She knew that they were almost nonexistent. If only she could stall long enough for Edmund to rescue her! Yet, she admitted to herself with brutal honesty, she had been in Plymouth three weeks now, and there still was no sign of him. True, she thought she had gotten a message from the old Indian, but perhaps it was not a message at all. Perhaps he really was senile, as the people in town believed.

The door swung on its hinges, and Benjamin entered. "I cannot stay, sister, I am off to petition the governor. But I did not want you to wonder at my absence and fear that I had lost faith in you."

She squeezed his rough hand affectionately and smiled at him. "How fares Abigail?"

"She is fine now, now that the damage is done." He snorted in disgust and shook his large head. "It was only the excitement of the events, combined with her growing pains. Had it happened at any other time, it would have been understood for just that. But with all this talk of witchcraft and the Devil, it has made the people talk of possession. I would never have believed that sensible people could be such fools," he muttered.

"And Mother Anna?" she asked hesitantly. How painful it would be if her stepmother joined those who accused her!

"Not her," said Benjamin. "She knows better than to be taken in by a young girl's hysterics. I went to the house and talked to her when Father was out. He and I find little to say to each other lately," he added with a trace of anger.

"How I wish I could see Mother Anna!"

"And she dearly shares your desire. Patience told me there had been a terrible argument. Father forbade them to even mention your name, and Mother Anna tried to stand up to him. I know not the details of what happened, nor do I wish to. But I do know that she is afraid to come here to see you. She disobeyed him enough to send you a message, though. She said to tell you that she believes in you. Her prayers for pardon go with me to the governor."

"That means a great deal to me," said Chastity softly.

"I only wish that others had such faith in you," said Benjamin with a shake of his head. "My success with Governor Bradford would be assured."

"Do you think you can convince him?" she asked.

"If I cannot get a full pardon right off, at least I should get a stay of execution until he has had time to study the case. I must go now, but shall return soon with good tidings, have no fear."

Chastity would not allow herself to hope. Although she was moved to know her stepmother's prayers went with her brother, the cheerfulness in his parting words had sounded hollow.

We do what we have to do, and we do it alone. Life is worthless unless we follow our beliefs, whatever they may be. Hannah Foote had said that to her, and Hannah must have known that she would be hanged for her beliefs.

Chastity's Indian grandmother had echoed the Quaker's words when she told her that each person must choose her own path and then must walk it alone. Even Awashuncks had said the same, and then gone on to warn her that each person, each path, had a price.

Well, she had chosen her path, and parts of it had been truly lovely. She had been blessed with the love of not one, but two wonderful men, and she had loved them in return. She had tasted real freedom, not the counterfeit brand that was preached in Plymouth, but the true kind of freedom where one could follow one's own destiny. In spite of what she had suffered, she had known glorious moments of happiness, beauty, and peace.

If her path was now winding its way to an end, she would face it bravely. She could step up to the ancient oak tree with a firm step. She would not shame the memory of her freedom by giving into the Puritans' reign of fear, by crying or begging for mercy. And she would not live if it meant that she had to live a lie.

Her resolutions were put to their first test when John visited her the following day.

He held the lantern high and peered at her face through the gloom as the door closed behind him. They eyed each other in silence for several moments, and he was finally forced to speak first.

"Where is my child?" he asked in a voice that cracked with emotion.

Chastity tossed back her shadowed curls and mocked him. "You heard Elizabeth, he has turned into a giant toad."

"Nay, it was my child, not the Devil's toad. It was conceived that day in the forest when you first tempted me. Elizabeth was wrong about that," he said, and Chastity thought she heard confusion in his voice. "Where is my child?" he repeated.

"He was stillborn," she said, too weary to explain. With a touch of surprise, she watched the news cut into him. He still had some human feelings then; she had doubted it before.

"I never wanted you to hang, Chastity, you must believe me." When she did not respond, he continued. "I only wanted you to come home to me. Can you not understand?"

His face had a haunted look in the half-light of the lantern, and Chastity noticed again how thin and drawn he had become. His shrunken cheeks and bony frame made him seem taller, and his golden hair was frosted with white.

"Chastity, speak to me," he begged.

"I have nothing to say to you, John," she said coldly.

"I love you. I could not bear the thought of you with another man. I had to get you back. If you truly repent, I will forgive you. You shall see."

"I see now that I am back, you and Elizabeth plan to watch me hang!"

"Elizabeth again! Chastity, you are my wife! I know not why Elizabeth spoke as she did. It was not wise of you to visit her and demand that she sign the book. . . . But of course, you did not do that. Did you? I think . . ." His voice faltered and he ran a slender hand through his hair and peered at her in confusion. "Step into the light where I can see your face."

"Nay," she replied, "my leg is chained to the wall, as you well know. You are paying for the irons."

He brushed that aside uncomfortably. "I tell you that I still love you. Will you say nothing?"

"I am tired, John, tired of lies. I do not care what you feel for me. I do not, cannot, and will never love you."

"You are just frightened," he said, trying to soothe her. "Do not despair, Chastity, I will protect you. They shall not hang you, I will not permit it."

"And pray what will you do to stop it, confess to your hideous sins?" she taunted him.

"Mine?" he asked in a strange high voice. "Nay, I cannot do that. The townsfolk would lose all faith in me. Why, they would probably not even believe my confession; there is too much evidence against you. They would think me bewitched! I will do anything to help you, Chastity. But before I can help, you must confess."

"I?" She looked at him in dumbfoundment. "Confess to what?"

"Why, to being a witch, of course," he answered almost gaily. "You will confess and be pardoned, and then I will preach a sermon on divine mercy and forgiveness. You will be welcomed back into the fold. You will return to me and all will be as it should be. The people here will forgive you, and so shall I."

Chastity looked into his smiling face in horror. The man must be mad to think that she would ever return to him! Why, even now his smile seemed innocent of all guile, and she had to bite her cheek to remind herself that all this was not just a terrible nightmare.

"I would rather be dead than return to you," she said forcefully.

Taken aback, John shook his head as if to shake her words away. "Is it the child? If it is the child, we can have others." He put his hands on her shoulders, and she could feel his breath on her lips. She could not stand it.

"John, listen to me carefully. I know that if I scream, no one will answer," she said slowly and clearly, letting each word sink in. "But if you do not take your hands off me this very minute, I will kick your good leg out from under you and break it into pieces to match the other!"

He froze in disbelief, his twisted scar showing against his gray skin.

"I mean it, John. Get away from me, I cannot bear the sight of you."

He whipped his hands behind him and took a step toward the door. "Witch!" he shrieked. "I was right! You really are a witch! You cast a spell on me the first time I saw you and made me burn with desire until I had to have you. I burn still! God help me to resist this fire that consumes me!" He threw himself against the wall and sobbed. "You have stolen my soul, there is no hope for me."

Words came to her, and she said them without thinking. "Leave, John, your hysterics bore me. I have little time left to me, and no wish to waste it with you."

"You ridicule me? You try to make me look the fool?" he shrilled in furious amazement as he turned to look at her.

"There is no need. You still fail to understand what I am saying. Frankly, John, I much prefer the rope's embrace to yours!"

Crazed hate twisted his face, and he snarled, "Witch-bitch! You think your Indian friends will save you, but you are wrong. Massasoit is a sick old man and his sons too worried about their lands to bother with the likes of you, no matter how many of them you took as lovers! I shall see you hang," he hissed as he left, "and I shall laugh!"

With a shudder Chastity realized that his mind was gone. John had retreated into his fantasies. Having nothing left to him but his demons, he now accepted them as real. If her own situation had not been so helpless, Chastity might have felt compassion for the tormented creature who had condemned her. As it was, all she could do was to shudder and turn away.

It was a weeping Benjamin who came to see her that afternoon.

"The governor refused to see me," he admitted sadly. "He sent word that the case was closed and he wanted none of it. God forgive me, Chastity, I have failed you!"

She found herself comforting the large man, who fell to his knees and buried his head in her skirts, crying like a child. As she smoothed his hair, she wondered at her newly discovered strength. She found it slightly ironic that she, who was condemned to hang, should comfort him, who was free.

"Hush, Benjamin," she murmured. "You did your best, none could ask for more. That is all anyone can do."

"But my best was not good enough, and in two days you will be dead!"

"Shhh, look at me. Nay, look!" she commanded, taking his head between her hands and tilting it upward. "See? There are no tears in my eyes. I am not afraid to die."

Indeed, a sweet smile hovered about her full lips and there was a calmness in her eyes. Benjamin, embarrassed by his weakness, wiped the tears from his own face and blew his nose soundly.

Awed by her serenity, he said, "They will excommunicate you on the morrow."

"It matters little, our Lord knows that I am innocent. Benjamin . . ." She hesitated, looking away, and then she decided to finish. "There is a chance, a very slim one I owe, but a chance nonetheless, that I will not hang."

"Nay, sister. I do not mean to grieve you, but you are wrong."

"Wait, do not interrupt me, this is difficult to explain. I have"—she paused—"friends that may still try to save me."

"You mean the Indians?"

"Yes."

"Chastity," he said doubtfully, "I would not put my faith in them. Whatever you were to them when you lived in Sowams, you are no longer. Remember, they are heathens, and their words are not to be trusted."

She shook her head sadly at his words. "Benjamin, if it is possible, I will be saved. If not, I will die. It is not really faith in my heart, simply a small piece of knowledge. I only tell you this because, if the Lord wills it to happen, I want you to understand. You alone have believed in me and tried to help. In all probability, my friends can do nothing. But just in case, I want you to know that whatever happens will be due to my friends, and not to the Devil and his legions."

"Do you really think they will come?"

"No," she said simply, "not any longer."

"Then there is nothing left for me to do but pray."

"And to be there for me, please," she said softly. "Let me see one loving face in the crowd, in case my strength fails me."

They made their sad farewell, and Benjamin left. As the door closed behind him, Chastity tasted a salt tear that had trickled down the curve of her cheek, and she angrily brushed it away.

I will not cry! she sternly reminded herself.

The next day was the Sabbath, and Chastity, bound in hand irons, was taken to the meeting house. She was forced to stand in the center of the broad aisle while John mounted the pulpit and two deacons and the ruling elders took their seats before him. The building was full; the congregation sat in a deathly hush, for this was a deathly occasion.

The reading of the sentence of excommunication was left to John, and the Puritans shuddered at its impact. There was something unearthly about the scene; it was as if the Day of Doom were being enacted, not in the next world, but here in the plain and decent house of God. Before their very eyes a young woman—one of them—was being sentenced to eternal damnation and torment. This is what they had been taught to fear all their lives. The room was as quiet as the grave.

Through it all, Chastity stood with her head high, her eyes fastened with contempt upon John's pale face. If he faltered, his parishioners knew that it was the Devil striving still to choke back the minister's holy words.

That night, her very last on earth, Chastity wasted no time in sleep. Instead, she tried to remember every pleasant moment she had ever had. In her mind, she saw again the periwinkle eyes that lit her mother's laughing face, a battered and much-loved poppet, the first sampler that she had labored over with so much pride, an orphaned lamb that she had nursed and raised.

Again she watched the ferns uncurl deep in the shadowed forest and touched with wonder the velvety silver-and-rose pearls of the pussywillows. She saw the bobolinks skim over the grassy meadows in dipping flight, and she laughed as she recalled the antics of a family of frolicking otters. She planted a tiny seed in the moist earth and watched as it shot up into a slender young sapling, pink explosions of cherry blossoms standing against its naked black limbs.

She felt the pleasant touch of her hand on the shuttle as colors took shape and texture on her loom, and designs, like living creatures, grew in her cloth. She danced again in her memory the ancient sun dance, her body nude and gleaming, and again she felt her skin warmed by the golden caress.

Her eyes misted as she saw the delicately carved cradle Benjamin's large and loving hands had fashioned for her unborn babe, and watched her cherished old Indian grandmother blow smoke rings into the air with delight.

Metacom, proud and noble prince of the Wampanoags, sang his song of love to her, and she felt a surge of tenderness that left her face flushed and her body weak.

But it was Edmund's handsome dark face, lit by eyes the color of the deepest blue waters, that she held tenderly in her dreams as the gray light of dawn began to filter through the cracks in her cell walls. It was Edmund's strong hand that gripped hers, his sweet breath on her neck, his rich voice in her ear that gave her strength when the door swung open on its iron hinges.

They had come for her.

Wordlessly, for no good Christian would speak to a soul that had been damned, they unlocked her irons, bound her hands behind her with a rope, and led her to a wagon that was waiting outside. The crowd of spectators drew aside as she mounted the cart. Children stared at her with morbid fascination as the constable urged the horse to action and the wagon creaked on its way. It slowly passed through the town and out toward Gallows Hill, drawing people the way that carrion draws flies. No Pilgrim, even the very youngest, would miss a spectacle like this one.

The low, rugged hills that rolled to the shore were colored with goldenrod and silver birch. The sky was the color of pewter; the smell of rain hung in the air.

Thunder will come, thought Chastity wryly, but not *my* Thunder.

The cart jolted to a halt on the steep ascent to the hill, a wheel caught against a rock. As the men rushed to help, citizens in the crowd murmured that it was surely the Devil holding the cart fast. But the mighty efforts of the men of Plymouth prevailed, and soon the cart rolled on.

The gallows tree stood in a clearing surrounded by heavy woods. Chastity began to tremble when she saw it. She cast about frantically for some sign of help and found none, until her eyes rested upon Benjamin's honest face. She managed a tiny smile and stood up bravely in the wagon when it rolled to a stop beneath the terrible tree.

A thick horsehair rope was looped about her neck.

"Chastity Cox!" John pushed his way through the throng and stood next to the ailing Elder Parkinson by the cart. "I give you one last chance to save your immortal soul from the eternal flames of hell! Will you confess to witchcraft and be saved?"

She saw his left hand shake wildly as he reached for the wagon to steady himself, and the corner of his mouth twitched uncontrollably. His icy eyes sent her a mute, pleading message.

She tossed her copper head with disdain and spoke in a clear, pure voice to the hushed assembly.

"I am innocent! This man well knows it, and God on his throne knows it. Your trial is a mockery of justice! If you hang me, you are all murderers, every last one. It will be on your heads!"

"Thou shalt not suffer a witch to live!" screamed John, his body trembling with rage. "Hang her!"

An arrow thudded into the wagon. The constable froze in fear. A chilling war whoop rent the air, and from behind the surrounding trees a fierce-looking war party of Indians emerged, their deadly bows drawn and aimed. A coal-black stallion appeared from nowhere, bearing a fearsome rider dressed in black, his face painted in a grotesque death mask.

"Let no one move!" he ordered, and Chastity's heart leaped at the sound of Edmund's beloved voice.

He rode over to the wagon and with a slash of his long knife severed the ropes around her neck and hands. They slipped to the ground and lay coiled about her feet, powerless to harm her now.

"Mohawks!" shouted an old man, recognizing the painted faces that encircled them.

"Cannibals!" cried someone in the crowd.

"Spawn of the Devil!" wailed another in terror.

"The Devil has come for his handmaiden!" screamed a woman as Edmund offered a hand to Chastity and she leaped up into the saddle behind him.

"Damn the Devil!" roared John in a flash of sanity. "This is just a man! Another of her lovers!" He threw himself wildly at the bridle.

The magnificent animal reared and John fell, clutching his chest in agony.

The crowd was paralyzed with fear as they stood watching their minister writhe on the ground. The horse had not even touched him! Surely this was the work of the Devil!

But Elizabeth Hutchinson was not awed. Seizing a knife from a man's belt, she darted through the press of bodies and hurled herself toward Chastity.

"You have killed him! My love is dead!" she screamed. Hate and rage contorted her young face. She was crazed and blind to all but Chastity's despised face.

So she did not see Benjamin, who, moving faster than he had ever moved in his life, pushed his way forward, stuck out his huge foot, and sent Elizabeth sprawling.

"The Devil has tripped her!" he announced in a loud voice, and he sent Chastity a solemn wink.

"The first person to move will be destroyed!" threatened Edmund. He wheeled his horse around and plunged into the protecting shadows of the great forest.

Chastity, her cheek pressed hard against Edmund's strong back, felt the muscles ripple under his soft shirt as he skillfully guided the stallion's flight. She held on to him fiercely. She was alive and reunited with her love. Whether it be to search for inland seas, to raise a family among the sloping hills of Virginia, or even to face a warn-torn England, Chastity would forevermore be by his side. They would share their songs, their sorrows, and their dreams. He was her beloved, her life, her immortal soul.

Soon the memory of Elder Parkinson, his mouth agape with shock and fear as Edmund released her bonds, returned to her, and she felt the tickle of a laugh start deep within her chest. Now she was truly free, and the laughter bubbled up and spilled from her throat, filling the still forest air.

Edmund, urging the galloping horse along secret Indian trails, heard the arpeggio of laughter that he so loved, and smiled.

Back in the clearing, no one moved for a long time. Finally one small boy dared to look behind him, and realized that the dreaded Mohawks had disappeared into the trees as silently as they had come.

The threatening skies over Plymouth burst asunder, and it began to rain.

❧ *Author's Note* ❧

UPON THE DEATH OF MASSASOIT, HIS SON WAMSUTTA, known as Alexander, became sachem. For refusing to sell the Pilgrims additional Indian lands, Alexander was arrested and taken to Plymouth, where he contracted a deadly fever. He was eventually released and allowed to return to Sowams to die.

Metacom, called Philip by whites, then became grand sachem. For many years he struggled to maintain peace, suffering the humiliations of having to bow to the decisions of the Pilgrim courts, paying tribute to their treasuries, relinquishing all Indian guns, and being forced to allow Puritan missionaries into Indian villages.

In 1675 John Sassamon, a Praying Indian and adviser to Metacom, turned traitor and was executed after betraying Metacom's secrets to Governor Winslow of Plymouth. The governor demanded that the executioners be punished by the whites. His efforts at peace thwarted, Metacom prepared for war and attacked the outlying Puritan villages on his lands. The Plymouth militia retaliated by storming his camp, only to discover that the Indians had been mysteriously forewarned and had escaped to safety across the Sakonnet River during the night.

The Nipmucks joined with Metacom, as did the Narragansetts, the most powerful tribe east of the Hudson. True to her promise of peace, Awashuncks refused to go on the warpath, and the Sakonnets remained neutral during the bloody war.

For almost two years the battles raged in Massachusetts, first one side winning and then the other. Indians, when captured, were immediately killed. No prisoners were taken. However, in the diary of a female prisoner taken by Metacom, it was written that the great sagamore was gentle and considerate to white women.

In the summer of 1675, Metacom and his remaining warriors were surrounded in a surprise attack. The powerful sachem was shot in the back by a Praying Indian turned traitor, and his body was drawn, quartered, and left to rot in the hot summer sun. Known leaders of raiding parties were executed. All the captives—men, women, and children—were sold into slavery. Indian lands were seized and sold at high prices to pay the costs of the war.

King Philip's War, the first organized resistance to white settlement in this land, was over. And in the words of the powah, "The Nipmucks, the Narragansetts, the Wampanoags, the tribes that had lived in these forests since the beginning of time, were no more."

Lady Vixen

Shirlee Busbee

Beautiful, headstrong Nicole Ashford was yet untouched by passion, but destined for adventure—and pleasure—beyond anything a woman of her time had ever known.

Outwitting a ruthless plot against her, she fled her aristocratic English home on a privateer's ship bound for the luxurious pirate havens of New Orleans—and exquisite abandon in Bermuda's hidden coves.

Yet the very daring of her escape plunged her into even graver peril, as captive mistress to notorious high seas outlaw, Captain Saber, whose savage passions made her a woman—but whose tender kisses plundered her soul!